Sands of Wonder Book 1

Daughter
of
Thieves

USA Today Bestselling Author
LICHELLE SLATER

Cover by Angel Leya
Editing by The Writer's Assistant
Formatting by Lichelle Slater of Dragon Scales Publishing

Other books by Lichelle Slater

THE FORGOTTEN KINGDOM SERIES
The Four Stones of Tern Tovan
(Exclusive to Newsletter subscribers)
The Dragon Princess
(Sleeping Beauty Reimagined)
The Siren Princess
(Little Mermaid Reimagined)
The Beast Princess
(Beauty and the Beast Reimagined)
The Phoenix Princess
(Snow White Reimagined)
The Crown Prince

Receive the prequel to *The Forgotten Kingdom Series* for FREE by signing up for my newsletter at:
www.LichelleSlater.com

CIRCUS OF THE STARS SERIES
Ringmaster
Marionette
Magician

Urban Fantasy
Curse of a Djinn

CHRISTMAS ROMANCE NOVELS
Secret Santa
Accidental Secret Santa

Sheblom
Dorus
Crehat
Zunbar
Ailorn Mountains
Balim
Halmu
Narshiz

Spells

Akshifak – I reveal you
Amsikik – I catch you
Anadi al-ma' – I call the water
Aouasif – windstorms
Ashriq – brighten/shine/light up
Barq – lightning
Ibtaqi – slow down
Iftah ya bowaba – open portal
Iftah ya simsim – open sesame
Inhar – collapse
Inhal – dissolve (remove spell)
Inshat – become active (such as energy/force)
Itrabati – be wrapped up
Itshad – be pulled
Jalid – ice
Salalem – stairs/staircase

To: Lucy Tempest

For being the best sensitivity reader,
Translator,
Spell-comer-upper,
And friend.

Thank you for all of your hep and
support with this series!
(You can read her books on Amazon!)

One

Little in this world is as timeless or numerous as the sands of the desert, and I was completely surrounded by it. As I milled through the crowd at the docks, just another faceless body pushing toward my destination, anyone would argue I was as significant as the grains of sand grinding between my toes. What they couldn't see was how deliberately I was invisible.

With neutral brown clothing and my face protected from the wind by a faded yellow scarf, no one could notice me. Not even when I bumped my shoulder against theirs and apologized in order to slide my hand down their arm to unlatch their bracelet. Or when I stepped on the heel of their boot, causing them to stumble so I could slip my hand into their pocket and lift a few stray coins.

To the people of Sheblom, I was Almas—the selfish thief who prowled the streets and stole their wealth.

And I was proud of that title.

I kept my attention on one particular ship that had just docked—the *Northern*, a ship burdened with traded goods. I'd lifted a couple of pieces from them before. They had just finished unloading crates with preciously packed cargo and organized them in neat little towers, ready to be moved to the wealthiest merchants in Zunbar.

One merchant walked with a man holding the manifest. They stopped by two crates. The merchant was vaguely familiar, though I couldn't recall if I'd stolen from him before or not. I rarely remembered faces, but I remembered houses and the items I stole.

"The serpent is from Kalekai. They made it with pure gold and emerald eyes. We traded your silk rug for it," the man holding the manifest said. He was from the ship, but dressed too properly to be a sailor, with a tightly buttoned jacket that pulled around his belly and a fluffy mess of white fabric beneath his sweaty jaw.

"And the dagger?" the merchant pressed.

The sailor smiled and lifted the lid of another crate, much smaller, revealing the dagger glinting from its bed of dried hay. "We traded the golden egg for it. Also pure gold, but as you can see, encrusted with pearls and rubies."

The merchant grinned with greed, making his eyes practically glow. "I see the merchandise with my own eyes and approve," he intoned, using the traditional phrasing for merchants confirming their goods.

The sailor handed the man his board, parchment, and quill for his signature. "It's been a pleasure doing business with you, Sir Midas. My men will deliver these immediately." He waved his hand toward a man and snapped his fingers, then pointed to the crate, likely telling him to seal it back up.

Sir Midas. I smiled beneath my scarf. *My next target.*

He was the . . . fourth richest merchant in Zunbar. Like every other rich merchant in the land, he lived up on the hill near the palace. If my memory served me correctly, he was known for trading fabric and more than once had tried to con my Aunt Jade into providing him with more opportunity to make money. I'd overheard her speaking with my father once. It was some ploy to hide jewels within the seams of garments she would make in order to be taxed only on the garments. Of course, Auntie had refused.

From the tales I had heard from other lands, it seemed a common thing—for the rich to look down on the poor from their homes atop a hill. I'd entered a handful of them, but always under my father's watchful eye. After all, rule number two of the thief code was to never get greedy. Father ensured I learned that rule by teaching me what items seemed insignificant to others and could be stolen without being missed, such as jewelry, candles, lamps, or silverware.

On rare occasions, however, Father would take me with him to obtain a more valuable item, such as the snake statue and dagger I had spotted on the docks. Those items we would essentially hold ransom until they offered a reward. I had only personally done that twice.

With it having been nearly a year since the last time— a rabbit statue the size of my hand—I could only imagine my father's pride when I approached him with this new endeavor. The forty thieves were growing in number. Since we started collecting outcasts, we had grown to well over forty members, and we needed more money to support everyone.

So I walked deliberately through the streets and exited the eastern gates of the city.

The walk to the small desert town in which I lived was long and hot and always offered me plenty of time to get lost in my thoughts. I hummed to myself while wondering if Father would go with me or if he would finally trust me enough to let me go on my own. After all, I was nearly sixteen.

In the distance, the horizon wavered with the heat of the sun as if it couldn't decide whether the sand dune marking my village was real or not. And then a figure took shape. Or rather, almost. It seemed simultaneously both far away and near.

I scrunched my brow and held my hand over my eyes to shield what I could of the sun.

The familiar turquoise turban finally took shape, and I grinned. "Mihrage!" I shouted across the distance.

The figure turned.

I ran as best I could through the sand, my feet sliding as they always did, and the nearer I drew, the more my second-best friend's form solidified.

"Where have you been all day?" he said to me long before I made it to him.

"The docks. Where do you think?"

"I imagined you would pester Taraji or even Aunt Jade." All I could see of his face were his striking blue eyes and orange skin. I often compared his eyes to the brightest parts of the sea, but wondered if his eyes looked like ice. His nose and mouth, hair and horns were hidden beneath his turban. Mihrage showed up in our village a couple of years ago, an orphan and Dalarian. He fit in perfectly with our band of outcasts.

I reached him, breathing hard, and tugged my scarf up to dry the sweat trickling down the side of my face. "I think we should make our way to the water and cool off."

Mihrage laughed. "It isn't even the hottest time of day."

"Precisely." I tapped my nose over my scarf and grimaced against the heat.

He shook his head with a slight roll of his eyes and

resumed walking.

I inclined my head. He seemed a bit lost in thought, so I pressed by saying, "What's on your mind? Where have you been all day?"

"I visited Madame Kiara's apothecary and purchased some more herbs. If Taraji is truly going to join the Desert Trials, she's going to need to take some healing ointment and other such items."

"You think she might join the trials? Is this one of your premonitions?"

"I haven't decided yet," he answered.

"Have you spoken with Taraji about it?" I looked sideways at him.

He shrugged noncommittally.

Taraji was my first best friend and the sister I'd never had. We had been raised together since childhood.

But Taraji had a gift I didn't—magic.

I was one of the lucky few women in Sheblom to lack the blessing of magic. It was fine. I survived without it. In fact, I couldn't help but think I was better without it. Only, the sultan and his grand sorceress weren't celebrating *me* in two days.

"You're being quiet," Mihrage said, breaking me from my thoughts.

"I was thinking about what I overheard at the docks."

From the edge of my vision, I saw Mihrage's white brows disappear up into his turban as he lifted them in surprise. "Care to share with me?"

I gave him a sly smile and shifted my gaze. "There's a jeweled dagger and golden snake being delivered to Sir Midas. I would have tried to steal them in transit but could have used some backup."

He shrugged innocently. "I'm not much of a thief. You know that."

"Something to do with your morals, if I recall? Which is odd, considering you live with *us* now." It was my turn to raise my brows at him.

He reached up and slid his fingers into the turban at his temple and I knew he was wiping at sweat and realized I felt sweat trickling down my spine and the back of my neck. At his movement, I reached back and wiped the trickle hanging on the curls at the back of my head.

"We're all born with our own gifts. You know that. Just because I don't like the idea of stealing from someone—"

"Do you not like it or is it that you *can't* do it?" I cut in. I scrunched my eyes enough to reveal my grin as my warm scarf clung to my lips.

Mihrage pulled the fabric from hiding his own mouth, showing me his pout. "Why do I need to be good at stealing when the thieves have you? I prefer meddling in mixing ingredients and creating healing potions and poisons." His eyes flashed with an almost cat-like glow.

"Oh please. You couldn't poison a rat, much less anyone else." I nudged him with my shoulder, the feeling of butterflies lurching into my stomach after doing so.

His grin softened and the right side slid upward higher than the left.

My mouth, already dry from the heat and walking through the desert, went suddenly even more dry and I choked on a cough, which sent me gasping for air. Tears welled in my eyes as I struggled to swallow my spit and wet my tongue enough to calm the coughing fit.

Mihrage pounded my back, as if that would help, and said, "Did you choke on your scarf?"

That was a much better alternative than admitting I choked on my own emotions or that I had feelings for him, so I only nodded. I coughed a couple more times before straightening again. "I'm fine," I croaked.

"You need to get one of those enchanted water skins."

I snorted. "Like I could afford *that*."

An object so precious as never-ending water in a land that was nothing but desert would cost a small fortune. And, of course, those who didn't do any sort of labor or traveling seemed to be the ones who actually owned them. Perhaps that should be the next priceless possession I stole, and not the golden serpent.

"I would think you could create a potion in a bottle that did the same. Or that satisfied anyone's thirst with a single swallow." I wiped the tears from my eyes.

"Hm. Not a bad idea." Mihrage stroked his smooth chin. At eighteen, he didn't have so much as a prickle under his nose, near his ears, or across his jaw at all. I often wondered if his kind, the Dalar, had any hair aside from their brows and the top of their head.

We walked around the edge of the sand dune that hid our village on one side and I fiddled with the frayed edge of the sleeve hiding my tattoos—markings I knew little about.

"Do you want to come with me to tell my father? You don't have to. I'm sure you have a lot to do, making ointments Taraji will never use."

Mihrage, now safe, removed the turban, which revealed his dark brown, dragon-like horns. They started at his hairline, one above each brow, and curved back and up. I could only imagine how impressive they would be as he grew older. I never asked why his left horn had a golden band around it, but I found myself wondering yet again as the sunlight reflected off of it. His braided white hair was nearly as long as mine, which was rather impressive. It was mussy from being wrapped up all morning, and he absently smoothed his hand over the top of his head.

"You seem confident she will not join the trials," he finally said, answering my statement about Taraji but not my question about joining me.

I shrugged and finally removed my scarf. "If she joins and completes them, she'll move to the academy. Taraji would never leave us like that."

Mihrage tucked his turban under his arm. "I hadn't thought of that." I followed his gaze to see his attention locked on Taraji's house.

My stomach dropped.

I sort of had a feeling he and Taraji might be interested in each other. I had caught them staring at each other more than once. But they'd never gone beyond exchanging looks and Taraji blushing. On the other hand, Mihrage seemed to flirt with me with nudging and laughing. Of course, he and Taraji had been spending more time together without me lately.

As if to confirm that thought, Mihrage turned his gaze to me and said, "I'm going to stop by Taraji's house and see how her practicing is coming along. We can meet up after you talk with your father."

I forced a smile onto my face. "Sounds good." The fake smile dropped as soon as Mihrage was far enough away he wouldn't see me unless he turned around. I pressed my wrist to my forehead and silently cursed myself. *You idiot. Mihrage is your friend. Why does it matter if he likes Taraji? If you really wanted him, you could chase after him and win him over. But you're friends.*

"Do you need some water, Caspara?"

I practically jumped out of my skin and dropped my hand to see my father standing beside me. "Don't creep up on me. And yes, please. Water sounds wonderful."

He kept his gaze forward, but his attention on me. "I couldn't tell if you had a headache from the heat or from trying to subtly let Mihrage know your heart yearns for him."

I scowled up at my father.

He put his hands up in a defensive posture.

"My heart doesn't *yearn* for anyone." But the blush burning up my back and likely across my cheeks revealed my lie. I turned around and walked into our home.

TWO

The village of the thieves had five squat homes pressed up against the sand dune, each of them one story. My father and I lived in one of the sixteen clay homes built in a crescent shape facing the dune. The center was our own personal square with a big, trustworthy well, posts for the camels, and benches for when the sun set and took the heat with it so we could tolerate being outside together.

There were a few pens for the couple of goats, sheep, and chickens we also kept for bartering or whatever other essentials we needed, like milk or blankets.

I hung my scarf on the hook inside the door of our home and lowered myself to one of the cushions on the floor to breathe in the significantly cooler air.

Father closed the door behind him. "What did you discover?"

I was grateful he wanted to talk about the reason I'd left that morning and not the awkwardness between myself and Mihrage. So I smiled up at him. "Two big items we can easily lift."

Father leaned his backside against the kitchen table and folded his arms, a proud smile on his lips, scrunching the corners of his eyes. Father was only in his late thirties, but the cost of raising a rambunctious and often unwilling daughter had taken its toll. He even had a tuft of graying hair at the front of his forehead.

"Go on," he prodded.

"A serpent made of gold. It seems insignificant, isn't that large, but will be something easy to take and even resell. It doesn't seem terribly unique. But the dagger is the real prize," I continued. "It's got red gold, pearls, and rubies."

Father stroked his beard as I spoke. I could see the wheels already turning in his mind and he finally nodded to me. "How do you think we should proceed?"

I was on my feet in an instant. "You're allowing me to plan it?"

"Your sixteenth birthday is drawing near, and to be quite honest, I cannot help but feel as though you are ready for this. You've joined me on a few of these types of assignments and have come out unscathed, so we can do it again. Just remember the rules."

I threw my arms around him, not caring he was damp from whatever work he'd been hard at that day. "I'm . . . I can't wait."

He squeezed me and relaxed. "You know, if you told Mihrage you liked him and wanted to take him on a walk along the beach or—"

"Baba!" I cringed and pushed away from him.

He burst into laughter, tilting his chin up to let the sound reverberate off the walls.

"Please. He's my friend! And I don't need your help with him."

Father's smile faded a bit. "I want you happy, Caspara." And then, as quickly as it faded, it returned, but the glimmer was missing from his eyes now, which told me he was hiding something. "Spend the rest of the day making your plans. Rest if you need to. Tonight, I'll join you in Zunbar and we'll fetch the treasures." He cupped my face and kissed the top of my head.

"I'm only turning a year older, Father. I'm not marrying anyone or going off to start a family."

"Good, because we have no dowry." Father's humor finally reached his eyes again.

I couldn't help but laugh with him, even if it was true girls my age were already being married off in exchange for money, livestock, social status, and so forth. Luckily for me, the thieves couldn't care less about those traditions.

If—*when*—we were successful in retrieving the snake and dagger and got the money for either selling them or claiming their reward, I would buy myself a birthday gift. It wasn't much, and I would never admit it out loud, but I had my eyes on a pair of new shoes that weren't split on the side and could actually prevent sand from getting in all the time.

With only six days before my sixteenth birthday, I had a lot to do in preparation. The thieves may not have celebrated traditions as others in Sheblom did, but we cherished birthday celebrations. Undoubtedly, Father had a feast assigned to various members of our clan, Taraji would have made her family make decorations, and Mihrage . . .

I froze at the side of my bed, where I'd gone after my conversation with my father.

How could I be so foolish? Mihrage hadn't gone to the apothecary to collect ingredients for Taraji to enter the desert trials and abandon us for the rest of her life. He'd gone to the bakery to collect ingredients for my birthday cake! It was bound to be love cake, since that was my favorite and I requested it every year.

Feeling much better, albeit also foolish, I changed into a set of clothing that wasn't sweat-drenched and sand-stained. I would switch to my darker thief's clothing when the sun set.

A cobalt-blue and red-orange-scaled lizard crawled across my bed.

Igborg, the pudgy, adorable uromastyx lizard I couldn't get rid of, snuggled against my leg in a movement that reminded me of a dog wanting to be scratched. He was the perfect companion. He blinked up at me with wide eyes, and I often imagined him as a dragon. If dragons were the size of a loaf of bread. And if dragons were native to Sheblom, which they weren't.

"Hey, *Habibi*." I reached down to scratch his head and under his chin. "I get to plan a raid on my own tonight. Can you believe it? I'm going to check with Taraji and see if she wants to help me plan it. You can come with me." I scooped him up and set him on his typical spot—my shoulder.

He hunkered down and held on with his little claws while I trotted back down the stairs and out the door.

"I'm going to Taraji's!" I called back to my father before his opened jaw could utter the question.

I knocked twice on Taraji's family door before letting myself in. "It's Caspara," I announced.

Taraji's younger sister, Isline, paused her hand-sewing project and scrunched her brows in a confused expression. "What are you doing here?"

"I'm looking for Taraji, of course. Where is she?"

"I thought you'd already be with her. Mihrage just left with her out to the field." She pointed in the wrong direction.

"The field" was a generous term for the patch of land

where dry grass and sticks that had once been bushes still clung to their roots. At Isline's confused expression, my stomach roiled.

"Thank you. I'll see you later." I left the house the way I'd entered and walked around the buildings, out to the field.

I knew better than to feel the way I felt. But I couldn't stop myself either. Which only made my guilt press in hard on my lungs and made it difficult to breathe.

I breached the top of the short hill and peered out at the field, where Mihrage stood in front of Taraji. She was showing him something in her hand and then held it out toward the sand. A small spiral of sand floated upward like a sort of miniature tornado and settled in her palm.

I was about to continue heading toward them but froze in my spot when Mihrage reached out and plucked some hair from Taraji's eyelash. They both laughed, the sort of high laughter that sounded too loud when people were truly happy.

I bit my bottom lip and tasted the metallic tang of blood.

There it was.

Out in broad daylight for me to see.

Mihrage loved Taraji, the beautiful, dark-skinned, charismatic girl I'd treasured my whole life. I should have felt happy for them. Taraji was bright, funny, and actually knew how to be a woman. She'd been raised by a mother, where I had none. Taught to cook, clean, sew, and whatever other motherly, womanly tasks needed to be learned. Father had done his best, but there were a lot of skills I certainly didn't have.

If I walked over now, I would spoil their moment. Their smiles would drop and they would step away from each other. I knew, because I'd done that just a few days prior and it had been the first time I really noticed there *might* be something between them.

I turned my back to them. I needed a glass of water anyway and had more important things to do, like steal the serpent and dagger that night. My heart sank to my feet.

"Caspara, is that you?" Taraji's voice rang out.

I lifted my hand to signal that I heard, but didn't stop walking. Hopefully, she hadn't suspected I saw them together and would continue doing whatever it was she wanted with Mihrage.

I stopped beside the well and lowered the bucket down into the water, letting it fall and crash to the surface of the water with a pleasant, solid splash.

"I called for you to wait up," Taraji said as she approached me, sounding out of breath.

I looked over my shoulder at her. "Sorry, I didn't hear. I was coming out to talk to you, but forgot I needed a drink of water."

Taraji raised her brow and fiddled with the gold earring dangling from her ear. "You forgot that you needed a drink of water?"

"Yep." I popped the *p* and started reeling up the bucket. "I get to run my own assignment tonight," I said, noticing Mihrage taking his time to approach us. Maybe he felt my jealousy and wanted to avoid it.

The jealousy made me feel sick, especially since I hated that I felt that way toward them.

Taraji's dark brown eyes brightened and she grinned. "You do? Kasim is going to allow you?" I smiled, the nauseous feeling fading with her oblivious joy. "What are you going to take?"

"A serpent and a dagger." I spewed all the details about

what they looked like, how I had spotted them, and who had them all while taking a few drinks of water directly from the bucket of water.

Igborg's head moved down and up with each spoonful of water, and I finally got the hint that he wanted some himself. I offered him the dipper and he set his face in the cool liquid to get a drink.

Mihrage leaned against the stone of the well. "It sounds like you have your work cut out for you. Sir Midas lives in one of the furthermost mansions." He had his arms folded over his chest and looked at me from beneath his eyebrows as if to say he had, indeed, seen me at the dunes, that he'd watched me walk away, and that he knew how I felt toward them both.

I hated his magical, sixth-sense gift. I casually shrugged my shoulder. "It won't be an issue for us. I'll go with Father tonight. We'll assess the grounds and see if we can get in and out, and then we can break in tonight if everything is clear."

"I might be able to help by conjuring up a sandstorm," Taraji offered, twitching her brows with a proud grin upon her face.

I was trying to figure out how that would actually help while busying my hands with Igborg. I pulled him from my shoulder and poured the rest of the water he didn't drink across his back, wetting it and cooling him.

"Or not . . . What's wrong, Caspara?" Taraji asked, hand on her hip in a way that looked very much like her mother.

I flushed, embarrassed. "Nothing is wrong. I'm nervous about tonight, that's all. Did Mihrage tell you he thinks you're going to join the Desert Trials? I told him that was ridiculous because you wouldn't think of leaving us." I smiled and nudged her ribs with my elbow. "Silly, isn't he?"

Taraji grimaced.

As if my stomach couldn't sink any further, it dropped through the heels of my feet and into the sand.

"You are?"

"Caspara, it's not—"

"Why didn't you tell me?" I interrupted, my tone perhaps a bit too sharp.

Mihrage straightened.

I lifted my gaze to him at his movement. "And you knew. You could have just *told* me while we were walking back!"

"It wasn't my place."

"Wasn't your place," I mocked and then scoffed.

"Caspara, I only just decided today," Taraji tried. "The day after tomorrow, I'll join the other sorceresses in the land. They're offering money to whoever completes the trials first. We could use that money."

"And if you finish the trials, you leave. Forever." I pulled away when she reached for me.

My best friend had hidden this secret. My second-best friend knew and hadn't told me. And the two of them were practically in love, and both of them were pushing me away. I was the third wheel of a wagon that caused it to clunk obnoxiously. It was better to remove the third wheel and balance a cart on two than suffer through an uneven load.

"I would never leave you," Taraji said, her brows etched with pain, her voice tight and unconfident.

But she knew the same as I—that the sorceresses left the main island of Sheblom and were shipped off to some secret island that held the Zauberin Academy. There, she would live and train to be one of the Sorceresses of the Sand. Only when she mastered her skill and was gifted an animal familiar would they consider her a "true" sorceress and allow her to return to the mainland. If she wanted.

"You kept all of this from me," I said. "You practice in secret and haven't shown me any of your tricks in *months*. Is it because . . ." I couldn't even bring myself to say it, but I cued Mihrage in on my question when I rubbed my hand down my right forearm. Across the sleeve hiding the tattoos.

Mihrage stepped in front of me, his white brows dipping into a deep scowl. "She would never do that. You know none of us care that you don't have magic. Plenty of women in the land are without it."

I exhaled through my nose and closed my eyes briefly, head lowered. I finally closed the gap between me and Taraji and wrapped my arms around her. "You're doing what's best for you. I can't blame you for that and I'll never resent you for it." But I let go and picked Igborg back up in my hand. "I have to plan this raid tonight. I'll see you at dinner."

Mihrage reached out and caught my upper arm.

Without turning to face him, I lifted my gaze.

"Caspara . . ." He wanted to tell me something. Perhaps he knew I was jealous of them, or he was sorry he had made me believe he liked me, that Taraji would always be my friend, and there would never be a way the three of us would be separated as friends, or whatever other nonsense he wanted to tell me to try and make me feel better.

Yet he said none of those things.

Instead, he lowered his hand and my heart lowered with it.

As I walked away, I barely caught Taraji whisper to

Mihrage, "What's wrong with her?"
And Mihrage answered, "She'll recover."

Three

A small headache climbed up the sides of my head while I stormed past my father and up to our shared room. Not wanting to think on anything else, I began pulling my black thief's clothes out for the night—until Igborg fell from my shoulder and landed on the shirt I held, effectively dropping it from my grip and onto the bed.

He looked up at me. Although we never held a verbal conversation where he could actually answer back, his glass-like eyes were always so expressive, I knew he was smarter than the average lizard.

Right now he stared at me with a look either telling me it was foolish to prepare so many hours in advance, or that I should go back out and speak with my friends. I knew he meant the latter, but I didn't care.

Father announced his presence behind me by coughing once.

I folded my arms across my chest, narrowed my eyes, and faced him. "What?"

"You never hide your anger."

"Taraji is joining the trials. She didn't even tell me." I busied myself by retrieving the patched-up bag my father always carried with us on raids, and then my own.

"Hm. If I recall, you spoke of her joining once. You

felt she would have a chance at a new life if she did." He walked over and grabbed the bag in my hand, forcing me to face him.

His soft brown eyes studied me with a look that made me feel like a child again, when he felt bad because he had to leave me alone for a few hours at night to slip away and steal food for us, or when I had to stay home with Taraji's family while he performed some secretive errand.

It was pity.

He felt bad for me.

I only realized I was clenching my teeth when I opened my mouth to talk to him and my jaw slackened. "The worst part is, I know I shouldn't be jealous." I let go of the bag and held up my arm. "According to you, my mother was a sorceress. My whole life, you've claimed these markings are some sort of prophecy, but I can't help but feel it's a curse suppressing whatever magic I might possess."

"Caspara, you've never had the gift of magic. You weren't born with it," he insisted. "But you don't need it. You're a talented thief, have quite the experience with your sword, and—"

"And yet I can't join my best friend on one of the grandest adventures of our lives. She'll leave and . . . and Mihrage will leave with her. And then what do I have? This?" I held my hands out to gesture to our pathetic home that, by comparison, would make most people in Zunbar happy with what they had.

Father looked around the room and his lips tightened ever so slightly in pain.

I didn't mean to hurt his feelings.

"Father, what do I have to live for?" I meant the

question fervently. My entire life, I'd wanted nothing but to be like him. I followed him everywhere. As I got older, I'd started sneaking off to follow him on his nightly raids until he finally just chose to train me and have me join him at his side. But now, with the very real thought my friends would leave, I didn't know what to do. "Will I take up the mantle of thief forever?" I wondered aloud.

"You've made quite the name for yourself as Almas," Father said.

I rolled my eyes. "The city thinks every thief is Almas. I'm not special."

He put his hands on my shoulders and leaned down to look me in the eye. "I never want to hear you say that again. You *are* special. You're the most special person in the world."

"Because I'm your daughter and you have to say that," I mumbled.

Father smiled. When he smiled, dimples showed in his cheeks and made my anger fade away like the pulling back of the tide. "Yes, of course because you're my daughter. But also because you *are* important. Telama never would have blessed you otherwise." He moved one hand down to lift my tattooed arm. "These markings aren't an accident, Caspara. They didn't happen as the result of a curse."

"They're a blessing," I said in a mocking, deep voice, because I'd heard him say this same thing a billion times. "But *you* never tell me what sort of blessing."

Father's gaze lowered to the markings and his thumb brushed the back of my hand. "When you were just born, I still lived with your mother. We were sitting side by side under the light of the window. You loved looking out at the trees, and Omar would sit on a branch nearest the window because you giggled when you saw him."

Father very rarely spoke of the past, before he was a thief. When he did, I felt it was a part of my father I'd never known, a part he resisted me knowing about him. I didn't dare move.

"One particular day, we were summoned . . ." He paused, his brows furrowed, and he lifted his eyes to mine.

"Please tell me," I begged before he could turn away.

He heaved a sigh. "I was summoned to the door. Telama, a wise woman who travels to people when they most need her, appeared. I knew who she was because Sultana Shahira once spoke a tale where she and the sultan would meet Telama in the streets, and the very next day they did. So when she arrived on my doorstep, I knew it was of the greatest importance." Father walked to our window and leaned his arm above it to look out at the expanse of nothing beyond. His lip tugged in a smile. His eyes were lost in the distant memory. "She told me she had a blessing for you. Your mother gave you to Telama and the woman's eyes lit up with this white glow."

I imagined the blind woman, gazing down at a mussy-haired infant with big brown eyes. Her hair was braided in two long braids, one over each shoulder, and her face was etched with years.

Father continued, "She said, *The power of one is in two most dear. When you discover your other half, your destiny will be made clear.*" He lowered his arm and faced me. "I don't know what it means. It was only a couple of years after that I . . . I took you and left."

Rubbing my lips together, I studied him. Father had never told me any of what Telama had said. Power of one in two? Other half? Destiny? "Father . . . who was my mother?"

Father's walls went up. His eyes pinched, his jaw tightened, and his shoulders rounded. "I think we need to get started on dinner and eat a mighty feast before your first assignment tonight." He walked past me and put his hand on my shoulder.

I turned with him and caught his wrist. "Baba, you owe me that much. It can be my birthday present."

"I'm afraid that if I tell you . . . that you may resent me for a very long time," he confessed.

"I may resent you more if you do not tell me."

Father scratched his beard. "I don't want to distract you from your raid tonight. So, let's make a compromise. You and I go and steal these things, and when we get home I'll answer any question you want to ask me."

I smiled. "Deal."

He held up his pinky finger and I linked mine in his and we both stuck out our tongue. It was a ridiculous promise "ritual" he'd done with me for as long as I could remember, and it left us both laughing each time.

Feeling far more lighthearted than a few minutes ago, I followed him down to the kitchen to help prepare a proper dinner.

If Father was being honest, and I saw no reason to think he wasn't, I might have some sorceress-given destiny. Maybe I did have some purpose in this life, even if I often felt like just another granule of sand being blown across the desert.

We spoke about the mission while preparing for dinner. Father liked my plan of going to the house and assessing the garden and house to see whether or not tonight was safe to enter. We needed to know the family's routine and plans in order to uncover the ideal time to slip in. Even more importantly, Father pointed out, we needed to know *where* the precious objects had been stored in the family home.

I realized then I should have followed the men who would have delivered them. I might have caught sight of where they'd placed everything. Father excused this error of mine, telling me, "You couldn't have known this would be your first job, which also means you had no idea how much preparation takes place prior to jumping in and stealing."

He was right.

We sat down to eat our *khoresh ghormeh sabzi*—one of the easiest meals to make because it was a stew with parsley, leeks, beans, and tonight Father even had fresh lamb to eat with it.

We left the dishes in the sink after eating and I finally changed into my thief clothing. I stood outside my front door, my scarf hanging from my head and Igborg hiding in my bag as if he were a tiny desert lizard in spite of being probably weighing almost five pounds. It might not have seemed much, but he was definitely noticeable.

Footfalls to my right drew my attention and I turned to see Taraji headed my way. I swallowed thickly and adjusted the bag on my shoulder.

"I wanted to apologize for earlier," she said. She stopped a short distance away and gnawed her bottom lip. "I should have told you about joining the trials."

"I know." The tightness in my chest suffocated me. "You've never made me feel inferior. I guess I'm just jealous, Taraji. You get to join the trials. You get a chance to have a better life while I'm . . . stuck here." I shrugged a shoulder. "I'm jealous you get to have an adventure." I offer an apologetic smile.

Her large lips spread, revealing her vibrant white teeth. She threw her arms around me and squeezed. "Adventure, ha! *You're* the one always going on adventures. You have no idea how jealous I am that you get to slink away like a cat in the night and you always come home with something good." She let go and stepped back. "Not to mention, you're one of the few thieves with a street name."

I rubbed the back of my neck. I didn't have the heart to tell her the title "Almas" was actually a man's name, nor did I want to admit to her that Almas had existed as long as our leader, Farhad, had crept the streets, and I *certainly* didn't have the heart to tell her the people overgeneralized to my actions because it was more convenient to hold on to that name than try and create a new one for me.

"Will you come with me to the parade?" she asked.

"I wouldn't miss it." I grinned.

She reached out and gave my hand a squeeze, her shoulders dropping in relief, and I echoed the same movement. It felt as if two Igborgs had been taken from my shoulders. Taraji skipped back to her house and I turned to face my father, who had just exited the house.

He said nothing but gave a knowing smile.

"Time to go steal! Maybe I can find a good luck charm for the trials and give it to Taraji."

Together, Father and I stepped into the night.

Four

Not a breath shifted the leaves of the ash tree attempting to obstruct my view of the front of the white marble house. I could only imagine how difficult it was to keep clean considering it was dropped in a sea of red sand. It stuck out as much as a pool of water in the middle of the desert.

Father and I had already scaled the wall. Protected by the darkness of the shadows, we were completely unseen. But in the silence that had followed us from the village, all I could think of was what my father had told me regarding Telama and her prophecy about my destiny. Who was I to deserve any kind of blessing?

"Climb up and look through the doors," Father whispered, his voice as silent as the wind and yet cutting through my thoughts and rooting me back into the moment I was *supposed* to be focused on.

I followed his gaze to the balcony nearest us. Lamplight glowed from it.

Somewhere in the courtyard was the gentle sound of a fountain.

I scoffed internally at the thought of having a fountain of running water. Precious water we desert folk valued above nearly anything else. If our well ran dry, we would have nothing, yet this family used water for nothing other than appearances.

Using the trellises, covered in crisp, dried vines thirsty for water, I easily made my way up the wall and gripped the white rail. As soon as my hands touched the railing, the light went out. Had we truly gotten so lucky that the family would be going to bed so early? A part of me wished they hadn't smothered the light, because I would have liked to better assess the room. Oh well, I would have to rely on my night vision.

With one arm steadying me on the balcony railing and my feet pressed firmly against the wall, I leaned as far as I could to view the front of the house. I had hidden my face behind my black scarf and a bead of sweat tickled down the back of my neck. I shivered and wiped it away.

The front door opened and Sir Midas, his wife, and their two children exited the house and loaded up into a cart.

"You've got to be kidding me," I muttered under my breath.

"What is it?" Father asked from somewhere below.

"The family is leaving," I whispered, keeping my eyes focused on the target. "How did we get so lucky?"

Father's clothing rustled beside me and I knew without looking that he'd made his way up beside me. "Last one up is a dung beetle."

I looked over my shoulder at my father.

His cocoa-brown eyes wrinkled in the corners with a smile, his mouth hidden behind the red scarf around his face. He pressed his weight into his palms, lifting himself up so his shoulders were over the ledge of the balcony.

"First one up has to eat it," I retorted. I pulled up on the railing from which I hung, lifting myself to grasp the top.

But Father was still somehow faster than me, in spite of being older, and expertly bounded up onto the balcony. "I've been thinking about how we should celebrate your sixteenth birthday."

I sat on the railing and swung my legs over before I straightened. "Father, I don't need anything special." I walked to the balcony doors and tested them.

Surprise—they were locked.

I dug my lockpick tools from the pouch on my belt, then crouched to peer into the black keyhole. "All I want is to know more about my mother. And you. Maybe the destiny Telama wants me to fulfill is hidden in the secrets you keep." I looked up at him from beneath my brows—a look he'd used on me as a child to get me to do as he wanted when he was fed up repeating himself.

I could barely see the details of his face in the moonlight, but there was just enough of a glint off his eyes that I noticed them dart to me. "Rule nine, Caspara," he said barely above a whisper.

Be as quiet as the shadows.

I snapped my teeth shut and concentrated on the task at hand. Using my hook, I pressed up on each of the five pins until I found the one that gave the most resistance— the binding pin. In record time, I located it, set it, then worked my way through the other four pins until each was set.

I stood and pulled the door open. "Baba."

He had been keeping his attention on the shadows around us, watching for any danger, and thus fulfilling rule number five of the thief code, *Watch each other's back.* Even if the thieves went out alone, we held this rule in more than one way. If another thief was in danger, we were to step up and assist them.

Father stepped back toward me, but his gaze was locked on something in the shadows across the streets, something I couldn't see in spite of my keen vision. He finally turned to me, gave a nod, and entered the room.

I stepped in after him and my jaw went slack upon seeing the massive room. The bed alone would fit probably four adults, but if the room were cleared of all the unnecessary furniture, we could have fit two of our meager desert homes side by side just in the bedroom.

The fire of jealousy and hatred burned in my belly.

This was the biggest reason why I didn't mind stealing from the wealthy. It was unjust that one family should possess so much while there were children begging on the streets for food.

The walls were painted blue and turquoise with silver designs stenciled on top. An enormous gold lamp hung overhead and a few hung on the walls. The bedding was silk, probably imported.

What would it have been like to have so much wealth? To have enough money I could buy a beaded pillow for no other use than to *decorate* my bed? Or to have an entire drawer filled with bracelets? I had only one, a brass one my father claimed had once been my mother's, and I only wore it for celebrations. I would don it for my birthday in a few days. But gazing down at the gold, silver, even turquoise bangles, I couldn't help but let the hatred bubble in my chest.

The poor didn't have a chance to rise above their stations.

Meanwhile, the rich got richer and greedier.

I always searched the woman's side of the room while Father took on the man's side. He walked past the vanity near the window, past the carved armoire, and to the far side of the room.

I swiped a good handful of the jewelry—bangles, earrings, golden chains, and broaches—enough that I could feel satisfied but not enough the woman would miss them. True, she might call to her husband, "Have you seen my bangle with the triangles on it? I can't find it anywhere." And he would call back, "Have you searched behind your vanity, my darling?"

I nearly laughed out loud at the thought.

I dropped the handfuls of jewelry on top of Igborg inside my pouch, but suddenly noticed my father had stopped in the middle of the room, his head tilted to one side.

"What is it?" I asked.

"How did you hear about the snake and dagger?" Father asked, seeming to have forgotten rule nine himself.

"At the docks. Why?" I took a few steps to peer around him.

On the table just steps away from my father were precious trinkets—a small dragon skull, a lamp with the nozzle scorched from being lit, and to my absolute astonishment, the dagger and snake statue.

My brows furrowed, likely matching the confused expression on my father's face.

I understood then why he asked what he did.

Because what were the chances that I not only overheard about these riches, but that the family whose house they were in would *conveniently* leave their home, *and* that we should enter the room in which they would be kept?

"This is such a coincidence," I voiced aloud.

"Too much of one," Father muttered. "Only someone who knows a thief would know how to set this up." He turned to face me. "We go to this particular house, enter *this* room first. Why? Because it's easier to enter the room nearest the outer wall where we are less likely to be noticed."

"Or the old man wanted to put his new prizes in his bedroom?" I offered.

Father gestured with an open hand to his side of the room. "Where are the men's things? Take a look at the jewelry you took. What size are they?"

Raising my brow and not following my father, I reached into my pouch and removed one of the bangles. It fit in the palm of my hand. Far too small for a woman to wear.

My mouth went dry.

This was one of the daughters' rooms.

My gaze darted to him. He was right. This was all too much of a coincidence.

Father grabbed my hand and had started to pull me from the room when he suddenly grunted and jerked backward, yanking my arm with him.

"What is it?" I asked frantically.

Father grimaced in pain.

We both looked down and spotted the golden serpent with its fangs stuck in the top of my father's boot. Its body coiled around his ankle and held fast.

My breath caught and I reached down to grab it, but my Father shoved his bag into my hands. "Take this and go now."

I blinked. "Are you crazy? We have to—"

"It's enchanted and I can't move. This is a trap."

"A trap?" I laughed because, well, it sounded ridiculous. Who would want to trap us? Maybe the guards because they were tired of Almas, but . . . Father's eyes were full of too much fear for that. "What is it you're not telling me?" I demanded.

He looked down at the serpent and then ran his hand over his face, withdrawing the scarf disguising it. "You have to leave."

My heart began to pound. "You want me to leave you? No! I'll carry the snake, and we can go to Madame Kiara. Surely, she can tell us a way—" He reached out again, gripped my arms and straightened me.

"You wanted me to tell you about your mother. I wanted to tell you tonight when we got home, but"—he heaved a big breath— "I do not believe I will make it home."

I shook my head, my words somehow caught in my throat.

"I'm sorry, Caspara. I should have been more open with you from the start. Your mother." He gnawed his bottom lip, still debating whether or not to tell me in spite of our current danger. "Caspara. What is the number one rule of the forty thieves?"

"Don't leave your baba behind?"

His expression didn't change.

I huffed. "Always be aware of your surroundings. But we watched them leave!"

He pointed to the snake's glowing green eyes. My hands suddenly went clammy and my mouth dry. The snake was indeed enchanted.

Father touched my chin. "This must have been set up."

"You think I was meant to overhear someone talking about a golden statue?" I asked sarcastically. I pulled away and ran to get the shirt I'd dropped on the floor. "I'll cover the snake with this and—"

"No, Caspara."

Footsteps sounded as well as voices, a good handful of them.

Guards.

Father's eyes were full of sadness, wishing we had more time. "Your mother is Roshanak. The Grand Sorceress. I'm so sorry I didn't tell you sooner. I know you have questions, and I will answer all of them when I get the chance, but you must go home."

"Baba—"

The soldier's voices were just outside the door. Luckily for us, the idiot merchant had locked it and one of the soldiers bumped into it when he tried to open it.

Father pulled me into his arms and kissed the top of my head.

"I'll get you out of prison," I vowed.

"I love you too, dune bug."

I gave my baba a playful scowl, kissed his cheek, hoisted his bag over my shoulder, and then bolted out the still-open balcony door just as the main bedroom door flew open and light filled the room.

Thieves got arrested now and then. It was part of the risk, but we always got ours out.

Yet, somehow the nervousness in my father's eyes made me wonder if maybe this wasn't any ordinary arrest. I hadn't even had time to process the identity of my mother when I skidded out the door and pressed my back up against the exterior wall.

And none too soon.

The door cracked and the sound of shifting metal from the soldier's armor filled the room.

My heart jumped into my throat when I heard a woman's voice. "Ah, Kasim. It has been many years, old friend."

I pressed my back as tightly as I could to the wall, as if it could absorb me if I tried hard enough.

"We haven't been friends for some time, Roshanak," Father said.

Roshanak. My mother. The news suddenly slammed into me and stole my breath. Grand Sorceress Roshanak, the most powerful sorceress in the land, the right hand of Sultan Zayne.

"Where is the girl?"

Me. She's looking for me. No, she could be looking for any other girl. But not even I believed myself.

"Who do you mean?" Father replied.

The woman laughed a shrill, annoyed laugh. "I know she was here with you. Do you think me a fool? I see no bag on your person. You never steal without having a way to get it home." The woman's voice grew nearer to me and I knew what I had to do—jump from the balcony and leave my father to be arrested.

Arrested by my *mother*.

Five

It wasn't much of a decision, jumping from the balcony, but I couldn't help but think if the roles were reversed, Father would never have left me behind. It wasn't fair he expected me to do something he wouldn't. But I leapt over the balcony and landed in the sand, rolling to absorb the blow.

I heard the exterior door open and slam against the wall just as I stepped back and crouched in the shadow of the mansion.

"Kasim, you disappoint me yet again. It is nearly her sixteenth birthday and I would think it's time . . ." Her voice faded as she reentered the room and the door closed behind her.

I couldn't hear anything else.

Me.

Unless there was another nearly sixteen-year-old girl my father knew and my mother wanted . . . she was looking for *me*.

My heart pounded hard enough I could feel it in my neck, as if I'd just sprinted the entire way from Zunbar to home. Why would the grand sorceress want a thief? Had any other thief been in that room, my question would have an obvious answer—to arrest them. But I couldn't believe the *grand* sorceress would be the one to fret about any ordinary thief.

More questions flooded my thoughts: why would a mother who hadn't been involved in my life suddenly come looking for me just before my sixteenth birthday? What if she'd been searching for me my whole life and Father had taken me from her?

I lingered in the shadows until I saw the soldiers exit the main entrance with my father bound between them. Seeing my father pulled me away from my questions, save one: why hadn't my father wanted me to be raised in the palace?

With my father's wrists bound behind his back and keeping his head high, he walked in the center of the guards. I could have sworn his eyes searched the shadows for my form.

My hands and legs trembled.

My questions could be answered later, as long as I saved my father. He always said I was the best lockpick in the land. I'd never personally attempted to break into the prison, but if I was as skilled as my father claimed, it would be no problem.

Mihrage had broken out of prison twice now. I wished he were there to help me. I should have asked for him to come, or accepted Taraji's help. Maybe she could have used her magic to distract the guards by blinding them with sand.

But "if only's" weren't going to help me undo what had already been done.

For agonizing minutes, I remained still to be sure no one followed in the shadows or watched from the balcony before I crept from my hiding spot. I climbed on top of the exterior wall of the manor and scurried like a rat across it before dropping into the streets on the other side.

I had been raised a thief, living with a handful of other outcasts in our land in the deserts outside of Zunbar. We stole from the greedy to support our own people and whomever we could in the city. But in all his years doing this, my father had never been arrested.

With every step I took to follow them, I resisted the urge to flee. After all, Father had ordered me to do so. I should have obeyed him. He would be mad at me later for not.

But a verbal scolding was better than sitting on my thumbs and fretting over his fate.

The back of my neck prickled and I paused at the corner of a building, catching my breath while looking around. *Rule number one* popped into my mind and I glanced in the direction from which I'd come to check my surroundings.

A shadow moved across the street and a few buildings down. The edge of a cloak?

Was I being followed?

My heart picked up speed and I listened carefully to the sounds of the night. Overhead, a cluster of bats called out, finishing their dinner of pesky mosquitos and gnats. A baby cried somewhere nearby. A bucket up an alley clattered and my heart jumped. But it was followed by the sound of a hissing cat. Just as my heart began to slow down, I heard the sound of beating wings and pressed myself tightly into the shadows.

But the hawk landed on the broken railing at the bottom of the steps.

"Omar?" I whispered. "What are you doing here?" I

demanded, as if the bird could answer me.

He rolled his head in my direction and fluffed his wings. Father's hunting hawk *should have been* sound asleep in our house, but he listened to Father about as well as I did. Still, he wasn't the type of hawk that should have been hunting at night.

I lifted my gaze in the direction I thought I had seen the shadow, but nothing had moved. I looked back at Omar. "You're not helping. If you want to, go make sure Kasim makes it to the prison safely."

The bird's eye focused on me as though contemplating whether or not to listen, then he spread his wings and flew away.

My pouch shifted and I patted it. "Don't worry, Igborg. Omar's gone," I said to reassure my pet lizard he wasn't going to become the hawk's dinner.

Even though I could have imagined the mysterious flutter of fabric in the shadows, I wasn't willing to risk any chance of getting caught. I took the alley instead of the main road and made my way to the prison.

I'd nearly made it to my destination when the hair on the back of my neck prickled again and my fingertips tingled. This time, I stepped into the nearest doorway and pressed my back to the door.

A hooded figure darted across the sliver of moonlight. They paused just at the edge and looked down the alley, their head moving left and then right. This was no coincidence. My instincts had warned me. Whoever this was had been following me. If Roshanak truly wanted me, as she'd told my father, this person could be one of her spies sent to collect me. If I were in her shoes, I would have done the same thing, and that thought almost scared me.

I took quick, short breaths, trying to stay as quiet as possible. The bags on my shoulder suddenly felt heavier than I'd noticed.

If I needed a way out, I knew to head south two streets and make a run eastward. If the figure followed, I could come up with a plan for which streets to disappear down within seconds, and then I would be out in the desert before they could ever catch up. The chances of being followed beyond the city gates were slim. In fact, no one had ever managed to follow a thief back to our village. At least, that I knew of.

The hooded figure went up the wrong alley, and I gulped a big breath of relief.

Father's voice telling me to go home echoed in my mind. But sucking in one last deep breath, I turned and ran as fast as my legs could carry me. I'd come this far and had evaded the figure for now. I had to finish what I'd set out to do.

The prison stood below the cliff on which the palace was built. I'd always been confused why they would keep thieves and murderers so close to the royal family, but then again the walls of the palace *were* heavily guarded. Not only that, but it would have been impossible for anyone to escape the prison, climb the cliff, and in turn the wall of the palace without being shot by the archers positioned on the roof of the prison.

Built of stone and mud, the prison hardly looked strong. Then again, I supposed it didn't need to be any stronger because the types of criminals who ended up there were men or women without magic and of the lower class. Those walls would never hold a sorceress. Not that I'd even heard of a sorceress ever being arrested.

The prison was a long, narrow building with several cells on either side—one of which didn't get an exterior window since it pressed right up against the cliff. Prison guards paced across the roof and one passed by the outer wall.

I'd lost sight of the group of men bringing my father to this location.

One of the blue tarps overhead decorating and providing shade to the streets of Zunbar snapped in the wind and my gaze lifted to it. I realized then that my nails were biting the palms of my hands and my scarf was clinging to my mouth. I lowered it to gasp a breath of fresh air.

Relax, Caspara. Thieves have been arrested before. First step, locate your father. Check the windows.

After checking to ensure none of the soldiers were near and I couldn't see the hooded figure, I ran to the first window of the prison. I gripped the edge with my fingers and pulled myself up to look through the bars and see if my father was inside. It was empty. The second one too. The third housed a sleeping drunk—I could smell the stench of him—and the fourth had a large man lying on the floor.

I wiped my hands, damp with nerves, on my pants for a third time and peered into the fifth cell.

"Baba?" I whispered at the figure standing near the door. I could barely make him out.

He rushed over and moonlight spilled over his features. My heart jumped. "I told you to go home," Father whispered.

"You know me better than that. I can help get you

out." I withdrew my lockpicks and held them out to him.

He wrapped his hand around mine. "Thank you. But you can't linger here."

I frowned. "I can cause a distraction and—"

"If you stand there too long, one of the guards will find you. Tell Farhad where I am."

"And ask him to answer all of the questions you held from me?" I didn't mean to sound as accusatory as I did, but the secrets hurt.

Father's grip on my hand tightened. "You're right. I should have told you sooner. I wanted you to be ready. I had planned to invite Jade so we could answer any questions you had, but . . ."

"Why?" I asked, my voice strained. I swallowed and made it stronger. "Why did you take me from her? Was she truly so awful you abandoned a life in the palace? A life where we could have lived without starving of hunger and thirst?"

Father studied my expression a long time with his cocoa-brown eyes, weighing his response and choosing his words as carefully as always. "Yes, you could have been raised in the palace, alongside Prince Abudar and Princess Mithra, with tables laden with food and wearing the finest of clothing. But Roshanak would have made your life miserable."

"And I'm just supposed to believe you?" The words blurted from my lips before I could check them. Father had never given me a reason to doubt him. He'd always been honest, his only secrets his past and my mother.

His eyes saddened. "No. I taught you better than that." The edge of his lip tugged ever so slightly in a heavy but proud grin.

Rule number eleven. Don't believe everything you hear.

Father's eyes suddenly darted to something over my shoulder. "Is he one of ours?"

I snapped my head to look back and spotted the hooded figure slinking toward me.

He froze when he realized I'd spotted him.

"I thought I'd lost him," I said breathlessly. My palms went clammy and sweat beaded my back as dread clawed at my stomach.

The man began running toward me.

"Go!" Father pushed my hand away. "I'll pick the lock. Tell Farhad. If I don't return to you by dawn, only then can he come for me."

I wanted to object, to tell him Farhad would send a whole army of our own to get him out as soon as I reached home, but the figure was within three strides of me and closing fast.

"Sands," I whispered.

I ran northward—the opposite direction of my unfamiliar shadow. I knew the back streets of Zunbar like the back of my hand. The alley I ran down broke out to the cliffs by the ocean and I followed a hazardous path down a dangerous pile of stones to the docks.

They clattered down behind me from the individual trying to keep up with me.

Once my boots hit the wooden slabs that made up the docks, I took off at a steady pace to the main street and then out the eastern gate. I glanced back only once and couldn't see the figure keeping up with me.

I hopped over the Dumue River and carried on southeast into the open expanse of desert beyond. I only stopped running when my ribs twinged and my legs burned from the effort.

The village of thieves lay in the dunes between the capital city and Dorus. To anyone who happened upon the village in the middle of the night, it appeared abandoned. After all, our windows were shuttered and lamps only lit when necessary. The forty thieves worked mostly at night, while everyone slept—including the heat.

I still had an hour's walk.

An hour to think to myself how this situation was entirely my fault. Because *I* had heard of the snake. *I* had told my father. *I* had planned—and failed at—the assignment.

A lump swelled in my throat and I dug into my pouch for my water skin. But no amount of water could help me swallow down the guilt I felt.

Igborg rumbled and I wiped a completely unnecessary tear from the corner of my eye.

"He's fine. I'm fine," I insisted. But I couldn't shake off the impending sense of doom holding on to my shoulders.

I'd always been one to jump to the worst possible scenario. It was a curse, I swear. One time, the rope holding the bucket for the well had frayed and the bucket had fallen in. I had insisted we would never be able to drink again.

Of course, I was five at the time and had no idea how easy it was to replace the bucket.

But even now, all I could think about was the grand sorceress holding my father in prison for some dark reason, like holding him hostage to get to me, or maybe Father was actually spying on the other sorceresses in the land and she thought she might get information out of him, or . . . my imagination was getting carried away.

Luckily, my village came into view and I began running again until I reached the council house and barged in.

The three men who stood at my father's side on the council looked up from the worn map resting on the table before them, each of them with an equally wide-eyed expression as the door bounced off the wall behind it.

My entrance could have been a little less abrupt, I supposed.

"My mother arrested him!" I had conjured up a conversation on the way there, and blurting *that* out certainly wasn't the plan. At least, not in that order. I shook my head and quickly backtracked. "I mean, there was a trap and Father was arrested by her, by Roshanak."

"He told you?" Farhad asked, completely off-topic.

"Did you see where they took him?" Babkak asked, sheathing the sword I hadn't realized he'd drawn until that moment.

I narrowed my eyes. "The prison, of course. Where else would they take him? You have to get him out!"

Farhad exchanged a silent look with Babkak. "It's risky."

"Why would she want Kasim?" Dablin added.

"She and Kasim have a history," Farhad replied vaguely, but exchanged a glance with me that told me he wouldn't reveal my secret if I didn't want him to. In my opinion, they should have realized the secret when I'd blurted that my mother had arrested my father, but I didn't care if they knew or not. Eventually, our merry band of thieves would find out one way or another.

However, Farhad continued before I could say anything. "You're certain he wants us to come now?"

I hesitated and shifted my weight on my feet. "Well, no. Not exactly." I lowered my gaze to keep the pressure of theirs off of me. "He said if he didn't make it back by dawn, to send help. I left him my lockpicks." I looked up from under my lashes.

As a child, I had used the pouting look to my advantage dozens of times. But not since I'd become a young lady. Not that I was trying to use it on the leaders of our people, but Farhad was practically a grandfather figure to me, and I wanted him to take action.

Farhad heaved a sigh and leaned his palms on the table, making the rickety thing creak beneath his weight. "Then you should go home and rest."

I blanched, blinking and straightening. "You expect me to walk into my *empty* home and have pleasant dreams while my father is locked up?"

"He isn't the first one of us to be arrested, Caspara," Dablin said. I knew he was trying to comfort me, but he was the youngest on the council and not even ten years older than me. His dashing smile didn't work on me.

I folded my arms across my chest and met his grin with a glare.

His smile faltered and he glanced at Farhad to clear his throat, as though silently asking if they were all truly going to sit and wait.

Farhad confirmed the unspoken words with a nod, then looked me in the eye. "Would you like to speak alone with me, Caspara? About anything you may have learned tonight?"

In honesty, yes. I wanted to beg for answers to all the

millions of questions I had, but my mind suddenly went blank at his offering. And I felt like a fool standing there, fuming like a stubborn child.

"No," I answered firmly, refusing his help. "Father can tell me when he gets home. If he isn't home by dawn and if you don't go to get him, I'll rescue him myself." I slammed the door so hard on my way out, something on one of the shelves inside crashed onto the floor.

Six

I sat on the roof of my home, staring up at the billions of stars overhead, my thoughts just about as plentiful. A knot had formed between my eyes, pulsing pain behind them and down the back of my neck. I was exhausted, emotionally and physically, and yet I couldn't sleep. I was watching the horizon for my father. Every shadow the moon cast made my heart jump. And every time, I was disappointed when the clouds parted and revealed nothing there.

Maybe I should have let Farhad answer my questions, if only for the sake of keeping me distracted. Midnight had long since passed and the moon was sinking lower to my right. I had been watching it from the edge of my vision. And every inch it sank, my stomach sank with it.

Igborg let out a high-pitched yawn as he stretched, his tiny claws extending out, and then he crawled onto my lap and curled up like a kitten.

I looked down at him and stroked his head. "I'm worried about Baba," I admitted.

He looked at me as if to say, "Me too," or "Then why are we sitting here?"

I couldn't argue with him because I didn't know either. Father should have picked the lock by now. He should have made it through the desert by now. The only reason he wouldn't have escaped would be if something happened, like the guards taking him and questioning him or catching him with the lockpicks, or . . . who knew what else?

The soft shuffle of boots on sand made me jump and look over my shoulder so quickly I nearly threw Igborg over the ledge and to the ground below.

"I didn't mean to startle you," Mihrage said.

My stomach dropped and I swallowed hard.

He wore only a cotton undershirt and his pants.

Biting the inside of my cheek, I looked back to the desert, in case something had changed during my five-second break in my vigil.

Mihrage lowered himself onto the ledge beside me. "Where's your father?"

I gritted my teeth and finally glanced sideways at Mihrage. "He was arrested."

Mihrage's brows lifted in surprise. "I never thought Almas, the grand thief of the night, would ever be caught." A playful grin toyed on his lips.

I threw him a glare.

He dropped his teasing smile and cleared his throat while running his fingers through his mussy white hair. It was only then I realized it was free from its typical braid, and it dawned on me that Mihrage had woken from his sleep to come up here and sit with me.

"I am merely surprised," he explained, breaking the silence. He placed his hand on my back. "Are you all right?"

I shrugged off his comforting touch. "Don't make me feel worse than I already do."

"That wasn't my intention," he said quickly. I knew it wasn't, but I was miserable. Why not make him miserable too? But the crease on his brow showed genuine concern.

Moving Igborg to the ledge opposite Mihrage, I pulled my knees to my chest. "He was supposed to be home," I whispered, finally admitting that I was worried. And as much as I wanted to pretend I was mad at Mihrage, I was secretly relieved I was no longer alone. "Can you sense anything about him?" I braved a glance away from the horizon to Mihrage.

He heaved a sigh and shook his head. "I'm afraid my premonitions don't quite work that way," he replied softly. "I can't always control them. I'm sorry."

"Whole lot of good you are," I said sarcastically.

Mihrage smiled, because he knew I meant it that way. He wrapped his arm around my shoulder, in spite of me having shrugged him off moments ago. The fireflies I should have felt buzzing in my stomach at his touch were asleep. Because he was my friend and nothing more. Because I would never do anything to hurt him or Taraji.

Relishing the silence and Mihrage's presence, I rested my head on his shoulder. It suddenly felt heavy and I needed relief from its weight. To make sure Mihrage understood I didn't mean it romantically, I said, "Where is Taraji? Shouldn't you be off on a midnight picnic with her somewhere?"

He chuckled, making my head bounce on his shoulder. "She's not one for midnight snacks. Not even midnight sitting on the edge of a building to watch the desert."

"Don't I know that? She stayed over once and we stayed up all night and she was a dragon the next day."

We laughed. It felt good to smile, to take my thoughts

away from the worry and negative thoughts I felt.

After some time, Mihrage said, "You should get some sleep."

I realized I had closed my eyes and actually had fallen asleep.

I quickly sat up and rubbed my eyes. "I can't. Not until Father is home."

Mihrage lowered his arm. "Your father will be fine. It's prison. The worst thing that could happen is that he might be forced to eat their awful food." He grinned again, trying to lighten my mood.

But he didn't know the means by which Father was arrested, or that he'd dropped information on me just before ordering me to leave him behind.

Not wanting to tell him just yet, I said, "I suppose you should know, considering you're the only one of us to have been arrested three times."

"Only twice," he countered in his typical way. "They didn't get me to the prison the third time."

A smile finally broke across my face because that third time was when Dablin had helped him escape and brought him to live with us. That was nearly five years ago, when Mihrage was only twelve and stealing to survive like most of the poor. He'd grown from a gangly boy into a tall and strong man in that short expanse of time.

"You'll be no good saving your father if you can't keep your eyes open tomorrow." Mihrage knew exactly what to say to finally get me to sleep. When I looked up at him, brow furrowed in question, he added, "I assume that's your back-up plan if he doesn't get home by dawn?"

I shuffled to my feet, picking up Igborg with me. Lazy thing didn't even open his eyes. "Farhad and the others are supposed to go get him."

"Mm. Right," he said and gave me a wink that told me he knew I wasn't about to twirl around in circles all day while everyone else went off to rescue my father. He knew me a bit too well. He'd always been a stickler for rules. "Just as well. I'm sure he'll be home by dinner. I'll see you in the morning, Caspara." He bobbed his chin in a silent departure, once again leaving me alone with my mind too tired to keep my eyes open.

I finally relented and went down to the room I shared with my father. I laid with my back to his bed. Everything from that night had been too conveniently perfect. Father had picked up on it the instant he'd spotted the snake, but what was it about the serpent that triggered his knowledge? What was it he saw that I completely missed? Had he sensed the enchantment that bound him to the room? Or was it a symbol he recognized?

I mentally made note of a new thief rule—*If it's too good to be true, it probably is.*

Igborg poked my cheek with his nose and then flicked his tongue over my ear.

"Igborg, stop," I groaned and pushed him off my shoulder. *Stupid lizard. Always hungry.*

I rolled over, but in doing so, I noticed light beyond my heavy eyelids. I peeled them open and, to my astonishment, it was daylight already. I muttered an unladylike curse and scrambled to get my shoes on and then my weapon belt with its reliable contents of small pouches, a dagger, and short sword. Oh, and a pocket on my lower back for Igborg.

As he squished his way in and blinked up at me, I wondered if I was feeding him too much, because he'd nearly outgrown the pouch somehow.

I'd found him almost a year ago while sneaking around a house in Zunbar. Igborg had wedged his body between a building and rock with a chunk of flesh taken out of his tail, puncture marks in his sides, covered in little sand ticks. I figured he must have been attacked by a bird and then left himself vulnerable to the ticks. Which was why he was always frightened of Omar.

For some reason, I couldn't bring myself to leave him behind to die, even though I knew he was in really poor shape. I'd taken him to the apothecary Mihrage frequented, and Madame Kiara had miraculously helped me nurse Igborg back to health. Once healed, I thought he would be thrilled to go back into the wild. But it seemed being hand-fed the best treats was far more rewarding than scavenging in the desert.

And I couldn't deny I adored him.

I stumbled down to the empty kitchen. My right foot had fallen asleep and burned fiercely at being woken to help me walk. I hoped I was early enough to meet Farhad, Babkak, and Dablin. Not bothering to grab so much as a roll to eat, I slammed the door shut behind me and ran for the edge of the sand dune just in time to spot someone leave around it.

"Farhad!" I called when I rounded the corner.

The small band paused and turned to look at me. They all resumed walking but one.

Farhad met me, already shaking his head. "You stay here, Caspara."

"But I want to come with you. I *should* come with you. It's my fault he was arrested, so I should be there to help you bring him back."

"We have it handled. Too many people will not only draw attention but could lead to us being discovered."

"I know how to slip through the streets," I countered.

He frowned, the gray hairs of his beard only accentuating the corners of his lips in a far more dramatic frown. "I'm afraid not, Caspara. Stay with Mihrage and Taraji. I'm giving you an order."

The last sentence was added because I'd opened my mouth to interrupt. I snapped my teeth shut instead.

"We'll bring your father home." Farhad set his hand on my shoulder. "I promise."

My stomach felt like I'd swallowed stones.

I was forced to watch them walk away.

I felt Igborg wiggle and start climbing up my back to sit on my shoulder, his signal that he was hungry. I wasn't in the mood to make something. And then I recalled Mihrage the night before said he would meet me at breakfast. Thank the sands.

Casting one more glance at the men headed off to fix my problem, I turned and walked back into the village. It was one thing to mess up. It was another entirely to be responsible for someone else getting hurt because of me. I'd broken rule five—*Watch out for one another*—and now Farhad and his group of *trusted* thieves had to use rule five to fix my mistake.

Why was I always making mistakes?

The door of Mihrage's house swung open before I could knock, and Taraji grinned at me. Her dark skin was accented by stunning brown eyes and obsidian hair. She'd done her makeup with silver. Although she'd always been one to look her best, the makeup attempts had only been over the last couple of days, which in that moment I realized was all in preparation for her joining the Desert Trials. That, or she thought she needed to catch Mihrage's attention.

She reached out and wrapped her arms around me. "Mihrage told me about your baba. I'm so sorry." She squeezed me.

I returned her hug briefly but pushed her back and stepped into the house. "We're getting him out. Everything will be fine."

"You mean *Farhad*," Mihrage said, emphasizing the name of our leader firmly, as if reminding me that "we"—he, Taraji, and I—were *not* part of that group.

I tightened my lips.

"Come get something to eat." Mihrage set the pan of breakfast on the table, which had three settings placed.

Bottling up my frustration with Farhad, I sat on the side of the table that had one plate, allowing Taraji to sit beside Mihrage.

They picked up on a conversation they had clearly been having before I arrived. Taraji was saying no one had ever died during the trials because the grand sorceress wouldn't risk that when trying to repair the relationship between magic wielders and non-magic users. It was true. In none of the fifteen years of the trials had anyone died. Become injured, frequently. Lost a limb? Sometimes. But death? Never.

"There's a first time for anything," I said sarcastically.

Taraji rolled her eyes at me. "As I said, Grand Sorceress Roshanak would *never* allow such a thing to happen." She turned to Mihrage.

The food on my fork dropped, accidentally drawing both her and Mihrage's attention back to me. I bit my bottom lip. *Should I tell them? Will they think differently of me if they know I'm her daughter? Her non-magic daughter living with thieves?*

Like an expert spear fisher, I jabbed the fork into my food and shoved it into my mouth to keep it busy, as if nothing happened.

"I will be fine, Caspara," Taraji insisted, misunderstanding, as if my fear for her losing her life were the reason I had dropped my food. She gripped my free hand and offered me one of her warm smiles.

It took effort to return it on my end.

Meanwhile, Mihrage watched me from under his brows in one of his silent, knowing ways that I was holding something back.

"Farhad wouldn't allow me to join," I grumbled to Mihrage.

Taraji blinked and her brows furrowed. "Why would you want to? You don't have magic." Again, she misunderstood our silent conversation.

Mihrage stood and carried the now-empty pan to his sink, then returned for our dishes. "Caspara is worried about her father, stone head." He leaned down and gave her a kiss on the top of her head.

Taraji's eyes alighted with understanding, but she gave him a quiet pout.

They truly were cute together. But that didn't mean I wanted to sit and watch them.

I rose to my feet. "Can we head for Zunbar?"

"Caspara, if Farhad didn't want you to join, it was for a reason," Mihrage said. "Why don't you come with me and Taraji to the Dumue River to—"

"Really, Mihrage?" I said dully. "You want me to do

what? Go fishing? Wash laundry? Or perhaps swim? Pretend like my father might not be in danger?"

"Capsara, it's only prison," Mihrage said.

Taraji stood and elbowed him in the ribs, making him wince.

"Ow."

"It won't harm any of us to go into Zunbar. Farhad didn't tell you that you couldn't go?" Taraji raised her eyebrows, the look asking the question.

I shook my head. "No. He said to stay with you."

Taraji smiled and faced Mihrage. "She'll be with us. Get your turban."

He folded his arms across his chest and leaned his backside against the counter behind him. "On one condition."

I rolled my eyes. "I won't try to come up with a rescue plan, if that will make you happy."

"Yes, it will. But I mean something else." He raised his brows. "Why are you so concerned for your father?"

I ran my fingers through my hair, using it as the opportunity to readjust it from having slept on it in a ponytail all night. And I told them everything. From sneaking in, to Father spotting the serpent, to trying to leave, and then him getting bitten.

There, I paused.

Because there was when he told me my mother's identity. And I didn't know how they would act if I shared it with them.

Taraji was leaning forward, because I'd stopped mid-sentence. "And?"

I swirled my finger around my hair and looked from Taraji to Mihrage and back. "And then he told me my mother was Roshanak and that he would answer everything when he got home."

Taraji gasped audibly.

Mihrage's arms slowly lowered.

"Which is why I need him home," I blurted. "I need him to tell me how she could be my mother. Why he took me away from her, why we don't live in the palace, why she's looking for me, because she asked for me, not by name but . . ." I drew a breath. "I worry his arrest wasn't a normal arrest because—"

"Because she knew you were there," Mihrage finished for me.

I nodded.

"Did you share this with Farhad?" Taraji asked, stepping forward to take my hand.

I nodded again. Suddenly, with the story out, my throat was all tied up and stupid tears prickled my eyes. I didn't need to be *this* worried, but how could I not be?

"I don't see anything wrong in going to the bazaar," Mihrage finally said. He took the brown headwrap from where it hung and twisted it until his white hair, horns, and face were hidden. He had more reason than most to disguise himself. After all, with orange skin, he would stick out more than even the pale people from the northern kingdoms.

Taraji picked up her purple scarf from the back of the chair and hid her face as well. "This will give us an opportunity to spend the day together before I head to the trials tomorrow. I could use a few last-minute things, I believe."

"I can finally get you a gift," I said, playing along. Of course, I did have to get her a gift to help her through the trials, but we all knew I was going to keep an eye on the guards and shadows for any sign of the thieves and my father.

Seven

More than once, I tried to offer a plan to sneak to the prisons, but each time I tried, Mihrage expertly interrupted and diverted the conversation to something regarding the heat, the docks, that he had made a few potions the night before for Taraji to take with her, and even that he could use some more and we should stop by the apothecary.

Each time, I scowled at him.

Each time, he ignored me.

We entered Zunbar late enough that morning that everyone in the city appeared to be about. All of them were preparing for the trials the next day, buying all sorts of food and spices for the grand meal they would have tonight in honor of their sorceress. None of them had a care in the world for anything but preparations for their personal celebrations. None knew my father had been arrested, and even if they did, not a soul would have cared.

I was reminded once again how lonely I felt in the crowd, just another dot of color on the painting, another seashell on the ocean floor. Insignificant. Small.

Taraji and Mihrage stood in front of me, brushing their knuckles against each other. I wanted to gag, and I definitely rolled my eyes more than once. Because I wanted that to be me.

I wanted to *mean* something.

As we walked, I lifted a few things here and there, but only to allow me to watch the shadows. More soldiers than usual dotted the bazaar, looking over the crowd.

Curious.

It made sense—they'd want to keep an eye out for people like us stealing while so many visitors were in the capital city for the trials. Yet, it somehow seemed like more than usual.

A flier pasted on the wall of a building caught my attention and I stopped dead in my tracks. It was a poster with a painting of a thief and the words "Reward: Almas" at the top. The image of the thief was me.

Well, me as a thief in black clothing and only eyes showing.

I concluded it was a rather useless painting since it was completely unidentifiable from anyone else passing through the city.

I sighed in relief and my gaze brushed past another flier but darted back. It was from one of the rogue sorceress groups.

"Overthrow corruption. Follow the trail. Find us."

Whatever that meant.

Still, I shuddered and stepped back into the crowd.

Magic didn't bother me. It never had. There was a lot of good in magic, like Mihrage's ability to know whenever we needed something, the lady in our village that could sense when we would get a sandstorm or rainstorm, Aunt Jade who could heal—though her magic required her to take on the injury, so she rarely performed it—Madame Kiara who helped people see their future, and even Taraji and her ability to manipulate sand.

I still didn't know what good *her* magic did specifically, but I didn't care.

It was what the sorceresses were *doing* with their magic that unnerved me most. Of course, I only knew what was rumored because I wasn't part of that world, but more than once we'd heard whisperings that some sorceresses were trying to overthrow the sultan.

Maybe that's why the soldiers were so many in number. Perhaps they were trying to identify any of the rogue groups of sorceresses. Perhaps they would make the trials a political statement.

Or, perhaps, the soldiers were present for an entirely different reason.

With still no sign of my father or any of the thieves, I stopped beside a table with little blown glass figurines. Taraji once told me that a sorceress received an animal companion once they mastered their magic. I supposed the figurines, which were animals, had been created specifically because of this.

Examining each one carefully, my sights lingered on a surprisingly intricate little griffin. The symbol of the royal family. They were the most abundant and varied in size from no bigger than my thumb to as big as my hand. My attention shifted to a cute little lizard.

As if Igborg knew I was thinking about him, he shifted in my pouch.

What would Taraji's familiar be? A mighty tiger? An owl? A camel?

The thought of a camel at her side, helping her cast spells, made me grin, and I *had* to have one. Casually glancing at the glass-maker and seeing he was busy with two women and their daughters fussing over a tiny bubble in the glass of a figurine, I turned and walked toward another booth.

With expert movements, my hand slid across the table, knocking the little camel figurine over the edge. I glanced over my shoulder just before stepping into the crowd and spotted Igborg pulling the figurine into the pouch with him. I grinned and turned around.

And ran right into a soldier, who snatched my elbow.

"Excuse me. I didn't mean to bump into you," I said quickly.

But the soldier held fast. In his opposite hand was the poster of the thief. He looked from the poster, to me, to his companion, and back at me. And I saw the moment where everything connected.

Because in my haste to get out the door that morning, I hadn't realized I still wore my black thief clothes from the night before.

"I . . . you're coming with us." He stumbled over his words.

"I don't think so," I replied. I stomped my heel into the top of his foot, making him bend over with a cry of pain. With his face closer to me, I pulled my right arm back and punched him in the nose as hard as I could.

There was a sickening crunch and my hand exploded with pain.

The soldier dropped to his knees, holding his face with blood gushing between his fingers.

"Sorry about the nose." Flicking my hand and gritting my teeth, I turned and pushed my way through the crowd.

"Stop that boy! Catch him! He's the thief!" the soldier's companion shouted over the bustle of the crowd.

Everyone turned to see what the chaos was,

inadvertently creating a much easier path for me to take. At one moment, I spotted Mihrage working his way toward me through the crowd, but I lost sight of him behind one of the booths as I slipped into an alley.

There was a loud whistle from one of the soldiers and more shouting.

I made it to the fork that led left or right, but the companion of the man I'd punched slid around the corner to my left. Right it was!

I ran that direction and turned to rejoin the crowd, slowing when I did so to try and appear as normal as possible. Removing my dagger, I cut the coin purse off the first person I came across that had one. I needed it for a backup plan.

Rule twelve—*Have a way out.*

But rejoining the crowd was a bad idea, because I hadn't taken into consideration that turning right took me west, *toward* the palace, and also toward the prison, which meant closer to more soldiers.

Sands, I thought.

"There he is!" someone in front of me shouted.

I met his eyes.

It was a fat man, pushing people back.

I rolled my eyes and pulled out the coin purse.

Sands knew I needed the money and I wished I could pocket all of the coins, but I decided self-preservation and distraction were far more important than buying anything in that moment. I slipped the knot free, grasped the bottom of the pouch, and turned it upside down to scatter its contents to the ground. It only took a moment for the nearest observers to notice the coins now shining from the red sand in the middle of the bazaar.

And then, chaos erupted.

The people who leapt on top of the coins created the perfect barrier between myself and the oncoming soldiers. I could only imagine Mihrage cursing my name, and if Farhad and the others were somewhere nearby, they would likely curse me too.

I jumped onto a nearby merchant's table, knocking a few of his blades off, and leaped onto the banner hanging over the side of the building behind his table. Using it as leverage, I scaled the wall up and onto the roof. I sprinted and flung myself across the gap between the building and the one beside it, landed, and rolled.

It wasn't my first time jumping and leaping from building to building, although it was always at night and far more carefully than what I was doing in that moment. My adrenaline and blood pumped in my veins, making me stumble more than once, and when I jumped to the third building, I cleared it so far that when I rolled, I nearly rolled off the opposite side.

I paused to catch my breath and collect myself, and then I dropped down into an alley. "That was too close," I muttered to myself.

My eyes widened and I turned to open the flap of Igborg's pouch.

He scowled up at me.

I gave him an apologetic smile. "Are you okay? I'm sorry. I had to run and get out and must have hurt you."

He stuck out his tongue and held up his hand as though to tell me I'd hurt it.

I reached out and touched his tiny claws. "Are you going to survive?"

He snorted and licked the back of his hand, like a cat

tending to a wound, although his eyes remained locked on me, telling me that it was all my fault and I would have to spoil him later for him to forgive me.

I smiled and closed the flap. "Silly boy."

Smiling to myself, I rounded a corner and spotted a soldier standing at the end of the alley with his arms crossed over his chest.

I skidded to a halt.

A deep scowl sat on his face. He blocked my path and looked directly at me.

How had he known I would be there? No one knew where the thieves lived, at least to my knowledge, and he couldn't have known that was the direction I would flee. There must have been more soldiers than I first thought.

After a quick glance over my shoulder, I spotted a second soldier blocking the path I'd just come from. To my right, a third soldier.

Sands. As if my day can't get any worse.

I was in trouble.

Behind me, one of the soldiers drew his sword. I scanned the nearest buildings for any way of escape. I didn't have time to think, only act, and my only way out was to get to one of the roofs of the nearby buildings.

Except, the apartments were three or four stories high in this part of the city. Clothing hung on lines overhead, but I knew none of those lines would hold my weight. There were windows, and the crumbling stucco would make for an easy climb.

"Don't do it," the nearest soldier warned and ran for me. He must have read my thoughts.

Wasting no time, I sprinted forward, closing the gap between me and the nearest wall, and launched myself at it. There was a small piece of exposed rock—just the right spot for my foot—which I dug into and pushed up to grasp the lip of the nearest window ledge. I hoisted myself up to stand on that ledge before I reached up for the next hand hold.

A bolt clattered against the wall right where I was about to place my hand, and I recoiled to look down at the soldiers below. But none of them had a crossbow. I lifted my gaze to the top of the building adjacent to where I hung and spotted an archer with his crossbow aimed at me.

The soldier holding his sword reached out and grabbed my ankle.

I kicked him off. I wanted to come up with something witty to say. Mihrage might have. But all I could think of was getting out of this mess.

"Come down, Almas," the first guard I'd spotted commanded. His beard really needed to be brushed.

I couldn't be arrested right now! Not when my father had likely been rescued. Everyone would be mad at me as it was for his arrest, but my getting caught would just be one more reason to prove I wasn't ready to be a thief without supervision.

And yet, as I assessed my situation, I knew escaping was futile.

I could try and climb to the roof with a very high probability of getting shot in the back and, if I did, suffer the consequences of potential infection. Or, I could give up to the guards. The consequence for stealing was losing a hand.

But in my case, if they had been sent by the grand sorceress, who knew what would become of me?

Before I could decide on my own, the archer released

another bolt where my second hand gripped. Although it only skimmed the side of my hand, the pain made me yank my arm against my chest and release my grip from the wall. Unfortunately, I leaned too far back, gasping when I couldn't reach forward and catch myself. I dropped from the building like a stone and hit the sand, landing flat on my back. My breath exploded from my lungs. I tried to gasp.

The three soldiers were at my side in an instant. One grabbed my right wrist, the other two forced me to my stomach, and they twisted my wrists behind me to bind me.

"Don't make it worse for yourself than it already is," the first soldier said. "You've already attacked one of us today and broken his nose. That's assault on top of theft."

I gritted my teeth as the ropes bit into my wrists, and as soon as they were secure, one of them unlatched my belt and pulled it away, removing my dagger, sword, pouches, and Igborg with it.

Blood rushed in my ears.

I didn't think my heart could pound any harder than it already was, and I struggled to keep my breathing steady.

Two men hauled me to my feet by my arms, and the first soldier stepped forward and yanked the scarf from my head, revealing my braids and feminine features—high cheekbones, narrow nose, all of it.

He stared with his mouth open.

They all did.

"A *woman?*" the second one hissed.

"Wait. Almas, the thief, is a *woman?*"

I rolled my eyes. "How dare I not be a man. What *was* I thinking?"

The first scowled. "That doesn't mean we'll go lightly on you. You've still committed crimes and we must take you to face your judgement. Take her to the prison."

The men gave me a sideways glance before the younger one ran on ahead.

"Keep it up with the sarcasm. It just might save you," the older guard mocked.

Eight

I was pushed into a windowless room, my bindings removed, and then the wooden door was locked shut behind me.

"May I have some water?" I asked.

"Sure. If you can find some." The soldier walked away.

I ran my tongue over my teeth. *Okay, Caspara. Think. You're here now. You did your best to try and escape . . . who am I kidding? You absolutely failed! Everyone is going to be furious! Shut up and think.*

I rubbed my fists into my eyes and turned in a circle to examine my room.

Four relatively thick walls and ceiling, a door with a barred window—which was the only window and source of light—and no cot to sleep on. Dirt floor. No lamp. A bucket in the corner emanated a putrid smell. I knew what that bucket was for. I would die before I would use that.

Or, hopefully, not.

Sucking in a breath, I pressed my cheek to the bar on the window and tried to look down the hallway. Unable to see anything beyond the wall, I called out, "Kasim?"

No one answered.

I cleared my throat and called louder. "Kasim!"

No response.

I closed my eyes and rested my forehead against the door. *He made it out.* I slowly sank to my knees in relief, because at least one of us was out.

My ears perked at the sound of voices echoing down the hall, and I leaned my ear against the window of the door to hear better.

"We must tell Roshanak immediately."

"I am leaving now and will return shortly. Make yourselves presentable."

A door opened and shut.

"How did we get so lucky?"

They all laughed.

Luck?

Coincidence?

Father didn't believe in coincidence.

My heart ached. Something bigger was at play here. As if on cue, my arm burned. I looked down and rubbed my hand over the tattoos. Maybe it wasn't that they were burning. No, it *couldn't* be that they were burning, because that had never happened before.

Was this luck *and* coincidence? Or was this something much bigger: fate?

I failed to see how being arrested was fate, but all of these actions had fallen into place. What if this was the beginning of my destiny, as my father had told me?

My temple pulsed and I massaged it, then lowered my body to lean against the wall. I had no dagger. No lockpicks. And they'd taken my belt, so nothing else. Not even Igborg.

I gnawed my bottom lip. They were fetching Roshanak.

In just a few minutes, I would meet my mother.

And I didn't know how that made me feel.

One thing I knew for certain, I wanted answers from my father first. I got up on my hands and knees and began searching the sand, just in case a previous . . . resident of my humble location had hidden anything.

Nothing.

I went to the door and tested the hinges.

They were iron. Newly replaced. I couldn't even get my dagger under the lip of the hinge pin.

Dejected, I peered out the window of my cell. A guard was roaming down the hall, coming back toward me.

"Excuse me. Could you tell me if you arrested a man by the name of Kasim last night?" I asked.

The man studied my face. "Why?"

I shrugged. "Just curious."

He shook his head. "I wouldn't know. I'm morning shift."

I stared at the man until he moved beyond my line of sight.

I was desperately trying, and failing, not to panic. I was absolutely helpless. There was no way out of here.

The main door of the prison opened and someone called the guards to attention. My heart pounded and I backed up. I wished I could hide in the sand and pretend I wasn't there. If Roshanak couldn't see me, maybe I could find my way out.

"This way."

I pressed my back into the corner of the room, the one along the same wall as the prison door, because they would have to open it to see me.

"She is in here. A young woman," an old man's voice

said. "As you know, the punishment for theft is amputation of the hand. But Roshanak—"

"We're still amputating hands?" That was a younger man's voice.

"Your Highness . . . we've always done this as a punishment. What would you want done instead?"

Highness?

My heart missed a beat in panic.

Was it the sultan?

"Where is she?" the "highness" asked.

The lock jingled in the door and the guard said, "Stand back, please."

"Why?"

"This is a common trick. Prisoners stand against the wall thinking they can hide and ambush us."

I rolled my eyes. Clearly, I wasn't as inventive as I imagined.

The door opened outward and the soldier, holding a lantern, stepped into my cell.

I folded my arms and tried to look as casual as possible, hiding in the shadows of my prison cell.

In reality, I was trying to use my arms to hold in my quaking.

A young man stepped in and my heart stopped.

Prince Abudar.

The future sultan of Sheblom.

Was standing in my prison cell.

He wore a stunning white tunic with blue embroidery, including little blue griffins around the bottom edge of the shirt between little hand-sewn swirls, and matching blue pants. His wavy black hair was parted neatly to the side, and he gave me a dashing smile that made deep dimples appear.

He was obnoxiously handsome.

But worse than his perfect square jaw and perfect smile and perfect face were his breathtaking eyes. They were golden on the outside with red sparking around the pupil, creating a shade of amber I'd only seen in stone.

He placed his hand on his chest and looked me up and down. "Aren't you a beauty to behold?" he said and then bowed at the waist. "My name is Prince Abudar."

I wasn't stupid enough to disrespect him. I wanted to keep my hand and head. Even if he thought his sly words would get to me.

"Pleased to meet you. Prince Abubu?" I gave a fake smile, feigning ignorance.

His brows dipped. "Um. Abudar."

"Right. Abu."

Beside him, the guard's eyes were widening.

Oh, I should really stop.

"Ah-boo—" he said slowly.

"I said Abu."

"No, A—you know, fine. Abu."

He waved his hand dismissively. "And you are?"

"Caspara, Your Highness," I answered stiffly and gave a tight curtsey. I wasn't going to be captured or wooed by his looks, and the curtsey seemed to satisfy the guard for now because he relaxed.

"A beautiful name for a beautiful girl. Just the type of girl I need." His gaze slowly drank me in, shifting with every curve, and I wondered if such a look flattered the other girls in the city. Of course it would. He was royalty. And even if we were from different worlds, I could understand why other girls might become infatuated with such attention.

"Thanks?" I said hesitantly.

Prince Abudar inclined his head. "Why are you in here?" He gestured to the tiny cell.

"Ask them. I was merely walking through the marketplace when I was grabbed by your soldiers and dragged here. They claim I'm Almas."

Prince Abudar's dark brows furrowed and his gaze darted to the soldier beside him. "Is this true?"

"That's why I wanted to speak with Grand Sorceress Roshanak. She's been looking for the girl." He didn't even acknowledge me.

Prince Abudar looked me up and down as if seeing me for the first time. But his focus lingered on my right arm.

I tucked it behind my back. "There's no proof I am Almas. I'm merely preparing for the Desert Trials tomorrow, and if I'm not home by dinner, my father will be extremely upset."

"Who is your father?" the prince asked.

I stupidly replied, "Sir Midas."

Prince Abudar's brows peaked. "Goodness. That is very unfortunate. Because we had them for dinner last night . . . and you weren't present." The edge of his lip played with a slight smile. "You're not so quick on your feet."

I set my jaw.

"I believe I know why Roshanak wants her. And I want her too."

The hair on the back of my neck prickled and I gritted my teeth in annoyance. I glared at the prince, not caring if he saw, because I couldn't help but think he was rather boorish.

Prince Abudar turned to the guard and opened his mouth as though to speak.

"I'm not doing anything for you," I said firmly. Prince or not, I didn't like what he'd said or how he'd said it. He *wanted* me?

Prince Abudar offered me another one of his dashing smiles that probably caused all sorts of girls to fall over him, but there was something in his eyes I didn't like.

I glared back in response.

"We'll see about that." He dipped his head in a bit of a bow. "I'll take her back with me."

Nine

Alarm bells rang in my head, warning me that this was dangerous. Dark thoughts slipped in—that if I went with him, I would never return home. That my mother had a dark side to her I never knew. And my father had kept secrets my entire life.

I supposed what scared me the most was the thought that discovering the truth would change everything I knew and was comfortable with.

"I told you I am not Almas," I tried. "Almas isn't just one person." I looked from Prince Abudar to the soldier and back.

Prince Abudar shook his head. "It isn't the name of *Almas* that I have heard, but your name. *Caspara.*"

"How?" I demanded and balled my hands into fists.

He turned to the guard. "I'll meet you outside. Make sure her things come with her." He glanced at me, down and up, one last time before exiting the room.

I wanted to stab his eye out with a stick for the way he looked at me, like I was some sort of diamond in the rough he could uncover, dust off, and possess. He made my blood boil and I barely knew him.

"Turn around. Chain her."

A soldier had entered with chains in his hands.

A sour taste crept into my mouth and I obeyed. Because the alternative wasn't something I wanted to tempt. I somehow kept my mouth shut and stared at the wall.

Mihrage and Taraji would be terrified by now. More likely than not, one of them had run back to the village to tell them I'd been captured. If Farhad just returned home with my father, then they would turn around and come back for me.

My father.

I could picture the disappointment carving lines between his brows and see his lips dip into a frown. Fear would be the next emotion.

The soldier chained my wrists behind my back, then he pulled me from the cell roughly, making me stumble over my feet. I threw him a glare but he either didn't see it or ignored it. I wanted to break *his* nose, but there was no breaking the chains.

I tried to swallow my nerves, but my mouth was bone dry.

Prince Abudar stood beyond the open door of the prison, out in the sunlight, talking to a small group of girls. He ran his fingers through his hair and the girl I could see under his arm practically swooned.

I rolled my eyes.

Oh, to be one of the rich who could afford feelings of flattery from the prince's attention. If only they saw what I'd seen just a moment ago in my cell, the hungry, greedy look in his eye when he looked at me.

A soldier beside the door held my belt out to me and I quickly looked it over to see if everything was there—my pouches and their contents, sword, dagger. The pouch which normally held Igborg was flat.

My throat clenched and I surveyed the room for any sign of him.

He was gone.

I thought about asking but didn't dare, because if he'd slipped out of the bag he could still be hiding somewhere and waiting for the chance to run. Or he may have escaped a long time ago. Maybe *fate* would be on his side and carry him home to tell Mihrage what had happened to me.

The soldier holding my arm took the weapon belt from his comrade and pulled me out into the sunlight.

"Excuse me, ladies," Prince Abudar said. He gave them a deep bow, then winked. "I shall see you all tomorrow morning, undoubtedly. And good luck to each of you."

"Thank you, Prince Abudar."

"We're honored, Your Highness."

The prince turned his attention to me only long enough to ensure the two soldiers had fallen into place at my sides to escort me before he led the way up the street. We passed dozens of homes, which slowly grew in size until they were as large as the mansion Father and I had slunk into the night before.

Had it really only been a day? And not even a full day at that—it wasn't even time for dinner!

The road curved and the cliff on my right evolved into the tall exterior walls of the palace. The only time I'd been so close was at night, and we never took the main road to get to the expensive houses.

And I was about to step beyond those foreboding walls.

"Your face has paled," Prince Abudar said.

I didn't look at him, nor did I answer.

"If it comforts you, you do not go to your doom."

"And I'm supposed to trust you?" I asked stiffly.

He smiled. "You're not used to being around those of a higher class, are you? You have no manners."

"I make it a point to avoid the upper class at all costs," I replied sardonically, eyebrows raised, and I finally challenged his look.

His lips pulled back in a grin that once again revealed his dimples. "In spite of what you may believe, I'm not going to harm you. Quite the opposite, in fact. I'm inviting you as a guest."

"Do you chain up all of your guests?"

Prince Abudar actually laughed.

I didn't.

We said nothing else to each other as I was walked through the gates. The courtyard was a different world. Flowering bushes, fountains of water, trees, and beauty I'd never seen hid behind the walls. I didn't want to look away, but we began ascending the steps to the front doors.

Two guards stood as sentinels. A third stepped forward and opened the door, then bowed low and greeted the prince. Prince Abudar nodded in reply and I entered the palace.

My jaw dropped and eyes widened. If I thought Sir Midas's home was grand, it paled in comparison to the beauty and riches of the palace. And the same visceral reaction I felt inside of his home echoed here. I snapped my teeth shut and ground them together.

"Send word to Roshanak to meet me in the practice room," Prince Abudar said to a servant who approached us.

The servant stole a glance my way as he turned, then took off in a dead sprint down one of the corridors.

My body shivered, not from cold but nerves. I drew a deep breath through my nose to try and quell them, and was grateful we had time to walk through the palace so I could compose myself before meeting Roshanak—my mother. I followed the prince until we ascended a staircase and went down a series of hallways until we entered a room bigger than any room I'd seen before.

Prince Abudar folded his hands behind his back and turned to face me. He nodded his head to the guard. "You may unchain her and go. I have it from here."

The soldier obeyed.

I gulped.

The door closed behind him and I kept my eyes locked on the prince while trying to assess everything around him. There were at least a dozen windows on one side of the room offering light, lamps glowing high overhead, and a wall filled with different types of weapons.

I understood what he meant by "practice" room. This was where he trained to be prince, more than likely.

I was about to crumple under the pressure of his gaze, about to demand what he wanted with me, when the door suddenly opened, making me jump and wheel to see who entered.

Abudar rolled his eyes.

Princess Mithra, Prince Abudar's sister, entered the practice room and eyed me up and down. Her lips sneered in disdain. "*This* is Almas?"

"No, this is Caspara," Prince Abudar corrected, gesturing a hand to me as if I needed an introduction in spite of them knowing full well who I was.

Not a moment later, a woman in a long golden gown entered.

Grand Sorceress Roshanak.

She didn't need to say it because, well, I looked like her. I had my father's eyes, but everything else was her. My narrow chin, thin and slightly upturned nose, high cheeks, full lips, all of it. I was practically a mirror image of her.

My insides roiled.

Because I didn't know how to react.

Roshanak stared at me with as much intensity as I did her. "You may leave us."

Prince Abudar blanched and straightened. "Roshanak, I need—"

"Now," she commanded, giving him a firm look.

The prince bowed and walked past his sister to leave.

"You too, Mithra."

"That's not fair, I should—" She stopped mid-sentence at the grand sorceress's look, then rolled her eyes and followed her brother out.

The woman who was my mother stood before me. She'd lived this close my entire life, and not once had I known. Not once had my father revealed her identity to me.

"I imagine you have thousands of thoughts flooding your mind right now," she said calmly, offering me a comforting smile. "Would you like to sit?"

"No."

Her brow twitched ever so slightly.

I sucked in a breath and lowered my hands to my sides. "I don't mean to sound impolite, but I don't understand why I am here."

She nodded slowly. "Kasim never told you, did he?"

"He did last night. When the snake bit him. Where is he?" I rubbed my fingertips against my palms, trying to give my hands something to do.

Roshanak crossed the floor to one of the benches under the windows. She motioned for me to join her, then took a seat on one of them. She didn't wait for me to comply, because I didn't make any move to do so. "Your father is safe."

"Where?" I demanded again. "Did he go home?"

She studied me with dark brown eyes. I had green flecks in mine. Like Father. Hers were . . . cold. Like the belly of a ship. "I'm afraid not. Not yet, at least. You see, Caspara, you are very important to me. I've been searching for you for the last thirteen years." Her eyes saddened and she looked down at her open hands resting on her lap.

I swallowed hard and braved a step toward her. "Why did my father feel it necessary to take me from you?"

She scoffed slightly. "He believed you would be corrupted by living in the palace. He was the son of a tailor, you see. He had been in love with Sultana Shahira before she volunteered to be Sultan Zayne's bride."

My brows dipped. I knew he had been close friends with Sultana Shahira, which was one of the reasons we knew Madame Kiara so well. They were sisters.

Roshanak's lips softened. "He didn't tell you that either?"

"N-no," I admitted.

She nodded. "I think a part of him will always love her. He would come visit her in the palace. He caught my eye. He was honest, handsome of course, and had the biggest heart of anyone I knew." She smiled fondly.

I felt myself relaxing. I wasn't shaking anymore, and I slowly walked nearer until I sat on the bench beside hers.

"He noticed me as well," she continued. "We fell in . . . passion. I don't know if you can call it love, because what we had was . . . different, I believe. When I had you, I think he stayed out of obligation." Roshanak moved her hair over her shoulder. It tumbled down the golden fabric in waves.

It wasn't a romantic story, but it made sense. If my father loved her, surely he would have told me as much. Perhaps their lack of love was the reason he never told me who she was. "But why would he take me and leave?" I pressed.

She lifted her shoulders. "He didn't like my beliefs toward the sorceresses. He thought I was rushing the kingdom too quickly to change." She dropped them with a sigh. "To be honest, I do not know the real reason. But I must know you're *my* Caspara. May I see your arm?"

At first, I could only stare at her. Father had told me the story of Telama blessing me as an infant, in my mother's arms. But it felt . . . wrong, somehow. Showing her my tattoos. My blessing. My destiny I didn't even know I believed in.

But I pushed the fabric up to my elbow, revealing the black tattoos that invaded the back of my hand and spread all the way up to my shoulder. They were symbols—or ancient letters, I didn't know—that varied in size and position, but covered my skin like an infection.

Roshanak rose to her feet, her smile widening with anticipation. She stepped toward me. "May I?" She reached a hand out.

Swallowing, still unsure, I begrudgingly nodded. She

hadn't actually answered why Father left, and maybe she didn't know because he never told her. Maybe she'd done something else my father didn't agree with.

She reached out and ran her finger from my elbow to my wrist and then back up with all four fingers. "Remarkable. It's been some time since I've seen these."

I pulled back. "I deserve to know what happened to my father."

Roshanak's dark eyes flickered for a moment, just the slightest of moments. It could have been the torchlight flickering, changing the look in her eye. "He is in prison. Here in the palace."

"What?" I jumped to my feet, yanking my sleeve down to my wrist. "Why do you have him here? He hasn't done anything—"

"He is a thief, Caspara. One of the best—or worst, depending on whose side you're on." She spoke as if it were as simple as that.

"You captured him for a reason. Last night, you demanded he tell you where I was," I said, leaning forward. "I was there. I heard you. You said it was urgent, almost my sixteenth birthday, and then you put him in here? There's more to why he's here than just being a thief. I'm not a child."

Roshanak lifted her chin. "You're correct."

I had mentally prepared for a defense and was caught a bit when she didn't further the argument.

"I have a proposition for you."

I narrowed my eyes and folded my arms across my chest. "Which is?"

"Has Kasim ever told you of his family vault inside the Dragon's Lair?" She rested her hands on her narrow hips.

I shook my head. "Only that I have a great, great grandfather, times a few more greats, who hid a secret in there or something. He hasn't told me that story since I was a child."

She nodded slowly. "Tomorrow you shall enter the trials and find the vault. In order to find the vault, you must follow the path of serpents I carved into the walls for you. They will be subtle, so most will not notice. When you reach the vault, you shall utter the phrase, *iftah ya simsim*, and the door will open for you. Once you are inside, you will locate an ancient lamp. Bring that back to me and I shall set your father free."

I stared at my mother a long time. I didn't know what I'd expected. Warm arms? A comforting hug? Answers as to why she'd never come for me, if she actually did love me? Yet, there she stood before me. Demanding I go into the caves and retrieve something for her.

"Are you blackmailing me?" I asked almost breathlessly.

Roshanak laughed lightly. "Don't be preposterous. I would never do such a thing to my daughter." She stepped forward and reached out to touch my cheek, but I turned my face away. She lowered her hand. "Kasim is alive and well. Bring me the lamp and you can return to the life you knew." She stepped back.

"Only if you let me see him," I said.

"Bring me the lamp and I'll let you see him. When he goes home with you. You may leave." She crossed to the door and opened it, then gestured with a hand for me to leave.

I felt . . . empty. Blank, like I didn't know what to

think. But one thought profoundly came to mind. "The Desert Trials are meant to challenge sorceresses, and you expect *me* to get through the challenges unscathed?"

"No. Quite the opposite, in fact. This is the safest way for you to navigate through the caves, because of the barriers that are in place. Should you encounter grave danger, the protections I put in place will allow you to enter the caves and try again."

That wasn't comforting at all.

She ushered me out the door, where a servant began leading me back through the palace.

Since the time I was a small child, I'd imagined a reunion with my mother. I had pretended she would laugh and smile and say she missed me. She would tell me she had been on a grand adventure and brought back gifts for me and stories to tell.

Instead, my mother wanted me to find a rusty, old lamp inside of a cave, during trials for sorceresses, in order to get my father back. And what choice did I have?

Ten

"Caspara?" a voice called to me. I'd been so consumed by my thoughts, worries, and anger that I hadn't even realized I'd passed through the streets of Zunbar and into the now empty bazaar. When I lifted my gaze from my dusty boots and sand-stained pants, I spotted a young boy.

Lycus grinned up at me from where he stood with his hands in his pockets.

Sitting on his shoulder was a plump, turquoise lizard.

"Igborg!" I practically shrieked his name. I ran over and pulled him into my arms and cradled him close to my chest. "Thank the sands! I was so worried about you. How did you get out of the prison? When did you leave? How did you end up with Lycus?"

I didn't care that he couldn't answer, I had to demand anyway.

And Igborg nuzzled me in response.

Somehow, having him back in my arms gave me comfort and I closed my eyes, letting his warmth seep into my hands.

"Mother is waiting for you," Lycus said. "Come on." The ten-year-old grabbed my sleeve and tugged me. Lycus was Madame Kiara's oldest child.

"I'm in a bit of a rush," I said. "Thank you for taking

care of Igborg."

"Mother said you would say that, but it's about your father." He waved again for me to follow.

My breath caught and my gut told me to go with him.

"All right," I relented. I reached up and stroked Igborg's spine.

"I fed Igborg for you, and I have a whole bag of seeds I've collected! I'll give them to you to take home. I also tried to catch a sand beetle today for him. He was almost as big as Igborg's head! I wanted to show you, but it dug a hole in the sand and disappeared."

I couldn't help but smile. I'd always liked Lycus.

When we reached the apothecary, the "closed" sign was up and only one lamp from the back room illuminated the main floor.

"Mother, I've brought Caspara!" Lycus announced when we entered.

"I'm back here, Caspara!" Kiara called to me.

I walked around the front counter and entered the back room. Kiara wore a red, gold, blue, and orange dress with intricate beading. Her black hair tumbled down her back in tight waves that must have been from wearing it in braids. The rich, earthy scent of coffee permeated the air as she poured it from the pot into two golden cups. People lined up for a chance to have a reading from her, but I had never been one of them.

Kiara's bright brown eyes glistened in a way that told me she knew more than I did. She gestured for me to take a seat. "I know the timing seems strange, but ever since Mihrage and Taraji stopped by earlier looking for you, I've felt the need to visit with you. And then Igborg showed up out of the blue." She smiled brightly in her warm way that always made me feel welcome.

I sat on the stool, which rocked to the left. One of the four legs was too short. "Lycus said you knew something about my father."

She nodded and scooted the coffee to me. "I can't receive inspiration for you, but Taraji told me about Kasim and I feel it may benefit you to have a reading. Drink." She sat on the stool across from me. "Your father loves you very much. More than his own life." Her gaze shifted to the coffee as I brought it to my lips to drink.

It was the perfect temperature, rich, creamy, and soft.

I licked my upper lip. "Then you know Roshanak is my mother?"

She nodded, her eyes apologetic. "I told Kasim to be honest with you, but he insisted on waiting until you were ready."

Kiara tilted my hand holding the mug toward my mouth. "I cannot tell you anything if you don't drink. Focus on your questions and let the coffee speak for you." She paused. "I can say Telama wanted the best for you when she gave your blessing."

I arched my brow and looked down at the tattoos on my fingers not hidden by the sleeve. "I don't want to talk about that." I drank the coffee as quickly as I could. Even though it was the most delicious coffee I had ever had and I wanted to savor it, I needed answers. I set the empty cup down and pushed it to Kiara, licking coffee from the corners of my mouth.

Kiara closed her eyes, muttered something under her breath, then looked down into the cup. She took my hand.

Her eyes widened when they locked on mine, and my mind was swept away from the room.

"You've ignored her the last twelve years of her life. Why the sudden interest?" Kasim demanded. He stood with his wrists chained over his head and his feet chained to the floor. His shirt was damp and sweat beaded his brow.

Roshanak paced back and forth in front of him, the beads of her lavish golden dress clattering against the stone floor like an ass's hooves down a cobblestone road. "Because I have solved the riddle of her tattoo and I must have her back."

Kasim's lip curled. "It is her choice, and there's no way she will choose you once she knows the truth. Did you tell her why we left you?"

Roshanak stopped in front of him and wrapped her finger around his beard. She smiled sweetly. "Based on what I've heard, she will do anything to keep you safe. She even offered to join the Desert Trials to help you. Imagine that. Completely without an ounce of magic in her bones, yet she's willing to risk everything for . . . you. Why? She's disappointingly more like you than I hoped."

His jaw flexed.

Roshanak leaned close to his lips. "We loved each other once, Kasim. Didn't we? I recall sharing many intimate moments together. One of which led to the birth of our daughter."

"A daughter you want nothing to do with until she has potential value to you." He spat, and the spit landed on her cheek.

A guard stepped from the side of the room and slammed the hilt of his sword into Kasim's ribs. Kasim grunted in pain and winced.

Roshanak grabbed the guard by the sleeve of his shirt

and dragged him closer so she could wipe the spit from her face on his shirt. "It's too late, Kasim. She will enter the trials and bring me the lamp. And then she shall finally be home."

"She already knows where her home is. And it isn't with the woman who abandoned her!" Kasim said through clenched teeth.

"We'll see about that, won't we, my love?"

As suddenly as the vision took me away it dragged me back, and I gasped for breath when Kiara's small room at the back of her shop came into focus. "That was my father!" I shouted, jumping to my feet. My heart thumped so hard in my chest it hurt. "What is she doing to him?"

Kiara didn't blink. Her eyes were glossed over and she stared just over my shoulder as if still seeing what wasn't there. Her hand remained tightly wrapped around my right wrist. "You must find your other half. The one who bears the same marks upon their arm. Discover who you are and fulfill your prophecy. Only then will the kingdom be safe."

"Will my father be okay?" I leaned forward to look in her eyes, hoping she would focus and answer me.

"Your father will be there to help you when you need him."

"Is Roshanak going to harm him?"

Kiara blinked slowly.

I shook her arm. "Kiara, is Roshanak going to harm my father?"

She drew a deep breath, closed her eyes, and let go of my arm. "What was that, dear?"

Tears filled my eyes. "Is my father going to be okay?"

"Your father?" She inclined her head and glanced at the cup. "Oh, I was going to say something about him."

She picked up the cup as if she hadn't seen it before, but her brows furrowed and she muttered, "I see nothing distinguishable."

"You just took me into a vision of him and Roshanak. Roshanak was saying . . . you told me I had to save the kingdom or something."

"Odd." Kiara stared into the cup for a long, silent moment, then shook her head and turned to me. "I rarely see full visions and, when they happen, I never remember them. I am sorry."

How could she not remember the vision she'd just shared with me?

With a lump in my throat, I stood.

Kiara hurried around the counter and embraced me. "I remember what I felt. It was hope, Caspara. I don't know what for. But you're more special than you think."

While I stared at her, she gathered a few jars and bandages, organizing them all into a bag. She even included some food. I watched, too lost in exhaustive thoughts to really see. She finally handed me the bag and cupped my face until I focused on her.

"I packed you some medical supplies and food for the trials. Believe in yourself, Caspara."

I nodded to her. How did she know I was going to the trials? My mind hurt too much to ask.

I remembered her hugging me one last time before I was outside of Zunbar without recalling how I'd gotten there, as my thoughts were consumed by what I'd been through.

The grand sorceress of Zunbar was my mother.

My mother was torturing my father.

I was to retrieve a lamp for her.

I was joining the trials.

Me.

A pathetic street rat with nothing to her name but a stinky lizard and a worthless tattoo.

Sand nipped at my cheeks as the wind threw it at my face. I had to get Father out of the palace prison, even if I had to risk the trials as a magicless participant. Because I couldn't bear to think of what would happen if I didn't.

Arms wrapped around me and foggy words tried to pierce my dazed state. "Caspara, I was worried sick about you! What happened? Caspara? What is it? Caspara. Are you there?"

I blinked away the face of my father. Farhad's face came into focus.

How had I gotten home?

Eleven

When Farhad patted my cheek, I finally noticed the group of men and women surrounding me, presumably gathered to rescue me. When he wrapped me in his arms, he half-lectured me and half-thanked the gods for my safe return, then grabbed me by the shoulders and said, "Where have you been?"

I met his intense gaze. "I-I . . . there were guards and . . . Prince Abudar and Roshanak . . ." I couldn't form a straight thought.

Farhad looked me up and down, then lowered his hands.

Taraji pushed him aside. "She needs rest. Caspara, you can come to my house. Mother won't mind feeding you too."

I nodded numbly.

For a brief moment, I caught sight of Mihrage, his eyes pinched in concern, but his face disappeared when Taraji pushed me toward her home.

I hoped Isline didn't want to talk tonight. I just wanted to eat and sleep.

Somehow, I knew Mihrage followed behind us.

Taraji led me into her home and announced my presence. She hurried to her mother and said something softly before returning to me. She silently took the heavy bag from my shoulder, said, "Go sit at the table," and then left the room.

Mihrage placed his warm hand on the small of my back and guided me to sit. He sat on my side, a spot for Taraji beside him. He rested his elbow on the table and leaned to look into my face. He silently tucked some hair behind my ear. "Your mind races tonight," he said softly, only to me.

I met his brown eyes, eyes that knew too much for his age. And I nodded. "In all directions. It hurts." I closed my eyes and massaged my temple.

He reached up and rubbed his thumb over my eyebrow, then repeated the movement across my other eyebrow. And then I felt his lips touch my forehead and all of the pain, all of the anxiety, the worry for my father, the lamp, the trials, all of it melted away.

My eyes blinked and when I opened them, Mihrage grinned at me. "What was that?"

He touched his index finger to his lips and straightened. No sooner did he do so than Taraji rounded the corner carrying a pot to set on the table. Silently, Mihrage stood to help carry other dishes for the meal.

Mihrage was still a mystery to me. In spite of our five-year friendship, he still kept a lot of his past history personal. I wondered if Taraji even knew. And judging by him hushing me, I doubted Taraji knew he could take away mental anguish.

I set Igborg on the table and commanded him to be polite.

He flicked his tongue at me and seemed to frown.

Babkak, Taraji's father, sat at the head of the table.

Mihrage took his seat beside me, then Taraji on his opposite side, and Taraji's mother sat across the table beside Isline.

Babkak nodded his head to me. "I know you've had a very busy day. Thank you for joining us for dinner." He offered a sympathetic smile.

I licked my lips but found myself unable to return his kind gesture. "Thank you for allowing me to visit. I . . . didn't want to be alone tonight."

Babkak offered thanks to Laverna, the goddess of thieves, for providing the meal and a way for their family to survive. He then asked her to protect her "servant," Kasim.

My heart ached, but it also felt warm. Babkak and Father had been friends as long as I could remember.

When I opened my eyes, a thought came to me. I leaned my head to the side and caught his gaze. "How did you meet my father?"

Babkak's food paused halfway to his mouth and he slowly lowered it back to his plate. He gave a single nod. "It was, sands. Shortly after he left your mother. It is uncommon to see men on the streets with a child in their arms. He had tried leaving you to live with his sister, Jade, but you wouldn't allow it." He smiled. "You wanted to be by his side always. But he wanted to do more than run a tailor shop beside his sister. After all, he was terrible at stitching, as you know."

I smiled fondly. "He tried to teach me to patch. I still have the squares of fabric I practiced on. You can't tell my stitches apart from his."

Everyone at the table smiled or chuckled.

Babkak took a bite, but shook his head. "Your father

always wanted what was best for you. I had seen him around, but he caught me stealing from one of the sailors at the dock and giving the coins to one of the beggar children. He asked why I would do such a thing. For some reason, I knew I could trust him. I told him about us and how we steal from the wealthy to give to those in need. I suppose he joined because he felt like his life had purpose knowing he was helping, and of course hiding you."

"He couldn't leave me behind?"

He nodded.

My heart warmed. Because I knew that to be true. Father had told me similar stories of trying to let Jade raise me, because I needed the influence of a woman's touch in my life. But I was grateful more than anything that he'd chosen to take me with him. Because it was difficult enough facing the thought my mother didn't want me— until now. I couldn't imagine being raised without either parent.

"Stories always lighten the mood," Isline said.

"Shall I tell you the story of how I tamed a Ryderion?" Mihrage asked, leaning forward with a mischievous grin.

Isline's eyes lit up. "Pretty please!"

Mihrage launched into a story about how he was crossing the west desert, on his way to Zunbar, when he came across the enormous desert creatures with plates of skin like armor and two horns on their noses they could fight each other with. He may have exaggerated the details, but the distraction was nice. He had managed to rope one in an attempt to ride it to Zunbar. He tied the rope around a horn while it was asleep and climbed onto its back, but when it woke, it stormed about the desert, flinging him until Mihrage could finally no longer hold on.

He claimed it threw him through the air and all the way to the eastern desert.

Isline laughed.

Taraji rolled her eyes.

Looking around the table, my heart twinged with pain. I'd never had a family like this. Most nights, it was me and Baba. And only if he wasn't off stealing something for the poor. In a few years, Taraji and Mihrage would have a family of their own.

I didn't blame my father. He had a daughter to raise in a land of thieves, and all I wanted to do was be like him. How else was he supposed to teach me? How could he teach the art of cooking or sewing when he didn't have time himself for those things? But I didn't regret the way I'd been raised. I loved the freedom of roaming the streets and getting into mischief.

Danger was thrilling.

There was a lull in the conversation as everyone continued eating.

I had finished and sat with my hands in my lap.

Isline asked, "Are you joining us for the parade tomorrow?"

I blinked.

"To send Taraji off," her mother added.

"Oh. I'm actually . . ." How did I explain to them I had to join the trials too?

Mihrage nudged me. "You're not alone, Caspara," he whispered. "We're all family."

Looking into his eyes, I realized if anyone understood what it meant to be lonely, it was Mihrage. He had made the forty thieves his home, his family. He had no mother, no father, no siblings. He was more alone than I was here.

He wasn't even with his own race.

I gave him a grateful smile.

He winked.

I drew a big breath. "Last night, when my father was captured, he told me who my mother is."

Taraji took my hand.

I squeezed hers. "She's Roshanak."

"The grand sorceress?" her mother breathed.

I bit my lip and nodded again. "I didn't believe him. But when Baba and I were stealing from that house . . . she showed up. The snake statue we were going to steal bit him when we were leaving. He told me to run, so I hid out on the balcony. And while I was out there, I heard her demand to know where I was. Then, today, when I was arrested, I was taken to speak with her. She . . . arrested my father because she wants me. I don't understand why, other than she is demanding I enter the trials tomorrow myself."

"What?" Mihrage asked, brows dipped in confusion.

"But why should you compete?" Taraji asked.

I shook my head and pulled up the sleeve of my shirt. "She was interested in my tattoo, but didn't say anything other than she wants me to go into my family vault and get something for her."

"Your family vault? Inside of the Dragon Lair?" Babkak asked. "I thought your father was making up those stories."

"I did too," I confessed. "I thought he just told me the stories to get me to sleep. But Roshanak wants me to find it and open it."

"What do you mean?" Isline asked.

I shifted the way I was sitting to get more comfortable

and filled Igborg's bowl with more water. "The way my father tells this story is much better, but I will try my hardest. Once upon a time, our kingdom was in chaos. Instead of a sultan to lead, there were six men trying to take sides they claimed were the opinions of the people. But those leaders didn't care about the land as a whole. Pulled in different directions by the leaders who meant well, the people were distanced from each other by lies and promises that could never be."

"Like the sorceresses are doing right now," Isline chimed in.

I hadn't considered the similarity, but nodded. "From what my father tells, my great, great, great"—I counted on my fingers—"great, great grandfather had a treasure unlike anything anyone had ever seen before. He used this treasure to bring peace to the land. But others sought this treasure and were willing to do *anything* to obtain it."

"Even kill," Taraji added dramatically, then stifled a smile.

Isline shoved some rice in her mouth and leaned forward. "What was the treasure?"

I shrugged. "That's part of the story I don't know. But seeing how Roshanak wants a lamp, I imagine that must be it. It must be enchanted in some way. Or just proof that I'm her daughter."

"But why don't you have it now?" Isline asked.

"Once there was relative peace in the land, my grandfather hid the treasure inside of the Dragon's Lair and sealed it behind a magical entrance protected with a password. He called himself a *sentinel,* a protector of the people. But he vowed that darkness would rise again, and only those who were his descendants could open the door and obtain the treasure within."

"But what is the password to get in?" Taraji asked, just as intrigued by the story as her sister, even though she'd heard it before.

"That's a secret," Mihrage answered. "She can't tell you the password or it wouldn't be a secret anymore."

Taraji shrugged. "I suppose."

"So your *mother* is asking you to get the lamp? And then she'll let your father go?" Babkak asked.

"That's what she says. To be honest, I don't know what to believe." I looked down at Igborg. He was licking my plate clean. "Father held a lot of secrets. I only just met my mother. I don't know who to believe."

"Believe your heart," Babkak said. "It will never lead you astray."

I lifted my gaze and smiled, but I wasn't sure I believed him.

"I'm excited you'll get to join me tomorrow," Taraji said, clasping her hands in front of her. "Do you have an outfit for the parade?"

I cringed. I'd completely forgotten about the expensive costumes the sorceresses wore during the parade. The trials were a big deal, they just never had been to me. "I'll have to stop by Auntie's shop and see if she has a spare outfit I can wear for the trials. Can I help clean up?" I stood when Taraji's mother stood.

She shook her head. "Certainly not. I have enough hands to help here. You need to bathe and prepare yourself for the trials tomorrow. Would you like to sleep here tonight? We can lay out an extra bed mat."

"I think I'd rather sleep at home," I replied softly, far less confidently than I intended. I scooped Igborg in my arm and he nuzzled my jaw. He made a happy grumbling sound.

Mihrage stood and opened the front door for me.

Taraji gave me a tight hug. "I'll see you tomorrow and go with you to Aunt Jade's."

"Okay." I smiled.

"I'll walk you home," Mihrage offered and closed the door behind us.

"I know the way. I can't get lost between here and there," I said teasingly.

He chuckled. "True. But Taraji insisted."

I didn't argue and we arrived at my house quickly. I paused at the door. "Thank you for whatever you did earlier."

He shrugged and pushed his hands into his pockets. "No problem."

"I thought you said you couldn't control your magic." I raised my eyebrows.

Mihrage grinned. "I can sometimes. That was a different form of magic than trying to spy on your father from miles away. All I did was ease the pain in your mind."

I felt my lip tug in a half-hearted smile. "Thank you." I took a deep breath and nudged him. "For what it's worth, I'm glad you and Taraji are courting."

His cheeks flushed a deep pink—a stark contrast from his orange skin—and he sheepishly looked away. "Thank you. I still care about you too, Caspara."

"I know." Even if it wasn't the way I wanted, he would still be a good friend.

He waved before he turned around and left and I entered my empty house.

I had entered my home plenty of times while my father was off on some job or task. However, the small room looked infinitely smaller and the dark corners felt significantly darker. Loneliness and fear crawled into my heart. I lit the bronze lamp on the bookshelf, and relief crept into the corners of my heart at the warmth of its light.

I walked up to the room I shared with Baba. Normally, I would have washed up before climbing into bed, but I was too exhausted. Still sticky from the sweat of the day, I kicked off my shoes and stripped down to my undergarments before lying on my bed. My gaze drifted to my father's empty bed just an arm's reach away.

What else didn't I know?

I looked down at the markings on my arm and wondered if the words meant anything. If they even were words.

I closed my hand in a fist and looked through the window at the gorged moon. Tomorrow night would be a full moon, and I couldn't help but see the symbolism of the Desert Trials lining up with one of the biggest celebrations in Sheblom—Schekombi. A celebration of life and the shifting season to winter, which was hardly much of a shift for Sheblom.

"I'm going to make you proud, Baba," I whispered to the moon, hoping it carried the message into his prison cell.

I rubbed my arm hard until I felt heat from the friction. Finally alone, I let the overwhelming feelings wash over me. Tears fell from my eyes and onto my pillow and I pressed my face into it as the bottled-up sob broke free.

I was afraid. And when I entered the trials, I would be alone as well—unless Taraji wanted to tag along with me throughout the trials. Unlike me, she *needed* to win. Her family needed the money. They needed her tuition covered. So tomorrow, when the time came, I would let her go on her way. Because that was the right thing to do.

I felt the sobs starting to die down because my arm burned again.

I braved a peek and could have sworn the marking on my arm had changed color, flashing blue or white. I blinked. It was just a trick of the light from the moon. The tattoo hadn't changed.

But I looked up at the moon again and bit my lip.

Igborg curled up in the crook of my neck when I lay back down and let out a squeaked grunt.

I patted his head. "You're right. At least I have you."

Twelve

Using my father's pouch, I packed the seeds Lycus had given me for Igborg, all of the supplies from Kiara, a bit more food for myself—I didn't know how long the trials would take—and my waterskin. For the first time since my father had been taken, I went to his side of the room. He had everything carefully organized. Blankets neatly folded against the wall, his bed tightly made, the shelf near the window lined with books, his prized dagger, a statue of Omar, and even Omar's perch—which had also been empty since Father was taken.

I knew I had little time, that I needed to get into Zunbar to Jade's shop to find an outfit that would help me fit in with the rest of the potential sorceresses, but maybe there was something among my father's possessions that would answer some of my questions.

I knelt on my father's bed and reached under the pile of blankets. Beneath that pile was a small box, and in that box were Father's most precious items.

When I opened the lid, I found it was filled with small things—one of Omar's feathers from the first time he molted, the fabric squares I'd practiced sewing on bundled up around a griffin feather pendant, which I wrapped back up and set to the side, a glass pebble from Piarya Beach, a red rock I had insisted was a treasure as a child, and a few other little things. The red rock was nothing special, but I vividly remembered that day by the river when Father had tried to teach me to fish.

He held the pole and explained how to throw the line out into the river, where the fish hid, and when he looked over at me, I wasn't paying attention at all. I was more interested in how different the rocks looked when they were wet. I took handfuls of them and set them in the water, then pulled them back out and watched in complete awe as the sun dried them, stealing away the sparkles.

Nothing in the box would tell me why he'd taken me away from Roshanak, or why she might want the enchanted lamp, or how the vault was even made. I looked over at the bookshelf and pondered searching my father's journals, but there were too many and I had too little time.

My answers would have to wait.

Igborg smacked his lips and rumbled a low growl.

"I know you're hungry." I hid the box of trinkets and memories before scooping him up as well as my burdened bag. It was going to be tricky carrying it around, but I would rather be prepared than wanting.

I didn't know what to expect in the trials. Taraji once told me that the trial changed every year. The cave system remained the same, but the way out changed as well as what sorts of dangers the sorceresses might encounter.

I still didn't feel like I had enough.

I needed a rope, perhaps a change of clothing too. Maybe I should have grabbed wood for fire. But I had to travel light. I couldn't look suspicious while the other sorceresses worked their ways through with magic.

Mihrage jumped down from where he typically sat on

the steps of his home as I headed past. He'd been sharpening a dagger. "You look ready."

I glanced sideways at him because for the first time since I'd known him, he sounded unsure of what to tell me. I paused and rubbed my hand up and down the strap of the bag. "I'm not."

"Erm. I'm sorry. I might be able to sneak in," he offered. His cheeks flushed a little, probably because he knew it was as stupid of an idea as it sounded.

I threw my arms around him and held tightly. "I'm going to be fine. How hard can it be? Besides, Roshanak told me she marked the way with serpent carvings." I stepped back and rubbed my hands on my pants. "I appreciate your offer, though. To sneak in and save my behind. Sands knows I need all the help I can get." I gave him a smile.

Mihrage grinned a goofy, crooked grin. "You'll blend in with them fine. I'm only worried about you finishing first. Imagine their shock if you get admission into the academy without being a sorceress!"

We both laughed and I was grateful for his comfort.

He remained by my side as I knocked on the door of Taraji's home.

She was the one to open the door and she looked me up and down. "Did you sleep all right?"

She looked absolutely stunning.

Her lips were painted purple to match the makeup around her eyes, which extended in a neatly manicured line all the way to her hair. Silver dots spotted beneath the purple at the edge of her eye. She'd braided the top of her hair back in four braids and left the rest in its natural and beautiful afro. Her kaftan was purple, silver, and white.

Mihrage's jaw hung slack.

I was pretty sure I reflected his expression. But I was much better at recovering and grinned like we were six again. "Wow! I don't even have words for how gorgeous you are. I want to hug you, but I don't want to wrinkle anything."

She rolled her eyes playfully, finally glancing at Mihrage. She lifted her brows and her grin softened into a little smile. "Cat got your tongue?"

Mihrage snapped his mouth shut. "I, uh, wow. I don't even know what to say. I'm . . . you look beautiful."

Taraji blushed madly and ran her hand down the front of Mihrage's shirt, pausing at one of his crooked buttons. "I'll be back before you know it. Don't miss me too much."

He stepped closer and I suddenly felt the pressure to look away and pretend to be invisible. Mihrage didn't care about Taraji's gown and pulled her right up to him. I watched a sand spider scurry over dunes left behind by footsteps while from the corner of my eye I watched my two best friends about to confess their emotions to each other.

Was now really the best time to be doing that?

"I'll be here waiting, when you get back. I'll help plan the grandest of feasts," Mihrage said.

Taraji giggled and traced her fingertip down his jaw. "I'll be back before you know it. I'll prove to them I'm just as good as the next sorceress."

"Better."

"Better," Taraji echoed.

My stomach knotted and I tried desperately to hold back a cringe because they pressed their foreheads together and I was positive they were going to kiss.

And then Igborg sneezed.

The two of them turned to look at me and I turned my back to them, starting to whistle while I walked away. I patted Igborg, who rested on my shoulder. But he turned to look back at them and watch what they were doing.

"I better go," Taraji said.

"Um. Yes. I'll see you in a few days."

I glanced over my shoulder and saw them awkwardly part. I should have let them have their moment, but there was some sense of relief that I didn't have to watch their awkward first kiss.

Taraji looked back at her house and shouted at the top of her lungs, "Mother, I'm going with Caspara to Auntie Jade's!"

"I'm nearly ready. Great sand dunes, Taraji! If we leave this early, we'll be waiting forever for the parade to start!" her mother called back.

"You don't have to come now. Finish getting Isline ready. I'll walk with Caspara." She rolled her eyes at me and giggled. "She's so dramatic."

"I'll meet you at Jade's shop, then!" her mother called back.

Taraji looped her arm in mine. "I know things between us have been tense. I still love you, you know."

"I know. And I'm sorry. I guess I've always been a little jealous that I don't have magic too."

She shook her head. "Not jealous. Hurt. I can't imagine what it is like being around me bragging about my magic my whole life, rubbing it in your face. And now learning about your mother." She gasped. "Caspara, what if Kasim took you away because you had no magic and he thought she wouldn't want you?"

My nose wrinkled. "Do sorceresses reveal themselves at so young an age? And I can't see my father doing that."

"Hm." She shrugged. "If you want, I can stay by your side through the trials. We can help each other."

I shook my head. "Taraji, this is your chance to be part of something better. If you have the chance to change your future, do it. You need to complete the trials."

She raised her brow at me. "Would you leave me behind?"

I didn't even need to think before answering, "If you knew my path would change my life for the better? Yes." I studied the buildings of Zunbar in the distance. The towers of the palace were visible as well as the guard towers atop the outer walls. "I don't think I'll ever get a chance to change my path. I'm pretty sure I'll forever be an outcast in Sheblom. Besides, since my father has no son, it's up to me to uphold his legacy. If I can get him back."

"You will," she insisted. "But if you weren't a thief, what would you hope to be?"

The tattoo on my arm tingled. My father's story of Telama and Kiara's words about my "other half" returned to my mind. But I'd never thought about my future the way Taraji did. I never set dreams. My whole life, I'd just sort of expected I would always be a thief. Nothing more. But with all of the recent events, and words like "destiny" being thrown around, I didn't know what I expected anymore.

I shrugged. "I don't know. I'll always be part of Almas, I suppose. Fate hasn't been too kind the last few days, so if it changes my path again, I think it would be futile of me to have my own dreams."

"Have you been spending time with Kiara?" Taraji teased.

I laughed. "Only last night."

"You did? And?"

I hesitated, my stomach dropping from a high to a low in a split second. "And my father needs me to save him."

Taraji let go of my arm. "You'll get him back."

When we arrived at Aunt Jade's tailor shop, she hadn't even opened yet. I knocked firmly on the door and glanced up the street. Four men with brooms walked in a row, sweeping the sand off the stone road in futility to prepare for thousands of guests in the street. Scents of breakfast faded in the morning and I imagined many of the young women close to my age giddy with the prospect of joining the academy, nervously getting their hair done and makeup perfect, trying to eat and keep it down, giggling and laughing with anticipation.

Taraji was one of them.

But not me. My entering the trials was for a far more important reason.

Jade opened the door, pulling a sheer shawl over her shoulders and nightgown. Her eyes widened in surprise. "Caspara. Taraji. What brings you here?"

"I need to borrow a decent kaftan," I said. "It can even be something someone returned."

Jade scrunched her eyes. "*Borrow*? What's Kasim got you into now?" She frowned and placed her hand on her hip.

I froze.

No one had told her about him being arrested. What would she say?

Her brows dipped, my hesitancy setting her on edge.

"What is it, Caspara?"

"H-he was arrested. I'll tell you everything."

Jade's eyes filled with worry and she stepped aside and let us in. She closed the door behind us and played with the chain around her neck.

I repeated the story of his arrest, added details of my own but spared the whole Prince Abudar part because Taraji would want to know every detail, and then explained Roshanak's command for me to enter the family vault and retrieve a lamp.

Jade's brows pinched in confusion. "Kasim and I used to try and find it when we were kids. Shahira even started putting together a map. But we never found the vault."

Taraji's eyes widened. "Sultana Shahira?"

"Is there another?" I teased.

Jade smiled. "We were best friends. We still are, to some degree I suppose, but our lives have taken very different paths."

My heart twisted, because I understood that feeling.

Jade looked me over. "I have the perfect outfit for you. You'll look like the other sorceresses. And I have no doubt you'll find what you seek."

Taraji cleared her throat. "Caspara needs a bath first."

I turned to her. "Ouch."

"Well, you do." She shrugged. "Have you seen yourself today?"

Jade chuckled. "Go upstairs, wash up, and I'll get dressed while you bathe. Then we can get you dressed and ready for the parade." Jade disappeared from my line of sight.

In our village, we had to collect well water and either warm it in the sun all day or heat it over the fire. But here in the city, they had running water, more than likely due to the magic of the sorceresses. Because of that, I may have relished my bath longer than necessary. I put a bucket of water on the floor for Igborg to soak in while I washed my body and hair, and then soaked myself until Taraji called my name.

I wrapped myself in a towel and looked down at Igborg. "Let's go, silly."

He slowly opened his eyes and then his mouth, a satisfied smile on his face.

I laughed and picked him up. After I wrapped him in a towel, I carried him down the stairs with me and handed him to Taraji. She giggled and snuggled him.

Jade put me in a rich emerald-green skirt with a top that crisscrossed over my breasts and around my neck, and had a matching sheer green scarf that covered my hair and left shoulder—barely hiding the tattoos there. She added a gold necklace and chains around my hips, then wrapped green fabric up to my left elbow and topped it off with a band of gold around my bicep.

I arched my brow at my own reflection. I couldn't recall ever wearing a dress, but I had certainly *never* worn anything as revealing as this.

"Wow. You'll make even Prince Abudar turn his head," Taraji said. She would be stunned silent when she learned I'd already met him and he'd turned his head even with me in my thief's clothing. I had a feeling any female would turn his head.

I felt vulnerable in that outfit. "On second thought, I think I'll just wear my other clothes."

"No. All of the girls are wearing something like this," she insisted.

"But how am I supposed to climb in this? Or run?"

"I think the skirts flow nicely," Taraji pointed out.

I pulled on the fabric. "Perhaps you could do pants that *look* like a skirt?"

Jade's lips parted and her eyes widened as though she had remembered something. "I actually have just the thing. I was experimenting for your birthday. Let me see here . . ." She walked over to a chest and returned with a pale-blue bundle of material. She set them down on the counter and held the first piece out to me—the skirt.

I frowned. When I stepped into it, however, I realized there were two legs. They were pants! My mouth gaped. "This is exactly what I wanted. They are so comfortable!" I looked at myself in the mirror.

The waistband was gold fabric, and when I pulled on the top, it was fitted perfectly to my form, which would prevent any excess fabric from snagging on rocks or whatever else I might encounter in the trials. It was the same shade of blue as the pants, but had the same gold as the waistband of the pants at the center of my stomach. A gold scarf with the same gold rhinestones as the pantleg rested over my shoulder.

I looked—and felt—more beautiful than I ever had in my entire life.

Would Roshanak even recognize me? Would Father, if he could see?

I dismissed the thought and faced my aunt.

Taraji's jaw hung open. "If you dressed like this all of the time, you would never have to steal. Men would give you what you wanted!"

Jade reached out and grabbed my pantleg. "The pants are even better, because I sewed in hidden pockets." She separated the folds of fabric to show me one on either side of my hips—nice, deep pockets. Inside the pleats and at the hem, she had smaller pockets and even a strap to hold my dagger. "I don't have one that will fit Igborg, I was concerned his weight would pull your pants down."

I looked over to the spot of sun he'd curled up in. "He does seem to be getting much bigger."

He was completely unbothered.

I slipped my hands into my pockets and grinned. "I can't believe you did this for me. Thank you." I embraced her.

"Happy early birthday." Her cheek pressed to mine and the smell of sandalwood in her hair reminded me of my father. "You know you can accomplish anything," she whispered in my ear. "You have Kasim's fire. You always have."

I let go and stood in front of the mirror.

Jade's eyes shimmered with tears. "You look so much like my mother."

I'd never met my father's parents. They had been killed in the streets years ago when Jade had been chosen to be the sultan's bride and they had tried to flee. The soldiers killed her parents and turned on Kasim, but Sultana Shahira stopped them. If the soldiers had killed him that day, I never would have been born.

As I looked at the details of my own face, I wondered if I had compared myself to Roshanak's features because I was *afraid* I would look like her, and that fear was what made me believe I did.

Jade retrieved a brush and I sat, allowing her to part my hair. She braided a small section by my temple, then somehow tied in a matching blue ribbon into my hair.

When she braided everything in one single braid, she worked in the smaller braid and ribbon.

I had never before felt truly beautiful. In fact, I'd never even felt like a woman. I'd never cared about gowns, makeup, or jewelry. Or perhaps a part of me did, but I knew Father would never be able to afford such things so I chose not to bother him with what I wanted. I looked so much older.

My father would have been impressed.

I smiled.

Taraji's mother arrived as we were finishing up and gushed over my outfit. She praised Jade while Taraji gathered her things.

"I need to cover my tattoos," I said as I stood.

"Why?" Jade asked.

"It's an identifying mark," I explained. As a thief, we always hid anything that would allow other people to remember our identity.

Jade stepped forward and took my hands. "Caspara, I don't think you should be ashamed of them. No one else has seen them but the thieves. No one will care if you have these marks. They're a part of you. Your identity. I think it's time for you to find that part of you and embrace it."

Before I could object, trumpets sounded in the distance.

Fate intervened once again.

"That's the start of the parade," Taraji said. She hoisted her bag over her shoulder. It matched her outfit perfectly. She turned and stepped out of the shop with her sister and mother.

"Will you watch me go?" I looked up at Jade, feeling heat prickle at the edges of my eyes.

She smiled brightly. "Of course I will." She wrapped me in a hug once more, then stepped back. I read in her gaze that she understood why my heart panged in my chest. Because my father wasn't there to see me.

But he would have been proud.

Jade handed me my father's satchel and I pulled it over my shoulder. "If you want, you can leave Igborg here and I'll watch him."

The lizard jumped to his feet and scrambled over to me and tried to climb my pantleg. Months ago, he would have been able to.

I laughed and helped him up. "I'd never leave you, Igborg. Silly boy." I kissed the top of his head and placed him in the bag. "Leave the food alone, though. And I mean it."

Somewhere inside the pouch, he grumbled.

Thirteen

The parade had already started when Taraji and I made it back out to the streets. People packed the alleys and stood in front of their shops, lining the main road for the parade. Men in fancy clothes led the way, carrying blue banners which displayed the royal seal of the griffin, and behind them walked men playing instruments. They were followed by young women in their best clothing—the potential new sorceresses for the Zauberin Academy.

I placed the strap of my father's bag over my head and readjusted the golden scarf on top of my head. But my thumb flicked at one of the frayed edges of the strap.

Taraji kissed her mother's cheek then stepped into the parade, dragging me with her. "Come on, we're going to end up at the back!"

I looked at Jade, who offered me a gentle, loving smile and motioned her hand toward the parade.

We stepped into the throng together, Taraji and I, and I thought back on what Jade said in the shop about her and Shahira living different lives. I didn't know much about my Aunt Jade, just that she was a seamstress and ran the shop herself when it should have been my father's birthright, but Father said she never complained. She'd never married. Never had kids. Never tried to get into the academy. I always wondered why. She seemed to have a big heart with plenty of love to give. A few months ago, I'd seen her flirting with the florist a few shops down from hers, and as I watched her face disappear amid all the others, I hoped it became something.

Because Jade deserved to be happy.

"Will you watch where you're going?" a girl in front of me snapped.

I looked down and realized I'd stepped on the heel of her shoe. "Sorry about that," I said.

"Hmph!" She turned away.

"Slept in a little late, hm?" a girl asked when we stepped in with the rest of them. She sized me up and rolled her eyes, then looked away, plastered on a fake smile, and waved at the crowd.

My lips tightened, but I said nothing in response.

There were dozens of girls. Maybe as many as fifty.

I reached my hand into my bag and placed my hand on Igborg for some comfort.

The girls around me laughed and waved at the crowd. Taraji got caught up in the excitement and joined them. The girls leaned to each other and spoke in giddy voices, thrilled they had an opportunity to show their worth to their family and strangers. I had no doubt many of them knew each other. After all, if I had been practicing my whole life to be a sorceress, I would probably have a group of friends I practiced with.

Taraji talked with the girl beside her.

Joining the parade was a terrible idea. I should have just found a way to sneak into the trials instead of pretending to be one of them.

We were directed west, down the same streets I'd

traveled the day prior with the prince of the land. We passed the palace and beyond, out into the desert. I'd never been into the western desert. The crowd followed behind us, but as we left the city behind, it was difficult to remain enthused. The people had stopped cheering and, in spite of it being relatively early in the morning, it was already hot and the waves of heat radiated off the sand, making it look like a river.

A girl beside me wiped her brow and looked down at the condensation on her fingertips. "*Jalid,*" she spoke.

My jaw dropped as I watched the sweat harden and cool into ice.

She rubbed those fingertips across the back of her neck and her gaze drifted to me. She smirked. "Amazing, isn't it? My gift is with water. I imagine that will be pretty helpful here. It doesn't get this hot in Halmu."

"You're from the oasis city?" I gaped.

She grinned. "I am. We took the river up north to get here. Not a terribly long journey, but much hotter than down there. I suppose the Ailorn Mountains help with that. What is your gift in?"

I hesitated, but shrugged. "Oh, you know. Sand stuff."

Her brows pinched. "What do you mean? Like, manipulating the sand or the winds?"

"Manipulation of the sands," I lied, stealing Taraji's power.

Taraji glanced sideways at me but didn't correct me.

The stranger smiled. "That would also be helpful here. I can't wait to see what you can do."

"Show off," the girl on my left muttered under her breath.

I looked over.

She was tall and thin and wore a purple scarf, but instead of silver accents like Taraji, she had gold accents. She looked at me. "She's sizing up the competition," she continued. "She's only talking to you because she wants to see what you can and can't do and see if she stands a chance in the trials."

I nodded and looked forward again. "I can't blame her."

The girl who had summoned the ice smirked. "They're called trials for a reason."

The front of the parade slowed to a stop, splitting into audience and participants. The crowd stood to one side while we stopped at the edge of a massive gulley.

Taraji grabbed my arm. "My heart is racing so fast, I can't stand it."

"Me too," I said softly.

"Welcome!" a voice rang out.

We all turned and faced a wooden platform that had been constructed a safe distance from the edge. Atop that platform stood Sultan Zayne in regal white and blue with golden accents. He wore the crown atop his head. His wife and the pride of our land, Sultana Shahira, stood at his side.

"I am pleased to welcome each of you to our proud capital city of Zunbar," he continued.

The crowd erupted.

Beside Sultana Shahira stood their daughter, Mithra, also wearing vibrant white, so pure it reminded me of afternoon clouds. Prince Abudar was nowhere to be seen, but strangely there was another young woman on the platform, standing near a man and woman I assumed were her parents.

Odd.

"I wish you all the best of luck over the next few days. Grand Sorceress Roshanak will explain the rules." He stepped to the side, revealing a gorgeous woman in a golden dress.

My throat tightened at seeing her again.

She stepped forward. Her black hair was braided with strands of gold and blue thread, and the wraps were coiled on the top of her head. Her cool brown eyes moved from girl to girl. With a bright smile on her face, she was regal and beautiful. "My name is Grand Sorceress Roshanak."

My mouth went dry.

Taraji leaned her lips so close to my ear, I could feel her breath. "She *is* beautiful. Just like you."

I didn't know why she found it necessary to tell me.

"I see such promise in each of you." Roshanak's eyes moved over the crowd.

I stepped a little behind Taraji and the other girl in purple, not wanting her to see me. I didn't want her to lock eyes with me and smirk, knowing the real reason I was part of the trials.

Roshanak gestured to the gulley behind us. "You shall enter the Dragon's Lair and work your way through ten separate trials. Should you encounter a situation where you could be killed, you will be transported back here safely and will return home with your family. Unfortunately, those who do not complete the trials will not be granted admission to the Zauberin Academy."

A few voices murmured.

So that's what she meant when she said if I failed I could try again, I thought.

"Areas that are not part of the trials have been safely

blocked off, and should you try to enter one of those areas, you will receive a slight shock. Those who complete the challenges shall be granted admission, and the lucky woman who completes first will be given the prize of twenty gold pieces."

A few people cheered and clapped.

"As you know, each sorceress is blessed with a particular skillset. For Sultana Shahira, it was the gift of storytelling. I have an affinity toward shadows. The purpose of the academy is to teach you skills beyond your special ability. In these trials, you may encounter situations where your ability cannot get you through. There will always be a way. You just have to be clever enough to figure it out."

Everyone erupted into applause.

Multiple magical abilities? That was possible? I looked sideways at Taraji, whose eyes were wide with the news.

"Did you know?" I asked.

She shook her head and her smile was so big, her cheeks had to hurt. "I can't believe it! I can actually learn more types of magic?"

"Shh." I chuckled.

Roshanak walked to Princess Mithra and said something only she could hear.

Princess Mithra held her head high as she descended the stairs to join us, finally old enough to be part of the trials.

If anyone was the epitome of beauty, it was Princess Mithra. Her gown had likely been prepared for months especially for this day, worked on, designed, perfected. She had blush on her cheeks and black lining her eyes with a streak of royal blue beneath them. Even though she was probably only sixteen years of age, she looked at least three years older with all of the makeup and the way she carried herself.

I nervously tried not to look at her while she turned and faced her proud parents.

"Where is Prince Abudar?" a girl with bright eyes asked when Princess Mithra reached us.

She stopped just a few people away from me. The princess smugly smiled. "He's pouting because he's not allowed to participate in the trials, being a boy and all. It's a rather big embarrassment to his betrothed." Her brow twitched and she faced forward.

The girls nearest her began whispering to each other, echoing the word "betrothed" and glancing up at the girl standing apart from the sultan and sultana.

I arched my brow. The girl was to be Abudar's bride? Good. Maybe having a wife would make him a bit more polite.

Grand Sorceress Roshanak clapped her hands and said, "*Salalem.*"

The side of the cliff on which we stood rumbled beneath our feet and shifted into stairs guiding down to the bottom of the ravine.

Roshanak smiled sweetly and held both hands up over her head. "Let the trials begin!"

The girls seemed to have suddenly lost all dignity and respect for each other as they shoved their way down the stairs. I was caught in the chaos and had no choice but to stumble clumsily. I was pushed to the outside edge of the steps. A shoulder bumped me, knocking me off-balance and causing me to step on a piece of shale. My boot slipped. I grabbed onto a nearby girl, but she pushed me away. My foot slid further and I dropped to my knees. Another bump and I would go over the edge.

But a firm hand grabbed my upper arm and hoisted me back to my feet. "Can't lose right at the beginning, that would be embarrassing." It was the girl with the purple scarf.

"Thank you," I panted.

"Don't mention it. Seriously." She slid back into the mess.

Where was Taraji?

I finally made it down the stairs and saw the girls had spread out across the sandy ravine floor, and all were headed for the cave entrance on the right-hand side.

That's when chaos erupted.

Out of nowhere, the girls started to cry out or scream and I watched in horror as the sand opened up beneath them in pits and began sucking girls down one by one. I skidded to a halt and watched a girl a few yards away from me claw at the slippery sand in a futile attempt to escape. But it was too late. If I tried to help, I'd be taken down with her. She reached for me, eyes pleading, before she disappeared beneath the sand.

I looked to the ridgeline where the crowd of onlookers watched from above, and the girl who had just disappeared before me reappeared in a puff of red smoke. She burst into sobs and fell to her knees.

She'd been cast out of the trials.

Two more girls at different distances from me disappeared.

More puffs of red appeared along the ridgeline—each a girl being sent home.

"Of course the trials would begin when she said they would," I muttered.

Everyone froze.

The pit the girl had just been dragged into was no longer there. I shifted my gaze back and forth to examine any sign of difference in the ground. One girl gingerly made her way toward the entrance of the cave, only to cry out just steps away as she was dragged into an unseen pit.

There had to be a safer way across the sand.

Taraji was in the center of the open ground. If I could get her, we could get across together. But I didn't know if the pits were just holes or caused by some kind of monster hidden beneath the sand. If I *actually* had Taraji's magic, I would probably have been able to move the sand and find out.

Another girl near the entrance held her hands out before her and uttered a spell I couldn't hear that sent a wave of wind to push the sand up into the air. I couldn't see whatever she saw, but she confidently chose her path. Those nearest her rushed to follow her steps. Her use of magic was a cue to the others to begin using spells to find their way across.

To my right, I spotted the girl in the purple-and-gold scarf picking her way toward the entrance. After taking a few terrifying blind steps to catch up, I fell into her steps. They were longer than mine, thanks to her height.

"Figured it out too?" she called over her shoulder.

"It's simple," I lied and glanced at her, but she wasn't looking at me now.

I looked over at Taraji, but she was also headed for the cave entrance, using her gift to shift the sand along her way. It seemed to bunch up in a crescent shape on a particular spot, revealing what appeared to be the outline of one of the pits hidden, and she avoided it.

I felt like I could finally breathe again when we reached the comfort of solid ground at the entrance of the cave. Just over a dozen girls had already arrived with more on their way behind us.

Taraji hugged me. "I lost sight of you on the stairs."

"I nearly fell off. Someone caught me." I glanced toward the other girl. Her eyes were locked on the cave wall.

"I'm so grateful you made it." Taraji let go and turned. "What do you think of this?"

Before us stood three doors: one made of faded wood with cracks and gaps between the planks, another in pristine condition and painted turquoise blue, and the final door painted red with gold hinges and a golden handle.

I followed everyone's gaze to the inscription above the doors:

Three entrances you see.
Ways in, there are three.
But what is it you cannot see
beyond the entrances three?
Choose the wooden and face a forest black?
The royal—a labyrinth—to find your way back?
Or shall one provide you a little shove
to help you enter the one above?

"A black forest seems easiest," a girl in a black dress quickly decided. She flung open the wooden door and disappeared.

"I feel like it's clearly the door to the right," a girl with fancy brown locks said. "*Above* implies help from the gods." She went through the red door.

Princess Mithra strode up to the middle door, saying nothing to the others before she too disappeared. Many of the girls looked at each other and several followed right after, merely because she was the princess.

Taraji was one of them, but I stopped her. "I don't think that's the way."

I noticed the girl in the purple scarf also contemplating following Mithra's steps while I read the passage again. But she turned to me and looked me up and down. "You're thinking something else?"

"I think the last phrase is literal," I said softly so only she and Taraji could hear. I'd followed her chosen path across the sands. I could give her a little hint.

"You want me . . . to push you through one of the doors?" she asked, confused.

Taraji folded her arms. "I think Mithra has an advantage, living with the grand sorceress and all."

I shook my head and stepped in front of the stranger.

I hinted with my eyes. "Look *above* the last door." I turned to Taraji.

Her eyes shifted away from me, up to the gap above the door on the far right of the overhang. Her eyes widened. "A fourth entrance?" she whispered.

"Or the third. For all we know, one of these doors could be transporting everyone who enters back to the grand sorceress," I said.

"That's insanity," Taraji objected.

"You don't have to stick with me," I reminded her. Her lips tightened.

"I mean it. Win this thing." I smiled and raised my

finger. "I completely forgot about this until now, but I brought you a good luck charm." I dug into my pouch and found the glass camel I'd stolen the day before and held it out to her.

"A camel?" Taraji wrinkled her nose.

Someone entered the door behind her.

"I think it's going to be your animal familiar," I said.

She laughed and accepted the small figurine. "But what if you're right?" Taraji said, her eyes drifting to the overhang.

The stranger stepped over to the red door. "If you give me a boost, I'll reach down and help you up. Call it repayment." She smiled knowingly.

We walked over and I interlocked my fingers before I set my hands on my thigh. She placed her right foot in my hand.

"Ready?" I asked.

"Almost." She placed her hands as high up on the wall as she could reach. "Okay. Now!"

With a grunt, I lifted with all my strength at the same time she pushed off. She was a tad heavier than I anticipated, but she still managed to grab on to the ledge. Hoisting herself, she got one arm up and grunted as she dragged herself safely onto and then over the lip. It wasn't graceful and certainly not how I would have done it.

"What are you three doing?" someone demanded.

Ignoring them, I took a couple of steps back while the stranger lay on her belly and reached her arm down to me. Like I'd done just the day before while fleeing from the soldiers, I dashed forward, kicked off the door, and launched myself up to grab her right forearm. She snatched mine at the perfect time. I kicked off the wall again and grabbed the girl's wrist with my left hand. She got just enough leverage to pull me up beside her.

"It can't really mean *above*, can it?" someone below muttered.

"No way, that's not a door. It says there are three *doors*."

"They're crazy."

"But they might be on to something."

Once I was on the ledge beside the purple-scarf stranger, I wondered. This *was* crazy. There wasn't a visible path, just gaping darkness, and there was no telling if this was the actual entrance. I could very well be wrong. Father had always told me to look for what others couldn't see, and this was definitely that.

But I also didn't care to win. I was only entering the cave to find my family vault.

I leaned over and looked down at Taraji. "Are you joining us?" I reached down to her.

Behind Taraji, girls were picking and choosing their doors. We were falling behind. Although I supposed it didn't matter.

"I . . . I'm going to follow Mithra." Taraji flashed me a smile.

I smiled back weakly. "Okay. Good luck, Taraji."

"You too, Caspara." She opened the middle door, painted the royal blue, and disappeared.

"We *could* form an alliance," the girl said from behind me. She stuck out her hand. "My name is Yasmin."

"My name is Caspara." I briefly shook her hand, then adjusted the gold scarf over my shoulder and wiped my forehead. Being out of the heat felt incredible, but if I had to scramble like that again, this outfit was going to prove useless.

I gave Yasmin a sideways glance, having noticed her staring at my arm. "What?"

"Your tattoos. They're intriguing is all. Let's get going before the others catch on." Yasmin was already on her feet and headed straight into the abyss.

If it came down to magic to truly get through each trial, I didn't stand a chance. But maybe my brains could be greater than magic.

Fourteen

Yasmin and I kept one hand on the wall as we shuffled our feet down the path. I kept my other hand on her back, because there was no light to see anything. Not even her. I couldn't help but wonder if I'd misinterpreted the riddle and should have gone with Taraji after all.

Without warning, I heard Yasmin's foot slip and she let out a cry. Her body jerked downward, and because I was holding on to her shirt, I was thrown forward and plunged into the black abyss. I screamed as I slid on my stomach down the steep slope.

We hit the bottom and tumbled, banging arms and knees and shoulders together.

Yasmin was the first to sit up and said, "Are you all right?"

My head slowly stopped spinning and I nodded. "I think so. Just a pain in my side that will go away. Maybe some bruising. Are you?"

"Yes." She nodded her head, a movement I could barely see because there was a source of light behind her.

I blinked and scrambled to my feet. We were in an enormous opening with a hole hundreds of feet overhead offering light that stretched down toward us like the white roots of the Dimeret plant. And then I noticed we were near the edge of a void. Stalagmites reached up from the inky darkness, and I wasn't entirely sure that darkness was just shadow. It seemed too thick.

Yasmin walked carefully around the edge on which we stood, eyeing the space around us. "There's no other way."

"No other way to what?" I asked.

She turned to me. "We have to get across. The only entrance I see is on the other side." She pointed. "We can't climb back the way we came. It's too steep. There's a ledge there" —she pointed up— "but I can't follow it beyond it stopping here. There doesn't seem to be a way to jump or climb up to anything in the ceiling. There are no visible steps or ladders or scaffolding. Seems to me, the only way across the void is to jump on the stalagmites."

I dusted smudges off my new clothing as I studied the stalagmites. "A few of them seem to have good hand and footholds. Almost like they've been made. That large one is nice and flat." I pointed to one just three stalagmites away. "I'm used to this sort of thing. I'll go first and you follow my path." I rubbed the sweat off the palms of my hands and walked forward.

"Stop!"

I halted. "What?"

"Your foot," Yasmin pointed. "That rock doesn't look right."

I looked down to where I was about to step. It was off-color from the rest of the floor. Just barely, but definitely not right. I stepped over it and nodded. "Thank you."

Yasmin kept her eyes on the floor as she joined me at my side. "I don't feel comfortable with you going first."

"Uh, why?"

"You want me to just stand here and watch you slip?"

I raised a brow. "Who said anything about slipping? I literally do this sort of thing every day. Maybe not over a void of who-knows-what looming below, or on stalagmites, but I run from the soldiers . . ." The sentence died on my lips and I quickly faced the void again. "I know how to jump and climb. That's all."

Yasmin relented with a sigh and gave a reluctant nod. "Okay, I'll follow you. Why do you run from soldiers?"

I merely smiled and winked. I studied the nearest stalagmites, carefully plotting my route. There was another large, flat-top stalagmite almost halfway across the void where I could stop and take a rest to plot out the second half of the way. Yasmin *should* be able to fit on it with me.

"This must be why the other girls screamed."

"Do we seriously have to slide down that?"

"Gross."

Voices echoed down from the way we'd fallen. Apparently, a few girls thought I was on to something, and they'd gotten there much faster because they were able to summon orbs of magic light. I could see the glow of their light before they reached the bottom.

I rolled my eyes.

"You two are just standing here?" one of the girls said as she adjusted her clothing and hair.

The other four girls fixed themselves too.

I refocused on my route. "We have to get across." Not wanting to waste any more time by standing and talking with people I didn't care about, I jumped to the first stalagmite to the sound of girls screaming. I gripped it with both arms and jammed my feet down to catch the ledge I'd noticed.

"You've *got* to be joking!" another said when she saw

I was safe. "We're supposed to climb like some sort of freakish cave monster to the other side?"

"No, we're *supposed* to use our magic to figure out a safe way across." I glanced back to see the speaker, a girl in a green-and-yellow dress. She stood with her hands on her hips, scowling at me with disgust.

"Maybe she can't levitate," Yasmin said flatly. "I know I can't."

"She has a point," a girl in pink said. "My magic is with living creatures. That's certainly not going to help me get across *this*."

Ignoring them, I jumped to the next stalagmite and—without losing momentum—onto the first flat-topped stalagmite. I wiped my hands on my pants again. It was a bit chilly, but my nerves were making my hands damp, not to mention the stalagmites were slightly slippery and the girls were annoying.

Yasmin kept her eyes on me. "Tell me when you're ready for me to follow."

"Just let me get to that big flat one," I said from where I knelt and pointed.

"Got it."

"*Akshifak!*" A burst of pink light filled the room, and glitter hit the edges of the stalactites hanging overhead, sticking to them and making them glow. But the light also stuck to the ledge Yasmin had pointed out and an invisible ladder reaching down to it. The spell revealed invisible scaffolding stretching across the void.

I scowled and turned to jump on the fourth stalagmite.

"A revelation spell," one of the girls said. "Is that part of your magic?"

I glanced back and saw the one in green nod. "Making

things disappear and finding them, then making them reappear. Seems to be handy."

The girl in pink stepped up to Yasmin. "You should follow us."

I glanced over at her, then back at the way I was headed. I was a good distance across. Almost halfway. And it would sort of be stupid to go back.

"Don't!" Yasmin suddenly shouted.

There was a click and I snapped my gaze to see one of the girls had stepped on the off-color rock. A groan radiated upward from the blackness, metal ground against stone, and there was a little puffing sound. The stalagmites began to move, but not just the stalagmites, the magical hidden scaffolding overhead moved too.

"Too late." Yasmin jumped on the first, then rapidly to the second and third stalagmites before they could get too far out of reach. I had to admit that I was impressed by her hidden skill. Perhaps desperate situations would make anyone leap across chasms?

Sensing her urgency, I retrained my attention to the big flat-top stalagmite and jumped. I had hoped to take my time and be careful, because moving quickly meant taking risks, and a slip of the foot or hand could drop me down into the darkness. Then I would have to start all over.

"Not that one!" Yasmin yelled just as I was about to leap.

My hesitation ended up being for my benefit, because the stalagmite suddenly dropped downward into the darkness. The shadows below engulfed the stone, which meant I had been right. Whatever was beneath wasn't only shadows. But by looking downward, I also spotted the orange light starting to glow beneath us.

"This is bad," I said aloud. I spotted another stalagmite getting closer and jumped to it, then finally onto the flat top, which I hit with my ribs and had to scramble on top.

Yasmin was right behind me, and I had to catch her by the wrist. I gritted my teeth and leaned back as far as I could, using my own body weight to leverage her as she kicked at the stalagmite. She finally tumbled over the top.

We both took a moment to catch our breath. The stalagmites were moving up and down, left and right, disappearing and reappearing in different places. Overhead, the scaffolding had broken apart and was forcing the inexperienced girls to leap from one to the next or time the passing of a piece just right for them to step onto.

"I'm beginning to wonder if the grand sorceress was being honest about the girls staying safe during this," Yasmin said. "If they plummet just right, they could hit a stalagmite and die."

"Not to mention the fire growing below us," I added.

She shifted her gaze downward and her eyes widened. "We need to move!"

"I'm watching. This one and that third one are on the same path. I'll jump on this. You get on that one." I didn't wait for her to confirm before I leapt.

"This is absurd," Yasmin complained before jumping onto hers.

"If you could summon a bridge, it wouldn't be," I said back.

I jumped onto the next one that passed but let out a squeal when it dropped. I had only a second to fling myself at the nearest one and try to scramble up it for a better angle. My feet were near the darkness, and I could have sworn I felt heat coming from it. The fire must have been getting closer.

Igborg scrambled up my side and onto my shoulder. His added weight on my arm made my grip tremble.

"I can't deal with you right now!" I shouted at him.

Igborg flicked his tongue against my cheek and then, to my horror, jumped.

"Igborg!" I screamed.

His sides stretched outward and then upward. To my astonishment, they were wings. He pumped his little wings and landed on the top of a stalagmite, then screamed at me.

I got the hint—that was the one I was supposed to get to.

I didn't have time to be in awe of my lizard.

I bit my bottom lip and scraped my feet against the stalagmite onto which I held. My arm strength waned. Finally, my right foot connected with a hole and I pushed up, jumping just as the stalagmite Igborg stood on dipped slightly as though to help catch me.

He flew to the next, and I followed behind.

Yasmin was already safe on the other side and reaching out to me. "Jump with all you have!"

I shook my head. My arms trembled. I needed to catch my breath and think about the timing, and—Igborg sunk his teeth into the back of my left leg and I jumped.

Yasmin caught me, though she didn't need to because I cleared the final gap perfectly, and landed on top of her, bringing her to the ground.

I lay on my back, panting.

"You have a pet dragon?" Yasmin asked, rolling her head to the side. She had a bit of dirt smudged on her cheek.

I sat up and looked at Igborg, who now looked like nothing more than the uromastyx lizard I thought he was.

He flicked his tongue.

"When were you going to tell me you're actually a dragon?" I scolded.

He cocked his head and looked at Yasmin, then me.

I heaved a sigh and dug into my pouch to get him a handful of seeds and my waterskin.

Yasmin glanced overhead. "I don't really want to sit here and watch this play out," she said with a frown. She got to her feet and walked briskly to the exit.

I looked upward at one of the girls dangling and sobbing for help. I wished I could. I looked around to see if I could possibly climb up and . . . but there was nothing. The leap onto the side on which I stood was too high up for me to get to without a ladder or rope.

And then I saw it. I jumped up to my feet. "If you get on that other platform, you can catch her!" I called out, pointing to one that moved in a lazy circle around a stalactite.

The girl in pink spotted what I meant and crouched. She jumped down at just the right time, then reached up and grasped the hips of the girl in green. "Let go!"

The girl in green sobbed but listened, and the girl in pink fell back, pulling her safety onto the platform beside her. The others started to follow her direction.

"Thank you!" they called down to me.

I glanced over my shoulder, the direction Yasmin had taken, and stepped back. They could find their way across from there. They were all safe now.

I picked up Igborg just as he snatched the last nut and gobbled it down.

Fifteen

"Why are you doing the trials?" Yasmin asked.

The corridor we walked down was lit along the ground with glowing moss. I was massaging my arms and we had been walking in silence a good while. When she spoke, I was taken back by the sudden question.

"I want the money at the end," I answered.

It was a better lie than telling Yasmin I was searching for a secret entrance into the treasure trove no one knew existed so I could save my father from the royal sorceress everyone else idolized, who happened to be my mother.

Yasmin stopped and eyed me. "You don't have magic, do you?"

For some reason, I felt like I'd been caught. But I frowned. "What gave you that idea?"

"No offense." She put her hands out defensively. "But why on the golden sands are you down here? This is *not* a fun way to spend the day."

I walked around her. "I already told you. I want the money at the end. Why haven't *you* used any magic? Are you not supposed to be here either?"

She turned and followed. "I have magic. But surely you know sorceresses rarely know magic beyond their specialty. Those who know spells in different elements are rare."

"I know. My friend, Taraji, can manipulate sand. She never would have made it across that chasm back there without me." At the thought of my best friend, my heart twinged. I hoped she didn't need to cross any trials like that. "What is your special ability?"

"Oh." Yasmin dragged the toe of her shoe across the moss, making it brighten. "I like light." She gave me a sheepish smile and summoned an orb of light to glow and lead the way.

I stopped and put my hands on my hips. "You're saying you could have prevented us from falling down back there?"

"I thought the cave would have torches," she replied innocently. The orb of light floated into the air when she lowered her hand.

I began walking again. "What Roshanak said at the beginning of the trials, about sorceresses learning other types of magic, was that true?"

Yasmin slowly bobbed her head up and down. "Yes, but not unless a sorceress is trained for years. We each have a gift, but cultivating that into real magic takes training."

"So, you are saying you aren't trained how to cast a spell to reveal hidden ladders?" I smiled.

"Afraid not." Her laughter echoed in the long hall. "But why are you going through all of this just for some gold? Is your family in debt or something?"

I ran my tongue over my teeth and began glancing at the walls for any sign of the serpent symbol Roshanak claimed would mark the path. "I need the money. I don't come from wealth like you do."

Yasmin didn't look at me. "There is no shame in that. A lot of people try to overcome their status."

"Who said I was ashamed?" I scowled.

"I didn't say you were, I just think a lot of poor people feel ashamed," she bumbled, trying to recover from her statement. "If it means anything, by your clothing and how beautiful you are, I had no idea."

Not knowing what to say, I furrowed my brows. "Thanks?"

"You know, the winner also gets the chance to dance with Prince Abudar at the celebration after. He's so handsome." She grinned and clasped her hands before her.

I rolled my eyes at her while I climbed over a giant boulder. "In that case, maybe I should make sure you win."

"Don't you think he's adorable? I mean, his smile . . ."

"Like I said, you can have him. Not interested. But I overheard Princess Mithra say his *betrothed* was present at the beginning of the trials."

I thought I saw her scowl, but she recovered. "But you *will* go to the celebration, right? Even if you don't win the coins, you can still participate in the food and music in the palace. And dancing, even if it's not with the prince. Do you dance? It's one of my absolute favorite things."

I nudged a glowing mushroom and it brightened, sending a sort of shockwave of light down the cave and lighting it further. "I do sometimes, but only when we have celebrations. Like tonight, while all of the hopeful sorceresses are in the trials, we have a big feast. Everyone cooks different parts of the meal and it's laid out on this long table. And we have a smaller table filled with treats." I grinned, vividly seeing everything spread out under the moonlight. "And then we take turns playing music and dancing with each other."

"That sounds fun," Yasmin said. "Maybe I can join you at your next celebration."

I shrugged. "Sure. Why not?" I had absolutely no intention of bringing her anywhere, nor did I plan on even continuing this "friendship" beyond getting through the caves.

We walked a while longer in silence, but I felt a gnawing in my gut.

"Look, you really should carry on without me," I finally said and stopped to take a drink of water.

Yasmin stopped with me and looked back the way we'd come. "Why? I thought you needed the money at the end. And, if we stick together, I can help you win so you get it. I'll still get admission anyway. That's all I want."

I offered her an apologetic smile. Why had I said that I wanted the money? "I don't want to hold you back if you want to win a chance to dance with Prince Abudar."

"I'll still get a chance to dance, just you wait." She winked and we began walking again.

I silently cursed myself because it would be impossible to leave her behind now.

"While we're stuck together, tell me about your family?"

"I'm a daughter of one of the forty thieves." I grinned widely so she would think it was a joke.

"I thought they were just a group of old men bent on stealing everything they can from those who have actually worked for it."

That didn't surprise me at all. Most people thought that's all we did. "What does *your* father do for a living?" I asked her.

Yasmin hesitated and then said, "He is a merchant. He owns his own ship."

"And how many generations is he?"

She gave a thoughtful frown and tapped her chin. "Maybe three? What's your point?"

"My point is, the rich stay rich. The poor can't work their way out of being poor. Not even help from the thieves changes anything."

"The thieves? You were being honest about being one of them?"

Our gazes linked. "Yes. And contrary to popular belief, we don't steal for ourselves. All of the money, horses, jewels, and food go to the poor in Zunbar, Narshiz, Halmu, Crehat, Dorus, and Balim. All over the country." The cave's path turned to the right and at the end, in the distance, was a glowing cavern.

"I had no idea," Yasmin mumbled.

"I know a woman whose husband is a sailor for a merchant ship. He works for three or four months at a time and comes home just long enough to give her his earnings to pay their rent and keep them out of debt. She begs for food for their two children while he is gone. She also weaves baskets and sells them in the bazaar. Yet, no matter how hard they work, they can't work hard enough or earn enough that they will ever be able to buy a home of their own, or rise above their status."

Yasmin wiped her hands on her scarf. "I didn't realize. I'm sorry."

"We can't change what we don't know," I said and patted her back.

We followed the tunnel for what felt like ages, until

Igborg climbed out, sat on my shoulder, and nibbled my earlobe.

I stopped at an alcove with a natural bench and sat. "I don't know about you, but I'm hungry. Want something to eat?" I dug into my pouch and pulled out a bundle of dried goat meat and nuts.

"Sure." Yasmin took a seat at my side and opened her own food.

"Do you have a good family?" I asked.

She pulled a piece of meat apart. "I'm really close with my mother. She taught me to believe there is good in everyone and has worked hard for me to learn compassion. I learn all about the business side of things with my father. We're close too, but not as much as me and my mother." She bit her meat. "I have a sister too."

"Are you close with her?"

She smiled almost longingly. "Not as much as I'd like. See, we both have magic. She's in the trials too. But with me being the eldest, I am the one who has trained the most and hardest, and all of the focus has gone to *my* schooling. Her schooling hasn't been as intense."

I nodded in understanding. "That must make your sister feel very alone."

Yasmin licked her thumb. "I think she accepts it. It's not her birthright, after all. It's mine."

We talked a little bit more while we snacked, but we heard voices nearing and took that as our cue to get up and begin our journey again. We headed toward the glowing cavern at the end of the tunnel. Yasmin rounded the corner first and stopped dead in her tracks.

I bumped into her shoulder.

The cavern was long and somewhat narrow, with an

underground waterfall and river cascading down the middle. Lining the water were the most unusual plants I'd ever seen. They had long, thin, white stems with a sort of hat on top.

"Midnight toadstools," Yasmin whispered, crouching to examine one as big as her hand.

Blue and green bulbs with tentacles dangling from the stalactites like jellyfish—I'd seen those dried up on the beach. Pink and purple stony plants grew up like coral at the bottom of the sea. And everything glowed through the darkness of the cave.

"I've never seen anything like this," Yasmin said softly, reverently. Her eyes examined every inch of the inside of the space.

"Neither have I," I replied. I walked over to the edge of the underground river. The carpet of moss lit up with white light every step I took, then faded away back to green. "The most plants that I've seen are the grasses and trees that grow along the Dumue River. Do you think the water is safe to drink?" I crouched and dipped my fingers into the frigid water.

Yasmin smiled, the dimple in her right cheek showing. "For all we know, it could be the fountain of youth the stories speak of." She joined me and knelt, eyeing the water, then the fall to our right. Her eyes were scrunched in focus. "It looks like there are steps up to the waterfall. I imagine the way out is behind it." Her spine was stiff, hands balled into fists on her knees.

I leaned back on my ankles. "You seem on edge."

Igborg crawled down my arm and lay his belly on the soft moss and twitched his head, sniffing the water. He dipped his head to drink it, so it must have been safe.

Yasmin touched her hands in the water, then wiped them over her face and stood up, flicking water from her fingers. "I keep expecting to see a giant spider fall down from the ceiling or a poisonous snake on the ground or . . . something. These are trials, remember? And we've gone a long way without incident."

I crouched to rinse my hands in the water. "Of course. I guess I just expected the challenges to be big. Can you do anything other than make magic light?"

"Are you saying I'm not any good?" She frowned at me.

I couldn't resist a smile. "Well. I mean, I haven't seen anything beyond your fancy circular torch."

"I'm powerful enough to win this, you know. I just don't need to."

"Yeah? Prove it." I rested my hands on my lap. I didn't care how powerful Yasmin was. I was only eager to see what magic could do. I had never watched magic other than Kiara's visions or Taraji moving sand around, and now seemed as good a time as any.

Yasmin stretched one hand out to the water and twisted the fingers on her other hand into the air. "*Anadi al-ma'.*"

My jaw dropped as the water pulled from the river to Yasmin's outstretched hand, then between that hand and her second, twisting and changing until the water took on the form of a dragon. It swam—or flew—through the air, around her head, across her shoulders, and then back down into the river.

"That was incredible!" I grinned like a child. "I thought you said your magic was only in light?"

Yasmin puffed out her chest. "I practice every chance

I get. I'm *trying* to learn other things. Now, let's get out of here before more people head this way."

I nudged Igborg with the toe of my shoe. "Hop on in. Yasmin is right. We'll stop and eat dinner in a few hours." Holding the flap of my bag open, I waited as Igborg tried to climb up my pant leg. I shook my head and pulled him off, then set him in the bag. "I don't understand why you didn't just fly in, silly. I know you're a dragon now." I closed the flap on him.

Yasmin led the way this time, stepping over and around vibrant pink mushrooms and yellow and orange flowers. She started up the stone steps.

I reached out and touched the purple leaf of a flower with a massive center, still unable to believe such beauty existed so close to home and yet completely unseen by anyone but those who would come this way through the trials.

At my touch, the petals around the flower recoiled and curled inward. The fuzzy center stems began shifting back and forth and I pulled my hand away.

I put my right foot on the bottom step, but couldn't lift my left. When I looked down, I spotted a tendril wrapping around my leg, already up to my thigh. I gasped and called for Yasmin just as the plant tugged on me, causing me to lose my balance and fall on my side.

"What did you do?" Yasmin shouted over the roar of the falls.

"I just touched it! Come get this thing off of me." I reached down and grabbed the tendril to push it off, but a sticky substance coated my hands.

"Oh no," I heard Yasmin say somewhere beside me. "Don't move, Caspara. Just freeze."

I tipped my head back to look up at her, still trying desperately to get away. "This flower is going to eat me, and you're telling me—"

"I'm serious, stop moving!" she yelled.

I turned my head to look at the plant I'd touched, but stopped moving. The center of the flower had opened up, revealing rows of pointed thorns that looked like teeth.

My breath caught.

The flower pulled on me, the vine stretched up to wrap around my hips. The tip of it poked my belly and I noticed little suckers like those of an octopus on the end. It was tasting me! My lungs burned and I desperately wanted to take a breath but feared it might notice and pull my leg into its mouth.

"*Barq*," Yasmin whispered.

A burst of light struck the plant and it collapsed in a heap, its tentacle falling limp to the ground with it.

My breath came out in a burst, and I gasped my inhale. "Thank you." I hurried to my feet and looked down at the translucent blue gunk on my hands and fingers. My brows furrowed. I couldn't feel my fingers.

Yasmin said nothing but dragged me to the water and shoved my hands into it.

I cried out as pain burned through my palms and up my arms into my shoulders. "Let go! That hurts! It burns!"

"It's poison," she said, holding me. "The cold will counteract the burn, but you've *got* to keep your hands in the water even though it hurts. You have to get the poison off."

A wave of cold washed up my arms and down the back of my neck. My tongue tingled. Nausea washed over me. My stomach roiled. I leaned forward, vomiting the snack I'd eaten just minutes ago into the water. A shiver crawled up from the base of my skull down to my toes.

Yasmin muttered a curse. "Do any of you have healing power?"

I lifted my head to see the girls who had followed us standing at the mouth of the passage. They stared at us with wide eyes. Not *us*. Me.

I wretched a second time.

"Can any one of you perhaps cast a spell to counteract poison?" Yasmin asked urgently. "She touched a plant that's poisonous and she's got to get it off of her."

"No," they muttered.

I managed to lift my head and look to Yasmin. "I-I have medicines in my bag. I don't know if . . . if any are an antidote."

Yasmin held on to my arms, holding me as I trembled. She let go long enough to search my bag. "Gouroot. Jipsweed. Nothing for poison that I can see. Do any of you have any herbs that might help?"

They huddled together and started digging through their pouches.

The girl in pink knelt at my side.

"I'm not exactly sure her getting poison on her skin is part of the trials. What if she actually dies?" Yasmin muttered.

"Grand Sorceress Roshanak said if any of us would be in a situation where we *could* die, we would just disappear. I'm sure they will have a way to heal her."

"I have lairgrass." The girl in green held out a pouch. "It will help with the nausea and pain."

Yasmin accepted it and pushed it into my mouth and under my tongue. "Do any of you have jewelweed?" she asked.

I closed my eyes. The lairgrass was bitter, a bit like cinnamon.

"I'm sorry, I don't."

"Me either."

"She can just return."

I heard them shuffling their feet, walking away, leaving me alone with Yasmin.

The nausea started to fade.

She let go of me and started rummaging through her own bag. I rested my shoulder on one of the boulders, but I was finally able to open my eyes.

"Take your hands out of the water," she instructed.

I did so and rested the backs of my hands on my knees, my body still trembling—from adrenaline, pain, or shock, I didn't know.

Yasmin rubbed something over my palms and I whimpered and had to bite my bottom lip to stop myself from pulling away.

Finally, the burning sensation began to subside, and I slowly managed to open my eyes and look down at the damage. My palms and fingers were swollen with blotchy red patches and little purple blisters.

"I have some healing ointment," Yasmin explained. "I don't know if it will help with the burning feeling, but it should work like healing a cut." Yasmin reached back into her pouch and found the bandages. She wrapped my left hand first, then my right. She tucked the bandage in and put the leftover supplies away. "Do you feel well enough to walk?"

I nodded. "But I need a drink of water first. I can't believe how quickly that made me sick." I reached into my pouch and carefully lifted my water for a drink. My fingers stung.

Yasmin was already back on her feet. "I'm sorry that happened to you."

I set the water pouch back in my bag and, with Yasmin's help, stood. "Thank you. Who knows what the poison would have done if you hadn't been here?"

"Paralyzed you. See? It's a good thing we stuck together!" She helped me forward. "Let's make it out without more injuries."

Sixteen

I felt much better after a few minutes of walking. I drank my water and even managed to eat some more food and keep it down. I'd kept the lairgrass under my tongue until it went tasteless, and then spat it out.

The passage after the waterfall was dark enough Yasmin summoned an orb of light to shine through the blackness. We reached a fork that broke off in three different directions.

"Okay. Which way?" Yasmin asked.

Using my knowledge about the serpents Roshanak had left behind for me, I searched the walls as subtly as possible. I spotted it. Or, at least I *thought* I did. It was near shoulder-height, and at first I thought it was a trick of the light.

The light from Yasmin's orb cast a shadow across the wall just right that I saw the open jaws of the serpent. While she was turned toward a different tunnel, I reached out and ran my fingers over the details of the carving. There was a curl of the snake's body and deep holes for the eyes.

It was definitely a snake.

I stepped back. "We should go this direction."

Yasmin turned to me and stepped up to my side. "Why

do you think that?"

"Call it a hunch." I didn't look at her before I entered the tunnel.

"Are you truly one of the thieves? Is this a thief trick? Hunches?" She skipped to keep up.

"Sort of. My father used to tell me to trust my instincts. It's rule number thirteen, according to him." I ducked around a short stalactite.

"Rule thirteen?" Yasmin gave the stalactite a wide berth.

I nodded. "We have a set of rules to live by. We aren't scoundrels." I threw her a smile.

She nodded, a thoughtful expression on her face.

"What do you want to do with the rest of your life?" I asked, thinking back on the conversation I'd had that morning with Taraji.

"What do you mean?"

"I mean, I'm sort of *doomed*, I suppose, to be a thief forever. What do you want to be? A seamstress? Sword fighter?"

Yasmin grinned, again revealing her dimple. It reminded me of Mihrage's dimple. "I want to be important," she answered. "I want to be remembered. I want people to hear stories of me, or the good I did. I want to survive history."

"Hm."

She looked sideways at me. "You don't think that's something to strive for?"

I shrugged and adjusted my pack. "It sounds lovely, but more like a story. It's sort of vague too. I can be remembered because I am Almas the thief, though it's not really me or *only* me. But . . . I suppose it would be nice to be remembered."

"What would you want?"

"Honestly? Being remembered for being me . . . I don't care about that. I think it would be nice to just *be* me. Whatever that means." I rolled my eyes and smiled.

Yasmin nodded slowly. "Perhaps you don't know what it means to be you because you haven't had the freedom to discover who you are? You've lived, as you said, being viewed as Almas. A thief. It's who you were taught to be. Maybe you need to uncover who you really are."

It made sense, and it sounded like it would be easy. And perhaps it would be, once Roshanak got what she wanted and my father came home. We could sit beside the fire at night and I could ask him who I was meant to be.

I absently rubbed my arm.

I found two more serpents and followed those tunnels until the passage finally opened to a low-ceilinged chamber with stalagmites and stalactites touching and creating columns. A light emanated from the opposite end, and when we were at just the right angle, it looked as if we were inside of a mouth.

Yasmin chuckled. "Looks like we've been eaten, doesn't it?"

"I was just thinking the same," I admitted. "Maybe this is the fifth trial." I raised my brows and feigned being scared.

"Fifth?"

"Sink holes, doors, chasm, and I'm counting the poisoned plant." I held up my bandaged hands.

"Ah."

Both of us looked to the left at the same time, though I

couldn't tell if it was because of instinct or because I had heard something. For some reason, Yasmin dispelled her orb of light, casting us in deep darkness my eyes weren't used to. She ushered me behind a column and we stayed low to the ground, but I saw through a gap between two thin stalagmites.

Princess Mithra entered from a side cavern, an orange ball of light hovering just ahead of her. "I can't believe it took us so long to get through that blasted maze. This was *supposed* to be easy for me!"

"How could you expect it to be so easy?" a second voice asked. It sounded male. "You couldn't just walk through the trials unscathed. Not even Grand Sorceress Roshanak would have allowed that. Otherwise, it would be obvious you were favored."

When Mithra wheeled around to her friend, I saw a scrape down her cheek. She pointed to it. "I might have a scar now, thank you very much."

"And things could have been a lot worse if I hadn't cut off the limbs of that tree." The figure removed the hood of their cloak and my breath caught.

It was a young man. His black hair was short and his right ear was pierced with a golden sword earring dangling from it. He was one of the palace guards. What was he doing here?

The young man reached out and rubbed his thumb over the thin scrape on Mithra's cheek while shaking his head. "It's not even bleeding anymore. You're going to be all right. And if you scar, you'll have a great story to tell."

Her eyes narrowed. "I don't *want* a story to tell. I don't *want* a scar disfiguring my face." She wheeled around.

He sighed and started after her. "How much further do you think before we reach the hoard?"

"I overheard Roshanak tell that useless thief she marked the way to the hoard with symbols of a serpent. I haven't seen any so far," Mithra answered without stopping or looking at him.

My breath caught. The *dragon* hoard? Why would they be headed that way too? Could it be the princess was after the same treasure as me?

The young man suddenly caught Princess Mithra by the wrist and pulled her to him. "Please don't be mad. I'm here because you asked me to be."

Mithra released a breath and relaxed in his arms. She looked up at him. "I'm sorry. You're right. If you hadn't been there, that tree could have crushed me." She leaned up on her toes and kissed his cheek. When she settled back on her feet, she looked up at him with a smile that reminded me of her brother. "I'm glad you're here."

The young man blushed. "It is only my duty."

I suddenly recognized him. He'd been in the cell with my father. He'd been the one to hit his sword into Father's ribs. My knees trembled. My hands went clammy. My dagger was in my boot and with a few short steps, I could take him by surprise and deliver my own blow to his ribs.

Mithra's lips curved up on one side in a sly grin. "You aren't at my side because of duty alone, Arash." She winked at him and walked out of his arms. "This way. I can feel it."

Yasmin remained still after Mithra and her boyfriend disappeared.

I was the first to straighten.

Yasmin slowly rose to her feet. "That was odd. Why is

Arash with her?" She seemed to be muttering to herself.

"The biggest question I have is, is Grand Sorceress Roshanak helping them?" I turned to Yasmin and went to fold my arms, but my hands still burned from the poison and I lowered them back to my sides.

Yasmin looked at me. "Should we follow the same path they're taking?"

I walked over to the passage Mithra had taken while Yasmin remained by the column. I couldn't identify any serpent carvings. "No. This isn't the right way."

I walked around the chamber, pausing at each opening until I came to one where light seeped through a crack overhead. I was grateful for the warmth, but the light was dim and growing dimmer as time passed. The sun was setting.

Light suddenly began to grow at the side of a passage ahead and to my left from a crack high in the ceiling.

The light settled on another carving.

I looked at Yasmin and gestured. "This way."

Yasmin's footsteps grew louder and she finally reached my side. "How are you so confident? The princess went that way." She pointed her thumb over her shoulder.

"You can follow her if you want. I can complete the trials on my own." It would be the *perfect* opportunity for Yasmin to leave me. I had no intention of allowing her to follow me to the hoard. If she didn't choose to leave on her own, I would have to leave her behind anyway. I couldn't risk her getting caught up in my mess.

Yasmin finally shook her head. "I'm sticking with you."

I sucked in a breath and slowly let it out. "This way, then."

It looked like I was going to have to leave her behind on my own. I would have to find a way to scare her off. I just wasn't sure how.

The light we had from some unknown source faded until Yasmin had to summon her orb of light again. My stomach growled for the fiftieth time, and Yasmin stopped when we found an opening inside of a small hall that wasn't big enough to be a chamber or even a cavern. The ceiling was barely high enough we didn't have to duck, but it was oval in shape and we would be out of the way should anyone want to pass by.

Yasmin flopped down on the ground and leaned her back against the wall. "I didn't realize caves could get so cold." She rubbed her hands together.

"We can start a fire," I offered when I sat beside her.

"Did you bring firewood with you?"

I rolled my head against the wall to look at her. "No. I didn't want unnecessary weight in my bag. Can't you just summon fire with your magic?"

"Even if I could, it still burns like fire. Which means it has to have something to feed it," Yasmin explained. "Since we don't have a fuel source, the fire wouldn't last long." She rubbed her hand across the back of her neck.

"That makes sense." I pulled a thin scarf from my bag and wrapped it around me. "Did you bring a meal with you?" I recalled that she had snacked with me hours ago, but hadn't paid attention to where she'd retrieved it from.

She nodded and reached into her pocket to produce a large bag. Before I could ask how on earth it fit in her pocket, she said, "It's enchanted. The bag, I mean. It can take on a smaller size and fit in my pocket, and then return to its original size without damaging the items inside.

Pretty neat, right?" She grinned proudly.

My lips tugged, but my heart sank. I couldn't even imagine how much that artifact cost. "That's really quite amazing," I agreed.

I produced my own food—cold rice with cold seasoned meat and nuts. Setting the bundle on my lap, I reached into the bag again and grabbed a handful of Lycus's seeds from Igborg's stash and poured them on the ground in a pile. I added a special treat, a piece of the dried meat.

Igborg hopped out and began munching on it right away.

I leaned my shoulder against Yasmin's for some warmth and used my fingers to eat my food, as was custom among the thieves. Yasmin, however, watched me with a slightly disgusted look on her face.

I eyed her.

She quickly returned to eating her own food with a spoon.

"You don't eat with your fingers where you're from?" I asked.

"No," she answered. "I didn't mean to stare, though. Fingers just get so . . . dirty. And you haven't washed them since the stream. And there could still be poison on your fingers."

I paused and looked down at my hands. They *were* a bit dirty, but I didn't sense any of the poison. "Normally, we wash our fingers before we eat. But I didn't pack soap and I'm not wasting my water on washing my fingers." I shrugged. "I just wish I'd brought a cloak with me. This scarf is pretty useless in providing warmth." I tugged on the scarf I'd draped over my shoulders.

"I have one in my bag we can share. Maybe we can curl up together too? Unless that's weird to you," Yasmin quickly added.

I studied her face.

She seemed embarrassed to even propose such a thing. But if either of us wanted to stay warm that night in the cave, we didn't have a choice other than to share the only source of warmth we had. Not only that, but when I woke in the middle of the night to continue on without her and get to the dragon's hoard, she would have the cloak all to herself.

"I don't mind at all. We need to stay warm," I agreed. "Thank you."

When we finished eating, we lay down. She curled up against my back and pulled the cloak around us both.

I actually felt a little guilty leaving her behind. She was a nice person and had helped me with my burns when the other girls had passed on by. Without Yasmin, I would have disappeared from the trials and Princess Mithra would have broken into my family's vault for some unknown reason.

I wasn't going to allow that to happen, no matter what.

Seventeen

Igborg's tail scraped against my left arm and his tongue flicked against my nose, waking me just as I'd wanted. However, I had no desire to be awake when it felt like I'd just barely fallen asleep. The orb of light Yasmin had summoned glowed dimly above her head. I held in a groan as I stretched and carefully slid out from under the cloak, then grabbed my bag and pulled it back over my shoulder.

Igborg scampered into the bag for warmth and I climbed to my feet.

I glanced at Yasmin and a pit of guilt grew in my stomach. I wished I had parchment so I could leave her a note that I was all right but had to leave for personal reasons. She would find her own way through this maze of caverns and trials, make her way out, and enter the academy just as she dreamed.

I reached out and tried to grab her orb of light. It wasn't tangible and my fingers swiped through it. I rolled my eyes and silently cursed myself. I would have to adventure on my own, blind and praying I could make it to the hoard.

Yasmin didn't deserve to be in whatever sort of danger I might face, especially if the serpents guided me beyond the safety barrier Roshanak created. Hopefully, she had set up the trials to go near enough I wouldn't have to travel outside of the barrier, but I didn't know.

The light from Yasmin's orb lit the path ahead of me a few feet, and when I reached the end of that light, I placed my fingertips against the wall to guide myself before stepping beyond the glow. When I tried to step out of the light, it stretched ahead of me.

Another step and the light flickered and shook.

I looked over my shoulder to see the orb trying to balance between me and Yasmin. I wondered if it would break away from her since she was stagnant, or if it would linger because she was the one who summoned it.

I braved more steps, finally entering the darkness.

Suddenly, the orb of light snapped to my side as if a string had been cut. It must have figured Yasmin could summon another if she needed. If orbs of light had any form of thought . . .

The path on which I walked began to slope downward and to the right. Warmth began to radiate up to me and I found myself smiling, grateful for the familiar sensation of heat the nearer I drew to it.

And then I heard a cry of pain.

It came from behind me.

"Yasmin." I looked down at my bandaged hands. I was *so close* to leaving her behind. She was a magic user, a sorceress, and she claimed to be powerful, so she *should* have been able to keep herself safe with her magic.

Metal clattered against stone.

I squeezed my eyes shut, cursed myself, and then turned around and ran back the way I'd come. The orb flew to keep up, and I skidded to a halt when I reached the alcove in which Yasmin and I had been sleeping.

I stared in shock.

Yasmin had her back pressed against the wall. A chain dangled from her left wrist. Short creatures, most barely reaching my knee or hip, stood before her. All of them held crude weapons—crooked daggers, hatchets, or spears—and wore loincloths around their waists. Their bottom teeth jutted over their top lips, and their ears were long and pointed. The way the magic orb lit the space made their deep, small eyes appear cruel.

Yasmin cast a spell that sent a burst of energy into the throng of creatures and sent those nearest her tumbling through the air.

One landed within arm's reach of me, and I realized then that they were goblins.

She was in the midst of summoning another spell when a goblin jumped and snatched the end of the chain on her wrist, and yanked on it.

Yasmin stumbled, her spell disrupted, and she gritted her teeth as she pulled against him. "Get off of me!" she shouted. She slammed her foot into the head of one of the goblins within reach and it struck a couple more, knocking all of them down.

Another goblin jumped up onto her back and she tried to cast another spell to get him off, but only ended up striking the ceiling above her head.

Apparently, spells weren't as efficient as swords in such close quarters.

I removed the dagger from my boot, aware of how gripping it caused my hand to sting, but I ignored the pain and jumped forward. "Get away now, or face my wrath!" I hollered.

The goblins all froze. Their skin was dark gray and

covered in marble-like lichen from living in the caves. I wondered briefly if we had unwittingly passed them by on our journey down this tunnel, taking them for boulders.

Yasmin stared at me with wide eyes, blinked, and then smiled in relief. "Caspara, you're all right!"

The goblins looked at each other, then one shouted, "Get the dagger girl!"

"Dagger girl!" they echoed.

The thirty or so little creatures turned their attention to me. They swung their swords and I dodged and parried their attacks. I kicked one, only for another to jump in and attack me, and they backed me toward a wall.

I'd been trained in hand-to-hand combat. I'd practiced with swords and daggers. But I had never been taught to fight creatures the size of small children, and certainly not in such large numbers. With the pressure off Yasmin, she was able to cast a spell that sent several goblins at the back flying again. They thumped against the walls, ceiling, and floor, then ran away crying.

A little dagger swiped against my arm, cutting a thin line.

I backed up and kicked one in the face with my heel, then dropped to my knees and kicked my leg out while I spun in a circle. I'd used the same move against a soldier in Zunbar a few days ago, and the move knocked over about five goblins. But for every one I managed to take out, it seemed as if two more took its place.

"Where are they coming from?" I shouted. I jumped back when one jabbed his sword forth, and I barely missed having my stomach sliced open.

"There's an entrance on the floor. I see it behind you!" Yasmin called. "*Ashriq!*"

The orb began to brighten and the goblins began to scream and retreat back into their hole.

"The light! It burns!"

"Retreat!"

"We'll find you! We'll return!"

"*Inhar*!" Yasmin commanded.

The light grew brighter and brighter until even I had to shield my eyes. Yasmin had said she only knew light magic, and yet she clearly had training far beyond what little she had claimed when she'd shown me the water dragon.

The floor trembled and I peered out from behind my fingers to see the rocks starting to collapse over a small hole I hadn't noticed.

But the trembling didn't stop.

"Uh, *inhal*," Yasmin said. The brightness of the light returned to normal. She snatched my hand and started to run, dragging me with her. "I may have triggered an earthquake."

Indeed she had, because the rumbling didn't stop when the hole was filled. A crack ran up from the wall to the ceiling. Rocks began to rain down. We ran from the room, but the rocks tumbled and fell behind us. Luckily, we entered a cavern and the fracture stopped at the tunnel's entrance.

I rested my hands on my knees, panting for breath.

The tunnel behind us was sealed.

"Well, there's no going back." Yasmin let out a relieved laugh.

I laughed with her and leaned my back on the wall. "You were doomed without me."

"I can't believe you left me in the first place." Yasmin

gave me a shove in the shoulder only to grimace and clutch her side.

My laughing stopped and I looked at her fingers to see blood seeping through them. "You're injured, Yasmin." I dropped to my knees and quickly reached into my bag for my powdered medicine and my water, likely similar to what Yasmin had used on my hands. I set out the small bowl and tapped the powder in, then added a little bit of water and mixed it with my finger. "Move your hand so I can see how bad it is."

Yasmin shook her head. "It's just a scratch. I'll be fine." She took a step and tipped over, catching herself on the opposite wall.

I reached up and grabbed her by her hips. "Yasmin, sit down. You must have been stabbed. And I know that your adrenaline is likely blinding you to the pain."

She drew a shuddered breath and shook her head again. "It's just a sting in my side from running. W-we should . . ." She slowly slid down to her knees and closed her eyes. Her entire form seemed to shudder.

Not like from the cold, or even from her current condition. It was as if her body was suddenly three and then one, and then her and not.

I watched her, holding on to the arm that was clutching her side. "Yasmin, what's happening?"

She swallowed. "Okay. It's worse than I thought." Her light voice took on a different tone. "N-not just my side. My . . . my leg too."

I realized she was using her other hand to hold a wound on her thigh. I gasped. "Yasmin! Don't worry. I-I'll help you. I have more bandages." I let go of her and dumped out all of the contents of my pouch so I could find every piece of fabric I'd brought as well as all of the herbs and medicine. "Lift up your skirt so I can help you with the cut on your leg."

"I'm not taking off my skirt," she said, her voice deep and somber.

"You don't have anything I haven't seen before," I pointed out.

But she looked at me from the edge of her eyes.

I hesitated. "Do you?"

She closed her eyes and let out a trembling sigh. "I'll need your help."

I helped her pull her skirt up. She lifted her hand, finally allowing me to see the wound, and I placed a bundle of cloth against the cut. It was only a couple of inches long, but deep and definitely needed to be sewn shut.

"Hold this," I commanded and pressed her hand against the bandage. I grabbed a new one, swiped it through the salve I'd made, and lifted her bandage to press the one with medicine on it directly into the wound. Using the bandage she held, I started tightening it around her thigh as tightly as I could. "I don't have a needle, but this medicine should help the wound heal faster and hopefully prevent infection. Madame Kiara is the best at such things. She gave me a whole bunch of ointments before the trials. Clearly not one for poison, though."

Yasmin grunted at the pain of me tightening her bandages.

"Sorry," I apologized, but didn't stop the pressure. "I've got to do the same to your side, okay?" When I looked up at her, my breath caught.

Yasmin wasn't a *her* anymore.

I almost fell backward.

Prince Abudar gave me a weak smile. "Surprise?"

Eighteen

"You have *got* to be kidding me." I stood and threw the bandages at him. "You lied to me this entire time? You disguised yourself as a *girl* to follow me around? You're despicable!" I began shoving my pouches back into my bag and looked around for Igborg.

The little turquoise dragon stood by Abudar's foot.

"No. I'm done helping Prince *Abu*," I said firmly.

"Caspara . . . I didn't follow . . . It's not the reason you think." Abudar's face was ashen. He'd lost a lot of blood from his wounds.

But the *boy* who had tried to seduce me, who said he *needed* me in the prison, who smiled at me like . . . like . . . ugh!

I threw my bag over my shoulder. "Come on, Igborg."

Abudar's eyelids fell closed and he slumped against the wall with his neck bent at an uncomfortable angle. His hand fell to the stone floor.

"Sure. Pretend all you want. It's not going to make me stay!" I kicked his foot.

He didn't budge.

Igborg climbed up on his knee and then looked up at me with his best puppy eyes. "Help." The dragon's small, high voice echoed both aloud and in my mind.

My mouth fell open. "You speak too?"

Igborg stuck his tongue out at Abudar. "Help."

I collected myself, snapped my teeth shut, and looked down at the unconscious prince.

I knew a little bit about healing, but not enough I could call myself an expert, and I certainly wasn't confident in my ability to help him. I looked back the way we'd come. The path was closed. No one could come that way.

If we stayed here, no one would find him.

If I left, I would be guilty of murder.

Unless he would just disappear and reappear at the side of the grand sorceress.

Unless . . . that wouldn't work because he *wasn't* a sorceress. He wasn't supposed to be there any more than I was.

I heaved a sigh and ran a hand down my face. "No. Roshanak said anyone who was in a situation where they could die would be sent home," I said out loud. "He'll be fine. We leave him, the magic will take him back, and someone far more qualified than me will heal him. Come on, Igborg." I turned to leave, but Igborg didn't move.

When I looked down at the dragon, he was nudging Abudar's hand with his small head.

I bit my lip.

Abudar was already in bad shape. If the magic was going to work regarding him being on the verge of death, he should have disappeared by now. Right?

"Fine, Igborg. You win." I dropped down to my knees at Abudar's side. Grabbing him by the shoulders, I tried to lower him onto his back, but I didn't anticipate his dead weight. When I tilted his stupid unconscious, muscled body backward, he fell fast and dragged me forward on top of him.

I flushed and thanked the sun that he was unconscious.

Even with a pale face, he was handsome.

And I hated it.

I pushed myself off of him and knelt at his side. Ignoring the stinging of my fingers, I pulled up the purple top that was undoubtedly Princess Mithra's. Where else would he get a female gown to hide in?

I couldn't get out of my mind the question of *why* he would disguise himself as a girl, and I tried to recall the conversation I'd had with him the night before. He'd said he needed me. Why? And he couldn't have possibly known I was going to be in the trials . . .

Unless he *did* know I would be in the trials.

Because Roshanak told him.

I set my jaw and felt the familiar tingle of pain behind my left eye that signaled an oncoming headache.

I pulled Abudar's shirt off completely, revealing his smooth torso. His muscles were toned. For some reason, it caught me off guard. I had expected him to be pudgy, I supposed, because royalty ate a lot. Or so I imagined.

And then I recalled he said his father taught him. Likely, Abudar meant his father *trained* him. With swords, hand-to-hand combat, and whatever else princes needed to know.

I cleaned out and bandaged the wound on his side— which was more difficult than laying him down. I had to keep rolling him from one side to the other to wrap the bandage around his stomach, and when it was too short to wrap around more than twice, I had to take the bandages from my own hands and add them to the end.

Finally, the *porcelain* prince was bandaged and would

soon be on the mend.

Exhausted, I leaned my back against the wall and rubbed the base of my hands against my eyes. They felt much better but still had a lingering burning sensation. When I looked down at them, the blisters had faded to little more than a rash.

Abudar could have left me behind then. *If* he was here for any other reason than to babysit me.

"So much for leaving him behind," I grumbled. I looked down at him and my brow furrowed. Because in the dim light, I could have sworn I saw something on his arm. "It can't be . . ."

I got back up on my hands and knees and motioned for the light to draw closer. Of course, it didn't budge, so I had to shift myself and lift his arm.

Prince Abudar had markings on his right arm from the tips of his fingers up to his shoulder.

Identical to mine.

I looked at his face. "Who *are* you?"

I traced one of the markings on his wrist while looking at the same one on my own.

We had the same tattoos.

Did he have the same prophecy as me?

Back at the prison, he'd looked at my right arm before I'd hidden it. When he took me to the palace, Roshanak had examined my arm as well.

Maybe . . . no. That was impossible.

But who else would have the exact same tattoo as me? Could fate finally be steering me in the right direction?

Could Prince Abudar be the "other half" I needed to find?

I scoffed at myself and shook my head, recoiling from

him to find the cloak he'd packed for himself. I laid it over him, keeping him warm and hiding the tattoo on his arm.

There was no way any sort of destiny would pair a *prince* and a *thief* together. It was comical, really.

Perhaps Roshanak wanted me to recover the lamp because she wanted proof I was Abudar's other half? Because, what if there was more to this? What if I wasn't actually his other half, but a distraction along *his* path to find her? Maybe this entire mission to find a magic lamp was actually my *mother's* way of forcing me to prove that I was her daughter.

My stomach sank.

I didn't have magic.

That was proof enough to me I wasn't special.

If I was supposed to be this miraculous, amazing person paired with a magical prince—the only male in our land I'd ever heard of with magic—then there was absolutely no way I would be born without magic myself.

I closed my eyes to rest them. Just for a moment.

Because my head was swimming.

Everything was crashing together, like swords clattering during a sparring match, and I could no longer make sense of my thoughts.

Exhaustion overtook me and I fell asleep.

When Igborg started snoring, I woke and found myself lying on my side.

Abudar was awake and eating something.

I rubbed my eye with my fist and sat up.

Abudar paused chewing when he saw me and reached back into my bag to hold a biscuit out to me. "Want one? They're pretty good."

"My aunt makes them." I snatched the one he offered

from his hand. "Why are you eating *my* food?"

"I don't think I have anymore." He took another bite of his biscuit and looked down at his leg. "You're not too bad with bandages, but you definitely need more medical training."

I lifted my eyebrow, pausing with my teeth half-sunken into the biscuit in my mouth. I chomped down and tucked the bread into my cheek. "Who is the one who stayed and helped you when I could have left you here to die?"

Abudar stared at me. He finally nodded. "I was teasing."

I dusted some crumbs from the corner of my lip. "When we met in the prison, you said you needed me."

The prince ran his tongue over his teeth. "I did."

"Care to share with me what it was you felt you needed me for? If it involves me and you doing anything together, I'll have you know I keep a dagger hidden—"

"No, no, no. Nothing like that." He waved his hand—biscuit and all—in the air.

"Then why?"

He ran his fingers through his messy hair. It wasn't complying. "It's nothing," he mumbled.

I narrowed my gaze at him. "Then why do you have the same tattoo as me, Abu?"

"It's Abudar," he mumbled, then lifted his arm and shifted his gaze from it to me.

I lifted my brow.

He heaved a sigh and folded his arms over his chest, then leaned fully back against the wall. "It's why I have magic."

"That doesn't make sense, because *I* don't have

magic." I shook my head at him.

Abudar frowned. "You weren't putting on an act before?"

I rolled my eyes. "Why would I? I didn't know you were . . . *you*."

"Well, I don't know what to tell you. I received a blessing from Telama as an infant, these tattoos appeared, and I was gifted with magic."

I sucked my tongue to the roof of my mouth. Perhaps the gods had mixed us up after all. What if I was *supposed* to have magic and didn't because of *him*?

Prince Abudar read my narrowed eyes, pinched brows, and scowl and relaxed his shoulders. "When I met you in the prison, I hoped Grand Sorceress Roshanak was right about you."

"Right about me? In what way?" I snatched my bag and dragged it to my side so he couldn't pluck another biscuit from my food.

"All she said was that you might be the other half, but that you had to prove yourself. Not even I know what that means." His amber eyes studied mine. I had to give him credit. He was being honest.

But there was a piece of this whole *blessing* he wasn't telling me.

I couldn't put my finger on it.

I hoisted my bag over my shoulder. "Good luck getting out on your own! Might be best to fall off a cliff at this point so you can teleport back to your precious palace and get help."

"Wait. Caspara, you can't leave me here!"

I grabbed Igborg and set him on my shoulder. "I can, and I am. You're bandaged up and healing, and I have something else to be doing. Prince or not, I can't just sit here and hold your hand. Someone is bound to miss you and come looking for you. Besides, now that you are healing and can walk, you can find your way out of the cave."

I heard Abudar grunt as I started away and braved a glance over my shoulder.

He was grimacing and holding on to the wall. He'd managed to get to his feet on his own but couldn't bear any weight on his leg.

Big baby.

"Have you heard of the dragon's hoard?" he called after me.

I stopped walking and faced him, successfully keeping my face stern. A couple of thoughts flashed through my mind—one, Mithra knew about the dragon hoard. We'd both heard her talking about it. This in turn meant either Abudar wanted to know what Mithra was looking for, he himself had overheard Roshanak tell me, or Roshanak had sent him to follow me. And lastly, if he *didn't* know about the hoard before coming down here, what in the sands of time was he doing?

"If I haven't?" I answered.

Abudar looked me up and down. "I don't think that's the case. You at least heard Mithra talking about it. But I assume you've heard of my grandfather, Khorshid? He was my mother's father."

"Yes. He was some mighty sorcerer who stole magic or whatever."

"He wasn't a sorcerer," Abudar corrected. "He had an enchanted staff that gave him power. But that's beside the point. The important thing is, he stole my mother's magic

178

so he could have his own."

"And?" I folded my arms, growing impatient.

"And I heard Roshanak tell you about the magic lamp." He took a breath while I narrowed my eyes. "I want to get that lamp back in order to get my mother's magic back." He paused there. Clearly wanting to add more and contemplating doing so. He finally said, "Because bound to that artifact is a jinni. One who can grant a wish."

I laughed and shook my head. "You want me to believe this . . . this . . . myth? About a jinni?"

He pushed off the wall and stood before me. "I don't care if you believe me, but I know that's why you're in here. Why else would a girl with no magic join the trials? It's *not* to enter the academy."

I tightened my lips and turned away. *What if there is a jinni?*

"I need a wish, Caspara. That's it. You can have the jinni after me. I just need it to wish my mother's magic back."

I wheeled back around. "And I need it to save my father's life! Why don't I find it, wish for my father's freedom, and then give it to *you* after?" I might have been sassing him a little. And I didn't care. Because down here, no one could punish me for it.

"I'm not selfish, you know." He stared at me. "I know you think I'm selfish. But I'm not. You need to understand. I'm always trying to do what's best for my country, and you cannot possibly understand what that is like."

I raised both brows at him and jabbed my finger into his chest. "Don't you dare say that I don't know what it's like to sacrifice for somebody else. Do you have any idea how many times I have gone without dinner so that children in my village can eat? Do you know how many times I've put myself at risk being arrested so that I can get money to feed pregnant mothers? Or widowed men? You sit in your palace with golden walls, the best clothing, food enough that you probably throw some to your dogs, and tell me that *I* don't know what sacrifice feels like? I dare you to spend *one* night out among your people. I dare you to spend one night on the streets in Zunbar and *then* tell me you understand what sacrifice feels like, Abu."

Abudar's jaw flexed. Some of the pride left his amber eyes and was replaced with anger.

I had struck a nerve.

But then he huffed. "It's *Abudar*, and I command you to give it to me first. I am the prince of Sheblom!"

I raised my brows and set my hands on my hips. "Oh mighty prince. If you are so blessed and wise, perhaps you should find your own way to the vault. Good luck getting in, of course. Perhaps our paths will cross again soon." I sneered at him and marched away.

"Caspara, you can't just leave me here. Get back here! I'll have you arrested if you leave me! Caspara!" Prince Abudar's voice faded as I got further away.

Prince or not, I wasn't going to let him boss me around, and I certainly wasn't going to allow *him* to use my family's treasure. *Especially* if it was a jinni.

ᴺNineteen

I had to admit being alone in the dark of the cave without light to guide me was definitely not easier than swallowing my pride and having Abudar by my side. It was terrifying. There were sounds in the deeper section of the cave that had my heart racing. Dripping water, the sound of scuffling that made me wonder if the goblins were coming back, and I could have sworn I heard breathing behind me at one point.

More than once, the toe of my shoe caught the corner of a rock or a crack in the ground. More than once, I stumbled. More than once, I spat a curse as I fell forward into the inky darkness and scuffed my hands and knees.

I should have stayed with Prince Abudar.

Even if he was slow, he at least had a magical form of light to protect me from myself.

But he'd lied to me, disguised himself, and . . .

. . . and had answered the questions I asked. Even if they weren't the answers I wanted. Even if I didn't like him, I was an idiot to leave him behind for more reasons than me not having his light.

The cave took on a gray color. Slowly, I began to see shadows and formations of the edges of the wall. I was finally able to at last see *something*. I couldn't identify the source of the light, but the passage split into two. I went to go to the right and felt a small shock, a tingling sensation that washed over my body.

This passage was out of bounds of the trials. If I stepped through, I wouldn't be protected by the magic the grand sorceress had created.

I turned away to go the other direction, but stopped barely two steps away.

I glanced from the corner of my eye and made my way to a dark spot on the wall near the entrance that was out of boundaries. My heart thundered in my ears because the spot on the wall could very well be a serpent carving, *or* an enormous cave spider. But the only way I could check was to touch it.

"Igborg, is that a spider?" I asked, my voice loud inside the empty cave in spite of the whispering. "I know you can talk now."

When he didn't answer, I removed him from my shoulder and held him out at arm's length toward the black spot.

He began to squirm.

"Tell me, Igborg!" I took a step back and tried to even my breathing. "Please tell me."

He finally gave up and said, "No."

I turned him so our faces were mere inches apart. "No you won't tell me, or no it's not a spider?"

"No."

"Igborg."

"No bug."

I pulled him to my chest and puffed the air out from my cheeks. Still wary, I reached my trembling hand out and touched the wall near the black spot. It was likely

Igborg was wrong in his understanding. A spider wasn't a bug. And he'd never seen a bug as big as him, so he could be wrong. But it could also be a scorpion, which also wasn't a bug, and Igborg wouldn't have been lying.

My hand started to tremble even harder. I patted the wall, hoping if it was a living creature, my patting would scare it off.

The black spot didn't budge.

I swallowed and slowly moved my hand toward it.

It still didn't move.

Finally, I slid my hand over and only felt bumps and ridges. Relief washed over me and I closed my eyes. "I'm really grateful Abudar wasn't here to see that," I muttered.

After fingering the grooves, I decided it was a serpent marking. Which meant I had to leave the boundaries. Which meant, if anything happened past here, I wouldn't be protected by the magic Roshanak had cast.

I had to.

For my father.

Because he would do the same for me.

I straightened and stepped through the unseen veil of magic. It tingled like a wave across my body and then dissipated. When I entered the pathway beyond, my tattooed arm burned with a warm-numb sensation.

I hoped it meant I was going in the right direction.

I rubbed it and carried onward with the same dim light guiding the way.

Just around the bend stood a solid slab of black-and-gray granite with a streak of gold through it. The massive piece of stone leaned on one side against the wall.

In the center of that granite slab was a golden seal, and in the middle of that seal was the symbol of a hand with an eye in the palm—a *hamsa*. I placed my hand on that symbol and felt energy rush through my body. I felt warmth all over and closed my eyes. My scalp tingled as if someone were playing with my hair.

I'd made it. This was my family vault.

Smiling, I opened my eyes and took a deep breath. "My name is Caspara. I am the daughter of Kasim. *Iftah ya simsim.*" The final sentence was the password Roshanak had given me.

The gold beneath my hand warmed and I dropped my hand when it got too hot to stand. When I heard the stone begin to grind, I took a step back and watched in wonder as it slowly rolled to the left, opening a black void beyond.

"It's true," I whispered aloud. I reached up and touched Igborg for comfort. "It's really true. Everything my father told me."

My heart swelled and I stepped into the darkness, walking confidently into a room I couldn't see. The same gray light that had guided me somehow shone behind me through the still-open door, revealing a few shapes I couldn't quite discern.

And then braziers on my left and right ignited—an enormous metal pot sat on top of a stand. Beyond the light, something glistened. I continued forward, and two more braziers lit. Every so often, the intentionally spaced lights ignited, adding more light into the vault. After ten pairs, the glittering in the darkness began to take form.

It was gold.

Piles and piles of it.

Gold and gemstones, like I'd never seen before.

A true dragon's hoard.

How could this be my *family's* vault? How could *my*

family be richer than the sultan? I could *buy* the kingdom if I wanted! Not that I did.

But how could Father know about this place and simply live as a thief? How could he struggle through starvation and holes in his boots and going without essentials?

I reached out and traced a painting on one of the columns.

"Maybe he didn't know," I whispered.

Even Jade said the two of them had searched but had never been able to find it. Maybe he had no idea just how much wealth lay inside. When my father told the story about the vault, he made it sound like a hole in the wall where a single precious item was placed, not an entire cave big enough to fit a dragon!

I crouched to look at a golden statue of a woman. Her fingers were poised with the index finger touching the thumb on both hands, one arm held overhead, and the other near her bosom. She wore a crown and her long hair cascaded down her bare shoulders, covering her breasts. A skirt covered her crossed legs.

Who was she?

"Where did all of this come from?" I wondered aloud.

I straightened, then turned in a circle, smiling bigger than I had in my entire life.

Father and I would never go hungry again. The forty thieves could sustain *hundreds* of families. Now I knew the location, I could bring Father back here and . . . I would no longer have to be Almas. Because we could give this fortune to the poor, helping everyone in Zunbar become a bit more equal.

Maybe I could finally learn who I was.

I lifted Igborg to look me in the eyes. "Want to help me sniff out this lamp I'm supposed to be searching for?"

"Help." He bobbed his head up and down, then dropped from my hand to the floor and scurried onward down the lit path.

I chuckled and shook my head at him. I still hadn't wrapped my mind around him being a dragon. We didn't have dragons in my land. They may have existed long ago, but where had he come from? Did he have a dragon family searching for him? Was he fully grown or a child?

I rubbed the back of my neck. These were answers I might never learn.

My footsteps echoed in the cave as I followed Igborg, almost as if there were another person in the cave with me. Somewhere in the distance, water dripped and plunked into a pool. I was unable to see anything beyond the ring of firelight, other than the light dancing off of shimmering surfaces of jewels and gold.

And then my right arm burned.

I looked down and saw the blackness of the tattoo taking on a sort of blue-yellow glow. My breath stopped with my feet and I looked around.

My tattoo had never glowed before. Yes, I'd felt it tingle, but now it almost burned.

When I looked around, there was a wooden chest with a purple pillow leaning against it, a small, rusty oil lamp, some gemstones I could easily fit in my pocket, and a jeweled dagger. There was a red velvet chaise chair with clawed feet, and a broken mirror.

I surveyed the area around me again. "Roshanak said to find a lamp . . ." I pursed my lips to one side of my face. "But what *kind* of lamp?"

My tattoos still glowed. I swallowed hard, slightly unnerved that they should be doing anything at all. I flicked my hand and tried to walk away, but my feet wouldn't move in the direction I wanted to go.

Igborg hopped on top of the chest and cocked his head to the side. "Here."

I crouched and Igborg jumped onto my shoulder. I lifted the lid of the chest to see it packed with gold. "What sort of person would hide a magic lamp with a jinni inside? Of course, I'm not sure I believe there's a jinni at all. It could have been a lie *Abu* told me," I said to Igborg, making sure to use the ridiculous name I'd come up with for him.

Igborg coughed, but it must have been a laugh.

I ran my fingers through the contents of the chest, back and forth, but all I found was gold, gold, and more gold. I even dumped half of the contents onto the floor until one piece clinked against something, knocking it from its perch on the purple pillow, and sent it tumbling into the path I'd walked down.

I rolled my eyes. "This is futile."

I turned and reached out to set the fallen object back where it belonged so I wouldn't trip on it on the way out. It was a lamp. My breath caught just a moment when I realized I'd seen the lamp sitting atop the purple pillow but had thought it too insignificant to be *the* lamp. I reached out and grasped the bottom. But as soon as my hand closed around the cool metal, a second hand gripped the handle.

I lifted my gaze to meet Prince Abudar's amber eyes.

"How did *you* get in here?" I glared and yanked the lamp, but he held fast.

He frowned and pulled at it too.

"How did you even find your way?" I demanded.

"I followed you. Didn't you wonder where the light came from while you were walking in the cavern? Now give me the lamp." He jerked hard, but my fingers were wrapped securely around its base.

"How dare you! You've lied to me, and now you're trying to steal from me!"

"It's just a stupid lamp. I was only picking it up to move it," Abudar argued.

"Oh, is that so, Prince Abu?" I held so tightly my fingers hurt and clenched my teeth.

He gritted his teeth as well and said, "It's Prince Abudar."

"Everything in this cave belongs to *my* family! You couldn't have entered if I hadn't spoken the password to get us in in the first place!" I sat down and pressed both of my feet against Abudar's wounded leg.

He let out a yelp and collapsed down onto that knee. "Oh, you're going to play dirty, are you?" He growled. His eyes bore into me. And then he placed one hand over mine and started to squeeze.

My fingers pinched between his fingers and the metal. I gasped. "That hurts!"

"Then let go. I already told you, all I have to do is make a wish and then you can have it!" he said sharply.

"I don't exactly trust you, *Your Highness*."

Abudar rolled his eyes. "It's not my fault you have trust issues."

"It's not my fault you didn't get here first. Now, let. Go!" I kicked at him again, but he dropped one hand to press my ankle into the stone floor before it could reach his leg.

"Do we need a truce?" he asked through gritted teeth.

My hand ached beneath his. My fingers were going numb. My ankle throbbed. "No way." I jerked my head forward to slam it against his, but he pulled his head to the side and I hit his shoulder instead of his forehead.

"Sands of time, will you stop?" he snapped. He turned his head and pressed it against mine.

"I can't imagine why they're arguing either," a voice said.

Abu's brows pinched.

My lip curled.

Simultaneously, we turned to look in the same direction.

A being with blue skin, yellow eyes, dark, blue-black hair pulled up in a high ponytail atop of their head, and golden and black clothing sat on a chaise with Igborg on his lap, eating a handful of his seeds.

"A jinni?" I blurted.

He flashed a smile more dashing than Abudar's, revealing pointed canines. "That be me."

Twenty

"Who are you?" Abudar asked.

In my surprise, I had relaxed my tension on the lamp just enough that when Abudar suddenly yanked, it jerked out of my hands and made my fingertips sting. I tore my gaze away from the stunning jinni to scowl at the prince. Abudar put his weight on a golden scepter he found on the floor and used it to get to his feet. Only, just before he could stand completely, I might have *accidentally* kicked it out from under him.

With all his weight on the staff, he collapsed to his hands and knees and let out a grunt of pain while he grimaced.

I gave him my most flattering smile and scooped up the fallen lamp. I walked over to the jinni, leaving Abudar on the floor. "My name is Caspara. And what should I call you?"

A sly smile slid across the jinni's face and his golden eyes shined. Up close, I realized his blue skin had gold specks all over it, like paint splatters, but they didn't smudge. His ears came to a point, and his black tunic was finely made without a speck of dust on it.

"Dear girl, you know I am far too clever to fall for that trick," he answered.

"Trick? I don't know—"

"Of course you know what I mean. If I give you my name, you can control me. But I shan't give my name, so don't ask again." He wagged his finger at me like when my father scolded me as a child. When he smiled, his pointed canines flashed.

The hair on the back of my neck prickled and I suddenly wondered if he was dangerous.

I swallowed hard. "You have to do what I ask anyway. I get a wish, right?"

The jinni didn't answer, and his smile didn't change.

I looked down at the lamp my great, great, great, great-grandfather had left behind for me. "My very great-grandfather hid you here long ago. It is my birthright to find you here and ask for your help. I have only one wish anyway, and—" My sentence caught in my throat when I looked at the jinni.

His head was lolled against the back of the chaise and he was snoring.

"I'm talking to you!" I shouted and slapped his foot.

The jinni opened his eyes. "Do you know how many stories like that I've heard?" He sat up and set his feet on the floor. "Let me guess, your wish is for riches, power, fame, or money." He tapped his fingers as he spoke, then patted his mouth with a feigned yawn.

"No, actually. I want my father back," I replied firmly, glaring at him.

He cringed, the movement dramatized by his eccentric eyebrows. "Can't bring people back from the dead. Well, technically I *could*, but it's horrific. They aren't ever themselves again and tend to stink after a few days."

I stomped my foot. "He's not dead. He's in prison."

"Ah, that makes things much easier for me." He rose to his feet, offering me his dashing smile a second time as he leaned forward until our faces were inches apart. "I take it you're not fond of the prince?"

Abudar grunted. "How did you know I'm the prince?" He was back on his feet, leaning on the staff and favoring his cut leg. Blood was seeping into the fabric of the skirt he still wore and I *almost* felt bad. My actions had reopened the wound, and it was already bad enough without my help.

The jinni tapped his head. "I'm observant and smart. And because Igborg told me *everything*." He grinned and set Igborg on his shoulder.

I frowned and pulled Igborg away. "He's mine."

"Fair enough." The jinni shrugged. "He seems to like you. He's smarter than you think, though, so don't talk down to him."

"I'll keep that in mind." I looked at Igborg, who seemed to be smiling at me. I placed Igborg up on *my* shoulder. "Don't be a traitor. But you also shouldn't have hidden that you're more than a lizard." I tapped his nose.

Igborg rubbed his head up against my cheek.

The jinni placed his hands behind his back and rocked back and forth from heel to toe. "I do have one question for you both before we get this whole wish thing started."

"What's that?" Abu asked.

"Are they with you?" The jinni pointed.

About five braziers away, Princess Mithra stepped off the pile of gold, holding Arash's hand to steady her as her feet slid.

Abudar's thick brows furrowed and he limped as fast as he could toward them. "What are you doing?"

"Abudar. Why are *you* here?" Mithra's eyes widened when she spotted her brother. I could have sworn I saw her hand slide into a pocket, depositing something inside. Her brows dipped. "Is that my skirt?"

"I told you I was going to beat you to the lamp, and I did. When I get my wish and tell the jinni to return Mother's magic, you can have it."

Mithra eyed him with confusion and looked past him to the jinni and me.

"Except I get a wish first," I called. "Before any of you."

"Actually, you and Prince Abudar must agree on one wish together," the jinni replied.

"What?" we said in unison.

The jinni sighed. "You touched the lamp at the same time. Therefore, you both get one single wish together."

Mithra rolled her eyes and began walking away.

"Where are you going?" Abudar demanded and limped after her. "I want to know why you're here with Arash." He grabbed her arm.

She pulled away. "I'm part of the trials, Abudar. I can go where I want and do as I wish. I'm not a child." Her eyes narrowed.

"But why are you *here*? In the vault?" he asked.

She twitched a brow. "For the lamp, obviously. You just found it before me."

Abudar's eyes tightened.

Clearly, the two royal siblings didn't get along as well as others believed. At least Abudar had been honest about that.

I slipped the lamp into one of the secret pockets of my pants and climbed over the nearest pile of gold. On the other side was a narrow path winding through the great treasures. I stopped long enough to fill my pockets with expensive trinkets and money before slinking expertly toward the exit.

"You know it doesn't matter if you escape with the lamp on your own," the jinni said, suddenly appearing beside a pillar I was about to pass, leaning his back against it with his arms folded. "You still have to come to an agreement with Prince Abudar."

"He's clearly too unreasonable for that. Too selfish." I gestured with both hands to the siblings arguing. "To be honest with you, though, I don't even need a wish. All I have to do is deliver the lamp, and you, to Roshanak and she'll free my father."

Their voices escalated and Mithra said something about not being respected while I made my way toward the exit.

"Abudar, that's enough!" Mithra shouted. "You always get what you want!"

The floor suddenly rumbled, a short burst, but with enough force to rock me.

Everyone went silent.

The sound reminded me of when Igborg would snort himself awake.

Speaking of Igborg, I felt him begin to tremble and looked at him to see his scales bristled along his sides, his belly as flat as he could go while still holding on to me, his eyes wide.

"What is it?" I whispered, lifting him into my hands while knowing this wasn't any sort of cave-in. The ground wasn't shaking.

There was a burst of air somewhere past Abudar and

Mithra.

"Dragon," Igborg's voice squeaked. "Hide!" He scampered down my arm, his tiny claws scratching along the way, and dipped into the bag on my shoulder.

I locked eyes on the jinni.

He was standing straight, eyes focused on the distance. "It couldn't be," he whispered to himself.

There was another rumble, this one longer and louder.

The jinni sucked in a breath. "In all the sands of time, I've never seen an ancient dragon."

As if on cue, a black shape slowly lifted itself from under the treasure. Gold, gemstones, statues, and even a throne tumbled from its back in a rush that sounded like wind.

"I-I'm going to guess this isn't part of the trials?" I asked. A rush of adrenaline ignited my blood and I stepped back, ready to run as soon as I could.

Abudar finally came to his senses. "Of course it is. We let it kill us, and we go back to the start with our lamp and get this sorted out. Hey, dragon!" He stupidly waved the staff he'd been using as a cane in the air.

My eyes widened. Could the prince *really* be that daft?

"Run," the jinni said.

Arash drew the scimitar from his hip and bent his knees, poised to defend the princess. "Your Highness, I don't think that's a good idea."

Mithra forced Abudar's arm down and put her hand over his mouth. "You idiot! The dragon isn't part of the trials. We passed through the protective barrier, remember?"

His eyes darted to the dragon now turning toward them. "Then what do we do?" he asked beneath her hand.

The dragon's red eyes focused on the three and let out a roar so loud the stalactites trembled overhead and I clamped my hands over my ears. Dust and rocks rained down from above.

"Run!" Arash shouted.

The jinni rolled his eyes. "I already said that." He gave me a mocking grin and said, "Hopefully, you'll still be alive to summon me forth soon, mistress." He blew me a kiss and disappeared in a puff of gold and blue smoke.

"Aren't you going to help get us out of here?" I demanded, shaking and rubbing the lamp, but the jinni didn't come forth.

Stalactites broke off and flew to the ground, jabbing into the gold like daggers, the dragon climbed to its feet, and I scrambled to scale a pile to get to the exit. Turned out, climbing gold was more difficult than climbing a sand dune.

Once I made it over the peak, I slid down the opposite side. I was ahead of the others.

Mithra was sprinting toward me while Arash flung Abudar's arm over his shoulders and practically dragged him toward the exit.

"We just have to get back through the barrier and then the magic will go back into effect," Mithra said as she passed me, but not *to* me.

Like an idiot, I stopped and looked back at the dragon now stretching its massive, bat-like wings. The torchlight revealed the spikes down the dragon's back in two rows and the spikes down the bone separating the fragile skin of its wings.

Father had shown me drawings of dragons in books and parchments, but I never imagined they would be this

196

enormous.

It opened its jaws, revealing teeth as large as swords. With another roar, the ground trembled so violently we all stumbled to the stone floor. I looked up and screamed as a rock fell from the ceiling toward me. I rolled, but it wasn't enough, and the boulder slammed into the ground and on top of my foot, pinning it to the floor.

I expected my foot to be crushed, to explode with pain, but it didn't. I opened my eyes and looked down to see it pinned between the boulder from the ceiling and another rock that created a pocket protecting my foot. There was pressure and I was sure it would be bruised, but luckily for me, it wasn't crushed.

I sat up and pushed against the boulder with all my might. It didn't budge. I scooted forward, grunted, and pushed again. When that didn't work, I leaned back and kicked at it with my free foot, but still it wouldn't move.

Igborg scampered out of the pouch and flew onto the rock as if he could pick it up with his small form or push it with his claws.

"G-Go," I said to him. "Fly out of here while you can! Go back to Mihrage. You like him."

Igborg hopped back down and nudged the lamp out of my pocket with his nose. "Jinni!"

I shook my head. "I have to save my wish for Baba."

"Caspara!" Abudar shouted.

I looked over and saw the three of them standing at the entrance of the dragon's hoard. Arash was pulling on him, trying to get him to leave, and Mithra was scolding him for not using his brain.

"I'm stuck!" I yelled back over the chaos of the dragon.

"We don't have time to run in and save her." Mithra had her hand on Abudar's chest and was pushing him back. "She's a nobody anyway. No one will miss her."

Abudar hesitated and glowered at his sister. "Her father will."

Mithra flinched.

While she hadn't been wrong, her words still stung.

If I died, what would become of my father? Would Roshanak bring him here herself to unlock the cave and retrieve the lamp from my body? And once she had it, would she kill him anyway?

If she did, it would be as if I never existed.

There would be no legends told of the brave thief who snuck into a cave for a magic lamp and died. There would be no fireside stories of how I saved the world or changed the life I knew. Not even a tale of any of my adventures, like how I saved the prince's life. Because who cared about me? I was just another grain of sand in a vast desert. A speck no one sees unless it strikes them in the eye.

Unwanted tears came to my eyes and I looked at the dragon headed my way. This was to be the legacy of Caspara—a nobody who amounted to nothing, like every other poor person in Sheblom.

I squeezed my eyes shut and pushed with all my might.

I would die here if I couldn't escape. I finally snatched the lamp and rubbed it, because I could still make a wish for my life and deliver the lamp to Roshanak without breaking any promise.

"You rang?" the jinni said. He ducked and managed to avoid a falling rock.

"I wish for you to get me out of here!" I shouted at

him.

He heaved a sigh and dusted some cave dust from his shoulder. "I cannot do that unless the other one agrees." He extended his hand toward the entrance of the cave.

"You're absolutely useless!" I growled at him.

"It isn't my fault you touched my lamp at the same time as him." The jinni pouted. "Let me know when he agrees." Before I could protest, the jinni disappeared again.

I shouted in frustration and pressed my fists into my eyes.

And then the weight on my ankle lifted and I opened my eyes to see Mithra standing several feet away, using a spell to lift the boulder.

"What are you waiting for?" she demanded. "Get up!"

I scrambled to my feet, held my bag in both hands, and limped as fast as I could through the exit with the other three. Arash dropped Abudar onto the ground and pushed against the granite slab. A vein in his neck bulged with effort and I limped over to help him. I pressed my hand to the *hamsa* in the center and it groaned closed. A plume of dust puffed out before it sealed the vault and the dragon behind it. Although I highly doubted the door would keep the dragon inside. Maybe the magic would.

I leaned against the wall, panting for breath and favoring my foot. "Thank you. You didn't have to do that."

"No. I didn't." Mithra sized me up and I couldn't read her expression before she flipped her hair over her shoulder and started walking down the passage to the right.

I lifted my hand. "I think that's the wrong direction. I

think—"

"Did I ask what you think?" She looked over her shoulder at me, eyes narrowed and lip curled. "I think I should know my way around. We came from this direction."

"But we didn't. We came from that way." I pointed the opposite of where she'd begun to walk. "And I think *I* would know, considering I'm used to navigating in the dark. Thief, remember?" I twitched my brows at her. I could be just as sassy as she was.

Mithra scoffed and placed a hand on her hip. "Now isn't the time to try and prove any sort of worth to me or Abudar. He's too high above your station for any form of attention."

I flexed my jaw. "Who said I want his attention? You don't need to be rude."

"I don't need to be nice either. Come on, Arash." She continued down the passage, summoning a pink orb of light.

Abudar was leaning so heavily on Arash, Arash could hardly walk. His purple skirt had torn up the side with his wound. The bandages were soaked through and bled so profusely, blood stained the skirt and trailed down his leg.

I ran around Abudar and Arash and grabbed Mithra by the arm. "But you're going the wrong way! Abudar won't make—"

"Don't touch me, filth!" She whipped around and shot a ball of energy, slamming it against my chest and sending me flying backward.

My shoulder struck the ground and I used the momentum and rolled to absorb as much of the blow as I could. When I got to my feet, I dusted off my knees. "Fine.

Go the wrong way. You're going to get lost in the caves and your mother and father will have to have other children to replace you and take over the throne." I fixed the bag on my shoulder and headed the way I *knew* was the way out.

An orb of yellow light caught up to me and I glanced over my shoulder to meet Abudar's amber eyes. He nodded weakly, then looked away.

Twenty-One

A scream echoed from behind me just as my body began to tingle in the magic barrier, signaling I was right all along and was going the right way back into the main cave. I looked over my shoulder as if I could see into the darkness beyond.

"Perfect Princess Mithra must have seen a spider." I rolled my eyes.

But the scream hadn't been one of fear.

"Or she realized I was right."

I heard muffled sounds I couldn't quite place. If they had fallen into trouble, Mithra and Abudar could use their magical powers to save them.

I was about to continue on my way when someone shouted my name. Arash, perhaps? Why would *he* yell for me?

Igborg hopped off my shoulder and flew to land on a rock the way we'd come.

"What do you think?" I asked.

"Help. Run," he said, bobbing his head up and down.

I ran my hand over my face and hair. Dust from the hoard fluttered into the air. I turned and limped back through the barrier and ran as fast as my foot would allow. The orb of light stayed with me. When I rounded a corner,

I skidded to a halt at the edge of a hole in the ground.

It was on a blind corner.

The orb lit up the space beyond and I knew there was no way Abudar could have jumped to the other side in his state.

If Arash and Abudar were leading the way, they would have fallen. If Mithra was leading the way, she could have fallen and grabbed onto Arash for help and pulled the other two in. But I couldn't hear anything.

"Abudar?" I shouted down. "Mithra? Arash?"

"Igborg help."

I turned to my trusty dragon.

He wiggled and flew off my shoulder and over the black pit. With a small huff and puff, a burst of fire flew down into the hole, revealing an underground lake. I didn't have time to be in awe of Igborg's ability to use fire, or consider how his fire could have helped Abudar and me stay warm when we'd tried to sleep.

The water far below churned as if something was beneath the surface.

"This entire cave has got to be cursed," I muttered to myself.

Arash suddenly broke the surface and gasped for breath. He sliced his scimitar into the water and propelled himself backward, toward the wall.

"Arash, what happened?" I called down.

He looked up at me, eyes wide. "There's something in the water! It took the prince and princess. You have to help me!"

"How am I supposed to do that? I don't have magic, and if I jump down there with you, then we're both at risk from whatever the creature is."

"I don't have magic either," he argued back. "Do *something*! Don't just stand there!" He barely managed to gasp a breath before he disappeared under the water.

My heart raced and I grabbed the lamp and rubbed it.

The jinni appeared and immediately looked down into the hole. "Well, you're in quite the predicament, aren't you?"

"Look, I've heard stories of jinn my entire life. Most jinn are free, wandering the desert and haunting people who dare cross them. I know you are a prisoner. A slave."

The jinni scowled. "That's not very nice."

"We can help you to not be a slave—we can set you free—but you've got to help us in return." I stared at the jinni, but he only folded his arms and narrowed his eyes in a way that told me he had no intention of helping. "Fine." I shoved his lamp back in my pouch, latched it shut, and jumped.

My breath was stolen the instant I hit the water. And I hadn't anticipated the weight of the gold and jewels in my pockets. I managed to swim hard enough to gasp a breath of air, but the treasure I'd taken from the hoard weighed me down.

My only choice was to dump it.

While my heart ached to let the precious gems and money sink to the darkness below, I pulled everything I could from my pockets, leaving me with the magic lamp and what little I had left in my bag.

I gasped when I surfaced again, but only just in time to see a blue, glowing tentacle in the water wrap around my ankles. I gritted my teeth and held my breath when it pulled me under. The only thing I could do was use my dagger to stab the monster lurking beneath the surface of the icy cold waters. I slipped the dagger from my boot and stabbed into the tentacle. The blue glow rippled upward, away from me, and lit up the form of an enormous octopus.

With the light it offered, I saw Arash feebly stab at the head as he struggled to hold his breath.

I couldn't see Abudar or Mithra.

I swam as fast as I could toward the octopus to help Arash, cutting any tentacle that reached out to me, but one wrapped around my waist just before I reached its head, then dragged me backward through the water and slammed me against the stone wall.

Stars exploded in my eyes and I grunted, expelling too much air.

My lungs burned.

My head ached.

I blinked against the stars in my vision just in time to see Arash go limp. His scimitar fell from his hand and floated downward.

This cave was determined to kill us.

I didn't quite know what happened next. I couldn't tell if the octopus threw me out of the water, or if something or someone dragged me out, but the next thing I knew, I was on my side on the stone floor, vomiting up water.

When I could finally breathe, I lifted my gaze and saw Arash up on his hands and knees, water dripping from his dark hair.

He cracked a relieved smile. "I can't believe you jumped in."

"I couldn't stand up there and watch you die." I groaned when I pushed myself up. My head swam and the edges of my vision started to grow black. I swallowed down another wave of nausea and closed my eyes.

"Oh no. Mithra."

I peeked my eye open to see Arash crawling to Mithra's form. He moved the hair from her face. Her lips were purple.

"You're not dying here." He leaned down, pinched her nose, and placed his mouth against hers, giving her breath.

Abudar lay beside her.

It wasn't lost on me that Arash had crawled past the future sultan to help the princess. As one of the guards of the palace, Abudar should have been Arash's *first* priority.

Abudar . . . didn't look well. In fact, he didn't look alive.

"A *thank you* would be nice. I can't believe I jumped in there. Now I'm soaking wet! Who knows what was in that water?" The jinni looked like a drenched cat, holding his hands out to the side, head down, and a sneer to boot. He shook his head and a ring of blue magic floated down from the top of his head to his feet, drying him instantly.

I blinked and gave him a once-over. "Wait, you're saying you rescued us?"

He flicked his fingers, even though they were dry. "Of course I did. I will never be found at the bottom of an underground lake in this gods-forsaken cave." He flung an arm out toward the lake. We were on a shore I hadn't seen from above.

"Thank you." I bit my lip and forced myself to crawl over to Abudar. My vision and body tilted to the left, but I gritted my teeth and focused on him.

When I reached his side and felt his neck for a pulse, there was nothing.

"He's not . . . breathing," I said weakly.

Arash looked over his shoulder at me. "Help him. You know how to do this, right?" He leaned down and breathed into Mithra's mouth.

I frowned. "Yes, but . . ."

I didn't want to finish with what I was thinking—that this would *technically* be a kiss, and I'd never been kissed. And Mithra had already pointed out I was worth nothing more than the mud under Abudar's shoe, so I shouldn't even dream of being so close to him. I shoved those thoughts aside and replaced them with reason. By law, or at least thief law, Abudar had saved my life back when I'd almost become plant-dinner. In return, I owed him mine. The prince would die without my help.

I pinched his nose, tilted his chin back, and hesitated before pressing my mouth over his. His lips were cold to the touch, but soft.

Behind me, Mithra began to cough.

"Try pressing on his chest now."

I looked up to the jinni

He lifted a brow. "If he's got water in his lungs, breathing into them isn't going to get the water out. You have to push on his chest."

I pressed five times, then repeated breathing into Abudar's mouth. I had to remind myself that Abudar had at least been kind enough to leave me with a bit of light when we parted, even if he had fought me for the lamp.

"Is he all right?" Mithra asked, her voice raw and tired.

"I don't know. He isn't breathing," I repeated to her before pumping on Abudar's chest for the third time.

Mithra dragged herself over to her brother's side. "Maybe you're doing it wrong." Her brows pinched in worry.

"You're welcome to take over," I replied impatiently.

She bit her lip and shook her head. The perfect black eyeliner was smudged below her eyes, and she genuinely looked frightened for her brother. Abudar would be pleased to know that.

I breathed into Abudar's mouth a fourth time. "Can't you use magic to help?" I asked Mithra.

She just stared at Abudar's face.

I glanced at the jinni, but he solemnly shook his head.

I leaned back on my ankles, spent.

Abudar might have been a prideful jerk, but he didn't deserve to die. At least not at the hands of a cave octopus. How noteworthy was that for royalty? He wasn't breathing, and if we had been in the boundaries of Roshanak's magic, he would have at least had the chance of being transported back to the palace.

My skull felt like someone was punching me on the back of the head and I closed my eyes. "Come on, Abudar." I pressed my lips to his once again and breathed three more times.

And then there was a gurgling noise and I sat up.

Abudar started to cough.

Arash acted quickly, rolling Abudar onto his side so he could expel the water in his lungs. "That's it. Get it all out."

Abudar drew big, deep breaths. His pupils were dilated and he took in his surroundings before Arash finally lay him onto his back.

"How are you feeling?" Arash asked.

"Thank you." Abudar looked up at the guard.

Arash shook his head. "Don't thank me. It was

Caspara."

Abudar's brows twitched and he turned his head.

I gave him a weak wave. "Now we just have to figure out how to get out of here. I just need to sleep. I'm exhausted." I closed my eyes again.

"Hey, whoa," Arash said.

Someone caught me as I fell sideways. I opened my eyes to see the jinni.

I swallowed. "I just need to sleep."

"You've got a terrible head wound, I'm afraid," he said. "If you sleep, you might not wake." His face was more solemn than I expected.

"That might not be so bad," I said before thinking. And then I frowned.

Arash got Mithra to her feet and touched her chin. "Are you okay enough to walk?"

"I'll be fine. My legs aren't hurt, just my arm." Mithra dragged her soaking hair to one shoulder.

Arash shifted his gaze from me to the jinni and back. "I have to help Abudar. Are you going to linger and help her?"

"I'll help her," the jinni answered. He didn't even wait for me to reply before lifting me to my feet.

Everything tilted and bile rose up into my mouth. I turned my head and expelled things I didn't know were still in my stomach. The jinni lifted me into his arms. I wanted to protest, argue that I was entirely capable of walking myself, but the pain in my head said otherwise. The jinni reminded me of the care my father would show me.

"I am never coming into this cave again." I wiped my chin with a trembling hand. My entire body shivered.

"Hopefully, you never have to," the jinni said. "Keep yourself awake."

But my world went black.

Twenty-Two

When I opened my eyes, I closed and reopened them twice before I realized I hadn't gone blind, but could only see the darkness of the cave surrounding me. After a moment of my eyes adjusting, I noticed a small glow to my right. I rolled my head that direction. The movement felt sluggish, as if there was a weight upon my neck that made it difficult to move.

Igborg was curled up on my stomach, his little body keeping me somewhat warm.

The light came from the jinni's golden freckles on his skin. He smiled softly when he met my gaze. He sat across from me with his feet straight out and his back against the wall. He silently gestured to the other three, who rested nearby.

I licked my parched lips. "Thank you. For saving me. Especially since it wasn't a wish and you didn't have to."

He reached out and lifted my hand, the one with the tattoos. "Perhaps I didn't *have* to. But you're different than most humans I've met. This mark, you've had it your entire life?"

I nodded. "A woman named Telama gave it to me. At least, that's what my father says."

"You don't believe him?"

My heart twinged and I pulled my hand away, my jaw clenching.

"Ah. He's lied to you in the past?"

"Yes," I answered softly, not wanting to wake the others. "He told me my mother was a sorceress, but he never told me she was the *grand* sorceress. He wouldn't tell me why he left with me either. I recently met her— Roshanak—and she sent me to find you to earn my father's freedom." I looked up at the jinni. "But if I can convince Abudar to help me with a wish for my father's freedom . . ." I heaved a sigh and slowly sat up.

Igborg grunted in protest and peeked an eye open to glare at me while I resituated him in my arms.

The jinni remained close but didn't press me for details. I didn't know why that was oddly comforting. His friendliness and calmness, and the fact he was intrigued by my tattoo, made me wonder if there was more to this jinni than I thought.

What if he wasn't a random jinni trapped in a lamp? What if there was a reason Roshanak wanted *him* specifically? Of course, I had no idea if it was typical for jinn to be trapped in lamps or other artifacts. I knew next to nothing of the magic world.

I leaned my shoulder against the cave wall. "What do you know of my tattoo?" I braved to ask.

His gaze rested on the markings. "The symbols aren't a language, if that's what you think," he answered, being intentionally vague and dismissive.

"If they aren't words, what are they?" I challenged, narrowing my gaze at him.

The jinni's lip curled. "Symbols."

"Care to share with me what they mean?" I asked in a

flat tone.

He touched his index finger to his lips. "I can't give you *all* the answers. Some you have to learn on your own. Now, tell me about this mother of yours."

I didn't appreciate the jinni's change of subject, but he clearly wasn't going to answer me. "She's wanted nothing to do with me my entire life." I stared down at Abudar.

"That's it?"

I arched my brow. "I can't give you all the answers," I replied in a bright, mocking tone.

The jinni flashed a grin, one that made me wonder if I'd crossed the line or somehow impressed him with my sarcasm. "In any event, the three of them have slept the entire night, as have you. You fell unconscious after I picked you up. Unfortunately, we're in another predicament."

I studied his bright eyes. "How?"

He gestured. "The tunnel has led us to a dead end. There was no way to get back up through the hole over the lake, and this was the only direction to go. We walked until we could walk no further. And there's only one way out now. Up." He pointed one finger straight up.

As I assessed the cave, I noticed we were stuck in a crescent-shaped space. I stared up at the hole in the cave roof. It was big enough we could fit. Though it was going to be extremely difficult to get Abudar out if he couldn't offer any help for himself.

"I don't have ropes. Abudar might, he has a magic pouch." I rose to my feet, leaning heavily on the wall behind me as the world tilted, but once I gained my footing, I examined the stone. "This will be easy enough to climb. The walls aren't wet here. And Mithra used a spell to get the rock off of me, so she could perhaps help lift us out."

"You're also out of food and water," the jinni added.

I bit my bottom lip and looked sideways at him. "You *could* help again."

He smiled. "You got a freebie already. Besides, where is the fun in that? I want to see what you've got, Caspara. What can a girl with no magical ability possibly do to save the prince, princess, bodyguard, and herself?" His eyes flashed gold and he disappeared in a puff of golden smoke.

"Some help you are," I grumbled and then heaved a sigh.

Cradling Igborg in the crook of my arm, I roamed the small space. The waning moon was still bright.

We had been in the cave at least two days, but it could have been three or even four. Father had tried to teach me how to keep an eye on the moon to track the days, but no matter what, I was always off by one or two.

I walked past the others, barely sparing a glance at Abudar. I didn't want to linger on him too long. He was still alive, covered by his cloak and a blanket that must have come from Arash, because Mithra also had a blanket, but not him.

My self-control failed me and I found myself watching Abudar. His chest rose and fell in deep, long breaths. I hoped someone had helped him get the bleeding to stop.

As I wandered, I found the walls to be solid and all the same—rough and made of sandstone. My hand grazed a ledge while I walked. I enjoyed the gritty texture of the sandstone. And then . . . I stopped.

I blinked and rubbed my eyes.

There was a line of light, like that which spreads out

from beneath a door when a lamp is lit beyond and finds every gap to reveal itself.

As I tip-toed toward it, the light remained fixed. It sat at the base of the wall. When I got nearer, I was stunned to silence to see a wooden door with a brass handle. How had the jinni missed this? He said there was no way out, that it was a dead end. He seemed to enjoy chaos and clearly wanted to see us struggle.

I gripped the handle.

Blue light flashed up my arm and the lock clicked.

Did my tattoos just unlock the door? I glanced over my shoulder to see if it was a prank of the jinni or if Abudar or Mithra had woken to unlock it with a spell. But they hadn't. Somehow, my touch had caused the lock to respond and open.

I turned back to the door. *Maybe this isn't the best idea to do on my own.*

But my curiosity won. Because, like the vault, anything could be inside.

I pushed the door inward. The hinges didn't utter a sound and when I stepped into the room, I heard the soft *schft, schft, schft* of something moving like the sound of wood on fabric. I saw no details of the room until I stepped across the threshold. And then I found myself standing in the center of a massive cave lit with golden lanterns dangling from the ceiling.

A woman with white hair long enough it rested on the floor sat before a loom, and nine more looms surrounded her in a circle. Smaller looms, about the size of a soldier's shield, were suspended in midair between the row of lanterns. Shelves carved into the wall held looms much smaller. Some the size of books, others even as small as a coin. Every possible nook and cranny of the room was filled with looms. Thousands of them.

The shuttles of each loom on which yarn was attached moved up and down through multi-colored threads stretched across the loom, like bars on a prison window, weaving in different rhythms and without a single hand touching them. Some were vibrant colors—reds and golds mixed with purple, yellow and green with white and black—while others were muted—varying shades of brown and white, grays and gold.

My attention finally settled on the woman. Her ancient fingers carefully threaded the turquoise thread over and under in a pattern only she foresaw. The rug she weaved was nearly complete—a breathtaking mix of navy, shades of gold, and turquoise. It was the finest workmanship I'd ever seen in my life, and I imagined even the sultan didn't own anything of such quality.

The old woman, likely sensing my presence, lifted her chin and turned her head in my direction. Her blind eyes gazed toward me and she smiled kindly. "A bit lost, aren't you, child?"

"I'm looking for a way out."

She nodded. "I'm afraid the way out you seek isn't going to be the way out you need."

My brows pinched. "What do you mean?"

"Your worth isn't dictated by gods or destiny, but by what you choose to do and who you decide to be." She finished the line on which she worked, then grabbed a pair of scissors and snipped the thread.

The rug shivered and she whispered to it as she held it tenderly in her arms.

"I have no idea what you're talking about," I

interrupted. "I just need a way out of—"

She placed her finger to her lips. "You don't *need* magic, young lady. Be who you were born to be. Who your father meant for you to be." She touched her fingers to her lips and blew me a kiss.

I shot up with a gasp.

"You were fussing in your sleep," Arash said. He knelt at my side and must have been looming over me, because he sat up quickly to avoid me smashing my head into his.

I blinked and looked around frantically. "Where is she?"

"Who?"

I jumped up, as quickly as my aching head would allow, and stepped over Abudar's legs and around Mithra, who was trying to fix her hair. I stopped at the wall where the door had been.

It was nothing but a solid wall.

"There was a door here." I patted my palms against the wall, frantically searching every crevasse for the handle.

"Caspara, you hit your head," Arash stated.

I scowled at him. "I didn't imagine it."

He raised his brows silently.

"I . . . suppose it could have been a dream. But it felt so . . . so real. She was weaving a rug." I stared at the wall as if my glare alone would summon the door to open it. I wanted to ask more questions, to find out what she was doing there and why, what were all of the rugs for, what did she mean?

"How do you propose we get out of here?" Arash asked, jarring my thoughts.

When I looked over, he was checking on Abudar's leg. With the light of the morning sun, I could see everything clearly. The bandage that I had wrapped around him must have fallen off in the underground lake, because I could see the gnarled wound, red and angry with infection already settling in.

Arash shook his head and removed his shirt, revealing his torso. It was nearly as fine as Abudar's, though he was a bit leaner. He was still physically toned and I wondered if he and Abudar trained together in the palace. He had a light scar across his left ribs and a few across his back. Someday, I would have to ask him how he got them.

"What about the way we came?" Abudar asked. He gripped his thigh above the wound, as if the tight squeeze would reduce the pain.

Without looking up from his work, Arash said, "We can't."

He pulled a dagger from his boot and sliced the shirt, then ripped it into a strip, cut the seam with his dagger, and continued to rip until the fabric spiraled, not breaking the strip and creating one long piece of fabric. Even I had to admit it was brilliant. With no more medicine, Arash began re-bandaging the wound, cinching tightly and making Abudar grit his teeth and flinch.

"We can't just sit here and die," Abudar said through his teeth.

"Who said anything about sitting?" I had made my way over to stand beneath the hole. I placed my hand over my eyes to study the edge and try to assess if it was weak and could crumble.

"Wait . . . you're considering climbing out?" he asked in bewilderment.

"It's either that or wasting our wish getting out, and I'm *not* doing that when my father's life is on the line."

Abudar tightened his lips.

I ran my tongue over my teeth. They were filthy. I was suddenly grateful Abudar was unconscious for our first "kiss." "I might not have magic. I can't cast a spell and get us all up there. I can't even use a spell to let anyone know where we are. But I am worth something, and I've got talents none of you have. One of those is scaling walls." I looked over at Igborg, whose tail stuck out from the bag he was rummaging through, likely searching for anything to eat. "Igborg."

He turned around and the flap of the bag rested on top of his head.

"I need you to fly up and look at the edge of the hole. If I climb all the way up there and the edge breaks, I'll fall and die."

His eyes widened and he scampered over to me. "Die?"

I crouched and picked him up in my hands. "That's why I need you to go see for me." I kissed the top of his head.

He huffed, spread his wings, and flew up to the hole.

I didn't think the distance was far enough I could *die*, but if I fell, I'd definitely break a leg or arm. Then again, with my head wound, if I fell and hit it, I supposed I *could* die.

Arash suddenly appeared at my side. "Even if you make it up there, how are we going to get Abudar out?" he asked discreetly, trying to keep his voice low enough so Mithra couldn't hear.

I raised my brow at him. "Does Abudar have a rope in his bag?"

He shook his head. "We didn't bring anything like that

either. I searched his bag looking for medicine to help with the infection."

I rubbed my dry lips together in thought. Maybe we should go back and get some water from the lake . . . then again, the risk of meeting up with the octopus wasn't such a great idea. "Mithra used a spell in the hoard to lift the boulder off my foot." I looked past the bodyguard to Mithra.

Arash turned his head to follow my gaze. "I could ask."

Mithra had managed to tie her hair back, but the pristine waves it'd been in days before had washed out from her plunge into the lake. In fact, everything about her was disheveled. Her white dress was practically brown now, smudged with dirt and cave grime. She was trying to appear busy by taking stock of what we had in our bags, but she kept glancing at Abudar.

I heard Abudar heave a sigh and mumble, "I'm not growing another head or anything."

Arash walked over and crouched at her side. "Mithra, could you use a levitation spell and get Abudar out through the hole?"

"Or summon a door to transport us back to the palace?" I asked. I meant it in jest, but if she could, we could have been out of there a day ago.

She narrowed her eyes at me and Arash rolled his eyes to look at me over his shoulder in a way that meant I should have kept my mouth shut.

"Those spells are too much right now," Abudar said shortly before Mithra replied.

"It so happens, those types of spells take a lot of energy and I haven't eaten in a day," Mithra replied sharply.

I shook my head and turned back to Igborg. "What do you think?" I couldn't quite see what he was doing other than hopping or moving around the edge of the hole.

He finally floated down to me and landed on top of my head. "Safe."

"Can you carry my pouch up there?" I looked up to see Igborg leaning over my head, his claws resting on my forehead.

"Yes. Why?" He tilted his head.

I looked at Mithra. "Summon me a rope and I'll climb out."

Her lips pinched as if she'd bitten a sour grape. "If I had something to start the creation, like a root or a snake, it would require less energy."

"Find one or make one, I don't care," I said.

Gripping the rock with my fingertips, I hoisted myself off the ground. Like so many times before, my toes found little ledges to cling to. I pushed up, gripped the next spot with my fingers, and continued doing so, focusing on a little at a time. In spite of being weary from lack of food and water, I knew the only way out of this was through me.

My arms began to tremble long before I anticipated. Exhaustion settled in and I had to let go with my right hand. I wiped it on the back of my pants to dry it off, then switched hands and repeated the movement. I pushed off with my leg to reach the next handhold and my thigh quivered.

I barely managed to hold on.

I licked my lips. The ledge was within reach.

"You're almost there, Caspara," Arash encouraged

from below.

Finally, my hands gripped the edge of the hole. My left hand slid on sand when I tried to drag myself up and I caught myself with my toes. I dried my hand again. With all I had, I pulled myself up to rest on my arms, then grunted, leaned forward, and managed to get my leg up. I rolled out of the hole and onto my back.

It might have been just as graceful as when Abudar pulled himself up on the cliff at the entrance of the cave, back when I thought he was a girl.

The afternoon sun beat down on me and, for the first time in my life, I was grateful for it.

I was out of the cave.

Twenty-Three

"Caspara?" Arash called.

"I made it. Give me a moment." I closed my eyes and willed my headache to disappear. It didn't. I rolled onto my belly and poked my head over the edge of the gaping hole. I could barely make Arash out against the halo of brightness from the sun.

"Can you see the palace?" he asked.

I placed a hand over my eyes and looked at the horizon, turning in a circle. The peaks of the Red Towers loomed in the distance. That was west. A few stony shapes were northwest, and finally I spotted the silhouette of the palace.

Far to the east.

I swallowed hard. "Arash, I think it might be too far away for us to make it there before we . . . well, die from our injuries." I looked back down at him. "At least Abudar. We have no more food, no more water, and judging by the distance, I'd say we're on the western side of the gulley we started at. What do we do?"

Arash held his hands out to his sides in a helpless gesture.

Mithra appeared at Arash's side. "Is there a root up there?"

"We're in a desert," I snapped back.

"Don't disrespect me!"

I rolled my eyes and massaged my aching temple. "So far, I'm the one getting us out of here. Can you summon a rope or not? Even better, are you possibly capable of sacrificing some of your energy and float Abu and Arash up here?"

"First of all, it's *Prince* Abudar to you," she scolded. "Second, I'm not sitting on my hands down here."

I gave her a big, fake smile. "Sure you aren't, Your Highness."

She said something to Arash that may have either been "I'm going to kill her" or possibly, "I need a skewer." I leaned more toward the first.

"We could use Prince Abudar's bandages," Arash suggested. "But if I take them off, he'll start bleeding again."

Mithra finally said, "I'm sending your lizard up with one."

Moments later, Igborg popped out of the hole with a rope in his mouth and my father's pouch in his claws. I threw my father's pouch over my shoulder and caught Igborg.

"You're so brave," I praised.

He smiled proudly, and when he did he dropped the rope.

I yelped and fell onto my stomach, barely managing to snatch the rope before it fell over the edge.

"Sorry," he apologized.

I reached out and patted him. "It's okay. How did you make the rope?" I called down to Mithra.

"I shortened my skirt a bit," she answered.

I nodded. "Good. Thank you. Arash, do you think you can climb up?"

"I'm going to," Mithra insisted.

I pursed my lips. "I think it might be a better idea if Arash came first. He needs to help me lift you and Abudar."

"Are you saying I'm fat?" her shrill voice called up to me.

I heaved a sigh and mouthed to Igborg. *I might just leave her down there.* "No, Mithra. I'm saying you won't be able to pull yourself up or climb, and I'm not strong enough to because I could barely climb out myself. If Arash comes first, he and I can pull Abudar and then you out of the hole."

"Why does Abudar get to go first?" she demanded.

I pinched the bridge of my nose.

Luckily, Arash was the one who said, "Mithra, he's dead weight. You're the best sorceress I know, other than my Mother, and you should be able to come up with a way to help us get him out of here safely."

"Mother?" I blurted aloud.

Arash didn't answer, so he must not have heard me.

Mother? I hoped he wasn't referring to *my* mother. *No. There are plenty of other sorceresses in the land. And mothers, of course.*

"Can you please hurry? It's blazing hot up here!" I called down. Maybe being in the cave wasn't such a bad idea after all.

"I'm coming up," Arash said.

I looked around and spotted a few large boulders nearby. I backed up and planted my heels against the edge of one of them, wrapped the rope around my left wrist and then waist, and leaned back as far as I could. "I'm ready!"

Arash's weight tugged on the rope, not nearly as bad as I thought it would be, like he was guiding himself on it, but somehow not putting his full weight on it. I didn't relax my grip at all. Most of the burns on my hands had healed now, but I didn't want to risk any further friction to my palms, if possible. The rope tightened around my wrist. My weary legs ached. Luckily, it was only momentarily.

Arash's fingers gripped the opening and then his full weight was suddenly on me as his fingers slipped off the edge. If I hadn't been keeping the tension, I would have lunged forward and skidded right back into the hole with Arash.

My right foot was starting to twinge in pain.

"Hurry!" I shouted. "I don't think I can hold you much longer."

"I'm nearly there. Don't let go!" Arash grunted.

I looked over at Igborg, who was staring at me. "Too bad you're not a full-size dragon. You could just pull him out on your own."

Igborg blinked at me, then hopped onto the rope and started trying to pull too. The rope went slack and Arash was struggling to climb the last little bit over the lip of the hole.

"Get me up!" Arash called out.

I dropped the rope and scrambled to the edge, falling onto my stomach as I grabbed both of his wrists with mine and pulled back with what little strength I had left.

Mithra made a noise from below and Arash flew up over the edge with a startled yelp and tumbled a short distance away.

He rolled onto his back and his head lolled to the side.

His face was beaded with sweat.

"You decided to use your magic anyway, hm?" I looked down at Mithra.

She rolled her eyes and didn't respond.

"Do you have it in you to help me with Abudar?" Arash's eyes darted to my wrists. He quickly sat up and took my hand. "You're bleeding. Is that from the rope?"

I nodded, still breathing hard, but more out of the stress of the entire situation. "Good thing Mithra found it within herself to use magic to get you out."

"Yes, or it would have taken a lot longer to climb out." He smiled and shook his head. His dark hair had a fresh layer of sand in it. "I don't know how you managed to get out on your own. I'm exhausted."

"Me too," I agreed.

He licked his lips. "We just have to get Abudar up. Mithra should have enough energy to get herself out with a spell."

I nodded.

"Okay, Mithra. Send Abudar up," Arash said.

I leaned over the edge and peered into the only sphere of light visible in the cave. All I could see was the end of the rope swaying against the dusty floor as though to sweep away the invading sand granules.

Mithra's voice floated up, and then Abudar's. I couldn't make out what they said, but Mithra appeared at the rope and wrapped her arms around it.

"He said send Abudar up, not you," I called back down.

"He's making me go up first."

I frowned, not believing a word she said, and rolled my eyes toward Arash to see if he believed her.

"I'll pull you up," he said without a moment's hesitation.

Heaving a sigh, I reached out to take the rope and help him.

"Keep your strength for Abudar," he said. "I can get her out."

I wasn't going to object. I had no desire to help the arrogant princess. While he heaved back on the rope, I sat and rested my arms on my knees. My left leg throbbed, along with my right ankle, clearly still injured from when I'd sprained it in the hoard.

Igborg lay in my shadow, flattened as low as he could get, his little sides moving out and in with quick breaths. I couldn't tell whether he was enjoying the warmth of the sun or wanted to stay cool.

At first, I had been grateful for the light and warmth, but the way the sun beat down on me, I could already feel sweat trickling down my back and I could only imagine how ripe I would smell in a few hours.

Waiting for Arash to get his *lover* out of the cave, I had a chance to look down at myself. My stomach dropped. The vibrant turquoise color of my birthday outfit was smudged with all the cave grime I'd lain on, rolled in, and dragged myself through, not to mention the sand from climbing out. A green smudge that could have been octopus blood or leftover poison from the plant stained my side. Perhaps Aunt Jade knew a sorceress who could use magic to get stains out of clothes. I hoped so. If my clothing looked that bad, I couldn't imagine what the rest of me looked like.

I watched sweat roll down Arash's temple and to his tense jaw. His green eyes reminded me of Father's and my heart twinged. I needed to get back.

"Finally," Mithra said as she reached the top of the hole.

Arash held her weight, the veins in his arms bulging. Knowing he wasn't going to be able to let go and catch her, I leaned over and grabbed Mithra by her forearm, planted my feet, and dragged her over the lip.

"You could have at least put some effort in with your legs," I said.

She met my gaze. "You know, when we make it back to the palace, I may have a word or two to say about your manners regarding how you've treated Prince Abudar and myself."

I gave her an unimpressed frown. "And what is that going to result in? My being arrested? Wouldn't be the first time."

She yanked herself away from me and scooted over to Arash.

I crawled back to the ledge and peered down. "Are you ready, Abu?"

"For the millionth time, it's Abudar," he said. But when our gazes locked, he gave me a wry and weary smile.

And that smile made my heart flutter.

Because he really didn't care that I'd given him a nickname. He might have even liked it.

Grateful the heat of the sun hid my blush, I threw the end of the rope back into the hole. "Grab on."

No sooner did the bottom of the rope slap against the stone floor than a tremble radiated across the sand in a giant ripple.

I slowly turned to Mithra. "That wasn't you, was it?"

Arash was looking her over, checking her arms for bruises and the cut to her face.

They looked at me simultaneously.

Mithra snorted. "How could that have been me?"

"Did you feel that down there, Abudar?" I asked.

"I thought it was just me." He looked over his shoulder. "Where did it come from?"

"Grab on to the rope. Mithra, if you have any more strength and can help us with getting him out, now would be a really good time to use it." I turned to her. "And for what it's worth, I'm sorry I've been short-tempered with you. I'm exhausted and just want to go home. I'm sure you can relate?"

She exhaled a built-up sigh and shook her head. Her brows softened. "I truly don't know how much more I have in me."

I took my position behind the rock, planted my feet, and held on to the rope with both hands. "Enough for one more spell, I hope. I'm ready, Arash. Abudar, we're going to pull you up on three!"

Arash moved quickly, crawling over behind me. He wrapped the rope around his waist and then planted his feet on the outside of mine, straddling me from behind. He held his right hand beneath both of mine, gripping the other end so tightly I could already see his knuckles growing white.

Mithra glanced from me to her guard and her lips tightened. I at least had enough sense to keep my mouth shut about how this could be her if she would just put forth a little bit of effort to help.

"Ready!" Abudar called.

"One. Two," I started.

The ground trembled so violently, Mithra stumbled and fell on her hands and knees.

Igborg let out a small roar and ran over to me, his eyes wide and frantic. "Help! Help! Dragon!"

No sooner did he squeak out the warning than an enormous plume of sand exploded about two hundred yards away from where we sat. A roar pierced the sky and the dragon slammed the enormous thumb claw on his wings into the sand as it climbed out from beneath.

My blood ran cold—a sensation I was not grateful for despite the heat.

It was the dragon we'd woken in the hoard.

In the bright late afternoon sun, I could see his full details—the vibrant red and blue scales, his golden belly, the six horns protruding from his head, and his griffin-like clawed feet. His eyes locked on us and he let out another roar that sent a vibration through the sand and stone beneath us.

"Pull hard and fast!" Arash ordered. He pulled before I was ready and the rope burned my hands.

I quickly fell into rhythm with him, dragging Abudar in seemingly slow strokes.

"We could tame that dragon and use it to our advantage!" Mithra brainlessly said.

"That's a great idea! Why don't you go try and give it a hug?" I said through gritted teeth. My arms ached already from pulling myself and Arash from the cave and they trembled. My grip was slipping. If we didn't get Abudar out soon, I was going to let go and I didn't think Arash could hold him on his own.

"Your sarcasm is not appreciated," Mithra said dully.

I snapped a glare her way. "I thought . . . sorceresses

were supposed to be powerful." I grunted. "So far, you've only proven how worthless magic is. Don't just stand there! Do something to get Abudar out!"

The dragon spread its mighty wings and began to beat them. The force sent wind and sand in our direction.

Mithra finally stretched forth her hands. "If I faint, you only have yourself to blame. *Itshad*!"

The rope began to pull on its own.

At the sudden release of tension, I fell backward and hit my head into Arash's. It might not have felt like anything at any other point, but with the injury already to my head, my vision exploded. Pain seared behind my right eye and through my temple, then down the back of my neck. I closed my eyes. The wound on my head pulsed in slow beats. And then I realized not only was my head throbbing, but it was in beat with the dragon's wings.

"Are you okay?" Arash said.

I looked up into the sky to see the dragon headed straight for us.

Abudar grabbed my arms and dragged me to my feet. When had he made it up? "We have to run. Are you going to be able to?"

I swayed and swallowed down a wave of nausea that hit when he righted me. "I don't think you can help either way," I pointed out, cradling the side of my head.

"Where are we going to hide?" Mithra argued.

"The gulley. There are all kinds of caves down there we can at least hide in. Follow Abudar," Arash said, taking Mithra's hand.

I adjusted the pouch on my shoulder and looked around frantically. "Igborg? Igborg, where are you? Where did he go?" I fruitlessly searched my pack, knowing full well he wasn't in there. It wasn't heavy. But when I looked around, he was nowhere to be seen. Though, I couldn't tell if my vision was blurry from the sand or from my head. "Igborg!"

"He must have scampered somewhere safe," Abudar said. He wrapped his arm around my shoulders and guided me in the opposite direction of the dragon, further away from the palace. "We have to run."

"But you don't understand. I can't leave him!" I tried to pull away, but Abudar was somehow stronger than me, even in his weakened state. Was I more injured than I thought?

"Maybe Igborg is going to talk to it and see if it will leave us alone?" Abudar suggested.

I finally looked at the prince. "That's what's got me worried. He thinks he's stronger than he is. And what if he only angers the dragon further?" I tried to swallow, but my mouth was too dry.

"Shield your eyes!" Arash suddenly shouted.

A moment later, a blast of wind hit us from behind, slamming sand particles against us. Normally, I would have covered my face with my trusty scarf, but I'd lost the golden one Jade had provided with my outfit, and I'd used my other one to wrap Abudar's wounds.

Wind howled in my ears and all I could see was red sand.

"*Inshat*!" Abudar summoned.

The sand and wind stopped and I peeked an eye open to see a shield around us. I turned to thank him, only to realize Arash and Mithra weren't in the same sphere of protection. In fact, they were nowhere to be seen.

"Abudar, they're gone."

Twenty-Four

Abudar's grip on me loosened briefly, but not before I felt a shudder pulse through him. When he did so, the shield around us broke a moment, allowing the wind through. I realized he wasn't going to be able to hold the shield long. He was just as exhausted and worn as me, if not more.

Abudar turned in a circle, dragging me with him, because he couldn't support his own weight. "Mithra!"

"We're over here!" she called back from somewhere to the right.

"Follow my voice!" he shouted.

The dragon's cry echoed down from up above and Mithra let out a scream.

Arash shouted her name in desperation.

Abudar hesitated, casting me a glance. In his terrified look, I read that he wanted to run to his sister's aid but didn't know if he dared leave me behind.

"She's your sister," I said and pulled out of his grip, then gave him a nudge. "Go!"

"Run with me." He snatched my hand and started running the best he could with a limp and through sand.

With my throbbing headache, I did my best to keep up.

"Arash!" he shouted over the wind.

"The dragon took her!" Arash sounded far away.

"Come to the sound of my voice!" Abudar yelled.

"What about Princess Mithra?" He was perhaps a bit closer.

"I've never been taught how to use a spell to tame a dragon," Abudar answered, perhaps a bit sarcastically. "I might be able to summon wind to try and disperse it, but the dragon may have summoned this sandstorm. And I don't know that my magic can counteract that of a dragon." I had a feeling Abudar was continuing to speak to help Arash find us.

"Can you please try?" Arash was so much closer now, but I still couldn't see him. And then, his silhouette came into shape. His arm was over his eyes as he blindly walked forward.

Abudar reached out and grabbed him, pulling him into the safe bubble protecting us from the violent wind. But like it had moments ago, it shuttered and Abudar grimaced. I squeezed my fingers around his and let him lean on me.

He slowly inhaled, eyes closed, and the invisible shield fell back in place. He relaxed his grip on my hand but didn't let go, and when he opened his eyes, his lips slanted into a smile that deepened his dimple. He didn't need to say anything. His amber eyes thanked me and he reached out and wiped something I assumed to be sand from the length of my nose.

Arash dusted off his face so he could open his eyes. "Thank you."

Abudar nodded silently and finally broke his gaze from mine.

I hadn't realized I was holding my breath and that the excitement in my stomach wasn't adrenaline from running, but from Abudar's closeness. The touch of his hand. The way he'd just looked at me.

"I will summon the wind, but the shield protecting us may fall. Be prepared to be hit by sand." He finally released my hand, closed his eyes, and moved both hands in opposite circles, palms facing each other. Orange light glowed between his hands and he exclaimed, "*Aouasif!*" Sand began to gather toward the magic orb, and he pointed both hands upward.

The orb slammed into the sandstorm with a dull sound like a crack of thunder. Abudar stumbled and Arash caught him. As Abudar had predicted, the shield around us wavered.

My eyes suddenly widened. Two winds. I grabbed onto Abudar's arm. "Abudar, won't that create a tornado?" I asked.

His face fell. "I hadn't considered that."

All of us looked upward toward the sandstorm, shielding our eyes. The wind from Abudar had a slight orange tone to it and the one from the dragon was red from the sand. As it came together, a giant funnel began to form.

"That wasn't supposed to happen." He spat a curse. "We need to run."

"Which direction?" Arash demanded.

"Go straight!"

We began rushing away. It was too pathetic to be called running, and we definitely had no idea where we were going.

"Your Highness!" Arash shouted.

Abudar suddenly struck my side and held on to my shoulders as he tumbled over me, then stopped with his body pressed to mine. He was on top of me and Arash on top of him.

"What was that all about?" I glared up at Arash.

"I don't know. This thing went flying by my head. I thought it was debris," Arash replied.

"I didn't hurt you, did I?" Abudar asked. Somehow, he'd poised his torso over me, but all his weight was on his arms and our hips.

This was delightfully bad. I'd vowed just days ago I wouldn't be taken in by his charms, and here I was unable to say a word because every time I looked at him, my tongue forgot how to work. My heart thundered in my ear.

I tried shoving him in the chest. "Get off," I said, but it was hardly forceful.

Abudar nodded, but his eyes darted to the side of my head. He took my chin and rolled it to the side. "In all the fuss over me, no one took care of you?" His gaze moved from my injury to me, brows furrowed.

I scoffed. "Why would anyone take care of a thief when the future sultan is at risk of dying?" I countered.

His lips tightened. He pressed himself to his hands, leaning further away from me, then put all his weight on his good leg so he could get up. "Arash, Caspara's wound is bleeding."

Arash raised a brow and looked down at himself, his shirtless torso, and then back to his prince. "I'm afraid I have nothing else to offer but my pants."

Abudar somehow found it in himself to laugh and shook his head. "I only have a skirt." He didn't have a shirt to offer either, unless it was in a bag somewhere.

We were quite a mess.

"Don't fuss over me. I'm going to be fine," I argued.

There was a scream overhead and Arash was on his feet in an instant, looking into the sandy, cloudy sky. "Mithra!" he shouted at the top of his lungs.

Abudar held his hand out to help me up, but I swatted it away. I couldn't let him know his dimpled smile was working on me. I had to ground myself in reality. The reality that everything would change once we actually made it home. That my father was still locked up in the palace, that Arash knew because he'd been in that room, and that Prince Abudar would likely never go against his father's will, not even when it came down to releasing my father.

I struggled to my feet on my own.

And then there was another scream, but this time it was longer and . . . growing louder.

My brows furrowed. I met Abudar's eyes and he shared my expression. We both looked around and then up.

I gasped.

Abudar threw his arm up in an arch. "*Ibtaqui, amsikik!*"

The shield around us wavered.

Mithra's white dress came into view a split second before it dawned on me. She was falling from the sky straight toward me. Had Abudar not acted so quickly, she would have landed on me and hurt us both. Instead, whatever spell Abudar had cast, Mithra slowed just feet over my head. He reached out to pull her from the air, but Arash was already there.

"How—" Abudar started.

"Why did the dragon drop you?" I interrupted.

Her side was gouged and dripping with blood. It

already stained her gown. She trembled, her brave and cocky façade gone in a moment of vulnerability. "Th-there was this little dragon. Igborg, is that his name? He kept biting the dragon. I-I don't un-understand."

"Igborg." I grabbed the strap of my father's pouch and twisted it around my hand in the same way my insides twisted.

"She needs medical attention immediately," Arash shouted to Abudar.

"We all do," I grumbled.

I saw Abudar glance at me from the corner of my vision. "What do you think, Caspara? You've been in a sandstorm, no doubt. What do we do?"

My limbs ached and I was positive everyone else was just as sore. We were all just as thirsty and hungry. Igborg was somewhere in the sandstorm fighting a dragon that should have slaughtered Mithra. The sky darkened as the winds began to collide.

And Abudar wanted me to get them out of it?

"Caspara." His touch made me jump and pull away. He held his hand up. "I'm not going to hurt you. Do you know a secret to get us out of the desert before it kills us?"

I looked down at Arash and Mithra, then back to Abudar. We were all covered in red sand, cuts and bruises. We would perish out here if I didn't share my little knowledge.

"Um." I blinked hard and tried to wipe sand from my face.

"I know you're worried about Igborg," Abudar added softly. "And neither of us wants to use the jinni for this."

"I'm not going to burst into tears or anything like that," I said harshly and glared at him. I rounded my shoulders. "In my village, the sandstorms come from the south. We can navigate because we watch how the sands move. But these winds are being pulled into a tornado, and I don't know that the sands will lead us in the right direction." I pointed down to a spot outside of the shield.

Both Abudar and Arash followed my finger. The mini dunes of sand were leaning in a particular direction.

"If what you say is true, we need to go that direction." Abudar pointed, glanced at the dunes, and then shifted his finger a bit. "That should be northeast, where the palace should be."

"Assuming we didn't run too far north, yes," I confirmed.

He licked his dry lips with his dry tongue and ran a hand over his face, wiping off some of the sand with the movement. "We don't have anything to bandage her up with. Keep your hand over her wound."

Arash adjusted his hand and Mithra cried out. "I'm sorry," he said softly.

Tears trickled down the side of her face, cleaning a small trail behind them.

"Wait," I blurted. Mithra's tears had reminded me of the inlet near Balim. "We're on the west side of the gulley. If we go further west, there's fresh water. I remember seeing the Red Towers when I was surveying to see how close we were to Zunbar. I think we should go toward them and find the water so we can all clean our wounds and get some water."

"It's a good idea," Arash conceded.

Abudar looked over his sister silently and finally nodded. "If I recall, Balim is just north of that inlet. One of us can go for help."

I nodded only to have my vision flash white, and I closed my eyes.

"Whoa," Abudar said. He grabbed me and held me upright. "That wound to her head is worse than I thought."

I dragged my eyes open. "I can walk. I just got lightheaded, that's all."

"Can I help you when you pass out?" Abudar raised his eyebrow at me, no smirk on his face.

When I should have been snarky, I hesitated. I met his look. Had he been Mihrage, maybe I would have let him help. Because I knew Mihrage. He was a friend. But Abudar was not a friend. More importantly, Abudar was the *prince*. Imagine how much trouble he would get in if his family discovered he'd helped a thief.

Except, I wasn't just a thief.

He wouldn't get in trouble because he wouldn't be helping a nobody. He would be helping the daughter of the grand sorceress.

"I'm not passing out," I finally said and looked away.

From the corner of my eye, Abudar tilted his head. "I'm not going to hurt you," he said softly, and I somehow knew he didn't mean physically.

I didn't answer.

Because he would.

Mihrage and Taraji, my best friends in the world, were both going to leave me. Taraji had likely finished the trials. Her determination could get her anything she worked for. She and Mihrage would move to the hidden island where the Zauberin Academy was. If I couldn't get my father out of prison, I would be completely alone. Abudar wouldn't be interested in a girl who could only be a thief. And even if he was kind, we were from different worlds.

Arash cradled Mithra in his arms and began walking the direction Abudar had decided. Abudar's shield had recovered, but I silently wondered if he was putting all of his effort into keeping it in place.

I followed after and let Abudar pick up the rear.

It was naïve of me to believe I had no reason to faint. I could feel how weak my body was, and the dull ache in my head had built to a drumming throb. It hurt to keep my eyes open. My feet dragged through the sand.

I felt a presence at my side and knew it was Abudar.

He said nothing.

I replied with nothing.

But I leaned against his side. He lifted his arm around my shoulders, coaxing me to hold on to him. I reached my left hand up and gripped his. He was pulling me forward, and I caught him hissing or grunting in pain now and then. The shield broke and sand started to hit us. I thought Arash muttered something to Abudar, but the prince didn't reply.

If we didn't get help soon, we would all die. Or Arash would have to run for help, seeing how he was the least injured of all of us.

"*Ahlan*, travelers. What are you doing out here?" a warm voice called out.

I barely managed to peek an eye open to spot a man in orange-red clothing, nearly blending in with the sand. His clothing reminded me of Mihrage. My stomach sank. Taraji must have been so worried. I wished I had learned to call Omar so I could send for help, or at least let my friends know I was alive. Not that Omar would hear me all the way over here anyway.

"We're trying to make it back to Zunbar," Abudar

said. His voice was barely strong enough to be heard over the wind. "These girls were participants in the Desert Trials and didn't make it back. We were sent to find them, but the sandstorm hit and we lost sight of the city." I didn't miss that Abudar avoided stating his title as the prince.

"These storms last for hours. You'll never make it back before sunset," the hooded figure stated. "And you all seem to be in very bad condition. Why don't you come back to my home? My wife can feed you and give you water. We can bandage up your wounds too."

"Do we trust him?" Abudar whispered to me.

"I don't know," I confessed. "We *do* need help."

Abudar's brow was furrowed, like he wanted to ask me if I knew which desert people were trustworthy, but I didn't know. "We do need help," he finally said.

The wind continued to howl and beat at us as we followed the man blindly. Somehow, a squat house came into view through the murky air. The man stopped and knocked on his door, announcing his presence.

"I've brought some people who need help. Shield your eyes, I'm opening the door." He stepped inside quickly, followed by Arash and Mithra, then me, and finally Abudar. The stranger closed and bolted the door behind us.

The wind howled against it.

The room was lit with a few lamps and revealed a surprisingly large space. There was a curtained-off section to the right of the main room and a set of stairs leading to a second floor. The building was constructed similarly to the homes in my own village. A painting hung on the wall that must have symbolized a religious entity—the head of a ram with its eyes closed on the body of a man with his hands before him in prayer.

The stranger unwrapped the scarf from around his face and head, sending sand tumbling onto his shirt and into the air. I couldn't help but stare. He had brown horns, just like Mihrage, and pointed ears. But his horns were larger and longer, and the scale-like plating over them was tipped with gold—I couldn't tell if it was painted or natural. The same plating stretched across his cheekbone. His long, brown hair was braided in hundreds of tiny braids and gathered all together on the top of his head, which he let down as soon as the scarf was gone.

"My name is Irilibus. We don't often get guests in the western desert." He hung his scarf on a hook by the door.

Arash set Mithra on the ground and knelt with her head on his lap. "Can we get her fixed while we exchange formalities?" he asked, his pitch a bit annoyed.

Irilibus tilted his chin down in a slight look of disapproval.

A woman I assumed to be his wife appeared behind him and approached Arash carrying a basket of medical supplies. She was breathtakingly beautiful. Her features were identical to her husband, but far more feminine. The ridges under her eyes were thin, and her jaw was narrow. Her braided hair was gathered at the back of her head and was decorated in gold and glass beads.

"How did this wound occur?" she asked.

"A dragon," Arash answered.

She and her husband snapped a look at each other and then back to us.

Mithra's teeth were gritted in pain and her eyes squeezed shut. She held tightly to Arash's hand.

"How in the wide ocean is there a sand dragon?" Irilibus asked. "He's been slumbering for centuries." His eyes darted to the religious painting and I realized it wasn't the head of a ram, but a dragon.

Maybe my head wound was as bad as Abudar claimed.

"We don't know," Abudar answered.

The edges of my vision were becoming blurred. I tried to swallow but didn't dare say anything.

"Regardless, you were lucky Irilibus found you," the woman said. "In your current state, the storm would have claimed you. You're clearly dehydrated and starving. How long has it been since you had a meal?" The woman, who still hadn't told us her name, had torn Mithra's dress to better reveal the wound in her side. In the lamplight, we all realized how horrific of an injury it was.

If Mithra was worried about the scar a tiny scratch would leave on her face, she was going to be disgusted by the scar the slice on her side was going to leave.

Irilibus gestured to the couch. "Why don't you two sit?" he said to me and Abudar.

I looked down at my clothing. "We're a bit dusty."

He chuckled. "We're used to a little sand. Please, sit. I'll get you some water." Irilibus walked over to the kitchen half of the main room.

Abudar kept his eyes on his sister while I took the chance to collapse onto the couch.

"Caspara, wake up." A hand brushed against my cheek.

I groaned and pushed at it. "My head is killing me. Stop touching me."

"You need to wake up. Open the door."

"Stop." I opened my eyes to glare at whoever it was touching my face, but found myself confused. I was lying in a bed. How had I gotten to a bed?

I looked over to see Abudar lying on the floor on his side, sound asleep. He wore a clean tunic, and a blanket covered him from the ribs down.

The wind outside had stopped.

I sat up, the ache in my head ebbing. There was no one and nothing close that could have touched my cheek. I brushed my hand over my face. I had distinctly heard a voice too. It had told me to go to the door.

Throwing off the blanket, I tip-toed around Abudar and ducked under the curtain to the main room. It was pitch black, but the moonlight snuck through the shutters and revealed the outlines of Mithra and Arash on the couch.

I must have passed out again. The last thing I recalled was getting to the little house during daylight, and now it was late in the night.

Trusting the voice in my mind, I unlocked and slowly opened the front door, grimacing immediately when the hinges groaned.

I heard the rustle of material and glanced over to see Arash quickly climbing to his feet, his guardian instincts taking over.

"It's me. Caspara," I whispered.

I couldn't see his face but knew he was looking at me. "What are you doing up?"

I shrugged. "A voice told me to look outside the door." I opened the door a bit more and peeked my head around it to look out into the desert.

A familiar shape was lying in front of the door.

"Igborg!" I shouted, not caring I probably woke everyone within a mile. I threw the door open and scooped him up and cradled him close. "You foolish dragon! What

made you think you could take on that big desert dragon?"
I turned around.

Arash had his hand held out toward Irilibus, who had a
sword in his hand and wore a long tan undershirt. Abudar
was behind him, looking very unprincely with sand-
crusted hair, sweat-streaked face, and a filthy purple
skirt—which no one had mentioned.

I blushed. "I'm sorry. I didn't mean to wake you all," I
said in a much quieter tone. "Igborg is back."

He nuzzled my jaw sluggishly. His little body was
freezing.

Abudar heaved a sigh. "Igborg is her animal familiar,"
he lied. "You know how sorceresses are gifted one by the
gods when they accept their true self? That's him."

Irilibus nodded and lowered his weapon. "You should
be more careful out here. We Dalarian are careful to
protect what is ours."

"I'm sorry." I gave him a weak smile.

Arash silently returned to where he'd been sleeping
and lay back down. Abudar motioned for me to return to
the room with the curtain in the doorway, the room I'd just
been asleep in. I complied and he let the curtain fall behind
us.

"How do you have no sense of safety?" he asked. "I
would have assumed you would be overly cautious, being
from the desert yourself."

"The eastern desert isn't so dangerous," I argued. "We
only have to worry about the desert animals." I sat on my
bed. My head didn't hurt as badly as it had before, but my
muscles ached. I was ready to be home again. I rubbed my
hand over Igborg's back to warm him up. He could have
frozen if I hadn't found him when I did. The thought made

my stomach sink.

"Where were you, Igborg?" I asked.

He purred. "Saving you."

I closed my eyes and stroked his soft side. "That was rather silly of you. You could have been killed."

"You would for me," he said.

"Well . . . yes. But—"

"Just thank him." Abudar ran his hand over his face and walked to his bedroll. It was only then I noticed the fresh bandages on his leg through the rip in his skirt.

"Why are you sleeping on the floor?" I asked.

He looked down at me. "Because you were on the bed."

"But you're the prince. You could have taken the bed and left me on the floor. After all, I'm used to it," I countered.

The edge of his mouth tugged in a little smile. "I may be royalty, but I'm not barbaric. You passed out from your head injury, so you needed somewhere comfortable to sleep." He lowered himself to the floor, and I didn't miss the grimace that crossed his face, nor the hand that went to his side.

"You still hurt," I pointed out.

"Yes. A little. It's not nearly as bad as it was, though." In the dim light of the room, I could make out a smile.

I reached up and touched the bandages that had been wrapped around my head. Since we were both awake, I thought I would ask him one of my most pressing questions. "Abudar . . ."

"Hm?"

"That tattoo on your arm is the same as mine. I was looking at it when we were in the caves. The symbol on your wrist is the same as the one on my wrist. The mark on your pinky is in the exact same spot as mine. What does it mean?"

He was quiet so long I wondered if he'd fallen asleep, but he finally said, "It is the marking of a sentinel. A protector of the land. When I was an infant, a woman named Telama visited and gave me her blessing that I should become one of those protectors."

The mark of a sentinel? Chills ran down my arms and I sat up a little more to look down at him. I could just make out the glisten of his eyes in the moonlight. These were questions I'd wondered my entire life and Abudar actually knew the answers!

"My mother believes this blessing is what gives me magic, and the ability to use such a variety of spells. Though she also explained that in other lands there are sorcerers, witches, and even necromancers who can use different magic. I've been training my entire life so I can be the sentinel the land needs."

Overwhelmed, I lay flat on the bed and covered myself and Igborg with the blanket. I looked up at the ceiling. A sentinel and Telama. I knew Telama, and Abudar had shared her name, so we *must* have had a connection. But what did that mean for me and Abudar? Was he the "other half" I was supposed to seek? Did that mean Abudar knew who I—*what* I was—the entire time we were in the cave? He mentioned the tattoos to me when he was helping me climb into the cave. Did he know all the way back in the prison? Is that why he took me to Roshanak?

"You think I am supposed to be the other one?" I asked aloud.

"I had hoped. It is why I reacted the way I did in the

prison, though you clearly misinterpreted it." I could hear his smile in the tone of his voice.

"Clearly," I agreed with an added chuckle of relief. Even though more questions had risen, so many had been answered, if only partially. But my head ached from all the thoughts rushing through my mind.

Abudar grunted and adjusted the way he was lying down. "I don't know how people sleep on the floor."

I sat up. "You can take the bed."

"No, I'm already lying down."

"But really. I'm used to it. And I'm less injured." I climbed off the bed, but Abudar reached out and put his hand on my foot.

"Caspara, I wasn't complaining. Just lie down and sleep. You need it."

"But . . ." Warmth shot through his touch, up my leg and into my belly. I didn't understand why he was letting me, but I climbed back in the bed. Either Abudar saw me as the sentinel he needed, or worse, he was actually kind.

Twenty-Five

Igborg sat on my lap at breakfast while I hand-fed him pieces of meat and berries from my plate. The blackberry juices spread across his lips and dribbled down his chin and I had to constantly wipe it off. But I didn't mind. My suicidal dragon was back in my arms.

Arash sat on the floor with Mithra, feeding her.

His actions made me roll my eyes in disgust. Her side was hurt, not her arms or hands. She was completely capable of feeding herself, but because Arash was her bodyguard and romantically interested in her, she took full advantage of his kindness. It made me gag.

"You find them as ridiculous as I do," Abudar said in a low voice. He sat at my other side and had been given a set of clothing with pants and a tunic—an outfit more proper for a man.

I raised a brow at him and smiled a bit. "That obvious, hm?"

He chuckled and drank the last of his water. "I have never been so fond of water."

I laughed. "I can't wait for a proper bath."

"Yes. You do stink," he teased and nudged me with his elbow.

"Speak for yourself, warthog," I countered.

"Ouch." He grasped his chest as if I'd pierced his heart, but his smile was bright.

The heat of a blush crawled up the back of my neck and I reached up to touch the bandages on my head, pretending to fix them just to keep my hands busy.

"We should leave as soon as possible so we can get home," Abudar said. "Mithra, please feed yourself and let's be on our way." He went to stand, but Irilibus cleared his throat and stood before Abudar could.

"Stay a moment longer. I'll gather some food and water for you all and help prepare you. Sierra, can you gather the food? I shall fill their waterskins at the well." Irilibus gathered our skins from where they sat on the couch.

"I can assist you," Arash offered as he rose to his feet.

Irilibus waved his hand dismissively. "I can manage the water. Check her bandages."

Arash frowned but complied. When he removed the bandages, I noticed Mithra's side had been sewn shut.

I turned to Abudar. "Did they stitch your leg closed too?"

He froze with his finger on Igborg's head as though I'd just caught him doing something he wasn't supposed to. He blinked and quickly straightened. "Yes. It's feeling much better now. Sierra also stitched up your head."

I reached up and touched the bandages and glanced at the woman cleaning up breakfast. "Thank you."

She smiled back at me. "You're welcome. We can't have you all develop infections."

"I suppose not." My smile widened and I heaved a breath then relaxed my shoulders. "We've been fighting for our lives for days. It's a bit strange to just . . ."

"Sit?" Abudar finished.

I nodded. I hadn't even noticed how close we were sitting, but Abudar's knee brushed mine and I had to remind myself he wasn't going to be interested in me. I was reading too much into his body language. In spite of that, my heart raced.

"Tell me about your dragonling," Sierra said.

My brows furrowed and I looked down at Igborg. It made sense that he was only a child. His speaking alone indicated as much. But it still felt strange to hear that he was. "He will eat anything you put in front of him, or at least taste it. He almost got stabbed by a scorpion once because of it." I smiled down at him.

Igborg blinked up at me.

"He came to me about a year ago. He was severely injured and I thought he was going to die. I figured he was a little desert lizard that had been caught and almost eaten by a hawk, and he was completely covered in nasty sand ticks."

"He must have been in a lot of pain," Abudar observed.

I nodded. "Madame Kiara helped me fix him up."

Abudar inclined his head. "Madame Kiara?"

"Yes. Her son Lycus adores Igborg. In fact, he gave us a whole bag of seeds for Igborg that we took in the trials." I tapped Igborg on the nose and he wiggled his body all the way down to his tail. I lifted my gaze to Abudar. "Are you surprised I know her? Your aunt is quite known in Zunbar. My friend Mihrage purchases her herbs at least weekly."

"I know, I just . . . it was a surprise for some reason. That's all. Maybe because we're more connected than we thought?" He scratched under Igborg's chin.

I braved a look at his tattoos again and bit my lip. *You must find your other half. The one who bears the same marks upon their arm.* Kiara had said that the last time we met. *Discover who you are and fulfill your prophecy.* I took in the room—Mithra and Arash speaking softly to one another, Abudar adoring on Igborg, Sierra putting the clean dishes away. And I *thought* I was beginning to understand what Kiara meant about "discovering" myself.

A few days ago, I didn't know who my mother was or why my father kept her identity hidden from me. Now I had uncovered my family's vault and obtained the lamp with Abudar. Abudar, who bore the same markings and prophecy as me.

I turned to Abudar to make the observation, to tell him maybe I really was this person he was looking for, when the door opened and Irilibus entered.

"I've returned with your water," he announced.

But he didn't close the door behind him. A woman in a red dress with orange and gold accents entered. Her head was covered and all hidden but her eyes, which were lined with gold.

I felt Abudar rise to his feet behind me. "What is this?" he demanded sharply.

But four, five, and then six other women filled the small space. I felt Abudar's sudden tenseness, and Arash had also jumped to his feet, but upon patting his hips must have recalled his sword was at the bottom of a lake in the caves.

A woman grabbed on to my arm. I tried to pull away, but she whispered, "*Itrabati.*"

A thin red thread wrapped its way around my wrists

and when I tried to pull it away, it didn't budge.

My eyes widened and I looked at Abudar. His eyes were darting back and forth and I wondered what he was thinking. He had magic. He could use a spell and knock them all away and get us out of here! I didn't even know who these people were.

Mithra's voice spoke quickly and a burst of light filled the room and blinded me.

The sorceresses in the room all began shouting things that were either spells or nonsense.

Abudar grabbed my upper arm firmly—or at least I hoped it was Abudar—and dragged me toward the door. I blinked away the spots of light in my vision and tried my best not to trip over my feet.

He grunted and a woman spoke the same spell again.

By the time my vision came back, I realized Abudar was on his knees and his wrists were bound behind him.

"This will prevent you from using any magic," one of the sorceresses said to me as she clamped a metal bracelet around my upper arm. It was cool to the touch, but nothing happened. She pulled me out of the house and into the morning sunlight and never-ending desert.

I looked over my shoulder and tried to drag my feet. "No. Stop! Arash!" I shouted the only name not associated with the palace, unsure if these women knew they were also abducting the prince and princess.

"They're being brought with us. Don't you worry yourself."

"But my bag. I need my bag, please. It's all I have of my father," I said.

The woman's eyes shifted sideways to look at me, and then she looked over her shoulder. "Be sure to bring their belongings!"

I prayed hard that Igborg had hidden inside of the bag, and that the bag still hid the confounded lamp with the jinni inside—the jinni we could *really* use some help from right now.

Looking over my shoulder again, I spotted the sorceresses bringing Mithra from the house, somehow being careful with her. She also bore a metal bracelet on her upper arm. Arash was pulled out next with lots of red ribbon binding his wrists, some pinning his arms to his sides, and then looser ribbon around his legs so he could walk, but tight enough he couldn't kick. He must have put up a fight.

Finally, Abudar was led out in the exact same bindings as Arash. But he didn't have a metal bracelet on his arm.

They didn't know he had magic.

I realized in that moment that I hadn't been naïve not to know he could use magic. No one knew. It had been a secret of the palace. By his own admission, it was rare a sorceress used magic beyond their particular gift. If the rogue sorceresses discovered the prince could use magic— a rarity in its own right—*and* that he could use multiple abilities, they would do anything in their power to keep him.

Our gazes locked.

He was still trying to figure a way out of this.

I had heard of the unrest among many of the sorceresses in our land. After Sultan Zayne's father, Sultan Hashem, decreed he was the one in power and no sorceresses could practice without punishment, those with magic had to hide. Many were punished for using their magic openly. Some were even executed. Many fled the land. Even more fled after Sultan Zayne was cursed by a shaytan, one of the most powerful demons from the underworld.

When Shahira volunteered to be his wife and helped banish the demon, she and Sultan Zayne had worked together to try and repair the kingdom's feelings toward magic users. However, a group of sorceresses felt they were owed compensation for all the years they'd been forced to be silent.

I tried to recall the poster I'd seen days ago at the bazaar when I'd seen the "wanted" poster of myself. I couldn't remember what they called themselves.

We walked in a tidy row. The city gates were guarded on each side by a sorceress in the same outfit as our captors, and when we entered them, a loud bell rang out. A cool, salty breeze greeted us as the wind came in from the ocean and straight through the rows of houses.

"Stop rushing," one of the women behind me growled.

I glanced over my shoulder to see Abudar pulling on her. My gaze was drawn forward again when the woman leading me finally stopped. We were in the town square and the people had come out of their homes to see what the commotion was.

Mithra was pulled up to my side, then Arash, and finally Abudar. Though, he walked forward to step between me and Mithra. One of the sorceresses stepped forward like she was going to stop him, but he stepped back in line just in time.

Her eyes scrunched, but she didn't make him move.

"We're in Balim," he said under his breath.

I tried to recall if we'd had any conversations of Balim, but all I knew was that we'd been walking toward it to find water. It was one of the cities on the northwestern part of the land.

"The Veil took it over last week," Abudar added in a mumble, trying not to move his lips, clearly picking up that I had no idea what he meant.

The Veil. The rogue group of sorceresses.

My eyes widened.

"We have before us the prince and princess of Zunbar!" one of the women said proudly. With their faces hidden and turned toward the crowd, I couldn't tell who was speaking.

The audience began to murmur and lean around the sorceresses to get a look at us.

"This is bad, Abudar," Mithra whispered.

"I think there's only one way out of this," he responded.

"You can't," she hissed.

"This lovely little group has walked right into our laps! Thanks to our trusty Irilibus and Sierra." One of the women gestured to her left, to where Irilibus stood proudly with his wife at his side.

Traitor.

"And as a reward for his service to us for delivering such worthy new recruits . . ." The same woman walked to him and Abudar stole a glance at me. "We gift you the location of the one who cursed your daughter. Seek him in the eastern desert where the forty hide."

Forty hide. That's my village! He-he couldn't be looking for Mihrage?

"Thank you, Shorix." He bowed.

Shorix bowed her head then turned back to us. "Separate the sorceresses from the men. With his children held, Sultan Zayne is sure to see things our way. Finally."

"Abudar, they can't know you have magic," I heard Mithra say.

"We can't get out of here otherwise," he said quickly.

The women stepped forward and grabbed us.

Mithra kept her eyes locked on her brother. "Don't."

Mithra and I were taken down a street toward a home near the shore, through the front doors and down a flight of stairs. Mithra was pushed into a chair in front of a window and I was forced into one across from her. Our red bindings magically reached out and held on to the chairs, holding us in place.

"It seems all of you have been through quite the ordeal, the way you're bandaged up. We will return shortly," the women said.

The door locked behind them.

I met Mithra's gaze. "If you have an idea, now would be a really good time to share it."

Twenty-Six

"If Abudar reveals he has magic, the sorceresses will do anything to keep him," Mithra said, confirming my fears. "I've heard a lot about The Veil from Roshanak. She insists they're not much of a threat, but more and more sorceresses seem to be joining their ranks. They've taken over this entire city." She gritted her teeth and pulled on her bindings.

I bit my bottom lip and looked at the door. "I have a dagger in my boot I can use to cut us free. If they grabbed my bag, Igborg will make his way back to us and he will help. Or . . . maybe me and Abudar could possibly agree this is a serious enough situation to wish for our way back to the palace." I paused. "What do you think they want?"

She shook her head. "You wouldn't understand."

"And why not?" I asked with a frown.

"Because *you* have never been oppressed! These women were outlawed by our land for decades. They've had to work in secret in fear of being caught, keeping their identities hidden."

I raised a brow. "Yes. You are right. I have absolutely *no idea* what that's like."

Mithra scowled at me. "Being a thief and being a sorceress are completely different," she bit back.

"You wouldn't know either. You're a princess."

"Are you kidding?" she asked, her voice shrill. "Do you know what it's like to have a magical *brother*? He's been doted on his entire life. I have had to fight for every bit of recognition while he walks into a room and everyone swoons over him."

I let out a bit of a laugh. "I actually understand what you mean. I felt that way when I first met him. I don't know why everyone falls over him."

Mithra's brows furrowed slightly and then her expression relaxed. "Hm. Maybe you're not as daft as I first thought." Her lips relaxed into a smile.

I glanced at the door. "What do you think they'll do when they discover I have no magic?"

"Let you go, I hope."

I didn't think that would be the case. Not when I was at risk of revealing their secret. I had to make sure that my own secret came out sooner rather than later, before they revealed any sort of plan they might have.

I jumped when the door opened and a single woman entered.

She walked to a third chair and lowered herself into it. "Salam, ladies. I know this may be a frightening experience for you."

"Being abducted? No," I said sarcastically.

The woman kept her attention focused on Mithra. "I am afraid there is a misconception regarding The Veil. I'm sure Roshanak has told you all of her lies."

"And how do I know what you speak won't be lies?"

The woman nodded. "That is a fair question, and one I am asked frequently." She removed the veil from her face, revealing a beautiful middle-aged woman with wrinkles beginning to deepen at the edges of her eyes and mouth. "My name is Shorix. I lead The Veil. I have brought you here for only one purpose, and that is to tell you the truth."

There was no way I was going to be able to lift my foot and acquire my dagger with the woman in front of us. I would have to wait until she left us alone. But once I cut our ropes off, we could easily fit out the window behind Mithra.

Mithra drew a slow breath through her nose. "And what truth do you allege has been hidden from me?"

"That the sorceresses have been suppressed in more ways than one. Your entire life you have been taught that the sorceresses are born with one magical gift and one only." She shifted her gaze to me. "What is yours?"

I fumbled to find the words, caught between being honest and lying. "Oh, well, I have some . . . skills, but not in, um, not in magic."

Shorix raised her brows and she looked me up and down. "Were you not part of the Desert Trials?"

"Not exactly. No." I cleared my throat and shifted.

"Liara!" she called and the door at the top of the stairs opened. "Take this girl out. She has no magic and is therefore useless to our cause. But leave the bracelet on, just in case."

I looked at Mithra. "I don't mind staying. What am I going to do?"

"I can't have you revealing our secrets."

"I thought you were speaking of truths," I countered.

The veiled woman spoke a word and the rope relaxed from the chair, but not the rope binding my wrists. Shorix said nothing to me but watched me with narrowed eyes.

The sorceress took me up the stairs and then back out

to the streets.

"Why are you here?" I asked.

"Because I believe in Shorix," Liara replied.

"And you feel you have to tie people up to get them to join? Did they tie you up?"

She glanced sideways at me. "We only bound you because of the prince and his bodyguard. We couldn't risk them taking you and the princess. Well. The princess. It's unfortunate you have no powers."

"I've made it this far in life," I grumbled.

Liara led me to a short house which had another woman standing outside the door. After surveying the village, I saw it was the only home with a sorceress guarding it. Abudar and Arash must have been inside.

When I was taken inside, I found both of the young men bound to chairs against the far wall. The chairs had literally been rooted into the floorboards like tree limbs.

Abudar actually looked relieved to see me, but his eyes darted past me to the door closing behind me. His brows dipped. "Where is Mithra?"

I was pushed to a chair by the wall and sat. "Apparently, their leader only wants to speak with sorceresses who actually have magic." My ropes once again latched on to the chair.

Liara left, leaving the three of us alone in the room.

"What does she want?" Abudar pressed.

I shook my head. "All I heard her say was that she wanted us to know the truth. She said Roshanak has been telling lies. That's all I know."

Arash's jaw tightened and he looked at the door again. "I don't know how to get us out of here. We can't break free of the ropes." He flexed and grunted as he tried to lean forward, proving to me they were as tightly held down as me.

"There *is* one little difference," I pointed out.

"What's that?" the boys asked simultaneously.

"I have the brains." I focused my attention on Abudar. "Can't you dispel the ropes?"

"I . . . *could*, but the only way out is the front door. The windows are all nailed shut." He nudged his head toward the nearest window.

Nails stuck out from all angles.

I chewed my bottom lip. Removing all of them would definitely draw attention. There would be no way for us to get all of the nails out before being captured. "While we were in the caves, I wondered if you could create a portal to transport us back to the palace. Is that something you could do?"

He scoffed. "No. Not that distance. I was only barely learning that skill prior to the trials. I've just barely mastered getting into the next room. I don't dare risk creating a portal that far away. We might end up on a different continent."

"*That* would be interesting," Arash said.

I pursed my lips. "Then . . . our only options are to go out the front door, break the window, or use our wish."

"Wasn't there a guard?" Arash asked.

I shrugged. "You're a guard too. Surely you know some guardly way to knock her out or something."

Arash's brow lifted so slowly I got what he was saying before he said it. "You have no idea how fighting really works, do you?"

"I know hand-to-hand combat. Maybe not as much as you and Abudar, but even I know a certain blow to the head could knock her out," I countered.

"Maybe we shouldn't jump to knocking anyone out," Abudar said. He scratched his chin on his shoulder.

"And we can't use our wish on that. There has to be another way," Abudar added.

"Oh, so you'd rather both sit here and wait for someone to rescue us?" I rolled my eyes and lifted my ankle to rest it on my knee, then shook my foot back and forth to try and jar my dagger loose.

"What are you doing?" Abudar asked.

"I have a dagger in my boot," I snapped.

He sighed. "I can get us out of the ropes, Caspara. That isn't the problem. Weren't you listening?"

I stopped and looked up at him. "Okay. Then *you* come up with an idea that isn't just saying all of mine are bad."

He glanced at Arash.

Arash shrugged but surveyed the room. "Maybe we don't use a portal all the way to the palace. What if you made a portal just to get us through the wall?" His brown eyes settled on Abudar.

Abudar pursed his lips and looked back at the window. "That . . . might actually work."

"I remember where the house is. The one they're keeping Mithra in," I said. "There were windows behind her in the basement we can get through."

Abudar said, "*Inhal,*" and the ropes on all of us sank to the ground.

We got to our feet and headed for the window, but I stopped and looked around. "Where are our bags?"

"In the corner." Abudar beat me to them and grabbed my bag.

I reached out for it, but he pulled away.

"I want to carry it for you."

I frowned. "Why are you so obnoxious?"

"It's my goal in life." He pulled it over his own head and shoulder, still smiling.

My cheeks immediately flushed. I tried to roll my eyes, but it was too late.

"Ow, careful."

I glanced over to see Igborg scrambling out of the pouch, his claws digging into Abudar's side and shoulder while Abudar shifted in awkward positions until Igborg sat on top of his shoulder.

Abudar eyed him. "There must be an easier way for you to get up and down. Like flying? Your claws hurt."

"Sorry," Igborg said. He sniffed at Abudar's neck, then hunkered down the way he did with me.

I chuckled and stroked Igborg's spine. "I'm glad you stayed hidden."

"Let's get out of here." Arash gestured with both hands toward the window.

Abudar held his right hand out to the window and turned his hand from left to right, his fingers spread. "*Iftah ya bowaba.*" Gold light flickered up his arm and across his tattoos, and a circle of orange light spun against the wall and revealed the grassy hill behind it.

Arash didn't hesitate before walking through. I followed after and Abudar brought up the rear. I led the way behind the houses until we reached the one in which Mithra and I had been held.

"Why are you so fond of this bag?" Abudar suddenly asked.

We had stopped and were leaning against the side of a

building across from our target. I glanced back at him. "It's my father's." I focused forward. "I'll go over and see if she's alone." I walked past Arash, who reached out and snagged my elbow to drag me back.

"No, I will be the one to do so. It is my responsibility." He frowned at me, then got on his hands and knees to crawl low and as soon as he reached the shadow of the house, lay down on his belly.

I folded my arms and leaned my back against the wall behind me, but glanced at Abudar still holding my bag with the lamp inside. I was still unused to seeing him wearing men's clothing. "So you dressed up in your sister's clothing in order to join the trials and find a lamp, hm?" I glanced at Abudar. "Or do you just like wearing her clothing?" I raised my brows, my lips tugging as I tried to refrain from smiling.

"A skirt *is* significantly cooler." Abudar grinned. "I heard Roshanak tell you something about the lamp and knew it could help my mother."

"But how did you make yourself a girl?"

"Ah." He held up his left hand and spun a ring on his pinky finger. The girl form of him I'd met in the caves took over him. "It's an enchanted ring," he explained. He turned it again and his true self appeared. "I have to concentrate on who I am and what I am. Which is why the spell fell when we were in the caves and I blacked out."

"You're such an idiot," I blurted. "You could disguise yourself as a sorceress and walk in and get Mithra!"

He blinked at me and looked down at his ring. "I don't know how that didn't occur to me."

"Can the ring change your clothing?"

He shook his head. "No. But I can look like Shorix."

Without a word, Abudar no longer looked like himself, nor did he look like Yasmin. He looked exactly like Shorix, only in the clothes Iribilus had given him.

"That isn't going to work," Arash said.

Without saying a word, Abudar created a portal back into the house where we'd been imprisoned. We split up and searched the rooms for clothing. I found a room and chest with clothes, but none of them were robes like the sorceresses wore.

"I've got one," Arash called just loud enough for us to hear.

Abudar was back to himself and putting on the clothing before he returned to looking like Shorix.

We then exited the building, *again*.

"I'll be back before you can forget my adorable smile." He winked at me, then walked around to the front of the house while I fumbled and was unable to come back with something to say.

How was Abudar able to make my knees feel weak?

How could a boy I barely know make me feel happy? Actually make my heart flutter? Make me think of all the good in the world and forget about my worries even if only for a split second?

I liked forgetting.

Twenty-Seven

Arash lay on his stomach by the window and I kept an eye all around us for signs anyone might be drawing near enough to blow our cover. After all, it was sometime before lunch and the people of Balim were busy. People passed by on the street side of the gap between houses that wasn't really an alley and each time I watched them carefully.

"What do you see?" I whispered.

"Mithra is alone," Arash answered in a low voice. "The door is opening and . . . I don't know if that's Abudar or not."

I bit my lip and leaned up on my toes to try and see over Arash and look through the window.

"Yes, it must be Abudar. He's undoing Mithra's bindings."

Relief washed over me and I smiled. We would get her out and maybe instead of trudging back across the desert, we could go to the shore just a few yards north, steal a boat, and sail around the north part of the main island of Sheblom to Zunbar.

Movement in the corner of my vision drew my attention and I had to look twice before it dawned on me. There were four women standing outside of the front door having a conversation, but the one who looked to her left had the same eyes as Shorix. The real one.

My stomach dropped.

"They're going up the stairs," Arash reported.

"Stop them!" I whispered. "She's outside the door!"

Arash looked over his shoulder at me, then the opposite direction to where I pointed. His eyes widened and he tapped his fingernail on the glass.

The women at the opposite end of the building turned at the noise.

I pressed my back to the wall and for some reason decided that meant I also needed to hold my breath. Meanwhile, Arash pressed himself as flat to the sand as he could. Even his cheek was resting against it.

Igborg flicked his tail and hopped from my shoulder. He landed on the sand with a soft sound and scurried into the open space.

My eyes widened, but I couldn't call him back.

He disappeared just out of sight and I gripped my worn and filthy top as my heart raced. I couldn't see what he was doing. What if they wanted to investigate?

"It was just a lizard. I will speak with her and see if she wants to join us. In the meantime, prepare lunch for her and the others. We need to treat them like guests in order to get what we want."

"As you wish, Head Sorceress," a few of the women replied.

Slowly, I peeked one eye around the edge of the building.

The women were dispersing, their attention no longer toward us. Igborg sat on top of a boulder, completely relaxed.

I heaved a sigh of relief and saw Arash raise his head. "Your dragon is smart."

"Thankfully. Did Abudar listen to you?"

He slowly shook his head. "I don't see them." With a grunt, he was on his hands and knees and then upright on his feet. He dusted the sand from his torso and mumbled something under his breath about needing a bath.

We all did.

But I didn't have time to worry about how much I smelled like sweat. Mithra and Abudar were somewhere in the house that the sorceresses had just entered.

Arash glanced at the window and backed up. "They just spotted Mithra's empty chair and yelled that she's escaped." He turned to run for the front of the house, but I caught him.

"We can't just barge in. Abudar has to have a plan."

His eyes narrowed. "My duty is to keep Princess Mithra safe and—"

"And if you barge in there, you don't know whether or not they will attack," I countered. "Have a bit of faith in Abudar." But even after saying it, my fingers itched to rub the lamp.

He looked toward the front of the house. "I'm waiting ten seconds."

I exhaled through my nose. I couldn't blame him. He *was* her bodyguard. I was also stupidly worried about Abudar, but I had to believe he knew what he was doing.

Mithra suddenly came sprinting toward us, her hands gripping her side.

Arash met her and wrapped his arms around her. "You're okay."

"Abudar got me out," she whispered. "But he's still

inside. He changed his appearance to another one of the sorceresses and they're debriefing him on hunting me down."

"I can stay here and wait for him," I offered. "But you two need to—"

"No," Arash said firmly. "All of us need to get out of the city before they lock it down."

My eyes widened. "You want to leave him behind? He's the future sultan!"

"And he can take care of himself," Arash argued. He kept his arm around Mithra and started guiding her behind the houses toward the city gates. "He's been trained for such a moment as this. With his ring, he can make his way out of the city unseen, but *we* won't be able to if we don't make it out before they warn the sorceresses at the gate."

"Won't they recognize Mithra anyway?" I asked. I grabbed Igborg then hurried after them. "She's sort of recognizable."

"She has a point," Mithra said. "What if we went out north? Along the coast?"

Arash stopped and looked in the opposite direction. "I don't know that Abudar would think to go that direction."

"Then I'll wait," I insisted.

Mithra eyed me up and down. "If I didn't know any better, I might say you have feelings for my brother."

I balled my hands into fists and glared at her. "Even if I did, I'm not stupid enough to think I have any sort of chance with him. Don't worry."

"Good. I like you, truly. But he is a prince and is already betrothed." She turned to Arash. "Let's just get out through the main gates. Find me a scarf and we'll blend in with everyone else."

I'd forgotten about Abudar's fiancé and recalled seeing her the day we'd begun the trials. She was pretty. Probably some form of royalty. Definitely a more worthy companion than *me*.

"Stop there," a voice said firmly behind us.

We all froze and turned to face one of the veiled sorceresses.

Arash stepped in front of Mithra.

"You can't go anywhere like that." She tossed an orange outfit into Arash's chest and then held another toward me.

"Abudar?" Arash asked.

He grinned and somehow his eyes still looked like his—and undoubtedly his smile too, though I couldn't see it under the veil.

Mithra and I hurried to hide our true identities beneath the clothing supplied by Abudar while we continued behind the houses.

"What happened in there?" Arash asked.

Abudar waved his hand dismissively. "I offered to go this way and check behind the houses to see if you had tried to sneak away. They're making their way to the gates though, so we have to run."

And we did. The short distance back to the main gates felt somehow farther than it should have. When we reached the end, Abudar led the way out from behind our hiding spot and into the main road.

I had taken the time to put Igborg back in my father's pack and hide it beneath the provided disguise. I also made sure to keep my distance from Abudar in spite of my heart racing and wanting me to be near him. We had to get back to the palace and everything would return to normal.

As we approached the gates, I held my breath. One wrong look and they might stop and investigate us.

The sorceress to our left nodded her head.

Abudar returned it.

I didn't. I was too nervous.

The woman smiled softly. "You must be new. Welcome and good luck with your tasks."

I nodded mutely.

And then we were out beyond the gates and it took everything in me to not break out in a dead run. I gasped a breath and placed my hand on my thundering heart.

Beyond the gates of Balim was the desert. To our right, the Red Towers. To our left, stone walls that had been shaped by the wind. We headed east between them, toward the palace. I didn't know this side of the desert had such beautiful natural structures, and it was fascinating to see.

We had made it out. Safe. The sorceresses wouldn't find us now.

"I don't suppose Irilibus and his lovely wife gave us any supplies?" Arash asked, turning to me.

I lifted one of the layers of orange and opened my pack. "We have water. And they did provide enough for lunch." I held up rolls. There was also a bundle of dried fish and lamb meat that Igborg was snuggling, and a few other pieces of food which weren't going to last us.

"I think we should hold off eating as long as possible," Mithra said.

I had to agree.

Igborg eventually climbed out and took his normal seat on my shoulder. Abudar dropped the magical façade, but he was stuck in the robes he wore. Luckily, he had a scarf around his face to protect it from the breeze. Arash also had a scarf on his face. I removed the bandage from my head and tried to use it to shield my own mouth from the sand, careful to keep the bloody side of the bandage away from my mouth.

Abudar fell back to walk at my side, even though I tried slowing down so he couldn't. He reached out and scratched under Igborg's chin, his favorite spot. "You're a dragonling, hm?"

Igborg blinked and tilted his head. "Yes."

"But where is your mother?"

He leaned to rub against my cheek. "Here."

"He means your dragon mother, Igborg," I said. "What happened to her? When I found you last year, you were gravely injured. I don't know how a dragonling made it into Zunbar in the first place."

"On a boat." He stepped up onto my shoulder. "Bad men took me. I got out. You found me."

"He must be too young to give more of a story," Abudar said. "But it surprises me that men would try to smuggle such a rare creature."

"Don't you remember last year?" Mithra said. "Your birthday?"

Abudar turned to his sister. "What about my birthday?"

"Mother and Father got you a rare and special gift for your sixteenth birthday." She raised her brows, hinting. Then she rolled her eyes. "It was a baby dragon, Abudar. Igborg was probably supposed to be your birthday gift last year."

He pulled his hand back and looked down at Igborg. "Mother and Father had a dragonling captured for me?"

"Maybe they figured you wouldn't get an animal familiar because you aren't a sorceress," she continued.

Abudar frowned and lifted his gaze to me. "In that case, I'm glad he found his way to you." He offered me an almost apologetic smile.

But it reminded me—I'd missed my birthday. My own sixteenth birthday. The most important celebration of my young life, where I was supposed to have a feast and wear the finest gowns and perform the ceremony that would cross me over into womanhood.

I looked down at my clothing.

I was supposed to wear this outfit to that celebration.

And Father was supposed to be at my side.

"What are you thinking about?" Abudar asked.

I shook my head. "Nothing."

"I'm really tired of all of this traveling," Mithra grumbled. "I can't wait to have a proper feast, a bath I won't leave for an hour, and my own bed."

"Hm. A bed." Abudar grinned.

Our small group left Balim behind and headed out into the open desert. I hoped that we would cross the path of the royal guards who were bound to come for the prince and princess because I, too, was tired of this adventure.

We were all too tired to speak.

Minutes felt like hours. The sun slowly lowered on the horizon. The bandage around my mouth was too thick to be comfortable and I ended up discarding it somewhere behind us.

Finally, Mithra stopped. "I can't walk any farther."

Abudar put his hand over his eyes, but we were too far away to spot the city. "I had hoped we could get closer."

"We don't even know how far away we truly are,"

Arash pointed out. "But we're absolutely too far away to be found."

"And we're being followed by a vulture." Abudar was looking up at the sky.

I followed his gaze and saw the large bird swooping lazy circles overhead. My heart jumped. "That isn't a vulture. Omar!" I called up.

The hawk took a wide turn then dove down for me. I held out my right arm and waited for him. He pulled up short and landed carefully, his strong talons gripping my arm. He leaned his head forward and nudged my chin.

He'd never been overly fond of me, but apparently he'd missed me.

I stroked the feathers on his breast. "What are you doing all the way out here? You're so far from home!"

He tilted his head sharply and blinked at me, then at Igborg.

Igborg had scurried to the shoulder opposite of Omar, but he leaned to watch the hawk with a wary eye.

"You have a hunting hawk?" Abudar asked.

I shook my head. "He's my father's, but sometimes he delivers notes too." I checked the strap around his leg and found a parchment rolled up. With trembling fingers, I took it out, then held it to Abudar. "Unroll it for me, please."

He looked at my shaking hand, but accepted and unrolled it.

I wanted it to be a message from my father. Or Mihrage saying he was on the way with Taraji. Or that the soldiers were coming to collect us. But mostly, I just wanted to know that my father was going to be okay.

"Dune bug, find the griffin feather. *Ana bahibik, ya*

habibti," Abudar read. He looked at me. "Who is this from?"

I took the scroll from him and looked at it over and over. "It's from my father." It was my father's handwriting. He could have written anything, and his only message was to tell me to find the feather necklace he had hidden?

What did this mean?

Twenty-Eight

"I was with him the night Roshanak arrested him," I explained to Abudar, Mithra, and Arash. We had sat down to eat our meager meal and drink our water in some shade we'd managed to find behind a squat tree. The shade was barely enough for one person, so we all sat back to back so at least our faces were shielded.

Abudar had asked about my father. I still hadn't figured out why my father would send me this note. I stared at two words: *ana bahibik*—I love you.

I couldn't help but feel those words were foreboding.

"What's it like?" Mithra suddenly asked. "Being a thief and living on the streets?"

"I don't live on the streets." I ran my thumb over the scroll and finally pushed it into one of my many pockets. "I have a home."

"Where?"

I looked up at Omar perched in the tree, waiting for me to send him away. "No offense, but I don't know that you wouldn't send someone there."

"Do you follow a schedule for when you steal?" Arash asked.

I turned to him. "No. And we only steal when necessary, like when we're running out of food or money, or if we notice there is someone in town who has a great need. Just last week, the blacksmith's daughter fell ill. He isn't one of the most poor, but he used all of their savings on medicine. We provided them with meals so they could eat."

"But that isn't stealing," Arash pointed out.

I lifted my brows. "I know." I rolled up to my knees. "I don't suppose one of you has the magical ability to write without ink?"

Abudar and Mithra simultaneously shook their heads, but it was Abudar who asked why.

"Because I want to send a note to my father. And to your soldiers to let them know where we are." I pursed my lips and pulled the lamp out of my bag and rubbed it.

The jinni appeared, all smiles, but his face scrunched in disappointment as he surveyed our location. "You still haven't made it out of the desert? Shame." His gaze fell on Abudar and he smirked. "At least these skirts are clean."

Abudar rolled his eyes.

"Jinni, do you have a quill and ink?" I asked. "I need to send a note to my father and another to the sultan and sultana." I pointed up to Omar.

The hawk cocked his head left and then right.

The jinni held his hand out and a quill appeared in his palm. I reached out for it, but he closed his hand. "One condition. Where is my little friend?"

I smiled and turned around. "Igborg, the jinni wants to see you."

Igborg crawled out of the bag and hopped up and down excitedly.

"I know you want to use my name, but you're sworn to secrecy," the jinni said. He crouched and picked up

Igborg.

"I know. Caspara will find it," Igborg answered.

The jinni handed me the quill.

I took the blank roll off of Omar's other leg and unrolled it, then knelt in the sand and placed the scroll to my knee to write. *Weh ana bahibak, ya Baba. Are you well?* And then on the opposite side, I wrote, *Tell them we're in the west desert. Need help.* I had to write small to get it to fit, but it worked. I rolled it up and placed it back in Omar's leg pouch.

"Take this to Baba," I said softly.

He ruffled his feathers.

"In the palace, if you can," I added. "If he's still there."

Omar spread his wings and took off into the sky.

I rubbed my collarbone with the tips of my fingers, silently hoping Omar could make it back safely.

"I think we should get going and travel as far as we can in the light," Arash said, climbing to his feet. He reached a hand out to Mithra to help her up.

"We will be lucky to find shade again," I mentioned.

They all looked at the tree and I knew we all felt the same thing. The shade of the tree had been a blessing of relief from the sun. We had no other protection from it but our clothing. But we had to leave it behind and continue across the desert.

I wrapped my scarf around my face and put my pack over my shoulder, then placed the other half of my roll and meat into my pack. I might not need it later, but Igborg definitely would.

"You've been rather quiet since we left Balim," Abudar commented to me as we began to walk.

I shrugged. "I don't have anything to say."

"Is that possible?"

I scowled, but my lips tugged.

He chuckled. "Did I say something, though? To hurt your feelings?"

My smile fell and I shook my head. "No. But don't be daft. Mithra announced you have a *betrothed* waiting for you when you get back."

He grimaced and his amber eyes darkened. "Yes. I'd . . . forgotten."

I snorted. "How do you forget about an engagement?" I turned and walked backwards so I wasn't looking directly at the sun. "It seems to me like I would recall something as significant as marrying someone."

Abudar kept his gaze forward. "Yes."

"You . . . don't like her?"

I thought I saw Mithra glance our way.

Abudar ran his tongue over his bottom lip. "It doesn't matter whether or not I like her. She seems like a lovely person. She's a princess from Kalekai. Our sources tell us that her kingdom was recently recovered after it was taken from her and her sisters when they were children. Since she is the eldest, she is the one who has been sent to form an alliance with our kingdoms."

I didn't understand anything regarding marital politics, or politics in general. "But if she is the eldest, who will rule her kingdom?"

He shook his head. "That was my argument. She needs an earl or nobleman as a husband so she can rule her own kingdom. Our union hasn't been confirmed yet, but I feel that may have changed while we've been gone. Roseline has had a lot of time with my father and mother."

"She sounds manipulative."

"Mm. I don't know if *manipulative* is quite right. She seems to be trying to help her kingdom out. Our wealth combined with her land, and her country will grow in strength."

"How does our country benefit from your union?"

He lifted his hands up in a meager shrug. "Better trading across her land. We excel at trading in the sea. We are the only stop between all three continents. But expanding across land would only benefit us more."

I mulled over the information. I felt trapped in my life as a thief, that I could never move beyond it because I had no magical abilities. I'd spoken with Taraji and Mihrage about it only days ago. But Abudar was the *prince,* and even he was trapped. Trapped in responsibility for his kingdom. I had the choice of who to wed. Was Abudar so lucky?

For some reason, I looked at him under a different light. Behind the careless grin, dimpled cheeks, and heart-stopping eyes was a boy barely older than me who would have to wed for the sake of his kingdom. He was forced to sacrifice his entire life for it.

I looked back at the jinni who, for some reason, had decided to walk with us. Igborg sat on top of his head, eyes closed.

"When we get back to the palace, I would like for you to tell me more about the sentinels," I said to Abudar. "My mind is too exhausted to take in new information right now."

He finally allowed a smile. "Okay. And maybe we can come to an agreement regarding our wish." He nudged his head toward the jinni.

"Abudar . . . if you overheard Roshanak telling me about the vault, you heard her demand the lamp from me." I raised my brows at him. "You might trust Roshanak, but after everything she's done, I don't think I can. So I need the wish to get my father out and keep the lamp away from her."

"I'll figure out a way to get your father out of the prison without using a wish or even giving the lamp to Roshanak," he insisted. "My father is the sultan, remember? He has ultimate power."

"And you can talk to him and get him to set my father free?" I studied Abudar.

He smiled. "After everything you've done for us, yes. And I'll even go with you to speak with Roshanak if you'd like, and if things go sideways I'll take the lamp."

I nodded. "Thank you, Abu. I mean it. I-I'm not used to having . . . people I can trust."

Abudar's dimple appeared again.

It was refreshing to have someone to lean on. Even if it was just for this one thing.

We walked.

And walked.

And walked.

And walked some more.

And then even farther.

And more.

I was shuffling through the sand, head bowed against the blazing light and heat of the sun when Mithra finally asked for us to stop.

"I truly cannot walk another step," she said, breathing hard. "My side is killing me and I'm almost out of water."

Arash looked around as if the landscape might have

changed within the last five seconds. There was no shade about. "It's a shame we don't have blankets for tonight. Or more water for the journey tomorrow." His statement was clearly aimed at the jinni.

I was almost positive the jinni understood too, because they locked eyes. But the jinni only removed Igborg from his head and sat down where he stood.

I shook my head at Arash. "He insists he can only act on a wish."

"You could have wished us back as soon as we were attacked by the octopus," Arash muttered.

"Yes, but I need the lamp to get my father back, and Abudar won't agree to that." I looked at the prince, casting all blame to him with a teasing frown.

Abudar raised his brows and poked my chest. "Don't blame me."

"Don't give me a reason to, tough guy." I leaned in until our noses almost touched. My heart raced.

"Oh, just kiss already!" the jinni said.

Mithra snorted.

I gave him a startled look. He was covering Igborg's eyes and had his back to us. Kiss Abudar? I had to admit, I would have liked that. Even if it was just once. Just to know what it was really like.

Abudar's lip tugged, but he stepped back and sat down before I could say anything to him or make an excuse. He pulled his cloak out and sat on it, then looked out toward the palace. The sun caused the spires to glint in the dimming light.

The jinni raised his brows at me and nudged his head toward Abudar.

I shook my head and sat nearby.

Arash took a drink of his water and lay down on his side so his back was toward the sun and shielded his eyes with his arm.

Mithra lay down behind him and rubbed her hand on his forearm. "I'm grateful you came with me. Imagine me having to be stuck with these two on my own."

He chuckled and rolled to face her. "That would have been tragic."

"How far are we from the palace?" Abudar asked.

"Maybe a few hours?" I said.

"We could keep going after getting some rest," he said.

I lay down on the edge of his cloak, just enough to be off the burning sand.

Abudar glanced at me, then adjusted so he too was lying down. "I hope they held off on the celebration for the closing of the trials. I've been longing for the feast."

I heaved a sigh. "I understand that. I missed my birthday celebration."

"Your birthday?"

"Yes. I turned sixteen." My lips tugged and my chest twinged.

He clicked his tongue. "I'm sorry. That's an important birthday. What do you usually get on your birthday?"

"My best friend Taraji, you met her at the beginning of the trials, makes a love cake." At the thought of it, my mouth watered. "We dance and celebrate. And I was supposed to perform the ritual where I become a woman."

"What is that?" Abudar asked. He folded his arm under his head.

"I wear my best clothing, and scarfs are braided together to create a rope, which is then laid in the sand.

The side opposite me would have vibrant flowers spread out like a carpet. My mother . . .” My voice hitched. I swallowed. “My mother is *supposed* to take my hand, but in my case it would have been Taraji’s mother. She would take my hand and guide me over the rope, which symbolizes my cross from childhood. And then the rest of the night is spent eating and dancing.”

“I thought you said you didn’t like to dance.” Abudar raised his brows.

I laughed. “I never said that. Only that I didn’t want to dance with Prince Abu.”

He grinned.

Our eyes were inches apart. Had he been any other boy, had he even been available, maybe. Maybe we could have kissed.

Twenty-Nine

It's impossible to say if anyone but Igborg slept that night. His little wheezing snores were the only confirmation that he slept soundly, without a care in the world. He didn't have to worry about saving his father, getting the prince and princess home, or what would happen once we got them back.

I held him close, though. Because I didn't ever *want* him to worry about such things. He was a child who needed protecting. I had bound myself to him when I saved him, and I didn't regret it one bit.

Abudar was pressed up to my back, and my embarrassment and hope kept my heart pounding, therefore keeping me warm. I could feel his strong body. And his arm was draped around me—whether intentional or not. It was comfortable.

And I hated it.

Why did life have to be so complicated?

I braved a look over my shoulder. The sky had turned purple in its transition from night to dawn, and the stars stretched out like billions of candles. And when I saw Abudar, with dirt smudged across his face and his hair filthy with sand, I almost gasped because his eyes peered straight into mine.

He rubbed his eyes with the base of his hand and sucked in a breath through his nose. "Couldn't sleep either?" he whispered.

"Not really," I admitted. "I keep thinking about my father. The note from him was vague. He could have told me anything in the world, and he told me to find his griffin feather pendant?" I shook my head. "It doesn't make sense."

"Maybe there's a note hidden with it he needs you to see?" Abudar offered.

It was possible. I rubbed my hand over my face and a shiver ran through me. The desert days were sweltering, but the nights were frigid.

Abudar pulled me closer to him. "Don't worry, I'm only doing this to keep you warm," he said, likely thinking I was going to protest.

I was grateful for the darkness, because maybe he couldn't properly see that I didn't want to pull away. "Abudar . . ."

"Hm?"

I wanted to tell him that he'd been kind to me, and I wanted to thank him for that because he didn't have to be. I wanted to ask him what it would take to see my father. I wanted to know what the laws were regarding royal marriages—though I would never dare ask because I didn't even know him.

What came out was, "In the caves, I saw this old woman."

"That's not what I was expecting." He chuckled a little. "Arash said you did. After you hit your head, right? Some sort of room?" His breath caressed my ear and goosebumps sprang up and down my arm. Abudar misinterpreted them and started rubbing my arm, which drew heat into my belly.

"Y-Yes. She was weaving a rug. What do you think it might have meant?"

"Maybe you saw one of the Fates." He chuckled softly so he wouldn't wake the others.

"Fates?" I looked over at him.

"You've never heard of them?" He propped himself up on his elbow and looked down at me. "Many cultures believe there are three old women who control the lives of humanity."

"Like a goddess?"

He shook his head. "Perhaps? It depends on what you believe in. One woman spins or creates our lives, another weaves them together, and the last decides when we die. Other myths say that they control our past, present, and future."

"Destiny. Fate," I murmured.

"Hm?"

I held my hand out with the tattoo. "Do you feel like our lives are controlled?"

"In more ways than our tattoos," he replied. He slid his right arm down my right arm and our tattoos sparked with a blue light that flickered across our tattoos and disappeared. "What was that?" he gasped.

I sat up and pulled away, then searched my arm. I blinked and turned to Abudar.

He sat up and held his hand out to mine, palm up.

I reached out and placed my palm to his.

He closed his fingers and I closed mine.

A tingling sensation spread from the tips of my fingers up into my arm, shoulder, and then neck. I smelled electricity, like lightning on a summer day, and dust with a hint of cinnamon.

Blue light flowed through our arms and into our markings.

I jerked my arm away and scrambled to my feet. No. I was a thief, not a sentinel meant to save people. Not hand-in-hand with the prince.

"You are my other half." He spoke in a low, fervent voice.

I faced him. "I can't be!" I tried to keep my voice low, but I was panicking. "I'm a thief, Abudar. I live in the eastern desert. The mattress I slept on in Irilibus's home was the first mattress I've ever slept on. I have to steal food when we run out of money."

"So what?" He got to his feet. "Maybe destiny, as you claim, separated us on purpose. Because you can relate to the people I can't and I can relate to those you can't. Our living in different places might help with that as we work together."

"Work together toward what end?" I asked. "Nothing's even wrong right now."

Abudar raised his brows, then pointed his thumb over his shoulder. "The sorceresses we just met?"

"I just . . . can't believe I'm the right one. I can't be. I'm not, I'm not important."

Abudar shook his head. "But you are. You're a sentinel."

"It's a mistake. My mother. Roshanak. She was right. I must be a distraction. I'm sorry I'm not that person you need." I grabbed my pack and Igborg.

"Caspara, please don't." Abudar caught my arm. "You don't have to worry about this right now. We need to get home first and release your father. You just learned Roshanak is your mother, and then your father was arrested. The revelation that you're also a sentinel is too much for you to have to handle right now. And you don't need to." He let go of me. "Learn about your role and then you can choose for yourself if you want to be one with me."

He looked crushed.

His eyes were sad, his brows soft, and his dimple was gone.

I licked my lips and looked down at my feet. "Okay."

"Okay." Abudar sat back down.

I swallowed hard and rubbed my hands on my pants.

"Must you both speak so loudly?" Mithra grumbled.

"Don't pretend you were sleeping," Abudar said. He ran his fingers through his hair, trying to get the sand out.

Mithra heaved a sigh and sat up. "When we get home, the first thing I'm going to do is bathe. And when I'm done bathing, I'm going to ask Father to erect shade from Zunbar to Balim. How else can people travel across the desert without dying?"

"Most people travel with tents," I said. "If we are traveling far, we use camels and have food and water too."

Arash groaned as he sat up. "I could sleep for a week."

"Me too." I rubbed my forehead and brushed my fingers across the stitches.

The sun peeked out and reached across the sand.

"Let's start walking," I said. "We have too much to do to wait any longer."

Abudar shoved his cloak into his own pack and started walking. "Come on."

I wanted to ask a billion questions, but couldn't think

of anything to ask. What Abudar and I had to do was figure out what everything meant. No, *I* had to figure out what being a sentinel meant. But Abudar was right. I had to solve one thing at a time, and first was my father.

"They're coming," Arash suddenly said.

Abudar raised his hand to shield his eyes and looked to the horizon. "I don't see anything. Wait. I spot them now."

We all shifted our attention back to the horizon, and sure enough, horses and camels trudged across the sand at full gallop. Omar led the way to us. Relief washed over me, making the ache in my shoulders and neck dissipate. I saw Abudar's shoulders drop with the same relief.

The first man who reached us called out, "Are any of you in need of medical attention?"

"We are all right, Captain Nadeem," Abudar called back. "Hungry and thirsty. Mithra is the most injured."

Captain Nadeem pulled his horse to a stop and assessed Abudar first. He looked Abudar up and down as though noticing the women's robes, but said nothing. He tilted Abudar's chin back and forth, searching for visible wounds, then demanded to see anything not obvious.

Abudar shook his head. "I've got a cut on my leg and side, but they've been sewn and are healing."

"Good. Princess Mithra, how about you?" Captain Nadeem turned to her.

"A cut on my side from a dragon."

"Dragon?" He glanced at Abudar.

He nodded to confirm it. "We accidentally woke it while we were in the caves."

Captain Nadeem hummed and turned to Arash. "And you?"

"Just a few scratches. Nothing else."

"And you, young lady?" he turned to me.

"Oh, I'm fine. Just a scratch on the head." I pointed.

"What *happened* to you? How did you get lost for so long?" Captain Nadeem went to his pack and returned with food for them to eat. "I expected to find you in worse shape than you are."

"We would have been, had it not been for some luck," Abudar said. "And if you hadn't found us so soon."

"Without the hawk, we wouldn't have." He looked up at the sky.

I held out my hand and Omar circled before landing on it. I stroked his breast. "You did good."

"You know it?" Captain Nadeem asked.

"He belongs to my father. I sent him with a message so you would know where to find us."

His brows dipped and he looked me up and down. "You must be Caspara?"

I nodded. "Yes, sir."

He looked over his shoulder. "Take them all to the palace. Arrest her."

My eyes widened. "What? Why? What did I do?" I gripped my bag.

Abudar stepped forward. "Captain Nadeem, with all due respect, Caspara helped get us out of the cave, and it's because of her the hawk found you. We would have perished in the cave days ago had she not helped. I demand to know why you're arresting her."

I sent Omar away and hid Igborg in my bag.

"My apologies, Your Highness, but it is by decree of Grand Sorceress Roshanak. You may speak with her when we arrive." Captain Nadeem nodded to his men.

They stepped forward, but Abudar blocked them.

"You don't need to bind her," he said in a low voice. "She won't run and she won't fight."

They looked at me and I was too terrified to move.

I clenched my teeth.

"I'll ride with her." Abudar turned to me and placed his hand on my back. "Get on the horse. I'll ride with you." He helped me onto the horse and climbed up behind me. He wrapped his arm around my waist. "I'm sure she only wants to speak to you."

I snorted. "She is arresting me! If she only wanted to talk, I wouldn't be under arrest. She wants the lamp, Abu."

He stiffened behind me.

I looked back at him. "I have to get my father free. Let's just make the wish to get your mother's magic back so I can give the lamp to Roshanak."

"I wouldn't if I were you," he said. "I'll keep the lamp and keep it hidden."

My eyes widened. "You *want* my father to remain in prison?"

"No, I just can't help but feel . . . if Roshanak *wants* the lamp, there's a reason why. I have a feeling in the pit of my stomach that the reason isn't good either."

"But I have to trade this lamp for my father's freedom."

Abudar shook his head. "I'll free him. I swear on my life. And if I can't . . . we'll use the wish."

I reached back and took his hand, my throat too tight to answer him. I faced forward again. For some reason, I believed him.

Thirty

I had never been so relieved to see the gates of Zunbar. As we entered the cobblestone streets, I felt like I could at least breathe again. I was closer to home than I'd been in days. Even if I had to be stuck in the palace, at least Father would finally be free. This nightmare was almost over.

When we stopped, the palace guards stepped toward me. Abudar slid off from the horse first, then placed his hands on my hips and helped me down. It was unnecessary. I'd dismounted horses before, but I was honestly grateful for his help because I was exhausted.

His hands lingered, keeping me close so only I could hear. "Go with the guards. I will speak with my father immediately and get this cleared up. But don't fight and give them a reason to harm you."

"You know me so well," I said sarcastically.

He grinned. "Much better than a few days ago." His hand slid up my arm and I almost pulled away, but then he grabbed the strap of my bag and moved it up onto his shoulder.

"Please keep Igborg safe," I whispered. "He's got to be starving. And will you send word to me if Omar returns? I would like to let my friends know I'm back and safe."

He nodded. "I will. Take care of her," he said to the guards as he stepped back.

I spotted Igborg peeking at me and I winked at him.

Two guards stepped up to flank me and directed me into the palace.

I had never seen such grandeur in my life. The guards walked me down a hallway with painted ceilings, extravagant mosaic tile floors, paintings and tapestries hanging on the walls, and vases and statues positioned on display in little cut-outs in the walls. Everything was overly expensive. A set of windows by the main doors of the palace were made of stained glass. I didn't know windows could look so breathtaking.

I was lost in the allure of the architecture, although I felt a pang of guilt for being so taken in by the wealth. Even the lamps that hung from the ceiling were made of gold and designed to the highest of standards.

To my surprise, they didn't take me down to a dungeon, but up a flight of stairs and to a white door with gold hinges and handles. One of them opened it and revealed the room beyond. Even as a guest room, it was far too big. It had a bed big enough for two people, a cute little chair by the window and a table beside it, a balcony framed by teal curtains, and beautiful pillows in bright colors stacked at the head of the bed. I walked directly to the window and looked over the city below.

It was odd to see the city from this view.

From here, no one could see the truth of the streets. No one could see the chaos of the docks. No one could smell the fish, the rot, or the sewage that was all part of Zunbar. From here, the city was a lie.

There was no question in my mind why Abudar

couldn't believe why I stole. From this perspective, the world was in order.

"Roshanak will be up soon," one of the guards stated. "A servant will follow with food and, I imagine, a bath." He and his companion stepped out of the room and closed the door behind them.

Somewhere in these walls was my father.

Somewhere was also my mother.

I ran my hand over my face.

Abudar was going to speak with his father, my father would be freed, and then he would get the wish that he wanted, I would go back to being a thief, Abudar would go back to being the prince, and to the rest of the world it would be as if nothing had happened in the caves. The world had turned while the four of us were gone, why should it stop now?

There was a knock on the door before it opened and Roshanak entered. Her violet gown touched the floor and was decorated with black designs and golden stitching. Her presence prompted me to straighten my spine and keep my hands at my sides, fearing that withholding such respect would result in some repercussion I couldn't anticipate.

She offered me a delicate smile. "Princess Mithra and Prince Abudar claim that you helped get them out of the cave. They even say you saved them."

I kept my eyes locked on her. "I did. And I demand to know about my father's well-being."

"You were gone so long, we feared you dead," she said.

I raised my brow. "My father might have, but not anyone else."

"I did," she insisted.

I balled my hands into fists. "You're avoiding my question."

Roshanak crossed to the bed and sat on it. "I know you have a lot of questions, Caspara. The biggest question you have is why your father took you and left."

It wasn't. My biggest question in that moment was whether or not she'd release my father, as per our bargain.

But she continued. "I loved you with all my heart. There was so much happening with the sorceresses back then. Kasim took you to keep you safe, but he was supposed to bring you back when I knew it was safe. He didn't do that. He argued that you shouldn't be raised in the palace, that you should be raised like he was."

I folded my arms across my chest. Father had mentioned on many occasions that he was proud of how he was raised. He showed me the house where he grew up, took me to the beach they used to swim at, and introduced me to people his family knew. But it didn't make sense that my father, the man who vowed to protect me from any danger in the world, would *choose* to keep me hidden from my mother unless she was dangerous in some way.

Roshanak placed her hands in her lap. "I don't expect you to believe me right away. We've only just met. But I can help you. By now, you've likely learned that you're a sentinel, and Abudar is as well?"

By not answering, I answered her.

She patted the spot beside her on the couch. "You are no prisoner of mine, Caspara. You can wash up and I will bring you some food to eat. Then you can rest and recover from your—"

"I want to speak with my father," I insisted.

"What?" She blinked, somehow surprised.

I straightened my spine. "I demand to speak with my father. Where is he?"

Roshanak's smile returned. "Of course you wish to see him. First, let's get you washed up. He wouldn't want to see you in such a state as this."

"He wouldn't care. What are you hiding from me?"

"Caspara, darling—"

"I'm *not* your darling," I snapped and held my ground. "You can do what you wish with me, but I demand you let him go."

"And where is the lamp you agreed to bring me?" she countered.

"Show me my father first and then I'll give it to you." She didn't need to know I didn't have it. Not until Father was out of her grip.

Roshanak heaved a sigh that caused her shoulders to rise and fall dramatically and then she stood. "I am afraid that—in spite of me being the grand sorceress—I have no control over what happens to the prisoners in this land. That is up to the sultan. Your father has held many secrets from you. He clearly never told you about the magic lamp. Did he ever tell you how he lost favor with the sultana?"

Lost favor?

My brows furrowed. Father said they'd drifted apart after she was married because they were from different worlds—like me and Abudar.

"Where. Is. My. Father?" I demanded, bringing her back to my question. "Tell me now, or I'm walking out of here and you'll never see me again. Sentinel or not. And I'll take the rusty old lamp with me."

She interlocked her fingers in front of her. "I'm sorry,

Caspara. But he is gone."

My breath hitched. "G-Gone? What do you mean?"

"He was executed." Her lips kept moving, but I couldn't hear anything else.

Executed.

He was executed.

The palace room faded away. My knees hit the ground, sending shockwaves up my legs, but the real pain exploded from my heart.

I couldn't breathe. I couldn't see. I couldn't think.

I visualized my father's face the last time I'd seen him, when he had started to tell me the truth about my mother. He'd written the note calling me "dune bug" and telling me he loved me because . . . because he knew. He knew that he would never see me again.

My throat burned with my sobs.

I never should have found the information about that snake. I never should have asked him to come with me. It was *my* fault he had been taken, and now my fault he was dead.

Gone forever.

I would no longer be able to laugh with my father. Tell funny stories. Make shadows with our hands in the firelight. He would no longer kiss my cheek with his prickly beard. I wished the ground would swallow me up like the sands had at the beginning of the Desert Trials. Only, I didn't want to return.

What did I have to live for now?

My body shook with my sobs. It ached from them. But I couldn't stop as every memory flooded into my mind.

I felt a hand on my shoulder and heard Roshanak say, "There is a bath prepared for you in the room through that doorway. Go soak. I'll send for food and then we can talk."

She left me alone.

Alone with my grief.

I didn't know how long I'd been on the floor, but my tears had dried and I had curled up in a ball. My ribs ached from crying so hard and my throat felt raw. *Get up and wash. You'll feel better.*

But I stared at the flipped-up corner of the rug.

I wanted Igborg. Taraji. Mihrage. My own room in my own bed with my blankets and the trinkets I'd collected with my father over the years. I wanted to go back in time and erase everything that had happened.

Eventually, I found myself on my feet shuffling to the room Roshanak had mentioned. I found a big tub filled with water. It smelled like lavender and jasmine. I stripped and slid into it, then scrubbed all of the dirt and grime from my body from the last several days. I even washed my hair twice.

And then I remembered the time Father would spend collecting and warming water for my bath and the special wooden fish he'd carved that would float.

And I was a puddle of tears once again.

I somehow managed to pull myself out of the bath and grabbed a towel to dry off. I found the long white cotton gown I assumed was a nightgown and pulled it on. Without the energy to do anything else, I wrapped my hair up in a towel and went to collapse on the bed.

But there was a knock on my door.

I let out a shaky breath and pulled the door open, anticipating a servant with food. I did *not* expect to see the prince standing on the other side. I only came to my senses when I noticed Abudar's eyes drift down and back up.

Igborg sat on his shoulder. His whole body waggled when he saw me and he jumped when I reached out for him. "Caspara," he squealed.

"I wanted to talk to you," Abudar said. He shifted uncomfortably. Finally, he met my gaze. "It's about your father." His eyes were sad, and his proud shoulders drooped.

I bit my bottom lip and curled my arms around Igborg. "I-I know. Roshanak told me," I whispered. "You promised! You swore to me that you would help him." My voice cracked and tears streamed down my cheeks once again.

"I did everything I promised I would do," he said softly. He took a step to close the gap between us. "I wish I could take this from you. I can't . . ." He stopped talking and pulled me against his chest.

"Did I hear the word *wish*?" The jinni appeared in the room.

Abudar shook his head and gave the jinni a stern look, making the creature's grin drop.

I should have pulled away from him. But I couldn't hold myself up while tears streamed down my face and pain I'd never felt before coursed through me.

Abudar held me. He rested his cheek on top of my head while I pressed my forehead into his sternum and sobbed. His strong arms held me up. And then he slowly pulled me to the bed.

He picked me up and laid me down. "You need rest."

I reached out and snatched the sleeve of his tunic. He wore a simple white shirt, apparently also ready for bed.

"What is it, Caspara?" Abudar asked. He reached out

and wiped some tears from my cheek.

"Nothing." I dropped my hand.

Abudar sat on the bed. "I don't want you to be alone right now. No one should be alone through grief such as this. I can sleep on the floor."

"Are you kidding? This bed is . . ." I shook my head and rubbed my eye. "My head is aching. You should go."

Abudar rose and I thought he would leave and go to his own room. Instead, he walked around the bed and climbed into it behind me.

I looked over my shoulder and saw he was lying on his back, hands resting on his stomach.

"You really don't have to stay," I whispered.

Igborg climbed over me and curled up between me and Abudar.

Abudar rolled onto his side and stroked his fingertips over Igborg's spikes. "You're wrong, Caspara. I need to stay. Because you need me."

I smiled weakly. "I don't need *you*."

"Course not." Abudar closed his eyes and said, "*Mushtaeil.*" The candles and torches went out, casting us in darkness.

I reached out and touched Abudar's hand. He closed his fingers around mine.

Thirty-One

"I'll always be with you, dune bug. All I want is for you to be happy. Be whoever you want. Find something to believe in and pursue it. Ana bahibak."

I was rudely dragged away from pleasant dreams of my father by an annoying knock on the door. When I peeled open my eyes, I was in the palace, on the softest thing I'd ever slept on and . . . Abudar grumbled beside me.

My heart jumped and I looked over.

He had shifted at the noise of the knock, and I'd completely forgotten he was there.

Sunlight peeked in through the curtains and spilled across him. His shirt was raised, showing the wound on his side from the caves. It was healing well. But my eyes drifted to his stomach. I shamelessly took in his muscled form before looking up at his face.

His black hair was a mess from sleeping, but he had cleaned up well from our desert escapade.

I had despised him for so long because he was rich and did nothing to help his people and I felt he flaunted his looks. But he'd been kind enough to stay with me when he probably shouldn't have, and done so much more for me. Not even my mother had stayed by my side.

Another knock, louder this time, and one of Abudar's eyes opened.

I sat up and stretched with a groan of protest. "I could sleep all day," I mumbled. I got to my feet and headed for the door.

"Wait!" Abudar whispered.

I turned to see him scrambling out of my bed. He ran his fingers through his hair while he walked to the bathing room to hide.

At the doorway, he paused and cleared his throat. "I shouldn't be here." And then he disappeared around the corner.

I opened the door and a servant stood with a tray of food enough to feed probably three people. Which was good, because Igborg needed to eat.

I stepped back, holding the door open. "Good morning."

She bowed her head. "Good morning to you as well." She crossed to the table by the window and set the tray down. "I am supposed to ask if you have seen Prince Abudar since you arrived?"

I shook my head. "The guards brought me straight here and I haven't left my room."

"If he stops by, will you tell him that his family is sitting at breakfast and would like him to join them?"

"Of course." I gave her a smile.

She curtseyed, then stopped at my bed and started making it.

"Oh, I can do that," I said. "It's not hard."

"It's my duty," she insisted.

Deciding it was better not to argue, even though Abudar hid in the next room, I sat on one of the seats and poured myself a cup of coffee because it smelled amazing.

Igborg hopped up on the chair beside me and then up onto the table.

The servant shrieked and backed up. "Hurry, lady! There's a lizard!"

"He's mine. It's all right. He's my friend." I reached out and picked him up. "See? His name is Igborg."

The woman eyed him and then me. "What a strange name."

"He is a strange little lizard." I grinned and brought him to my lips to kiss his head, then set him back on the table and gave him a plate with fruit and some of the lamb.

She opened her mouth to ask another question or say something, but chose not to, and finished making the bed by piling the ridiculous amount of pillows back on it. She told me to have a good day and finally left.

Abudar exited the bathroom. He must have taken the time to organize himself, because his hair was smoothed down and his clothes righted. "They're having quite the feast this morning." He dipped his eyes toward my tray of food. "Must be in celebration of us returning home. I should invite you to come with me." He shoved his hands into his pockets.

I gestured to my nightgown. "This is not what one should wear when meeting the sultan and sultana."

He laughed. "I suppose not. I'll have a servant bring you some clothes. I imagine Mithra won't miss any from her closet."

"Oh, don't give me her clothes. The last thing I want to do is give her a reason to despise me more than she already does." I sipped the coffee and closed my eyes. I had never tasted anything so delicious.

"She's not that bad."

"She hates you."

He lifted a shoulder in a shrug. "I think it's more envy than hatred. She's been a bit moody lately. I think it was in anticipation of the trials. Hopefully she'll calm down now that they're over."

The conversation between us paused.

I set my coffee down and ran my fingers through the tangles in my long hair and watched Igborg devour a piece of melon. I lifted my gaze to Abudar. "Your family is waiting," I reminded.

"Right." He blinked and sighed before taking his hands out of his pockets. "I'll be back sometime today, when I get the chance. Unless you need me before then. Just ask a servant."

"I would like to visit my father's body," I said softly.

Abudar nodded. "I'll make arrangements for you."

"Abu?"

He grinned enough to show his dimple. "I think I'm growing fond of that nickname."

My cheeks flushed. "Thank you for staying with me last night."

"No one should grieve alone." He bowed at the waist, the first proper princely thing he'd done since we met, and then he left me alone to finish my breakfast.

My mind felt numb while I ate. I had so many things to think of and no desire to do so. My head ached from the fog of crying—and from the wound. I needed to have Baba sent home to be washed and prepared for burial, I needed to find out *why* he had been executed, figure out what to do with the lamp, and what to do about Roshanak.

She had sent me to find the lamp, and my father was

executed before I could return it. Even if I had returned with the lamp and given it to her, he would still be gone. It didn't make sense to me.

A servant brought a black gown for me to wear and I put it on, then asked her to send for Roshanak or one of the royal family, because I needed to take care of things. I must have dozed off in the chair, because I woke when my door opened.

Roshanak paused and smiled. "I didn't mean to wake you."

"I wish to see my father and have him sent home for burial. Please."

Igborg was curled up in my lap, still sleeping and snoring slightly.

"He has already been sent home," she said. To my surprise, she too was in black and she knelt by the chair at my side. "He passed a few days ago."

"I missed his funeral too?" My voice struggled to get out.

Roshanak reached out and grasped my hand. "I will take you to visit him later today."

"Why would you allow for this to happen? You and I had an arrangement!" My voice found its volume and I pulled away and stood, taking Igborg with me. I set him on my bed and wheeled to face my mother. "You wanted me to return with the lamp, but he was executed *before* I even had a chance!"

"Caspara, lower your voice."

I raised my brows. "Lower my voice? Because you're embarrassed that I'm angry with you? I have every right to be. You broke your end of the bargain."

"You didn't uphold your end either. You didn't return

with the lamp." She rose to her feet. "Or did you?" There was a glint in her eye that demanded an answer I wouldn't give.

I narrowed my eyes. "You can search this entire room and you'll find I don't have it. If I did, I would wish for you to disappear from my life."

Roshanak blanched.

Even I was a bit surprised the thought had left my mouth.

She folded her hands together. "You're in pain. I understand. Perhaps you will feel better if I take you to the library and we discuss what being a sentinel means?"

"Do you *really* think that's what I want right now?"

"I think it would be wise of you."

I clenched my teeth. "If I go with you, will you let me go home after? And don't you dare say I'm home now."

Roshanak let out a calculated breath and nodded. "Yes."

I grabbed Igborg. "Then I'll follow."

I didn't want the distraction, but perhaps more questions would be answered. More importantly, I hoped I would be able to find one of the palace exits so the next time I was alone, I could slip out. Because I didn't trust that Roshanak would honor our deal. She'd already proven she couldn't be trusted.

Roshanak silently led me through the halls and down two sets of stairs until we reached the main floor. She opened a set of blue doors and revealed a beautiful library.

I'd seen books. I had five of them at home. But there were hundreds packed on shelves in this library. Roshanak went to one of the tables, which was already covered in books and parchments, carefully organized, and gestured to one of the seats.

I set Igborg on the floor. "Don't eat anything," I warned.

He blinked at me and looked around, then started meandering around and sniffing things.

I sat on a purple cushion.

"To be a sentinel is to be a protector," Roshanak began. "Ages ago, before sultans ruled the land, back when people wandered from place to place, when jinn roamed free and gods lived with mortals, there was relative peace. There are stories of one jinni who upset the balance. He was mischievous and a trickster, a being never true to his word and always willing to worm his way out of a bargain." She pushed some papers toward me, drawings of a dark-skinned being with gold dots that looked very similar to *my* jinni.

"Did he have a name?" I asked. I didn't want to show interest, I barely wanted to even speak with her, but I had to know.

Roshanak nodded. "Every jinni does. But they will never tell you their name if asked. It must be learned. This particular jinni was Taylin. We know because it is written here." She pointed to the slanted writing at the edge of the page. "I have searched for years to discover his name."

"Who is Nahir?" I pointed to another name in the text.

"The only woman he loved." She turned a few pages to a drawing of a woman. "Nahir sought help for her tribe and was willing to do anything to help them. Even if it meant making a wish to Taylin. As a cruel joke, Taylin enslaved her for as many years as there were people in her tribe—one hundred and fifty-three. But as cunning as Taylin was, Nahir was beautiful. The jinni fell in love with her, and she in love with him."

Had my jinni done that? Was my jinni Taylin?

Roshanak continued. "But performing magic in this way comes at a cost. Hearing of a jinni willing to grant wishes, the mortals had begun to seek out Taylin. The trickster was a master of granting their wishes in ways they didn't expect. A woman who wanted to be separated from her husband was turned into an ass. A man who wanted a lover's hand was turned into the ring she wore upon her finger. One day, Taylin granted the wrong wish to the wrong person." She turned more pages and showed me a drawing of a faceless man.

"No one knew who it was?" I asked.

"There is still debate on whether Taylin banished the gods himself, or if he caused such unrest the gods left of their own free will. Either way, the gods have never been seen on this earth since. No one knows if this man was one of the gods. But whoever it was, they exacted revenge against the disloyal jinni. He enslaved Taylin, as Taylin had enslaved Nahir." She pointed to the image of a lamp that looked exactly like the one from the vault.

Taylin *was* my jinni. He was the jinni trapped in the lamp. Roshanak wanted the magic lamp because she wanted the jinni. She wanted Taylin.

And I needed to know why.

Licking my lips, I relaxed the way I sat and leaned forward to act more interested. "But what happened with Nahir?" I asked, staying on the topic and not daring to stray for fear Roshanak would pick up on my plot.

Roshanak sighed. "When granted her freedom, Nahir was distraught because she could no longer be with the man she loved. Taylin was bound to the lamp, and the lamp was hidden. She pleaded to be left to weep tears forever, which is why the river that cuts through Sheblom is called Dumue."

I shook my head. "That is tragic. Why have I never heard this story?"

"Because most people don't have the knowledge of books." She gestured to the room. "Not only that, but after this happened, mortals raged battles against each other. Some tribes were destroyed. Others banded together and created kingdoms. Taylin was forgotten. Until a man found him and made a wish for the power to bring peace to the land. In response, Taylin thought he would be clever and fractured the power into two separate people. If the man, Tulum, could find his other half, together they could calm the raging battles and bring peace once more."

I felt a tingle prickle up my arm and glanced down at it.

From the corner of my vision, I saw Roshanak nod. "You're right. Your tattoo. Tulum finally found his other half in the form of a young, blind woman named Telama."

My heart jumped and I looked at her. "I know that name. Father said she is the one who gave me the blessing that gave me this tattoo."

Roshanak nodded. "He was right. I'm glad he told you that. Because together, Telama and Tulum calmed sultans and kings, brought prosperity to the land, and even furthered our knowledge. They called themselves sentinels. Like you and Abudar are now."

It all strangely made sense. If I hadn't already met Taylin, I wouldn't have believed most of it. Even if it still sounded more like legend than truth, my arm had tingled and confirmed to me at least part of what she said was true.

"Things in our land . . . seem to be relatively peaceful," I pointed out. "Even though there are typical struggles with the poor, the only major problem is with The Veil. But even then, what harm have they truly caused?"

Roshanak shook her head. "Nothing serious yet, thankfully. But I believe we are sometimes granted the gift of being able to foresee our futures and given an opportunity to calm it before we reach our tipping point. I'm afraid that, even with the knowledge of who you and Abudar are, the storm still rages. I have overheard that The Veil plan to take all of the sorceresses to their hideout, regardless of whether or not the sorceress wishes to join their side. They hope to convert all of them to their cause."

I had seen that first-hand when me and Mithra had been dragged away. "Mithra met with their leader, Shorix. She told us that you lied but wouldn't tell me anything further because I have no magic." I looked away, feeling ashamed when I shouldn't because I was before the most powerful woman in Sheblom.

She reached out and took my hand and traced her finger over one of the tattoos on the back. "Caspara, I am embarrassed to admit I thought I was the cause of you having no magic. I was afraid I had punished my daughter or cursed her. At that time, those years ago . . . your father took you from me because I was unstable." She lifted her eyes to meet mine.

"This isn't what you told me before," I said, a bit of an edge to my voice.

"I was embarrassed to tell you the truth. But I see now what an incredible woman you've become. Back then, I couldn't handle the thought that my beautiful little girl would never know the feeling of magic, never know what it was like to learn spells, to feel that power grow within her. I selfishly pushed you away."

Tears stung my eyes. "You threw me away because I didn't have magic?"

"No, no. I didn't throw you away. I thought you didn't have magic *because* of me. I didn't know if I had done something wrong while I was pregnant with you." She sighed. "It is hopeless trying to explain it now when I can see so clearly the woman you've become. But I would like you to stay in the palace with me now. Living here is much easier than it is on the streets. You won't have to steal to survive, you won't have to go without a meal, you will have a bed to sleep on, and your little lizard can stay with you and have all the food he wants too." Roshanak looked over at Igborg, who had climbed up on top of a pillow on the couch and was spinning in a circle before lying down.

I pulled my hand away from her touch and set it in my lap. I looked down at the papers and recalled my father's voice from my dream urging me to find a cause and fight for it. Maybe my mother was right. Maybe she had wanted the lamp all along to find a way to help our people because she didn't know if Abudar and I would be able to. Perhaps . . . I might actually have something to fight for with Roshanak. And there might have been truth to her statement that she had nothing to personally do with my father's execution, but it was all the responsibility of the sultan. I could be placing blame on the wrong person.

"I might not have magic, but I have other skills. Can I be trained to use those?" I lifted my gaze to her.

She smiled. "Yes. Arash and Captain Nadeem can help

facilitate your training."

"And Prince Abudar?"

Roshanak's brows lifted and a smile slowly appeared on her lips. "I had a feeling you two were fond of each other."

"It's not *that*. He's got to be just as well trained as Arash, and . . ." I couldn't hide my blush and cleared my throat. "I just thought he might help. Especially if we're supposed to work together."

"He has other responsibilities too, I'm afraid."

I rubbed my hands on my lap.

Roshanak gathered the parchments together and tapped them against the table. "Would you like to begin training now or do you need time to absorb this?"

I looked at the drawing of Taylin. I understood *how* the sentinels came to be. I didn't know *what* they were, though. Guardians? Okay. But how were *we* supposed to contend with The Veil? "I'd like to talk with Abudar about this. I think we have a lot to figure out together."

"In the meantime—" Roshanak started.

The library doors opened and Mithra entered, followed by the young woman I'd spotted the first day of the Desert Trials. Abudar's *betrothed*.

Roshanak stood. "I think it might be good for all of you young ladies to spend some time together. I'll see you at dinner," she said to Mithra as she exited.

Mithra turned to me. "It's true, then? Roshanak is your mother?"

"You didn't believe me?"

Mithra's brow raised, a silent acknowledgement that she hadn't.

"You must be Caspara. I'm Roseline." The girl

stepped forward and held her hand out to me. She had golden hair, almost white, and big blue eyes. I hadn't realized just how beautiful she was. Her skin was porcelain, but she had little freckles over her nose and down across her cheeks. She was far more beautiful than me.

"Yes." I awkwardly shook her hand. "And you are the fiancée of Prince Abudar."

She spread her lips into a smile, but it surprisingly didn't reach her eyes. "Yes, I am. He's supposed to announce it tomorrow at the celebration."

I bit my bottom lip. And there it was. My truth. Everything I knew and feared. Survival versus reality. My head twinged and I brushed my fingers over the wound on my head. "I suppose I should congratulate you."

"I am happy for it." Again, Roseline smiled. Again, it didn't reach her eyes. She walked to one of the many bookshelves and removed a book, then sat down and began to read it.

"It looks as though Roshanak told you of the sentinels?" Mithra's eyes darted to the table, then my arm, and back up to my eyes. "Does this mean we'll be seeing more of you?"

I nodded slowly. "I guess."

"You'll like being here. Come find a book and read." She found her own book and took a seat, then patted a cushion nearby.

Was this what it was like to live in the palace? Do nothing but read?

I glanced at Igborg.

Would that be so bad?

Thirty-Two

I spent much of the afternoon reviewing the parchments and pages Roshanak left behind and learned that there had been six sets of sentinels before Abudar and myself. We were the seventh pair. There was significance of the number seven, and I understood Roshanak's insistence on recovering me.

In Sheblom, seven was a holy number. We didn't work the seventh day, the seventh child was always held to the highest standards, we wore our wedding ring on our seventh finger, and so forth.

Igborg hopped up on the table and sat down right on my hand, which was holding one of the books open.

I blinked and rubbed my eye with my available hand. "What?"

"I am hungry."

I looked around the empty room.

Mithra and Roseline had left long ago. Mithra had tasks to attend to and Roseline must have thought me dreary company in my black clothing. We'd been given tea and finger sandwiches sometime around lunch, but now it was late in the day and definitely time for dinner.

"I am a bit hungry myself," I confessed and stood. I picked Igborg up and set him on my shoulder. I was halfway to the door when it swung open and a man stood in the doorway.

"Ah, Madame Caspara, Grand Sorceress Roshanak has requested your presence at dinner."

I raised a brow. "Dinner with the royal family or only her?"

"Only her. Follow me, please." He headed down the hallway and I followed.

The smell of the royal dinner permeated the air and I couldn't resist stealing a glance through the open doors into the dining room as I passed. The servants were just finishing up setting out the dinnerware—two plates stacked on top of each other, too many forks and spoons to know what to do with, and two different sizes of cups.

I was led through a side door and out onto a patio in a section of gardens I didn't realize the palace had.

Roshanak sat at a table with one chair across from her, sipping from a teacup. "You look like you've had a long day. Sit and have some tea. It will help with your head." She set her cup down and poured another glass for me.

I took my seat and laid Igborg down on the table.

Roshanak's eyes drifted over to him. "I saw Abudar walking with it yesterday. I didn't realize it was yours. A companion you picked up in the desert?"

"Yes. He's . . . all I have. Sometimes." I picked up the tea and held it in both hands. It was cool enough I could touch the glass without it burning and closed my eyes. "Are we going after dinner?"

"Going where?"

I opened my eyes and locked them on her. "To visit my father."

"Oh. Yes, I forgot we had agreed to do that. Mithra

and I had a very busy afternoon." Roshanak put on a polished smile and leaned back for the servant to put the food down on the table.

My heart twinged and my stomach sank while my eyes narrowed. It was the same warning sensation I got when people lied. Taraji used to joke that this sense was a magical power of mine. It wasn't a power, it was instinct.

I kept my gaze locked on her eyes. "You had no intention of taking me. That's why you left me alone in the library all afternoon."

She shook her head. "I told you, I had tr—"

"I know what you said." I set my tea down and grabbed Igborg right as he sank his claws into one of the rolls.

He squeaked and somehow managed to lift his back legs and secure it as I lifted him from the table and stood. I set my other hand beneath him to hold him and the roll so he didn't drop it.

"Where are you going?" Roshanak stood. "Caspara, I will take you after dinner."

But how could I believe her?

I was already back inside the palace before she could finish her sentence. I stormed down the hallway, not bothering to look at the dining room this time because I could hear conversation and had no desire to see Abudar sitting beside Roseline, even though I was a bit curious to see the sultan and sultana up close.

Once clear of the dining room, I ran out the front door and through the courtyard, down the path leading to the front gates, and demanded the guards at the gate allow me to leave.

They exchanged glances and then looked at the palace.

"We haven't been given permission, young lady," one said.

"I don't care. You can't make me stay, I'm not a prisoner!" I snapped.

The other guard heaved a sigh. "I know, but our duty is to make sure your life isn't at risk."

I narrowed my eyes and wished I had gone back to my room to grab my father's pouch, because I was going to climb out of there. I put Igborg on my shoulder and stormed to the wall and tried scaling it, but the confounded dress made it difficult for me to put my feet where they needed to go.

"What are you doing? Come down! You'll fall!"

And I did. Luckily, it wasn't far, but I landed on the same ankle I had hurt in the caves. It cramped and I fell to the ground.

"Are you mad?" the first soldier accused, dropping to his knees at my side.

"I climb all the time." I got to my feet, but he grasped my arm and started pulling me back to the palace. "What are you doing? I demand you let me go!"

"I'm under strict orders that you're not allowed to leave the palace grounds."

I tried to drag him back, but he held fast.

He shook his head. "Please don't make me fight you. Things will be easier for you if you obey the rules."

"I've got her from here."

We both looked to see Abudar approaching us, leading a horse by the reins. He still had a bit of a limp in his gait and seemed to be almost using the horse to support him.

I blinked. I hadn't anticipated *him*.

Abudar stopped at the edge of the path and motioned

for me. "You'll get there a lot faster on horseback. I'll take her," he said to the guard.

The man reluctantly released me. "It's not going to be my neck on the line."

"I'll tell Roshanak myself." Abudar stepped up to my side.

It would have been a lot more dramatic if I had jumped on, Abudar behind me, and we rode off into the sunset. But the confounded dress didn't allow me to straddle the horse the way I knew how, and I ended up tearing the seam on the right side. I grabbed the edges of the hole and tore it the rest of the way down, creating a slit that went up to my thigh.

Finally, I managed to get onto the horse and smoothed my hair. "I'm ready."

Abudar was smiling his crooked, closed-mouth grin, his dimple mocking me at the humiliating moment I'd just endured. But he said nothing and straddled the horse behind me. "I'll bring her back," he vowed.

Not willing to argue with their prince, the guards opened the gates and we exited.

Being back on the familiar street was comforting. A few of the merchants were collapsing the curtains around their stalls or carrying their wares back into their homes. A handful of children giggled as they chased a ball down the hill. An elderly couple with graying hair sat on a bench. The old lady placed her head on her husband's shoulder. The noise of the docks echoed to us.

I finally glanced over my shoulder at Abudar. "What made you bring a horse out to me?"

"I saw you walk past the dining hall. I knew Roshanak wanted you to eat with her, so when you marched by, I realized something must have happened. Mithra mentioned Roshanak told you she would take you to your father's grave and hadn't, so I figured that's where you were headed. I grabbed my favorite horse." He shrugged. "I also knew the guards had been told not to let you leave. My father and mother want you and me to begin training together and find out what it means to be sentinels."

"They think I'm so unstable that I need a babysitter?" I scowled.

He laughed. "Not at all. I might have told them you're a bit feisty." He moved his hand from his leg to mine in a teasing way. Or, at least that's how I hoped he meant it.

"Abudar." I grabbed his hand and put it back on his leg. "I only left because she promised. All I wanted was to see him." An unbidden lump seized my voice and unwanted tears prickled my eyes. I was so tired of crying.

"She shouldn't have made such a promise and not upheld her end." He wrapped his arms around me.

I should have pulled away or told him we shouldn't be seen like this because he had Roseline, but just for a moment I embraced his warmth.

And then he lowered his hands because he must have felt the same way.

I wiped my tears aside and we entered the desert.

Abudar nudged the horse into a trot and we arrived in half the amount of time it would have taken us to walk to the home of the thieves.

I spotted the familiar dune that hid our village and cleared my throat. "This is close enough. I can walk from here."

"I said I was taking you."

"Yes, but . . ."

"But what?"

I glanced over my shoulder at him. "You're the future sultan of Sheblom and I'm taking you to the den of the forty thieves. How do I know you won't turn around and attack them?"

Abudar looked hurt. "Why would I do such a thing? You're putting your trust in me, and I am in you. We're allies now."

I wasn't so sure, but returned my attention forward. "It's just around the dune. Where the light is coming from."

"I can't believe you live this far away from the city."

"We can't risk getting caught."

We rounded the corner of the sand dune and my heart swelled. Everyone in my village wore black and were gathered in our little square. They had food out and candles burning on my doorstep with colored sand decorating it in mourning.

I reached out and gripped Abudar's hand that was holding the reins, then jumped off the horse and sprinted toward my people. My family.

Mihrage took off running toward me. I spotted him by the well, and he must have had one of his premonitions that it was me before I entered the light. "Caspara!" he announced to everyone.

I slammed into his chest and he enveloped me in his arms.

Taraji was at our side in an instant and wormed her arms around my waist and gripped me with just as much intensity.

I broke into sobs as my emotions washed over me— relief at seeing my friends, happiness that Taraji had made it out of the trials, comfort seeing the thieves all mourning for my father, and reprieve that I was home.

I had foolishly thought I was alone, but I wasn't.

I always had the thieves.

"Who is that?" someone asked.

I turned to see Abudar surrounded by men. I dried my cheeks and let go of Mihrage and Taraji and hurried over to him. "This is my friend." I put my hand on Abudar's back.

"He's got some nice jewelry," one of the shadows said. It sounded like Babkak.

I realized for the first time that Abudar had a small golden ring in his left nostril. "We all wear jewelry," I stated.

"What's his name?" I saw the firelight flicker across Farhad's face.

Abudar cut me off before I could make something up. "My name is Abudar."

"The prince?"

The crowd murmured.

I took Abudar's hand, gave it a reassuring squeeze, and then directed him to follow me into the square.

Abudar stood confidently, shoulders squared, spine straight. He was a different version of Abudar. One I hadn't met yet. This must have been his prince side, trained and poised. He nodded politely to those staring.

I turned him to face Farhad, now lit by the flames. "This is our leader."

Farhad's eyes flashed and he drew me away from Abudar's side. "What is he doing here?" he scolded. "You're giving our identities and the safety of our location to the prince?"

"He's not going to harm us," I objected.

"His father killed yours. Do you not feel that's reason enough not to trust him?"

I placed my hand on his shoulder. "Farhad, I've spent the last week with him. We helped each other through the Dragon's Lair, he helped me when I got injured, and he's the one who brought me here when no one else in the palace would. Not even Roshanak."

"You've been with your mother?"

I nodded. "Only today. We just arrived back from the desert last night."

Farhad glanced back at Abudar, who was watching me from the corner of his eyes. "You trust him?" he asked after a long moment of scrutinization.

"I never thought I would say this, but yes. With my life."

He nodded. "That's good enough for me. I'll invite him to join our feast."

"Don't scare him too much." I offered him a smile.

Farhad rolled his eyes, but a smile played on his lips. He left me and approached Abudar. He leaned close so their noses nearly touched.

I saw Abudar bristle, but he didn't move otherwise.

"If you tell anyone our location, prince or not, we will be obligated to end your life and theirs so our location remains hidden."

"Understood, sir."

Farhad looked him up and down, then sneered. "Good. Now." He straightened and a grin spread across his face. "Let's celebrate the return of our Caspara!"

Everyone cheered.

As though nothing had happened, music broke out.

Children ran up to Abudar to meet him, then the women in our village shook his hand and introduced themselves and their families. The men were last. Abudar seemed to relax the more people spoke with him, then two of the most elderly women took him by the hands and dragged him to one of the tables overflowing with food.

Aunt Jade appeared from the crowd and pulled me into her embrace. "It is so good to see you."

"I'm so sorry," I said, my voice cracking.

She held me out at arm's length. "For what? Caspara, you did nothing but try and help your father. You didn't fail him. You never could." She wiped at the tears on my cheeks while her own filled her eyes. "He was always proud of you and always will be. Never be ashamed of trying to save him." She pressed her lips to my forehead. "Enjoy your time with your friends."

"Thank you, Jade." I hugged her again before she slipped back into the crowd.

Mihrage folded his arms and leaned his shoulder to mine. "I'm glad you're safe. Seems you made an important ally."

"He's my other half." I held up my tattooed arm. "He's the other sentinel."

Thirty-Three

"Are you going to save him?" Mihrage asked me, watching as the women who had dragged Abudar to the table began piling his plate with food.

I tilted my head. "Not just yet. I'll let him sweat a little."

"I can't believe you know the prince," Taraji said, appearing on my other side.

I looked at her. "I know. Hey, did you finish the trials?"

She grinned proudly. "Yes! I get to begin attending the academy next month!"

"I'm so proud of you!" I pulled her into another hug. "I knew you could do it."

"Thank you. I can't even tell you the chaos that happened after the trials when the princess didn't appear, and then word spread that the prince was missing too."

Mihrage let out a low whistle. "The entire city was searched from top to bottom."

"Tell me more. I know Abudar would like to hear too." I finally walked over to Abudar as he was waving his hands and insisting he had enough food as it was.

I sat at his side and Mihrage and Taraji sat across from us. "I'll take it from here, grandmothers."

"Welcome home, Caspara." One of them ruffled my hair and walked away, excitedly talking to her friend about how they were lucky to have met royalty before they passed from this earth.

"What is the purpose of the feast?" Abudar asked, leaning toward me. "They couldn't have known you were coming."

"We celebrate the day of the funeral and then three days after someone has passed. I'm assuming today is the third day." I looked to my friends, who confirmed with nods. "This is Mihrage. And this is Taraji. You met her at the trials."

Abudar's brow furrowed in thought.

Taraji's nose wrinkled. "I met him?"

I raised my brow. "Remember the girl in the purple dress who climbed up into the space over the doors at the entrance of the caves?" I pointed to Abudar.

Her eyes widened. "That was *you*?"

He winked. "Yours truly. Although, I was wearing a disguise."

Taraji clapped her hand over her mouth. "Why?"

I exchanged a look with Abudar. "It's a long story."

"I also have to point out . . . Mihrage?" Abudar nudged his head, hinting toward Mihrage.

"What about him?" I asked, picking up one of the bowls to serve myself a much-needed meal.

"He's the same as Irilibus."

I'd never seen Mihrage's expression change so swiftly. His face dropped and his eyes widened. I could have sworn his skin took on a lighter shade of orange.

"You know that name?" I asked.

Mihrage swallowed hard. "Y-Yes. He's the one who exiled me from my people." He pointed to the golden band wrapped around his left horn.

With a gasp, I realized we needed to warn him about what we'd heard in Balim.

Abudar beat me to it. "The Veil told him you live here," he said. "And that you cursed his daughter?"

Mihrage shook his head. "I did nothing of the sort." His attention zeroed in on me. "Remember how I explained to you that I can't always control my powers? That I sometimes see when I don't want to? I warned him about something that would happen to his daughter. When it did, he blamed me. He still blames me for it. He branded me a traitor and exiled me."

"But we never saw his daughter," I pointed out, exchanging a glance with Abudar.

"They may have kept her hidden or sent her away." He looked down at the top of the table.

"What happened?" Abudar prodded.

Mihrage shook his head. "I don't want to answer that."

"But why would he still want revenge?" Taraji asked.

"I . . . don't know." Mihrage looked out toward the desert. "But if he's coming, my presence puts all of you at risk."

"We have enough chaos to handle right now," I interrupted. "It will take him days to get here, and that's only if he left when we did."

"You think you traveled faster than him?" Mihrage lifted his brow in a challenging manner.

"He's got to search the desert for us." I took a bite of my food. "But you can go into hiding if you feel you need to. Move into the city with Jade or head further east to Dubar. Maybe we can even keep you safe in the palace?" I looked at Abudar. "I could use a friend in there."

"I'm not friend enough?" he asked, his cheek filled with

food. His eyes had a playful glint.

"You have princely duties to attend to, I'm told," I replied, recalling my mother's words earlier.

He rolled his eyes. "Don't remind me."

Taraji suddenly gasped. "Caspara, this is our favorite dance! Come on!" She jumped to her feet and ran around the table to grab on to me.

I'd barely eaten five bites of my food. But she was right. It was the first dance I'd learned as a child and one that always made me happy. For some reason, as a child, I used to think everyone in the world would stop and watch me dance, that the stars oversaw and whispered to each other about the little girl who danced like a fairy.

I swallowed the food I had finished chewing then joined her in the center ring. One of the other girls who had joined us handed me a scarf, and Isline handed one to her sister. We all put our scarves together, forming a circle with them in the middle. The music started out slow but happy. We began walking in a circle in rhythm with the music, then every other girl crouched and stood. When we stood, the other set of girls crouched. As the music picked up, we stepped back from the circle, then held our scarfless hand out toward the audience, palm up.

I smiled at the friends I had known my entire life and my feet fell into the memorized steps. I lifted the scarf into the air and looked up at the sky.

My father was now one of the stars looking down at me.

A star twinkled and my heart swelled. Father was winking at me and I could practically hear him say, "*My little dune bug.*"

The music picked up, as did our dancing, and soon the scarfs moved back and forth while we spun in circles. I brought my scarf into both hands, held it up into the air with my palms pressed together, then brought my hands down and pushed my scarf out away from my body, pointing them toward the audience.

The music was coming to a close, but it wouldn't end. Because the last part of the song was to pick a partner.

Taraji spun in a circle, her skirts twirling out away from her body, and she swooped her green scarf around Mihrage's neck. He stood and shimmied his shoulders, leaning over her as she bent backward, mimicking his movement while still holding the scarf.

In the past, I would have chosen my father or a child near my age.

But I glanced at Abudar. He was focused on Mihrage and Taraji but seemed to sense my gaze, because he met it.

I stepped up before him. "Do you feel up to dancing?"

"I think I might know this one." He tilted his head. "The question is, can you keep up with me?" He smiled so widely two dimples appeared in his cheeks.

I laughed and flung the scarf around his neck. "The question, Your Highness, is can *you*?"

Abudar got to his feet and fell into the steps like he was an expert. I wondered if learning to dance was one of his assignments as a prince.

When we reached the circle, I dragged the scarf from around his neck and he took the opposite end. He tugged it upward, leading me into a twirl that ended with his arm around my stomach and the scarf wrapped behind me. I tilted my chin up to look into his eyes.

The rest of the world melted away.

Everything slowed down.

His breath brushed my face and smelled of anise, but he

smelled like vetiver—earth, dry wood, and cotton. And either his footsteps slowed, or the world did. He turned in a slow circle with me, then pulled the scarf, making me spin away from him. We fell into step back to back and nearly tripped, then both burst out laughing.

The rest of the dance was a flurry of movement and color.

He then switched roles with me, spinning into me and making me the man in the dance with my arms around him.

Abudar looked over his shoulder and down. "You're cute from this angle."

"Only that angle, hm?"

"This one as well." He spun out and brought me back in like the dance had begun. Only this time he leaned down and touched his forehead to mine.

His feet stopped.

Mine obeyed.

I'd never been so close to anyone.

My heart raced in my chest and I breathed hard, not just from dancing but from the anticipation.

"You have something on your chin," Abudar whispered. He rubbed his thumb against my jaw.

"Maybe I wanted it there for later."

He chuckled and the sound resonated in my head.

I closed my eyes, wanting desperately for him to press his lips to mine, because . . . why not? Why couldn't he kiss me? Fall in love with *me*?

"Caspara," Taraji whispered.

Abudar's nose brushed against mine and our breath mixed, but our lips didn't touch.

"Caspara," Taraji said a little louder.

I turned my head, glaring at her because how dare she

interrupt my first kiss with the boy whose life I'd saved by almost kissing him? But by breaking away from my dream with Abudar I realized the song had ended. Possibly for a long time. And everyone in the village was staring at us.

I let go of Abudar and stepped back, blushing from head to toe.

"I didn't mean to embarrass you," he said. I didn't miss the hurt in his voice.

"It's not that," I said quickly. "It's only that . . . you're—"

"The prince?" He twitched a brow. "I get it." He tried to smile.

"No, Abudar, it's not like that."

A new song picked up and everyone in town stepped out to dance.

My stomach sank and all the happiness I'd felt just a moment ago was gone.

Taraji looped her arm in mine. "Come see your father's grave."

Silently, I walked with her. Mihrage followed and I imagined Abudar was alongside him.

"When we got out of the caves, I overheard Roshanak speaking with the sultan and sultana," Taraji said. "They were pretending not to be concerned but were talking about Mithra and how she should have already been out."

"Don't be hurt," Mihrage said to Abudar.

"By what?"

"Caspara. She was raised alone by Kasim. Well, him and the rest of our village."

I wanted to look back, to let Mihrage know I could hear him, but a part of me wondered if he knew that. Of course, Taraji was carrying on about how the soldiers were notified and a few were even sent into the exits to begin searching when Mithra didn't appear that night.

Mihrage continued. "She's a good person, but I think she's always been afraid of getting close to new people because everyone in this village is raised to be careful who we trust. That might be why her actions are so confusing to you. I imagine she shows interest and then pulls away?"

"Maybe a little," Abudar confirmed. "But it might also be because my parents have arranged my marriage for me."

Their voices fell and I picked up their words sparsely like "someday" and "hope" and "better not hurt her."

The light of the celebration faded and revealed a path of candles leading to our small cemetery and one headstone in particular.

Taraji released my arm and gave me the opportunity to approach my father's headstone on my own.

It was a low piece of marble with his name carved into it.

A lump formed in my throat. I knelt in front of the headstone and kissed my fingers before touching it. "Hello, Baba." I took a handful of sand from the turquoise bowl and spread it in a line directly in front of the stone.

A bowl with purple sand, and others with yellow, green, blue, and red sat organized on my right. I took yellow and sprinkled it in arches so it touched the turquoise line. I added green dots, finishing the simple artwork I left for him. With each grain of sand, I silently tried to remember every good memory I had with him. From snuggles at night as a child to teaching me how to hold a dagger, how to pick a pocket, and how to dance.

Oh, how we would dance.

He would let me stand on his feet and then he would

twirl me around.

He would make little cookies and we would laugh when they burned because we were busy making shadow puppets on the wall.

"Remember all those things, Baba?" I asked, smearing my colored fingers across my cheeks and then my forehead. "I'll always remember you. I'm sorry we didn't get a proper goodbye. You'll be in my heart and part of my life forever. I'll keep you with me." I leaned up on my knees and pressed my lips to the headstone.

Taraji leaned over and took a handful of red sand, added a circle around a small flower, and then knelt at my side.

"I should have been here with him," I whispered. "I should have been in the prison with him and been at his side when he was . . ." I tried to swallow.

"If you were beside him when that happened, you would never remember the good." Taraji took my hand and looked down at the colors staining my fingers. "You were meant to remember the good."

"I miss him so much. It kills me to be here without him. I can't just talk to him whenever I want to." I reached out and traced his name. "How am I supposed to do this without him?"

"I don't know. But you're not alone. You know he's always going to be a part of your life. He'll always find a way to help you." She rested her head on my shoulder.

"I know he will." Warmth washed over me and I closed my eyes.

We sat in silence for a long while. I watched the torchlight dance across the stone. Igborg showed up with his belly bulging. He walked through the edge of the colored sand I'd placed and then reached up and rested his clawed hands on the stone, leaving behind baby dragon prints.

My feet tingled and I finally stood.

Abudar and Mihrage were standing silent and I gave both of them a grateful smile.

"Thank you for staying with me." I hugged Mihrage and then looked up at Abudar. "I mean it. I appreciate it."

"You're welcome." He lowered and lifted his eyes.

"I need to go to my house and retrieve something of my father's."

"The griffin necklace."

I tucked hair behind my ear. "You remembered?"

"When it comes to you, of course." His gaze roamed my face. "I have never been to a funeral. Is it tradition to do the chalk on your face? Taraji didn't." He gestured to her.

"Only the mourning family." I looked back at my father's stone.

"Do you wear it more than once?"

"No. But I will for the rest of the night." I lifted Igborg and rubbed red sand down his spine. "We will." I kissed the top of his head.

"And then we will dance the night away," Mihrage said, his arm around Taraji's shoulders.

I grinned. "Yes. In celebration of his life. Are you going to get in trouble for staying out late?" I turned to Abudar.

"You spent a day in my world." His knuckles brushed mine. "I want to spend a night in yours."

Thirty-Four

"I've been thinking about our wish," Abudar said as he walked by my side toward my house.

My stomach dropped a bit and I looked sideways at him. This was the wrong place and time to talk about his mother's lost magic.

"I think we should wish for you to have your father back."

I stepped over the sand art on the doorstep and into my home. "The jinni said he can't bring people back from the dead."

"I don't mean *back from the dead*." He stepped in behind me just as I turned to look at him and we ended up with our chests practically touching and me looking up.

My breath hitched and I stepped back. "How can we wish for him to come back but not have him revived from the dead?"

Abudar ran his fingers through his hair. "I've read in books that there are some magical artifacts that bind someone's soul to it so they live on. In fact, my parents met a prince and princess from Ashwyra years ago and Father spoke to him about a magic staff that claimed to be a wizard that was fractured into various artifacts or places."

I stepped away from Abudar and lit the lamp beside the

door to offer light in the small kitchen. "I don't know, Abudar. Father wasn't magical. What good would it do to have him trapped in some sort of artifact? And what should happen to him when I die? Will his soul forever be trapped there?"

He sighed. "I didn't think of that, I suppose. I'm just trying to help."

"I know." I offered him a little smile.

I walked past the desolate kitchen where I would make my father his meals, and up to the room I shared with him. Light from the burning torches outside flickered through the open window, giving me just enough light to find my father's "treasure chest." Everything he had kept safe there was now mine, even if they were just trinkets to remember him by.

I stopped just inside the doorway and sucked in a deep breath. "I'd like to take his blanket with us. And a few other things."

"This is your bedroom?" Abudar asked.

I had already walked to my father's bed and lowered to my knees while looking at the prince. "Not exactly up to your expectations?"

"I . . . I didn't know people lived like this." His amber eyes examined my trunk, which held every piece of clothing I owned. The lid was broken—something Father kept saying he would fix but never got to. Abudar looked over my bed, then to the small wooden partition that allowed a bit of privacy to dress. "Where do you bathe?" he suddenly asked.

I reached under the pile of blankets and retrieved the small chest of treasures. "Oh, we never bathe."

Abudar's eyes darted to me.

I grinned. "Never."

He rolled his eyes. "Ha ha."

"We take water from the well outside and warm it over the fire if we have time, or use the warmth of the sun. Then we usually stand behind our house and just wash with that bucket of water." I withdrew the bundle of mismatched fabric squares from my sewing days, before I became an expert at *not* sewing. I unwrapped it to reveal the pendant Father had told me to retrieve.

The griffin feather pendant.

The white gold had been delicately hand-shaped with grooves of the feather, and its tip was a stunning orange shade of gold. I'd only seen it once as a child.

"What is that?" Abudar asked as he knelt at my side.

I shook my head. "I don't know. But Father told me to retrieve it in his last note to me that Omar brought, so it must be significant. When I was young, he always told me that I would understand. Someday." I ran my fingertip over the grooves. "For him, every question would be answered *someday*."

"That must have been frustrating to you."

I nodded. "Hurt, I think, is a better word."

Abudar set his hand on my shoulder.

White light suddenly filled the room, radiating from the griffin charm. Its light spread up the tattoos on my arm, and with it the sensation of warmth. When I looked over at Abudar, his markings glowed with the same light.

We locked eyes.

The room flashed with bright white light, and then we were no longer in my home.

A fire crackled to my left and Abudar knelt on my right, his hand still holding my shoulder. To our right was a stunning lake, and somewhere nearby a waterfall. Massive trees towered overhead, but moonlight brightened the night sky. The billions of stars were so close, I felt that I could reach out and touch them.

"My, my, my, look at how much you've grown."

My attention shifted beyond the firelight to an old woman waddling unsteadily. She sat with a groan onto a pillow. Her long, gray hair was loose and hung down her back and over a patchwork shawl that hung over her shoulders. Her gray eyes were focused in our direction.

"Telama," Abudar said without a moment of hesitation. He dropped his hand, knelt forward, and touched his forehead to the ground. "I am honored to be in your presence."

I, however, hesitated, caught between imitating Abudar and not. Because this was the woman who had given me my tattoos. She was the woman who'd blessed me with this miraculous destiny I was supposed to fulfill, one I didn't even understand.

She chuckled. "Sit up, Prince Abudar."

He complied but remained rigid and respectful.

"Caspara, you have many questions that need to be answered. The one you must first know is Kasim only ever wanted what was best for you. Everything he did was to protect you. Unfortunately, he believed that also meant keeping certain things secret from you until your sixteenth birthday."

My fingers tightened around the pendant still in my hand. "What else did he keep from me?"

"The reason he raised you amongst the thieves was because Roshanak couldn't come to terms with raising a daughter without her same abilities. The idea of being the grand sorceress and having a daughter without magic was too much for her to bear. One day, she took you into the city . . . and there she left you.”

My eyes widened and I thought my heart stopped beating because pain seared through it like I’d never felt before. “Sh-she abandoned me?”

Telama nodded, her face solemn. She gestured to the flames, which took form into little people and the city of Zunbar. I recognized Roshanak carrying a bundle in her arms. She went down to the docks and set me in one of the many open crates.

I recognized that spot.

I’d passed it hundreds of times, not once knowing that my mother had left me there to either die or be found by someone else years ago.

“How old was I?” I whispered.

“Not even a year.”

“But this was *after* you came and gave me a blessing,” I pointed out.

Telama nodded.

“Which means my mother didn’t even see worth in me as a sentinel?” Anger boiled in my chest and my markings burned, slowly taking on a red glow.

“She didn’t fully understand what it means to be a sentinel,” Telama explained. “Had she, I don’t think she would have chosen her actions. Kasim returned that night and found you gone. Roshanak admitted what she’d done and he left to find you. When he did, he never returned to the palace.” She reached out and placed her hand over mine.

The edges of the metal pendant bit into my fingers until I slowly relaxed them.

“I cannot say whose actions are the best. We all make

mistakes. In training Prince Abudar, Roshanak learned how powerful the sentinels truly can be, especially with their powers combined, and she knew in order for Abudar to reach his fullest potential, she needed to find you. And you, Caspara, can reach your full potential with Abudar at your side. You have so much more worth than you realize, even though you know it."

My brows furrowed. How could I know something but not realize it? I also couldn't believe that my mother's mistakes would include casting out her only child. Or that she had lied to me yet again. She claimed she had been unstable and Kasim took me away from her.

"Now, Prince Abudar." She moved her touch to him. "You too have many questions racing through your heart." Her lips spread into a smile. "Like your father before you, there are difficult choices in your future. Choices that will change the course of the kingdom."

"How do I know what the right choices are?" he almost whispered.

Telama lifted her hand and placed it on his chest. "You will know here. And sometimes, young man, you are faced with two very good choices that will lead you down good paths either way. Do not live your life wondering 'what if?' because a man caught in the past will never be able to see his future."

Abudar nodded slowly.

"I can only say you've been raised your entire life with such potential. It's at your fingertips. Your confidence is one of your strengths. Make your decisions and stand by them. There may come a time when others will try to sway those convictions. You're also concerned with Mithra."

He heaved a sigh. "She's been acting . . . differently

since we returned from the caves. Even Arash has pointed it out to me. She's . . . almost nicer. I know it doesn't sound like it makes sense, but she's never nice to me like this."

Telama nodded slowly. "I cannot tell you her future, but I can tell you it is wise to be wary. She is like you, able to be swayed. Do what you can to keep her on your side, but do not feel guilt if she chooses her own path. You cannot control her."

Somehow, for the first time, I realized Telama reminded me of the old woman I had walked in on. The one in the hidden weaving room inside the Dragon's Lair.

I blinked and leaned up on my knees. "Wait. Are you one of the Fates?" I blurted.

Telama's lips spread into a grin. "Gavair mentioned you accidentally found her."

"So you are?" I gasped and clamped my hands over my mouth.

Telama pressed a bent finger to her lips. "I help to know what is present while Gavair is in charge of the future and end of life. We call ourselves the Weavers."

"You actually did see that old woman in the caves?" Abudar murmured, eyes widened.

"I guess I did."

"I have told you all—"

"Wait," I interrupted, cutting Telama off. I swallowed hard. "I don't mean to interrupt and I know you can't answer *all* of our questions, but I interrupted your conversation with Abudar."

He shook his head. "I don't think I have questions she can answer right now. It seems I need to return home and have a conversation with Mithra first."

Telama nodded. "You both know who you are. Caspara,

it's time to make your decision of who you want to be."

"The pendant!" I held it up. "What does it mean?"

"You will have to learn that for yourself."

The lake and fire faded away. Telama's wise face disappeared.

I knelt on my father's bed back in my home.

Abudar drew a breath and leaned back on his ankles. "That was unexpected."

"And not nearly as many answers as I needed." I heaved a sigh and looked down at the pendant.

"If she answered them all, there would be nothing for you to live for. You'd already know your fate." He groaned as he rose to his feet, but extended his hand down to me to help me up.

I set the pendant back in the chest before tucking the chest in my arm as Abudar pulled me to my feet. I examined my room. I could stay there, be a thief, and do everything my father had trained me to do.

Or, I could accept my role as one of the sentinels.

I might not have had a lot of answers to my questions, but there was one Telama *had* answered. I *was* a sentinel. She had chosen me. It didn't matter that I didn't understand why. And the only way to see if I would be any good at being a sentinel would be to train beside Abudar.

Which also meant leaving my home behind.

Stepping out of my comfort zone wasn't something I was good at, but I had to try.

My fingers tingled and I looked down to see the tattoo on my middle finger take on a more navy color as opposed to black. But it could have just been a trick of the torchlight.

I spent a few extra minutes collecting my clothing and put them in the bag I often carried when I went on assignments with my father. Abudar folded my father's blanket, at my request, and went downstairs to wait patiently.

I bit my bottom lip as I surveyed my empty room. My father would never lie in that bed again. I would never throw my shoe at him because of his snoring. We would never stay up far too late sharing stories.

With a deep breath, I squelched my pain and went downstairs to where Abudar stood.

He nodded to me and opened the front door.

After taking everything from me, Abudar urged me to rejoin the celebration while he—I assumed—loaded everything onto the horse we'd taken from the palace.

Mihrage dragged me back to dance, stealing my mind away from grief.

Taraji took my hand and soon Abudar was part of the dance again.

We danced until my feet ached and I finally sat down at the table with my food and ate bits of the now cold meat.

Abudar flopped down across from me, still chuckling from dancing. "I think your people put any celebration in the palace to shame."

"How is that possible?" I asked.

"Because you're carefree." He watched those still dancing. Most of the children had been sent to bed, and the elderly had left. "All of you, including you, Caspara, let go. You act silly and laugh, you make up dance moves and aren't ashamed if you step incorrectly."

"Dance is supposed to be about feeling emotions and feeling your body," I said.

He looked at me sideways. "It's not like that in the palace. You'll see at the celebration tomorrow."

I chuckled. "You're going to be positively exhausted. Two nights of dancing in a row is going to wear you out." I rubbed my foot.

"Not if I get to . . ." He didn't finish his sentence and looked away quickly.

My brows pinched. "Get to what?"

"Nothing. Did you want to sleep here one more night or shall we return to the palace?"

I wasn't satisfied with his answer, but Abudar was already on his feet. I wanted to stay and have breakfast with the thieves. I wanted to have that final celebration. But my heart ached just looking at my house, and I knew that even with Abudar there, I wouldn't be able to sleep in my bed.

"We should go," I said softly. "I'll visit in a few days."

I spent a few extra minutes saying goodbyes to everyone. I thanked every single one of them for celebrating my father's life. I hugged Jade long and tight until we both had tears. We didn't even say anything. We didn't need to.

I found Igborg passed out cold on one of the empty plates and cradled him in my arms while I stopped by my father's grave one last time.

"I'm going to make you proud, Baba," I said to him. I leaned down and kissed the top. As I straightened, I touched the headstone and my tattoos glowed white. "If I had any wish . . . I would wish for one last conversation with you. One last chance to tell you how much I love you. I think that is what I would wish for."

I said my final farewell and left the graveyard and returned to Abudar's side.

He withdrew his hands from his pockets. "Are you ready?"

"I know what we should have asked Telama for." I

moved my skirt so my leg reached through the slit to climb up on the horse.

"What's that?" he asked.

"We should have asked her what to wish for."

Thirty-Five

I woke up feeling more rested than I had in days. Igborg was sitting on the window's ledge, looking out over the city. It might have been a trick of the light, but I could have sworn he'd grown bigger in recent days.

I reached up and touched the pendant on my neck and remembered the night before. Abudar had held me close while we danced and rode. He'd looked down into my eyes like he'd known me my entire life. And maybe a part of him had. Because every time I looked at him, I felt the same way. Perhaps it had something to do with our being sentinels and everything.

There was a knock and I heaved a sigh.

The only time I was forced awake at home was if Father had something important worth interrupting me for. Or if I had chores.

"Yes?" I called.

The door cracked open. "Pardon me for waking you, but Grand Sorceress Roshanak asked for me to fit you for dresses, especially for the celebration tonight. And Sultana Shahira would like a private meeting with you."

I sat upright. "Shahira? I mean, the sultana?"

The servant nodded.

I swallowed hard and climbed out of the bed.

The servant ushered me over to stand in front of the mirror, then began measuring me with a ribbon. A second young woman appeared and began jotting things down, including colors and whatever numbers the first woman said.

"I think you'll look particularly dashing in orange."

I raised my brows and looked at her reflection. "You want me to wear orange? No. That's awful."

"Or green?" the younger woman asked.

I suddenly recalled the dress my aunt had made, the green one she'd first had me try and wear. "My aunt Jade might have a dress left," I mentioned.

The older woman's eyes widened. "Your aunt is the seamstress Jade? Good heavens! We are sending the measurements to her. We shall let her know of your desires and then send you to her for the fittings."

"Or bring her to you."

I smiled. "I think she would appreciate that very much. But will she have time to make a new gown for this evening?"

"Hm. That is a good point." The older woman tapped her chin.

"She *did* have a green gown she attempted to have me wear to the trials," I mentioned. "It was beautiful."

"Ah! Yes! And if we have to change the color, we will. Thank you, Caspara. Oh, and this is for you to wear in the meantime." She gestured to the deep blue dress hanging from the privacy partition. The way it shimmered in the light, one might easily mistake it for black, and it had silver stitching on the hems.

"This is . . . breathtaking," I said. "I shouldn't wear this."

"Nonsense. I can help you put it on if you wish. Though you should wash up first." She excused the younger servant.

No matter how much I attempted to object, I finally found myself taking another bath, though I didn't wash my hair. I washed off the sand and the colored chalk from my father's funeral celebration.

The woman told me her name was Hera and she was in charge of making sure I was taken care of. She combed out my hair, then rolled it around a thin towel from the ends up until it reached the bottom of my skull. She worked some sort of hair magic and twisted the ends of the towel into my hair and pinned it in place.

"There we are," Hera grinned. "Tonight, when we let it out, it will be in lovely ringlets. Now, the makeup."

I pulled away. "No. I don't wear that."

"But you will tonight. I insist." She held up the dress and helped me put it over my head. It was sleeveless, so my arms wouldn't have been caught, but I couldn't deny I was grateful for her help. There were at least three interior layers I was positive I would have gotten tangled in without her.

Hera stepped back. "Did you have a chance to eat?" She looked over at the small table, which had a tray but no food.

Igborg looked at me innocently from where he'd curled up on the foot of the bed.

"No, I'm afraid not," I said.

"Then I shall set another place so you and Sultana Shahira can dine together. This way!"

I wanted to object and tell her I wanted to avoid the sultana. But I was living in her palace, and at least for now I would begin training beside her son. Unless she was planning on throwing me out into the streets, like my mother.

I shook my head and silently reminded myself that I didn't actually know Shahira and I should be honored to meet her. More than that, she had saved my father's life years ago. If Father trusted her, so could I.

Igborg's nails clattered against the tile as he scampered behind us.

Hera knocked and opened a door to a rather small room with only a couple of couches, a desk beside the window, and cushions in the center of the room around a low table. "You will wait in here. Make yourself comfortable."

I fidgeted with my fingers.

Igborg found himself a comfortable pillow. "I want to fly. Can I?"

"Not right now, but I'll take you later, okay? After lunch."

"Oh yes. Lunch." He licked his lips.

I laughed and crouched in front of him. "You would eat nonstop if I allowed you to."

"I'm growing."

I blinked. "I thought you were getting bigger. And you seem to be talking more too."

He nodded.

"But how big will you get?"

He tilted his head. "Sand dragon might know."

"You are *not* going to try to speak with him," I said firmly.

He heaved a sigh. "Maybe later."

"No, not later. It's not happening."

The handle moved and I quickly straightened and ran my hand over my stomach, which suddenly felt uneasy. The door opened and the sultana of Sheblom entered the room. A beautiful orange tiger strolled in behind her.

Igborg froze.

She smiled softly. Her eyes were bright and full of kindness. "I've been wanting to speak with you, Caspara. Welcome to the palace." She walked forward.

"Sultana." I bowed and then remembered I should probably curtsey, but I wasn't quite sure how and stepped on the back of my dress, nearly tripping myself.

"You don't need to be formal with me. I was raised in Zunbar too, with my sister. Kiara has spoken of you and Igborg before." She crouched and stroked Igborg. "Lycus is extremely fond of you. He says you're going to get as big as a house. Do you think you'll get that big?"

"Igborg hopes so!" he said excitedly, tilting his head back and forth so she would scratch every bit of it.

"Abudar has already told me he is a dragon. The little one we were supposed to give him for his birthday last year, if I'm not mistaken." Shahira straightened. "I am glad he found his way to you. This is Navid, my familiar."

I stole a glance at the tiger. "If you don't have magic, why is he still here?"

Navid sat down and looked at Igborg. Igborg was smaller than his head. "Because I am still bound to her. Someday, her magic shall return. Then we shall resume working together."

"Abudar tells me you two are rather close."

I hesitated, for a brief moment misunderstanding Shahira was alluding to me liking Abudar, but I realized she was still speaking about Igborg. I grinned. "Yes. Igborg is everything to me now. He's my only family aside from Jade."

"That's not true." Shahira reached out and took my hand, her eyes suddenly full of sadness. "I knew Kasim well. He was my closest friend beside Jade. We grew up together."

My heart ached and I tried to swallow the lump in my throat. "I've been wanting to ask. Why? If you knew him, why allow him to be executed?"

She sighed and walked to the window and closed it, shutting out the warm air. "I didn't approve of it. Neither did Zayne. In fact, I wouldn't call what happened a proper execution at all. We haven't done one of those in decades."

I stepped forward. "Then what *would* you call it? What happened?"

She gestured to one of the seats.

Had I been with Abudar, I would have refused. I would have refused even with my mother. But I relented and sat down on the couch.

The sultana sat beside me and placed her hands on her knees. "When Kasim fell in love with Roshanak, I was thrilled. When I was younger, a part of me always hoped I would marry Kasim."

My breath hitched. "You loved my father?"

Shahira smiled fondly and nodded. "I did. He even offered to take me and flee the country before I discovered what was happening inside the palace with Zayne and my father. He was always a protector. After I married, we knew we could never be together. It wasn't in our destiny. By him falling in love with Roshanak, I could at least keep him close as a friend."

"But what happened? How was he executed?"

"I still don't understand," she confessed. "When he was first brought here, we didn't know. In fact, it wasn't until Abudar spoke to me the morning of the Desert Trials that I knew. Roshanak imprisoned him in the dungeon, insisting he was a spy feeding information to The Veil. She also insisted that during his most recent break-in he threatened the lives of the family, and had her men not been there, he would have killed one of them."

"That's a lie," I snapped. I gripped my skirt in fists. "I was there that night. The family wasn't even home!"

Shahira reached out and placed her hand on my knee comfortingly. "I believe you. I spoke with Kasim myself. While you were all gone in the trials, Zayne and I consulted with Roshanak. Zayne commanded she release him. She didn't agree. Of course, she was right that he is technically a criminal."

I rolled my eyes. "Stealing from the rich to give to the poor shouldn't be considered a crime."

"Stealing is always a crime." She raised her brows and I wondered if that look was what mothers gave their children before a scolding. I wouldn't know.

I folded my arms.

Shahira placed her hand back in her lap. "Roshanak insisted on punishing him for his crimes, so Zayne said he could pay a fine. Kasim agreed. And then . . ." Her eyes saddened.

Navid placed his massive head on her lap and she set her hand on top of his head.

"Captain Nadeem came to us and informed us your father was found in his cell. Dead. I investigated the best I could with those I trusted, and a part of me believes Roshanak may have had a hand in it, but I cannot figure out why. Why would she kill him? What should she gain? Killing him wouldn't bring you to her. It just . . . doesn't make sense. Even now. I'm afraid it's not much of an answer for you. And for that, I am deeply sorry."

I met the tiger's eyes, staring at him because I was trying to wrap my head around this information. "No one saw how it happened? Were there any clues as to how he died? That he is really dead and it wasn't a spell?"

"Not that we could find. I truly am sorry, Caspara."

What was I going to say in response? My father was dead. Roshanak was suspected, but without proof, couldn't be punished.

"Did he ever take you cliff diving?"

I lifted my gaze to the sultana, relieved for the change of subject since overthinking my questions wouldn't answer them. I fondly recalled the cliffs behind the palace that were the best place to cliff jump. "Yes. A few times."

She smiled, her eyes wrinkling at the corners when she did so. "I want to hear all about you."

"I . . . don't really know what to say." I picked at my nails. "I was raised by the forty thieves, trained to steal and fight. To fend for myself. Father taught me everything he could. Though I never was any good at sewing."

Shahira laughed. "To be honest, neither was your father. He never wanted to take over his father's shop. He would have, though, out of duty. But he couldn't sew a button to save his life, let alone an entire outfit."

I joined her laughter. Because hearing her speak of him made me want to know more about what he was like before I was born. "Were you there when he met Roshanak?"

She nodded, her smile saddening a bit. "They really were in love with each other. At least, that's what it looked like to me."

"Telama told me she left me on the streets."

Shahira sucked her cheeks in and looked down at the table. "I think . . . perhaps that is a conversation you need to have with her." She lifted her gaze back to me. "That was a very worrisome time for all of us. The Veil had appeared for the first time and had taken five sorceresses. Roshanak told me she worried that if The Veil took daughter of the grand sorceress, they might be able to blackmail her or even the throne." She really believed it.

"It's hard for me to believe that," I said. "Then again, there is much I didn't know about my father."

Shahira smiled. "He was always a bit overly protective. He was willing to die to keep his family safe the day Jade was chosen to be Zayne's wife. Do you recall those stories?"

"Only a little," I admitted. "All I know of that day was that the sultan was choosing and killing his wives."

"Yes. Only it wasn't Zayne. It was my father, who was his Vizier at the time. After my father murdered thirty-nine women and stole their power, he stole mine as well. By stealing the magic of all forty of us, he was granted power himself. But I destroyed his staff, and by the grace of the gods, he disappeared from this world and was trapped and hidden."

I blinked. "I didn't know all of that. I did know that you chose Roshanak because you wanted to mend the relationship with the sorceresses in the land."

She nodded again. "Because my father had chosen the sorceresses to kill. And Zayne's father had outlawed magic being performed in the open. He and I disagreed with his father's philosophy, so we've been working with Roshanak to help all of the women in our land."

"It's admirable, I suppose."

Shahira's lips tugged into a smile. It reminded me of Abudar, and I was grateful the servants brought food in just then. They set the tray before us and left.

I started to eat, giving myself an excuse not to talk and busying my hands so I stopped picking at the dress.

"Abudar mentioned to me today you two connected last night. That your tattoos glowed." She looked at me from beneath her brows.

I licked my lip. "Does he tell you everything?"

She laughed. "Yes. He and I are very close. He's my miracle child. I nearly died while giving birth to him. And when he was visited by Telama and showed prowess in magic . . . we've become very close."

"That sounds like me with my father."

Shahira watched me a moment, then said, "I don't mean to put you on the spot. But what do you hope to do with your life from here on?"

"To be honest, I don't know." I shrugged and took another bite of my food. "Taraji, my friend, she asked me that days ago. Goodness, over a week now. I just expected to always be a thief, but now . . ." I looked at my tattoos. "I guess I'll be whatever I'm supposed to be."

"He's excited to start training with you, you know?"

I lifted my gaze and saw her smiling in a coy way. "Who?"

"Abudar." She resumed eating, but that smile lingered.

I was both flattered and embarrassed.

We finished our lunch, with Sultana Shahira changing the topic to Jade visiting to help with my dress, then shifted to Mithra wanting to see if I really had no magic, and then back to Abudar training me—though I honestly didn't know how he would do that. Was there a book—a training manual for sentinels? Journals Roshanak hadn't shown me?

More than likely.

Thirty-Six

I stood in the hallway, pacing back and forth. Jade had spent the last three hours adjusting the green gown I'd tried on in her shop the day I left for the Desert Trials. The emerald top crossed in the back and the front, covering my breasts and wrapping around my shoulders and ribs. She had attached two golden chains to pull the two straps together at the back to keep them from sliding up or down.

The matching green skirt she had embellished with a gold waistband and a layer of gold fabric in the skirts so if I spun in a circle, the gold and green flowed together. Of course, Hera made me put on a layer of kohl makeup, darkening my lids in a way that accentuated the green flecks in my light brown eyes, and then she added a thin layer of gold liner and three green dots beneath it.

When my makeup was done, she released my hair from the updo she'd created and my hair flowed down in beautiful waves I'd never seen before. She placed some head jewelry on top and shoved me out the door.

Now my stomach knotted with nerves because I felt more out of place than I had in my entire life. I was used to being in shadows, wearing clothing that covered me, and dancing with my friends. Not being a guest in the palace, wearing makeup and *this*, out in the open for all to see.

The hallways bustled with servants scampering back and forth, carrying trays of fresh food, empty trays, or trays with empty or full glasses.

I sucked in a final breath, pulled the door open, and stepped into the massive ballroom.

It was packed with people. I recognized some of the noble families, but there were lots more. They must have been families of the girls who had completed the trials. There was a giddy sort of buzz in the air because, after all, they were here to finally celebrate that victory.

Young men mingled with the girls, flirting and doing their best to charm them.

I rolled my eyes and passed by. But my heart jumped when I spotted Taraji with Mihrage, both of them setting food on their plates. "Taraji! Mihrage!" I pushed through the crowd until I was at their side.

Taraji did a double-take and her jaw dropped. "Caspara?"

"Oh, stop it. It's not like you don't recognize me."

"I almost didn't. I've never . . . holy smokes."

I blushed and bit my lip. "Too much?"

"No!" she blurted. She grinned so big I knew her cheeks had to hurt. "You're going to get a lot of attention tonight is all. Just brace for that."

Mihrage leaned down. "Or one set of eyes in particular?" He twitched his brows knowingly.

"He doesn't feel the same," I mumbled. "He can't."

"Why not?" Taraji put a grape in her mouth.

I looked toward the musicians.

In front of them, Sultan Zayne stood beside his wife, both talking. Mithra had just walked in and joined them.

"Because—"

The man playing the flute let out a long, single, low note, drawing all eyes to look to the front of the room.

Sultan Zayne straightened and stepped forward. "Welcome, everyone, to the palace. Tonight we celebrate the return of my son and daughter, Prince Abudar and Princess Mithra."

The crowd cheered loudly.

"But we also celebrate those of you who proudly completed the Desert Trials several days ago."

Again, the crowd cheered. A few whistled.

Roshanak entered and stepped into the crowd, not drawing attention to herself.

"Eat your fill, dance until your feet hurt, and congratulations on your entrance into the Zauberin Academy!" He turned and cued the musicians to begin playing while the crowd cheered.

Several people immediately stepped to the center of the room and began one of the dances.

I scanned the crowd for the only person I wanted to see.

Abudar was on the dance floor in line with the men. The women stood opposite of the men in their own line. I felt a pull to join him, but as I stepped into line, I realized I'd stepped into line beside Roseline.

She watched the girl on her right, trying to mimic the quick movements as best she could.

I reached out and touched her hand, drawing her attention to me. "Just feel the music," I instructed. "Feel the beat with your feet." I picked up my skirt to show her my feet. "Let your legs absorb it and then your arms. It doesn't have to be perfect." I smiled.

She gave me a nervous smile in return. "What if I mess up?"

"That's part of the fun." I winked.

Roseline swallowed hard and imitated the way I moved my arms. We weren't exactly in sync with the rest of the women in the line, but I wasn't about to let Roseline feel incompetent on her own. Even if she was Prince Abudar's fiancée.

The line of women approached the men.

My heart panged when Abudar reached behind Roseline and took her right hand, then set his hand on her waist with her fingers in his. As if it couldn't be worse, I saw him meet my gaze before he did so.

I set my jaw.

I was going to make him just as jealous.

The young man I had approached took me in the same position and I stole a glance at him. He wasn't bad looking. In fact, he was pretty handsome. His jaw wasn't square like Abudar's, but his chin was dimpled. He also didn't have as wide a nose as the prince's. All in all, he was a worthy boy to make Abudar jealous.

Because I wasn't going to be the only one that night feeling hurt.

I made sure to smile and stay close with my partner. I let him spin me and bring me back in. We faced each other and I reached my hands over my head and waved them in the air—as the dance moves were, and he stepped close to me so our bodies almost touched.

"My name is Ferin," he said.

"Caspara. Pleased to meet you, Ferin." We stepped to the side, forward, and then left so our left hands touched, our arms both at right angles. "What do you do, Ferin?"

"My father is the royal jeweler. I'm following in his footsteps."

We turned in a circle.

I kept my smile on my face. "That's impressive."

"What about you?" he asked.

"Oh, I'm a thief."

He laughed and I laughed with him, like it was a joke I'd made even though he had no idea how honest I was being.

From the corner of my eye, I saw Abudar turn his head and look at me.

I didn't acknowledge him.

"I noticed the tattoos on your arm." He spun me again and wrapped his arms around me from behind while we stepped forward. "That must have been painful."

"Not too bad," I said, suddenly self-conscious about them. Maybe I should have hidden them beneath sleeves. "Do you have any?"

"No. At least not yet."

The song ended and Ferin bowed. "Can I have another dance with you?"

I stole a look at Abudar, who was kissing the back of Roseline's hand. I looked up at Ferin and gave him my hand. "Yes. But I need a drink first."

"I will wait."

I meandered over to one of the tables laden with food and took a glass of water to drink. My eyes settled on a beautiful, fluffy cake on the table and my heart jumped. It was a love cake.

"You should have a piece."

I looked up to see Abudar reaching for a knife to cut it. "Why is that?"

"I had them make it for you." He looked at me from the corner of his eyes while he made the first cut. "Didn't you say it was the cake you usually have for your birthday?"

How could I not stare at him? "You did this for me?" I asked softly.

He set the piece of cake on a plate and held it out to me. "Happy birthday, Caspara."

"Abudar, can you show me how to do this dance? It seems to be one with multiple dance partners," Roseline said, eyes focused on those dancing when she could have been focused on him.

Abudar took Roseline's hand. "Yes. Come with me."

I stared after him, my heart and stomach fighting with each other to understand if I was flattered or annoyed. But Abudar had had the royal kitchen people make a cake just for me. Just for my birthday.

I took a bite of the cake and smiled.

It was delicious. And perfect.

I took two more bites and spotted Ferin headed my direction. I would have to finish the cake later.

We fell into another dance. Only with this dance, we had to switch partners. I switched to Abudar the first time.

He put our palms together and stepped forward and then back. "What are you doing?" he asked.

"Dancing? Aren't you?" I raised a brow.

"I mean with him." He nudged his head toward Ferin.

I smiled. "I'm afraid I don't know what you mean."

We switched.

I spun around with the three other boys in the circle before I returned to Ferin. He took my right hand and lifted it into the air. I ducked under and twirled, then he brought me close to his chest. I pushed off and spun to Abudar again.

"I was only thinking perhaps you should dance with someone else," Abudar said, picking up our conversation again.

"I didn't come with anyone, in case you forgot that, Your Highness." I stepped back, curtseyed, then clapped with everyone else dancing.

He frowned and put our hands together a second time. "I know you didn't."

I waited until we were close and leaned in so our noses almost touched. "Are you jealous?" I whispered.

He fumbled for words, but we switched partners again.

I had to confess it was an absolute delight to focus on making Abudar jealous by dancing with all the boys I could while he had to stick with Roseline. Why shouldn't I have fun? I'd never been to a celebration like this, and certainly never danced with so many boys before, let alone so close to my age.

In fact, at one point I completely forgot I was striving to make Abudar jealous because I was genuinely having fun.

It was at that point that the music stopped and Sultan Zayne stood. He motioned with his hand for Abudar to join him.

Abudar took Roseline's hand and they walked through the parting crowd until they stepped up to his father's side.

In spite of all of my effort, jealousy crept into me. Foolish. I knew it too. Abudar was never mine. Sands, I'd only known him a whole week and a half, or however many days it had been.

"This evening, we make a proud announcement. I'm sure many of you have seen Crown Princess Roseline of Kalekai and possibly even danced with her. We are pleased to announce her engagement to our son, Prince Abudar." He stepped aside, positively beaming.

I clenched my teeth.

There was a polite cheer, but I imagined most of the girls in that room had their heart broken that night.

None as deeply as me.

Mithra stepped up to my side. "You didn't applaud the announcement," she observed.

I turned with her to get a drink. "Should I have?" I asked.

"I've seen the way you look at him. You can't possibly think he would *choose* you to marry." Mithra sipped from her glass.

I took my own from the tray and shifted a cold glare to her. "First of all, I said nothing of marriage. Abudar has been a good friend to me and—"

"It should stay that way." Her eyes darted up and down. "Roseline is a good person. She'll take care of him. Besides, she's royalty." Mithra glanced to her right and I followed her gaze to see Arash wearing a stunning royal blue uniform that had to belong to the palace guard. He looked dashing.

"You're saying that, even though I'm Roshanak's daughter, I have no worth? Because I don't have magic like you? Or money?" I asked her.

Mithra looked back at me. "I didn't say you have no worth. You're a sentinel. Clearly, Telama saw something in you. I just hate seeing your heart broken when there was never even an option for him." She offered me a little smile and I realized she really was trying to be kind. Sharp and blunt, but at least she was honest.

I finished my drink and set the empty glass down. "I may excuse myself soon. I was out late last night at a funeral celebration and I'm weary." I walked away from her.

Taraji somehow managed to find me and dragged me

over to Mihrage, who was pressed up against a far wall, avoiding all people as much as possible.

"I don't know why you came," I said, eyes moving to his obvious horns. "You hate showing yourself."

Mihrage heaved a sigh. "I couldn't let Taraji come on her own."

Taraji shoved the last of her treat into her mouth. "This has been the most fun I've ever had. Can you believe we're in the palace?"

"I might be staying here for a little while," I admitted.

They both turned to me, eyes wide.

"Roshanak is my mother. Abudar is the other sentinel. I need to learn what that means for me and try and train, I guess."

"That's exciting, isn't it?" Mihrage said.

I nodded and glanced over my shoulder. Everyone had been congratulating Abudar. His eyes glanced up now and then to survey the crowd and I wondered if he was looking for me. Another song began.

"Oh, Mihrage, one more dance!" Taraji grabbed his hand.

"Aren't your feet dying?" He groaned, but had a big smile on his face.

"Yes, which is why I said only one more." They pushed through the crowd and onto the dance floor.

Once again, I felt like just another girl in the crowd. People would see me and not remember me. Another grain of dust stuck in a boot.

I had decided to head to bed and was making my way through the crowd when a hand snagged my wrist.

When I turned, I was surprised to see Abudar.

"Can I have a word?" he asked. He turned us toward the

wall that had four enormous stained glass windows and a closed door.

"I suppose. As long as it's only one."

Abudar's dimple appeared with his grin. He dropped my hand and I followed him back through the crowd. He opened the door, which Arash stood beside, and exited first.

Arash cleared his throat. "You look lovely tonight, Caspara," he said.

"I, well, thank you. And you look nice too." I flushed and stepped out with Abudar.

Arash closed the door behind me, leaving me alone with Abudar in a courtyard with a beautiful tree growing in the center, four stone benches, and flowers growing at the base of the tree.

"Whoa."

"Mother has spent a lot of time bringing some green to Sheblom. Her friends from Fidsa sent the flowers." Abudar sat down on the bench and stuck his feet out while he closed his eyes in brief relief.

I glanced at the windows and realized that the stained glass prevented anyone from being able to see us, which meant Abudar could let down his princely façade for a moment of respite. I sat on a different bench, feeling relief to my feet as well.

Abudar sighed and opened his eyes. "I'm sorry that announcement came as a surprise to you."

"It wasn't exactly a surprise. I met Roseline yesterday." I looked down at my dress and smoothed it out over my knees.

"Do you like her?"

I shrugged. "She seems kind."

The silence between us stretched.

I lifted my gaze to Abudar. He was staring up at the night sky.

"I enjoyed our time together last night," Abudar finally said, breaking the silence.

"Don't," I said firmly and stood.

His brows pinched and he straightened and turned to me. "Don't what?"

"Don't do that. Don't pretend that you and I can care for each other."

"Caspara, I don't know how else to tell you that marrying Roseline—"

"Is political. I know."

He stood and reached out for my hand.

I didn't offer mine in return, and he dropped his.

His eyes revealed the hurt he didn't show anywhere else on his face. "You live your life so freely. I wish I could be like you."

"Abudar, my life is a mess. How could you *want* to live like this?" I gave a bitter laugh.

"At least you get to choose who you want to be with. At least you get to choose what you want to be. At least . . ." He ran his fingers through his hair.

I folded my arms. "Why haven't you spoken with your father about this?"

He shook his head and glanced at the windows. "Because everything about it makes sense."

"He got to choose who he married," I pointed out.

Abudar shook his head. "No. Mother volunteered, but his first wife was arranged. They got lucky they were childhood friends and Mother was some form of royalty from an uncle or whomever." He set his hands on his hips and looked back at me.

"What do you want me to say?" I asked. "That I have feelings for you? I'm pretty sure we've both made that obvious, but those feelings could be mixed up because we're supposed to be allies." I lifted my right arm. "You're my other half, after all."

"You feel the same way?"

I rolled my eyes. "Abu. Really?"

He stepped forward.

But I stepped back when my heart jumped. "Abudar, we can't."

He flexed his jaw, then closed the gap between us. He cupped my face in his hands and pressed his lips to mine.

My mind went blank.

His lips were soft against mine, his breath hot, his touch firm but gentle. He broke the kiss because I stood frozen. But I quickly reached up and put my hand on the side of his face, our eyes locked together.

He lowered one hand to my lower back and drew me close to him.

This time, I returned the kiss. My heart slammed against my ribs, and my hands trembled from adrenaline and desire.

In a perfect world, this would have been everything we needed.

But the world wasn't perfect.

Abudar was engaged.

I pulled away, stepping out of his touch.

The pain that pulled his brows and made him open his mouth shot through me too. Tears stung my eyes. I slowly shook my head.

He dropped his hands to his sides and his gaze to the ground. "It's not fair," he whispered.

"I'm sorry, Abudar." I sucked in a breath, pushed the

tears down, and left him behind in the garden.

I didn't stop once as I pushed my way through the crowd, because I wasn't going to be able to hold the tears back much longer. Finally, I made it into the hallway and tears rolled down my cheeks.

Abudar was right.

This wasn't fair.

Thirty-Seven

Over the next several days, I did an expert job avoiding Abudar altogether. Roshanak managed to fill my days by lecturing me about magic and where it came from. She said that the markings on my arm probably reacted to Abudar's magic, and we reviewed more history of the sentinels. Finally on the fourth day, she sent me to the training room. The same room I'd been taken to the first time I visited the palace. It was there Roshanak had demanded the lamp.

I entered the training room and froze with my hand still on the handle.

Abudar was in the midst of sparring with Arash. Shirtless.

I pushed down my emotions, reminding myself I couldn't like him. We were only to be friends. That didn't stop me from staring at the two. Even Arash was good to look at.

Arash stepped forward and I cringed a little, expecting Abudar to take the upper hand and elbow him in the face. He went to do so, but Arash somehow bent his head backward and dodged the blow, then used his right hand to shove a wooden dagger against Abudar's ribs.

"You're dead," he panted, grinning.

Abudar rolled his eyes and shook his head. "I should

have seen that coming."

They stepped back and bowed to each other.

"You could have practiced some of that nonverbal magic Roshanak has been pestering you about." Arash walked to one of the benches and retrieved a towel to wipe his face.

"You wouldn't stand a chance if I did that." Abudar laughed.

"Right." Arash turned, finally spotting me. "Caspara," he said, surprised.

Abudar looked over his shoulder and eyed me.

I felt a bit of a sting. We hadn't seen each other since he kissed me. I had avoided him at all costs and was pretty sure he had been avoiding me. At least until now. I couldn't wait to get some of my anger out toward him.

I was wearing a new outfit Jade had made, but more like the style I preferred—pants. The outfit was still nicer than what I was used to, but at least it felt like me, and even more importantly, it made Abudar's gaze linger.

"Roshanak wanted me to come and practice with you," I said, placing a hand on my hip.

"I've been dying to see this," Arash smiled. He sat down and gestured to me. "Go on, Abudar. Show her what you've got."

Abudar twitched an eyebrow but set his towel and water down, then returned to the sparring floor. "Do you prefer to start with a staff?"

I walked over to one of the weapon stands and took a sword similar to my own. "Are you afraid of getting an owie?" I tested the weight and balance by twisting it in my wrist. I looked over at Abudar and raised my own brow.

"You want to use sharpened blades?" He frowned and

nodded, but took his own sword, full-sized and straight. "I'll try to leave your hair and clothing intact." He gave me a teasing smile.

I narrowed my gaze. "I haven't ever practiced in a fancy room. We'll have to see if I can handle it," I said sarcastically.

"Ladies first," Abudar gestured with his free hand to the open practice space.

"Where is your skirt, Abu?" I asked.

His brows lowered and he *almost* glared. Because he realized I wasn't entirely teasing.

Arash snickered and Abudar definitely glared at him.

"I shouldn't hurt your feelings in such a way." I patted Abudar's shoulder as I passed and took my position. I was going to embarrass the prince as much as possible, so I held my blade a bit too high, then leaned a bit too far back, making him believe I wasn't completely competent.

Abudar took his own position and his gaze took all of me in.

He made the first move, a simple step and jab, which I knew meant he would anticipate me blocking and then he would spin or jump back. Which he did when I leaned into it.

But when he stepped forward again, I grabbed his wrist, ducked under his arm, and rammed the hilt of my sword into his ribs. The *thud* was satisfying to hear.

He grunted.

I stood behind him.

Abudar quickly turned on his heel to parry another blow and his eye scrunched.

"You do remember my father trained me," I said.

"Let's see how much a tailor knows." Abudar didn't

hold back. He stepped forward, drawing his weapon high and low, slicing through the air in a relentless barrage of offense.

I blocked each blow, the metal vibrating into my hand and wrist, then up my arm. Each blow made me grit my teeth as my anger began to build. I knew I couldn't keep up with his pace, so I dropped to my knees and kicked.

He anticipated it. After all, in the caves I'd kicked his wounded leg out from under him. He jumped back and swung low.

When I met his sword, I twisted my own, causing it to slide down his blade toward the hilt. I twisted it again, locking the hilts together. I grabbed his wrist and pulled with all my strength to throw him over my shoulder. But Abudar's feet were planted and I didn't budge him.

I growled and used the movement as leverage to get back to my feet. I spun my back across his arm to again come behind him, but he whipped around in the opposite direction, pulling us further apart. I had hoped to smash my elbow into his stupid face.

"You need some refining," Abudar commented.

"You need some creativity," I countered. "You stick to the same movements."

"Yet you haven't punctured a single offensive attack." He once again stepped forward and met my blade, forcing me to backpedal.

I stomped my heel into the top of his foot, making him yelp. I fell to my knees and crawled between his legs, but grabbed his ankle when I went to stand.

Abudar cursed but somehow managed to catch himself, spin around, and put his sword up to deflect a blow. I took advantage and kicked at his knee. He caught my foot and twisted it, spinning me so my back was to him. He yanked.

I fell against his chest and he wrapped an arm around my throat.

I elbowed him in the diaphragm, but he grunted and held on, tightening.

"Tap my arm so I release you," he ordered.

"No," I growled. I kicked up behind me, aiming right between his legs.

Abudar grunted and doubled over, loosening his grip enough I could slide out from his grip. He grimaced. "That was unfair."

I smirked, amused I had finally hurt him. "In fighting, anything is fair." I took the upper hand, swinging my blade in offensive attacks. He leaned back and I kicked him in the ribs, causing him to fall over.

I jumped to poise my blade at his throat, but he rolled out of the way and kicked my ankles. I yelped as I fell on my back onto the hard stone floor and found myself looking up at the ceiling.

Abudar rolled on top of me, straddling my hips, and put his blade under my chin. "I win."

I tried to catch my breath as I glowered up at him. "Get off."

He leaned down and his rich, woody smell wafted to me, mixed with sweat. "Or what?" he challenged, a smirk on his lips.

This moment may have been romantic to some.

If they didn't know Abudar had chosen to follow tradition instead of fight for his heart. Unless he truly didn't think I was worth it.

I narrowed my glare, swung my blade as a distraction, and thrust my empty hand forward and into his nose.

"Ow, sands!" Abudar dropped his sword and clutched his nose.

I rolled, shoving him off of me, and got to my feet.

"You broke my nose!" he shouted.

"I did not. It didn't crunch. It's not even bleeding, you big baby," I said, dusting off my clothing and catching my breath.

Arash jumped to his feet, clapping.

Abudar glared at him through tears. "Whose side are you on?"

"You're the one that challenged her. She just saw it through." Arash put his arm around my shoulders. "Father would be proud of you."

I raised my brows and leaned away to eye him. "Father?"

Arash's brows dipped and he glanced at Abudar, then back at me. "She didn't tell you? You mean this entire time you haven't known?"

"Known what?"

"That . . . you're my sister?"

I pushed Arash away and stepped back to stare at him. *Sister?* No one had mentioned I had a brother. Not even Telama!

Arash heaved a sigh. "Well. Surprise." He grinned.

"We have the same father?"

He shifted his weight from one food to the next. "Yes. And the same mother too. I'm sorry, I had assumed you knew."

I looked to Abudar for confirmation.

Abudar was touching his nose and looking at his fingers to see if there was any blood. He glanced up at me and rubbed some tears from his eye. "It's true, if that's what your look means. Roshanak has raised him in the palace with me. Unless she kidnapped him from a different couple, he's your brother."

"But . . . how? I mean, Roshanak kept you."

Arash shook his head. "I don't know. To be honest, I only have one memory of you when you were little. You bit my finger."

I couldn't help but keep my gaze locked on him. "I don't believe you. I saw a vision with you in the prison with my father. You helped harm him." I glared.

Arash grimaced. "In my defense, I didn't know he was our father prior to that. You aren't the only one our mother has kept secrets from."

"No. I don't believe you. I'm getting really tired of all of these lies." I pushed past him and stormed to the door.

"Caspara, we're not done with training!" he called.

"I am!" I slammed the door shut behind me.

Igborg was jumping on my bed when I entered. He was jumping and flying around the room, then landing, clearly practicing.

"Sands. I promised I would take you outside every day and we haven't gone yet." I held my hands out to him and he tumbled from the air. I caught him. "I'd rather spend time with you anyway. Come on."

"Okay."

Igborg was getting heavier as well as bigger. I cradled him in both arms as I made my way to the courtyard I'd been in a few days ago with Abudar. When he'd kissed me. And I'd kissed him back.

I rolled my eyes at myself.

I was stupid to think he would choose me when he could have a princess.

I set Igborg on one of the benches and folded my arms to watch him fly into the tree.

"I'm getting rather bored being locked up in my lamp with no one to talk to." I knew it was the jinni before I saw him in the shadows. His golden eyes watched Igborg. "What have I missed?"

I rolled my eyes. "I'm a sentinel. Abudar is my other half, but that makes no sense because he's getting married to some princess from another country. And do you know what makes it worse? He kissed me!"

"No!" The jinni appeared in front of me and grabbed my hands.

"Yes! *After* his engagement had been announced. And you won't believe what I just discovered. Arash, the soldier, is my brother!"

The jinni shook his head. "Your life is complicated."

"You have no idea." I sank onto one of the benches.

Igborg jumped from the branch and stuck his wings out, slowing his fall toward the ground. He spread his wings again and flapped them to propel himself upward and higher into the tree, growing a little braver.

"I feel like I uncover a part of myself and then lose it. I think I belong somewhere and then don't. I just want to go back to how things were," I said, looking down at my hands.

"I could make that wish come true."

I looked at him sideways. "What if I told you I know your real name?"

He grinned, fangs showing. "I wouldn't believe you."

"Your name is Taylin. You're the jinni that created the sentinels."

"Well then." He lifted his head, elongating his neck in a proud position. And then he reached out and touched my hand. My tattoos glowed blue and the gold on his body responded by glowing too. "I knew you were a sentinel the moment you summoned me. When I woke to find *both* sentinels tousling and arguing over me . . . it was flattering, but am I correct you didn't know who you were or the importance of it?"

I shook my head. "I do now. At least, most of it. I'm just beginning to train, though."

Taylin's lips curled in a sad smile. "I worked hand in hand with the six sets of sentinels before you through the years. I have never seen two argue such as you and Abudar. Do you truly hate him so?"

I flexed my jaw and pulled my hand away from him. "He's selfish."

"You're hurt."

"Everyone I know hurts me. That's why I hate making friends. Now that I don't have my father and Taraji and Mihrage—"

"Your father is lost?" Taylin asked.

I shook my head and lowered my gaze to my hands.

"Hm."

"He was killed. Whether by execution or murder, no one seems to know," I said softly. "But no one seems to really be trying to find the answers either. You know what I would wish for?"

"Before you speak, please don't wish for me to bring your father back from the dead. I was being honest about that," he interrupted. "And I can't grant you *every* wish you want. And while I can grant most wishes, you must be careful with *how* you word the wish. Because even though you are my master and I nothing but a humble servant, I have the freedom to interpret your wish any way I see fit."

I looked up at Taylin. "What do you mean I am your master?"

Taylin folded his arms and pursed his lips to the side. Finally, he said, "You know my name. That means you get three wishes. You and Abudar no longer have to agree on one. Congratulations."

I blinked.

Igborg descended from the balcony in a far more controlled way and landed on one of the benches, but slid off the side and into the sand.

"Three wishes?" I rubbed my hands on my knees.

I could wish to be sultana, then I could help the people the way I saw fit. But the thought of being a sultana terrified me. Besides, Shahira was doing a wonderful job. I didn't want the weight of responsibility for an entire nation. What if there was a war? Or drought?

I could wish for magic. I was the daughter of a grand sorceress, without magic in a magical world, and I was a sentinel—possibly the only sentinel in the history of sentinels—without any glimmer of magic in a follicle of my hair.

Or I could wish for Abudar to fall in love . . . no. No, that would be unfair.

"Well?" Taylin said, his voice sounding bored.

I shook my head. "I don't know. I mean, Abudar said we needed to work together to help our people. Do you think he really wants to help them?"

Taylin didn't answer, and his stance didn't shift. The only way I knew he was alive was that he blinked.

"Fine. Don't answer me." I stood.

Taylin dropped his arms. "You're mad at *me*?"

"No! I'm . . . thinking. Because I don't want anything

for myself. Other than possibly asking for people to stop hiding my life from me. You already said you can't bring my father back. I could wish for direction in my life, but I already have that from Telama and this stupid tattoo." I ran my hands down my face and turned to him. "If *you* could wish for something, what would it be?"

He shook his head. "I can't change the past. But I would wish to be mortal. To live a full mortal life and die instead of being stuck as a jinni for eternity. I've lived enough lives, I'd like to live just one."

"You . . . want to be mortal?"

Taylin's lip tugged. "Pathetic, hm?"

"No. Not at all." I looked up at Igborg. "I do have one wish."

"What's that?"

I smiled to myself as I watched Igborg fly down yet again. "I wish for you to return Sultana Shahira's magical abilities to her. That her ability to weave stories through spoken word will occur in the way she states, just as she was able to do before her father stole that magic from her."

Taylin blinked at me. "You want to give up one of your wishes for the sultana? Someone you barely know?"

I nodded. "That wish was the only reason Abudar entered the cave. It seems like a pretty admirable reason to me. He tried to help my father. The least I can do is grant him the wish he wanted."

Taylin smiled. "I think you're pretty admirable yourself. Your wish is my command." He snapped his fingers and a puff of gold, sparkling smoke plumed from beneath them.

Thirty-Eight

My door flung open and I jumped to my feet, heart racing. I scowled at Abudar. "You can't just barge in like that. Are you insane?"

He walked to me and pulled me into a hug. "I don't know how you did it, but I know it was you."

"Um. What?"

"My mother. Her magic is back." He stepped back, his face positively radiating from his smile. "How did you make the wish without me?"

I cleared my throat. "Do you have the lamp on you?"

He dug into his pocket and pulled it out.

I took it from him and rubbed my thumb down the handle. I could be honest, or I could lie. Lying seemed like the better choice, all things considered. But I held it up. "I learned the jinni's name. Roshanak wanted him specifically. He's the one who helped create the sentinels."

Abudar's eyes widened. "You're kidding."

"I'm not. And because I know his name, I get three wishes. So I used my first to help your mother." I walked over and set the lamp on the table.

Abudar took a moment before he said, "Caspara, I didn't deserve that."

"And why not?" I faced him. "You've been nothing but

kind to me. You saved my life, took me to see my father, handled me making your nose black and blue." I smiled.

Abudar didn't. His nose was indeed bruised, but not broken.

"Your mother deserves her magic," I added, feeling a bit awkward. "Did . . . do you want the other wishes?"

"No." He finally tugged the corner of his lips upward. "You constantly surprise me."

I wanted desperately to be flattered, to flirt by tucking my hair behind my ear, but I knew it would be useless. Abudar was claimed by someone else. So I nudged him in the shoulder. "You know me. I'll always be full of surprises." I cleared my throat, realizing how awkward that had been, and strolled over to the foot of the bed. "Um. You can go now, I guess."

Abudar chuckled. "I'll come collect you for dinner."

When the door shut, I sank into one of the chairs at the table and put my face in my hands. "How am I so pathetic with him?"

Igborg nuzzled my cheek. "You are happy."

"And I don't feel like that's right." I turned my head. "He's engaged, Igborg. To be married. I know it doesn't make sense to you. I need to do something to stay busy. I'm going to go practice with Arash or something." I snagged the lamp and shoved it into one of my pockets.

Igborg jumped off the table and scurried after me.

I recalled back in the caves when Arash mentioned to Mithra that his mother was a powerful sorceress. I should have known then that he was my brother.

My *brother*.

I still couldn't wrap my head around it. The revelation had only added more questions to my life. Why did my father take me and leave him behind? Why didn't Father ever tell me about Arash? Where was the harm in that? Maybe he thought I would be jealous of Arash for getting to grow up in the palace and have the life I envied.

When I made it to the practice room, I didn't find Arash. The room was vacant. I dragged one of the dummies into the center of the room, took the sword I'd been using for practice, and fell into the memorized steps my father had taught me.

But I began to let my anger out and slammed the blade against the straw-stuffed dummy. Harder and harder.

Abudar—stab.

Wishes—stab.

Secrets—stab, stab, stab.

Arash—slice.

The doors suddenly flew open and I wheeled around with my sword pointed forward, panting hard and sweat trickling down my jaw.

"Sands, Abudar! That's twice today!" I lowered my sword.

He stood in the doorway, eyes wide. "I've been looking all over the palace for you." He ran to me. "Caspara, your village is in danger."

"What do you mean?" My stomach knotted.

He grabbed my hands. "A group of soldiers was sent to your village. Roshanak is going to annihilate all of them."

My eyes widened. "Why would she do that? They aren't a threat!"

He shook his head. "I don't know. I sent a—"

"There are families! You met them!" I pulled away and dropped the sword to the ground. "You are going to get me out of this palace so I can warn them before she reaches them." I took off running out the door.

"Caspara, wait." Abudar caught up to me and grabbed me. "In spite of how fast you may run, you will never outrun the soldiers. But I can try that spell."

"The portal? I thought you said it wasn't safe across long distances."

He shook his head. "If we have your father's bag, that might help strengthen the portal because it's a physical object from that location. You'll need to keep your mind on every detail, as will I."

I nodded. "Okay."

We went back to my room and I grabbed my father's bag and held it to my chest.

Abudar wrapped one arm around my waist and I wrapped my arms around his chest. "Stay close."

"Are you sure this is a good idea?" I asked.

"No. Are you ready?" he asked.

I slammed my eyes shut. "Just get this over with."

Abudar began to say, "*Ash'in*—" but was cut off by the jinni loudly clearing his throat.

We both looked at him.

Taylin rubbed his nose, then pointed to the window.

"I truly don't understand him," Abudar mumbled.

I let go of Abudar and walked to the window and opened it. When I leaned out to see what Taylin was pointing at, I gave a startled cry. A rug floated through the window and swirled around me, wrapping me in a tight hug.

"What is this?" I gasped.

Taylin grinned. "Looks to me like a magic rug."

I lifted my gaze to him. "Magic? As in enchanted?" My eyes widened. "Like what Telama's sister was making! What was her name? It was . . . Gavair." I shook my head and held my hands out.

The carpet touched its corners to my hands. It was blue and gold, the exact same rug I had seen her whisper to. I had watched her *create* this rug.

"Remarkable." Abudar stepped up to my side and reached out and touched the edge of the rug.

It floated down to the ground, lying flat.

"I *think* it wants to take you for a ride," Taylin said.

The rug rippled and flew out the window, but when I leaned out to see where it went, it was floating at the window's edge.

I looked back at Abudar. "This might be safer than trying a spell you barely know."

He rubbed his jaw and looked at Taylin. "This isn't a trick?"

Taylin sighed. "In spite of my history, I actually like you two. I didn't summon it. Caspara did."

"I did? How?"

Taylin pointed to my arm. "Your arm was glowing while Abudar spoke about your village. You were wanting a quick way to arrive, I imagine, and it answered."

"You're saying I created this?" I looked at him skeptically.

"No. It was already created. But it came to you. Much like Igborg." He waved for me to go out the window. "You don't have much time to lose." Taylin smiled. "Don't forget to bring me." He disappeared.

I snatched the lamp and shoved it in my pocket.

Abudar shook his head. "You first? I'll steady your hand."

"Why not *you* first?" I asked.

"Because I can actually catch you if you fall." He raised

a brow.

With Abudar's help, we moved the table under the window and I leaned out. Abudar gripped my wrist firmly and I grabbed his before I set a foot on the rug. It somehow remained steady, even though it floated in the air. I lowered my other foot, then stood up, still holding on to Abudar.

The rug didn't move.

I glanced at Abudar and slowly lowered myself so I sat cross-legged on it. "It feels sturdy," I said.

Abudar finally released my hand, then climbed out the window and onto the rug behind me. "I can't believe we're doing this right now. Do you truly believe it was made by Gavair?"

"I don't know what to think." I stroked my fingers over the rug's perfect stitches. The smooth silk threads reminded me of the shirt my father used to wear for special ceremonies. I swallowed the lump forming in my throat.

Abudar drew a deep breath. "Let's save your village."

The rug shot forward and up into the night sky.

I screamed and gripped its sides. Abudar leaned against my back, holding just above my hands, keeping both myself and him from falling off.

"This is insanity!" he shouted over the wind.

I laughed. My heart felt somehow free, even as we climbed, and then the rug smoothed out and floated over the sands. I reached out as if I could stroke the clouds around us.

Abudar's arm slid around my waist as he straightened. "Next time, not so abruptly," he mumbled to the rug.

I kept my eyes on the desert below, trying to identify from the sky where my village was. Like my first time in the palace, I couldn't help but think how different everything looked from so far away. The city of Zunbar disappeared quickly, and soon we were over a rolling sea of sand.

"I see your village," Abudar suddenly said. "I see the torches."

My brows furrowed and I focused on where he pointed. My stomach dropped. "Abudar, that isn't torchlight. It's fire."

My village, my home, was already in flames.

"H-How did they beat us here?" The words came out tight, strangled, desperate for an answer.

"I don't know. But they must have left. They had to have plenty of time to escape."

I looked at him over my shoulder and his brows were pinched in thought.

The rug landed and we stood in the middle of the village.

I shook my head as hot tears stung my eyes. I ran to the nearest home, Mihrage's home, and threw the doors open. It was vacant, but vases had been shattered, pillows torn, and lantern oil glistened on the floor. It just hadn't caught fire yet.

"Mihrage!" I shouted twice. When he didn't answer, I ran out and for the next home. I could barely see through my tears. "Taraji! Farhad!"

Sorrow overwhelmed me.

What was I to do?

My father and the thieves were my only family.

"Taraji!" I screamed as loud as I could.

"Caspara, they must be safe." Abudar grabbed my arm.

"You can't possibly know that!" I shouted. I slammed my fist against his chest. "Let go!"

"Caspara . . ." Abudar's eyes softened with pity, but he let go of me. "I sent—"

"I'm not going to be a sentinel," I said firmly. Anger burned in my chest.

His eyes widened. "What? You have to!"

"No, I don't." I turned away and headed for the cemetery to see if the invaders had desecrated it.

"Why this sudden anger toward me? After everything?" Abudar's voice was deep in anger and he started following me.

I stopped and faced him. "My father was *murdered*, Abudar. No one tried to find out what happened to him. No one looked for clues to see what happened, your mother told me. Don't you see how wrong my life is? How everything bad happens to me?"

Abudar's jaw flexed.

"*Everything* I know and love has been taken from me." Tears finally broke. "This?" I held up my arm. "This isn't a blessing. It isn't a destiny. My life is a curse. Perhaps Roseline will help you find the one who is actually supposed to be your other half, because it *can't* be me." I wheeled back around and stepped on the path leading to the graveyard.

"Could there be a place where your people would run?" Abudar said. "A hidden cave or something they might have escaped to after a warning?"

My head pounded. "If there were, I would never tell you."

I heard him stop following me.

"Caspara, I'm sorry," he said.

I balled my hands into fists and stopped in my tracks. From where I stood, the headstones looked untouched. I turned slowly and faced Abudar. "Sorry that you're selfish? That royalty take and never give back? You saw my humble home. While you live in a room big enough for a family, your people starve. Destiny?" I let out a bit of a manic laugh. "Destiny has taken everything. I'm done with destiny. Forget this tattoo. Forget being a sentinel."

His eyes narrowed. "I brought you here."

"*After* the soldiers destroyed everything!"

"I warned your people!" he shouted back, pointing his finger to the ground. "I sent a message warning them the soldiers were on their way and telling them to hide. *That's* why you're not finding anyone. If you had stopped yelling for just a moment, I could have told you when we arrived."

"Yeah. Right." I scoffed.

"I'm sorry I couldn't stop your father's death. You know that happened before we got back to the palace, before I could intervene."

"You should leave."

"I'm not done talking to you yet." He grabbed my arm. "If your father died in our prison, I can find out why."

"Don't you touch me!" I shoved him away and ripped my arm out of his grip. "You think I don't know how the guards found their way here? You told them where we are! That or your father followed us. I trusted you with the secret of our location and you betrayed me. Not just me. *Them.* You and I are done."

Abudar's jaw was flexed so tightly I knew he clenched his teeth. He finally relaxed it and shook his head. "I'm not my father. But your father wasn't perfect either."

I closed the gap between us so quickly, I didn't know I could move that fast. "Take that back."

"No."

I swung my fist with everything I had. It connected with Abudar's jaw and he flew into the side of the nearest building. The tattoos on my arm rippled from the tips of my finger to my shoulder.

His shoulder cracked against the wall and he grunted as he hit the sand.

I gasped and stepped back, then looked back down at my arm. One of the symbols turned red. I looked back at Abudar.

He held his shoulder as he got to his feet. "I was raised to do whatever was necessary for the good of the land. It is my responsibility as the prince to protect my people, even if it is at the cost of my own life. *We* are the guardians of our land. You're supposed to be at my side. But if you don't want to help, I won't force you."

"Help against sorceresses who have every right to learn whatever magic they please?" I shouted.

He shook his head. "I wish you luck in whatever future you make for yourself. If you change your mind, you know where to find me." He turned away and walked back into the courtyard.

He was a selfish, spoiled liar who used others when it was convenient for him to do so. He'd led me on, even *kissing me* while knowing he would marry someone else. How could he think he could have a fiancée and me on the side? I was right to not fall for his charms or fake kindness. If I had kept my head about me, I wouldn't have.

And to think he had the gall to lead the soldiers here! Yet, even if Abudar hadn't been the one who divulged our location, he could have done more to stop them. But who was I kidding? The sultan and sultana wouldn't even search for clues to who killed my father. Why wouldn't they attack my people?

Between him and the world, I was done. I was going to rejoin the thieves and never leave them again. Life with the thieves was safe.

Rule number fifteen, if it's too good to be true, it probably is.

My heart sank.

I should have been better aware. I knew and ignored so many signs.

Angry at myself and the world, I wiped the tears from my cheeks and walked back into the village.

The rug lay on the ground near the well, and Abudar was nowhere to be seen.

I collapsed to my knees and willed the sand to swallow me up. Take me away. Take the pain away. Igborg nuzzled my hands. I barely had the energy to register he had somehow made his way there before I pressed my forehead into the ground and let out a sob.

"If you don't breathe, you're going to pass out," Taylin said from right beside me.

But I couldn't lift my head to see him. I didn't *want* to see him.

He grumbled something in a language I didn't understand, and then I felt him draw me into his lap, like my father used to do when I was a child. "I've seen a lot of sorrow in my existence. I try to stay as far away from it as possible."

I sobbed into his shoulder.

The jinni rubbed his hand over my back in soothing motions. He rested his head against mine. For some reason, his touch and presence brought relief to me. "You are very hard on yourself, you know. If only you could see yourself and realize how much good you've done, how much you've already achieved in your young life."

I finally lifted my head and scowled at him.

Taylin smiled. "Who got the prince and princess out of the cave? Who saved the prince's life? More than once, I might add. You have skills no one else in the palace has."

I scoffed. "And who put her faith in a stupid boy with a fiancée who did nothing but sit on his hands while everything fell apart?"

Taylin tilted his head. "If none of your people are dead, and if the soldiers didn't arrest them, where would they go?"

I frowned.

He raised his brows.

"The Dumue River, I suppose."

He set me on the ground in order to get to his feet, then took my hand and pulled me to my feet. "Then we go and see if Abudar spoke the truth about his warning."

I bit my lip. "He's going to get lost in the desert if he's walking back to Zunbar." I looked over at the rug. "Perhaps you should collect him and take him home first? I might never talk to him again, but he doesn't deserve to die in the desert after just returning home from it."

The rug floated off into the night.

Taylin frowned. "Well, now how are we going to get to the river?"

"We walk." I set Igborg on my shoulder and looked around at the destroyed village before entering the desert in the direction of the river.

Taylin grumbled but followed at my side.

I approached the riverbank with apprehension. Each step I took I feared would confirm my darkest thoughts. Until I spotted a flicker of light—a reflection of the moon on a blade near the hidden entrance.

My heart jumped into my throat and I ran as fast as I could.

When I got within fifty yards, I called out, "Farhad, is that you?"

The blade flashed again and a hooded figure stepped out from the safety of darkness. They withdrew their hood. It wasn't Farhad, but it was Babkak. "Caspara?"

I threw my arms around him, relief flooding over me. "I went to the village and saw it burned down and hoped you'd all fled here."

"We're all accounted for," Babkak confirmed. "If you hadn't sent that warning to us, we would have been arrested, or worse." He ruffled my hair like he did when I was a child.

I peered up at him with brows pinched in confusion. "I didn't warn you."

He tilted his head and looked at Igborg sitting on my shoulder. "Igborg did. He flew out to us a few hours ago and warned us."

I turned my attention to my dragon.

He ruffled his wings and smiled. "I did. Prince Abu told me to."

I stared at him, speechless. Abudar said he had warned my people, but I hadn't believed him. I had blamed him for the destruction of my home and the death of my people. But he had warned them after all. I hadn't even given him the chance he deserved. Worse, I had accused him of revealing our location.

Guilt sank my heart.

"Come in and get some rest. You look positively exhausted." Babkak guided me into the dug-out cave with his hand on my back.

The cave had been carved out of the side of a large dune. The dune was actually the structure of the hideout, carefully hidden with some kind of magic that kept it there without blowing the sand off.

Inside, the people of my village were pressed tightly together, most of them asleep. A lantern hung overhead, offering a warm glow to the gloomy hideout.

Babkak silently gestured to a bedroll, and I walked toward it.

Mihrage bolted upright. He shook Taraji awake, then jumped over those still sleeping and pulled me into his arms and held tight. I felt Taraji wrap her arms around me from behind.

I rubbed my hand over my arm.

Abudar didn't deserve to take the blame for how I felt, but I was confused as to how I should feel toward him.

I'd searched my entire life for a purpose and ignored everything that led me to being a sentinel. Because I wasn't strong. Or smart. I wasn't able to even win a fight against Abudar. How could I do that against any sort of enemy?

Thirty-Nine

The thieves made arrangements to head south, toward the Ailorn Mountains. Our village was completely decimated. It could be rebuilt, but now the royal guard knew where the hideout was located. We would return to one of the caves where the thieves had first been formed.

I looked over to a group of children playing nearby and realized they were playing with Igborg, who was scorching the sand with little puffs of fire. He was so carefree and relied entirely on me to teach him what to do and who to be.

"We have everything packed onto the camels," Mihrage said. "How are you holding up?"

I shook my head and ran my hands over my face. "I have never felt so lost."

He put his hand on my back and guided me down to the river. He leaned against a tree. "You've always been brave. Always the first to jump into the ocean or fight. You've got a lot of courage."

"But?" I mumbled.

"But you never give yourself enough credit for any of that. Caspara, you don't have to be anyone you don't want to be, but maybe it's time for you to figure out who you *need* to be." Mihrage wrapped his arm around my shoulders and pulled me into a hug. "We're your family and will always be here. We'll support whatever you need to do."

"I don't know how to be a sentinel. And to be honest, I don't think Roshanak or Abudar know either. I don't trust either of them. Roshanak might have killed my father, and now that I've yelled at Abudar . . ."

He shrugged and let go. "Then maybe you and Abudar need to figure that out together."

"Dablin is nearly here," someone announced.

Farhad clapped his hands. "Prepare to leave."

Dablin rode in on his horse and jumped off before it came to a full stop. He grabbed Farhad by the arm and led him away from the group. "The Veil moved through the city last night and took every sorceress they could find."

"It is good we are leaving now." Farhad started covering his face with his scarf.

"There's more. There are rumors Prince Abudar left with Caspara last night, but he never made it back to the palace."

I pushed Mihrage away and hurried over. "What was that about Prince Abudar?"

Dablin kept his voice low. "When did you last see him?"

"In our village. I sent the magic rug to take him back to the palace, though."

Dablin eyed me.

My stomach dropped. What if the rug wasn't summoned like Taylin said? What if it was enchanted by one of the sorceresses of The Veil and I was responsible for Abudar being kidnapped by them?

"Farhad," Babkak called.

All attention shifted to the top of the dune where Babkak walked with a hooded figure following behind him.

"What is it?" Farhad asked.

Babkak stepped to the side and extended his hand. "This man requested an audience with you."

"I will cut directly to the chase." The man removed his hood, revealing horns and orange skin. "My name is Irilibus. I am here to request custody of the criminal, Mihrage."

Epilogue

MITHRA

Why did Abudar constantly have to stick his nose where it didn't belong? What was it in his brain that made him think he needed to be the hero of everything? I'd been lucky the night he took Caspara to the forty thieves. Had he not done so, I wouldn't have been able to send the spy to follow them. Of course I felt guilty destroying those homes, but I couldn't allow Abudar and Caspara to continue with their forbidden relationship.

"I still don't understand why we burned down their village," Arash said. He sat on the foot of my bed, watching me.

I leaned against the window, my arms folded. "It was unfortunate I had to take such drastic measures, but I had to break them apart. Even with Abudar's engagement to Roseline, he and Caspara were growing too close. If they bond as sentinels . . . I can't have Abudar getting more powerful than he already is." I faced Arash and ran my thumb over the ruby I'd taken from Caspara's vault.

Arash was fiddling absently with his earring. It was his tell—that he was thinking of something. His dark eyes looked up at me as I approached him. "And what is your goal with giving him to The Veil?"

I heaved a sigh. "I didn't *give* him to them. They saw an opportunity and took it. Unfortunately for him." I leaned down and kissed Arash's forehead, then tilted his chin up with one finger and kissed his lips. "It gives me a reason to meet with them without suspicion. And perhaps I can learn more about my power that Roshanak has kept hidden from me."

"I can't help but feel a bit guilty. Prince Abudar is my friend, and I actually like Caspara. She means well," he said. "And what if you get caught?"

I smiled and tapped his nose. "You worry too much."

Arash shook his head and gently grabbed my wrist. "No, I don't. What if my mother becomes suspicious? You know how she is."

"I want you by my side, Arash. I need you." I slid my arms around his neck and sat on his lap. "Will you stay with me? You're already my bodyguard."

His neck flushed red and he slowly nodded. "Of course I'll stay at your side."

I kissed his forehead and rose to my feet. "I need to speak with my parents and see what their plan is with Abudar. Roshanak will likely want to plan with me too."

"And what are you going to do?"

I slid the ruby into my pocket. "I'm going to visit with Roshanak and plan how to get my big brother back." I smiled. "And then I'm going to get rid of him on my own terms."

The Sands of Wonder series continues in:

Guardian of Thieves
Sands of Wonder Series Book 2

ALSO BY LICHELLE SLATER

THE FORGOTTEN KINGDOM SERIES
The Four Stones of Tern Tovan
(Exclusive to Newsletter subscribers)
The Dragon Princess
(Sleeping Beauty Reimagined)
The Siren Princess
(Little Mermaid Reimagined)
The Beast Princess
(Beauty and the Beast Reimagined)
The Phoenix Princess
(Snow White Reimagined)
The Crown Prince

Receive the prequel to *The Forgotten Kingdom Series* for FREE by signing up for my newsletter at:
www.LichelleSlater.com

CIRCUS OF THE STARS SERIES
Ringmaster
Marionette
Magician

Urban Fantasy
Curse of a Djinn

CHRISTMAS ROMANCE NOVELS
Secret Santa
Accidental Secret Santa

ABOUT THE AUTHOR

Personal dragon trainer, lover of glitter, writer of fantasy.

Reading has always been a huge passion, from The Hobbit to Goosebumps. Some of my fondest memories are at the library or being read to, and when I embarked on my journey of becoming an author, I did so with the dream of sharing the worlds in my mind with others.

I currently live in Salt Lake City, UT with my adorable King Charles, Perseus, and work full-time as a special education preschool teacher.

I am a USA Today Bestselling author and was nominated for "Unforgettable Book of the Year" for The Beast Princess and "Mind-Blowing Fantasy of the Year" for The Siren Princess at Penned Con 2020, and as "Best Debut Author" for Step Right Up (now Circus in the Stars: Ringmaster) at UtopiaCon in 2017.

Join my reader group on Facebook:
Lichelle's Book Wyrms

Follow Me Here

Instagram
@LichelleSlater_Author

TikTok
@LichelleSlaterAuthor

Amazon
www.amazon.com/Lichelle-Slater/e/B01MSU34EN/

Goodreads
www.goodreads.com/author/show/16150296.Lichelle_Slater